"You're fronting for gangsters, Mr. Franks. You've set up a perfect company — two perfect companies, each relying on the other — through which Pascara and Flamini and Dukes are cleaning their money." Waldo paused, enjoying himself. "You've got the biggest car wash in town, Mr. Franks. You're cleaning up millions of dollars from numbers and from loan sharking and from prostitution and from drugs and from protection and from larceny. From where we're sitting, Mr. Franks, you seem a pretty important guy to an awful lot of people. . . ." Waldo stopped once more, looking toward Tina. "You, and your wife."

"No!" said Franks, holding out his hand like a man trying to ward off something unpleasant. "No, wait! I can explain it. Everything can be explained."

Waldo laughed openly, and Schultz joined in, sharing the same joke. "We had a bet," said Waldo. "Johnnie and I. Just how long would it take one of you to say you could explain it. Everyone always says it, you know? Everyone always says something like that."

Recent Titles by Brian Freemantle from Severn House

Sherlock and Sebastian Holmes

THE HOLMES INHERITANCE
THE HOLMES FACTOR

Charlie Muffin

DEAD MEN LIVING
KINGS OF MANY CASTLES

AT ANY PRICE
BETRAYALS
DEAD END
DIRTY WHITE
GOLD
HELL'S PARADISE
ICE AGE
THE IRON CAGE
THE KREMLIN CONSPIRACY
THE MARY CELESTE
O'FARRELL'S LAW
TARGET
TWO WOMEN

TO SAVE A SON

Brian Freemantle

This title first published in Great Britain 2006 by
SEVERN HOUSE PUBLISHERS LTD of
9–15 High Street, Sutton, Surrey SM1 1DF.
This title first published in the USA 2006 by
SEVERN HOUSE PUBLISHERS INC of
595 Madison Avenue, New York, N.Y. 10022.
Originally published in the USA only in paperback
format under the title *The Choice of Eddie Franks.*

British Library Cataloguing in Publication Data

Freemantle, Brian
    To save a son
    1. Mafia - Fiction
    2. Money laundering - United States - Fiction
    3. Witnesses - United States - Fiction
    4. Suspense fiction
    I.   Title
    823.9'14 [F]

    ISBN-10: 0-7278-6335-5 28.95

Printed and bound in Great Britain by
MPG Books Ltd., Bodmin, Cornwall.

Prologue

". . . Come on! Come on, Eddie! Harder, you've got to try harder! Nicky's winning! He's doing better! Harder, Eddie! Be the best, always try to be the best. . . ."

Eddie Franks jerked awake, sweat-soaked from the dream he hadn't had for a long time, immediately concerned for Tina, beside him. She slept on, undisturbed, and he relaxed slightly. Franks lay in the darkness, trying to remember the last occasion. Actually in America, he supposed. Not the first time, when he really had been a refugee. Later, at college—he turned again to his wife's indistinct shape—when he'd realized how much he loved her, and was learning from the opposition of her family, the family who'd taken him in, that although they'd done everything to make it seem otherwise, he was still an outsider when it came to marriage. And always would be.

". . . Nicky's getting better results! Better grades! Harder, Eddie! Try harder! . . ."

They'd had to give in, over Tina. And he would go on showing them, vowed Franks. He'd show Poppa Scargo and he'd show Nicky Scargo and for different reasons he'd show Tina. Now that his father wasn't around anymore to obstruct and hold him back, he was going to show *everyone*. Be the best.

1

PART ONE

Pride goeth before destruction,
and a haughty spirit before a
fall.
                              Proverbs

1

Eddie Franks wanted to feel more: to know some emotion. It wasn't fitting; it was disrespectful, like his bad-dream relief that morning at no longer being held back by the old man. His father was dead; about to be buried. A father who had loved him and cared for him and tried to protect him. "I was determined you'd survive," the old man had always said, "determined we'd both survive."

Eddie wished he could remember some of that time, for himself. The stories were a further source of guilt. They'd seemed exciting—adventurous even—when he was young. Not terrifying as the old man intended. Later, when he'd grown up and seen the films and read the accounts and knew it was all true, Eddie had still been unable to imagine what it had been like. Actually to *believe* his mother had left the apartment in Liberec one morning to buy bread and never returned, snatched from the street by a Jew-hunting squad and dispatched to a camp his father had never located. Or to imagine how the old man, after his search failed and the pogroms began when the Sudetenland was annexed, had really carried him, papoose-fashion in a wrap across his back as he trekked across Europe, always frightened, always trying to elude the squads that his unknown mother had failed to evade. Running became a way of life: *the* way of life. Until England. It was in England that the old man changed their name: from Frankovich to Franks. His given name, too. Isaac became David. Still Jewish, but not so identifiably so. Edmund was kept, but inevitably shortened to Eddie. His father had explained that changing the name was part of running. And it wasn't even the original intention to stop. He'd intended moving on to America when he could.

Which was why he'd sent Eddie on ahead. The U-boat sinking in 1940 of the *City of Benares*, with the loss of so many wives and children heading for American safety, deterred a lot of men from sending their families across the Atlantic, but not the newly named David Franks. It was an acceptable risk to a man who had walked one step ahead of his pursuers throughout Europe with a whimpering baby strapped to his back.

The approach had been made to David Franks before Eddie arrived in America; before the name change from Frankovich to Franks. To pass initial immigration formalities, his father had been required to provide a lengthy account of his European flight. Within weeks of providing that information he had been interviewed by a recruiter for a disinformation division nominally attached to British external intelligence. It was an environment in which Eddie's enterprising, survival-conscious father flourished; he was fluent in every language of the European countries through which he'd wandered.

The job—and the recognition and the prestige—meant for his father more than just the fact that London would not be a temporary resting place. It meant that when the conflict was over—and there were citations and even medals for David Franks for what he had done in that conflict—there was a wide network of people and a seemingly endless number of open doors for a life in peacetime.

David Franks was one of the few people in Britain to recognize that after the sacrifices and the deprivations of the war years, people would want to enjoy themselves. And so—having known unhappiness for so long—he set about making other people happy.

Some of the wartime-opened doorways were into banks and financial institutions. David Franks had no trouble borrowing money—about which he showed a care only possible from someone who had never possessed any—and with that money he established amusement arcades and facilities immediately adjacent to the holiday camps the more adventurous and entrepreneurial developers were creating.

It meant David Franks was not locked into debt when the immediate postwar celebration times became latter-year boom and expansion times. And he could move quickly, when he had to. From the safe sidelines David Franks studied the holiday business and anticipated the moment when people would want to cross the channel by ferry and airplane instead of by landing craft and assault plane. It was still cautious anticipation. Unlike some of the later businessmen, the old man didn't consider building his own hotels in Spain or Italy or France. Or even leasing existing

6

facilities. He contented himself with block bookings, always a runaway number of units in the various countries, and moving gradually toward an upper, moneyed end of the market.

Which really meant fear, Eddie knew.

His father had been terrified—what else could he have been?—fleeing through the Nazi-occupied countries. He'd gained surface but fragile confidence during his wartime service with the propaganda divisions, sufficient confidence to take the chance that had worked during the immediate postwar period and then the expansion to the Continent. But by then—by the time the returned Eddie had finished the expensive prep schools and gone back again to America to study at Harvard, because the Oxford or Cambridge education upon which the old man set his heart was not possible—that fragile confidence began to chip. When Eddie urged expansion—actual hotel purchases and the leasing of airplanes—his father argued continuing caution, content to watch other people's fireworks. David Franks had found his sanctuary and was satisfied with it, a successful survivor who never wanted to run again.

Eddie Franks stopped the reflection, turning physically from the whitely new gravestone. Tina answered the look, smiling sadly at him. If his still-nervous father hadn't sent him to America—not once but twice, he realized—he would never have married Tina and now be awaiting the birth of their first child. As if aware of his thoughts, Tina Franks cupped her hand protectively over the bulge that shaped her expansive mourning dress. Would his son—Eddie had already convinced himself the child would be a boy—find as much difficulty expressing emotion over him as he did over his own father? Eddie hoped not.

It would be easier, for his son. He'd grow up safe and protected and know what was happening to him, all the time. For Eddie, his own mother's abduction and his backpacking across Europe had only ever been stories; the reality was standing on a wind-blasted dockside at Southampton in 1951, proudly conscious of his American clothes and his American sneakers and his acquired but soon-lost American accent and—because he wanted to impress—his American chewing gum, and being embraced by a complete stranger and being called "son."

And not feeling like anybody's son.

Eddie Franks felt then like he had always felt. Alone. Eddie's eyes remained on his American wife, self-irritation filling the emptiness. How could he wonder about his ability to love—or

7

lack of it—when he loved Tina so absolutely? And his love for her *was* absolute. He became aware that she was nudging him into reaction and that the service was over. He smiled, in apologetic concentration, thanking the rabbi for performing the funeral anyway, after his father's prolonged lapse from the faith and his own complete disinterest in it. He passed over the sealed envelope containing the donation, emptily agreed to remain in contact, and then solicitously took Tina's arm, to help her back to the car.

They drove unspeaking for a long time, until the car was approaching the M-4 on the route to their country house at Maidenhead. Tina said suddenly, "Your father was very proud of you, you know. I think that's the first thing I ever remember him telling me. How proud he was."

Franks looked to his wife, pleased at hearing her say it. The secret, hidden difficulties he had in reacting to his father's passing didn't make him a man incapable of normal feelings or love. It was particular to the circumstances of his early life, that's all. Quite understandable, considering those circumstances. He had always been a dutiful, obedient, loving and loyal son. Certainly his father had never had cause to suspect the inward irritation; no one had. Franks smiled at his wife, who did not know—and who would never know—the promises he had made to himself. He said: "He'd have reason to be prouder."

Tina frowned back at him. "What do you mean?"

"He was satisfied: content," said Franks. "I'm not. I'm not content at all."

The baby was born precisely on the date the gynecologist gave and was a boy, as Franks expected. It was an easy, uncomplicated birth, and at Tina's suggestion they called the child David, after Eddie's father.

"You said it would be a boy," she reminded him.

"Everything is going to work out like I said," anticipated Franks, almost boastfully confident. He added, "And it's all for you."

That was an unnecessary lie, he thought in immediate self-criticism. Materially he supposed it was for Tina. But on that hidden level there was another reason. The Scargo family had provided him with a home—first on the Lower East Side and then, as they prospered, in Westchester—and with love as they felt able to give it. But always there had been the enforced competitiveness between him and Nicky, Tina's real brother. The booming-voiced Enrico had chided one to play softball better

8

than the other. Stipulated the runs they had to get in baseball, criticized them when they failed, and praised one against the other if one succeeded and the other didn't. *"Harder, Eddie; try harder."* Now, at last, he was going to be able to; at last he was going to show them. And beat Nicky.

2

It did not take long to initiate what he wanted, even for someone of Franks' impatience. Because of his father's restraint their banking record was impeccable, no overdraft on any account. But there was a reluctance when he made his applications in the managers' and directors' sterile, polish-smelling offices, as if people imagined he still needed his father's backing. He got the loans, although not as much as he wanted; it made him careful in the spending, which later he came to believe wasn't a bad thing.

The holiday growth was already underway in Spain, but there were still sufficient openings. Franks decided he didn't have time for the delays and restrictions of building his own hotel. He was lucky with the bankruptcy of another company, able to buy a hotel already virtually constructed and pick up the block-booking airline seats from the same bankruptcy. He got grants from a Madrid government anxious to encourage tourism, and used the signed and contracted Spanish agreement as collateral for the next approach to British banks—for an overdraft double what he'd asked before—and succeeded in getting three times the original. He held back again from building, instead launching a London takeover of a struggling company that already owned two hotels, was under-capitalized, and had hesitant family directors anxious to escape. He got the company cheaply, without fully expending his borrowed funds, so there was sufficient capital from the Madrid agreement to refurbish them to a high quality. It was a positive decision, copied from his father, who had always recognized the snobbishness of people and who had geared himself for a clientele who imagined they could afford something more expensive than an ordinary package holiday, even if they couldn't.

9

He graduated from block bookings on other companies' airlines, leasing instead entire aircraft with the agreement that they could be painted and ascribed to his own company. His heavy TV advertising had champagne as the theme, champagne flights and champagne accommodations and champagne service; it wasn't until the customers were in his specially painted and hostessed sections of the airport that they discovered the champagne was Spanish, not French.

Franks repaid the English overdrafts as quickly as before and this time persuaded the impressed Spaniards to increase their grants. Doubling his credit in London was practically a formality this time. He began purchasing completed villas, and for the first time he committed himself to the construction of apartment buildings.

The expansion from the mainland to Majorca and Minorca was natural. Increased business meant increased aircraft leasing, an arrangement which proved not only to be safe but practical because it produced tax advantages to offset his consistently high cash flow. From the Mediterranean islands he went into Tenerife, and, having decided his Spanish base was sufficient, Franks moved into France and Italy. He only bought existing properties—villas and apartment houses as well as hotels—although it was more difficult than it had been in Spain to get government support. He still managed assistance of up to sixty percent of the purchase prices.

Newspapers began referring to Eddie Franks as a buccaneer, and there was speculation in the City pages just how much he would be worth if he went public, instead of retaining the businesses as private, limited companies, restricting the directorships to himself and Tina, and filling the subsidiary positions with accountants and lawyers. Franks didn't want to go public. Although his rise justified the description "meteoric," he had always been able to achieve sufficient capital through the banks, and had no need for a public share issue. Franks considered going public a danger; there were too many predators in the City, adept at takeovers, and, having worked practically to the exclusion of everything—even Tina—Franks didn't intend being a takeover victim.

Tina insisted she understood and was proud of his success—and he didn't doubt that she was—but Franks frequently regretted the absolute commitment that had been necessary. It would, he honestly recognized, have placed a strain on any marriage less secure than theirs. David was three when Tina became pregnant

10

again. This time the baby was a girl, the birth as easy as before. Tina said she wanted to call it Gabriella, and that was the first time he'd been aware of her mother's Christian name.

Franks suggested that the baby be christened in America, with Tina's family, telling her it was his way of saying thank-you for all the sacrifices she had made. Which it was. But he was anxious to go to America so his surrogate family could learn how successful he'd become. He'd tried harder, just like Enrico Scargo always told him to. How well would Nicky have done, by comparison?

3

They sailed to New York with two nannies: a motherly, big-bosomed woman called Elizabeth, who was an already established part of the household as David's nanny, and a second nanny for the baby. The leisurely crossing on the *QE-2* allowed Tina a five-day rest, but there was a nostalgia involved as well. It was the first time Franks had sailed *to* America since the hazily remembered evacuation voyage; for the to-and-from education trips he'd always flown. Franks wanted as much contrast as possible from that first time and hoped the Scargo family would recognize it.

The arrival came near to the pattern Franks was trying to create. All the Scargo family were waiting, as they had been for the wartime docking. Not just Tina's mother and father and Nicky, but the cousins and aunts and uncles whose names Franks couldn't remember and failed to catch during the shouted, laughing, and sometimes crying introductions. Franks knew it was for Tina's benefit, not his this time, so he stood slightly back to let her enjoy it. Mamma Scargo cried openly and Enrico seemed affected, too, covering the need to swallow heavily by clasping Franks in the sort of enveloping embrace that he had once been used to. Only Nicky seemed completely controlled. He embraced his sister, certainly, but the greeting to Franks was a formal, hard handshake, accompanied by an immediate up-and-down examination, and Franks felt like the refugee he'd always been.

11

There was a cavalcade of limousines to the Westchester house, where the tables were set in the garden under awnings for the welcoming lunch. Enrico proposed toasts to his grandchildren, and his wife sat throughout the meal cuddling the baby protectively, at the head of the table. A floor had been laid across the tennis court and the screening taken down, and in the afternoon an orchestra arrived and there was dancing for the younger people.

Although the voyage had been relaxing, Enrico insisted they would be tired after the journey and ended the party early, before midevening. Inside the house then, Franks was aware for the first time of the effort to which Tina's parents had gone. A room adjoining their bedroom had been decorated as a complete nursery, with animal motif wallpaper, a tinkling, rotating mobile depicting the Jack and Jill nursery rhyme, overly large stuffed toys, and a basketwork crib festooned and primped with broderie anglaise. Tina, who'd cried already, cried again. Franks thanked them, and the Scargos smiled, happy at the appreciation of their gesture.

While Tina and her mother watched the children being bathed, Franks and Poppa Scargo went downstairs. The sitting room overlooked the tennis court, and when they entered, Nicky was at the window, watching the reluctant departure of the last stragglers and the caterer's efforts to clear up. He turned at their entry and, unasked, went to the drinks tray and poured brandy for his father. Enrico took it without thanks, accustomed to the service.

"Eddie?" invited Nicky, back at the drinks.

Franks hesitated, not wanting a drink but aware they might consider it rudeness if he refused; it was the first time they had been in any sort of proper family situation since the arrival. "Thank you," he accepted. As the man he'd been brought up to regard as a brother handed him the goblet, Franks said, "How are things with you, Nicky?"

"Couldn't be better," said the man.

"Tell him," instructed Enrico proudly.

"I've been made a partner," disclosed Nicky. "Two weeks ago."

Fleetingly Franks had the impression of déjà vu. This was how it had always been between them, each having to parade their successes to the other. He supposed it was fitting that Nicky got the first opportunity.

"That's pretty good," said Franks, recognizing Enrico's

12

need for his true son to be praised. After his graduation from Yale Law School, Nicky had specialized in corporate law, going first to a Wall Street brokerage firm before transferring into one of the smaller law practices. Franks would have thought he was still too young for a partnership and wondered if Enrico had bought the entry, with some sort of investment.

"It's better than good; junior vice president is phenomenal after three years!" said Enrico. He was a red-faced, large-bellied man, physically larger than Franks remembered, who seemed to have grown into the role of patriarch he'd performed that afternoon.

"*. . . Come on! Come on, Eddie! Harder; you've got to try harder! . . .*" Franks blinked against the echo in his mind.

"Made your first million yet?" Enrico demanded abruptly, giving Franks his chance.

Franks hesitated; he'd forgotten a lot of Enrico's exuberance, too. He said, with intentional modesty, "Actually, I have. I've been lucky."

"There's no such thing as luck in business," boomed Enrico, whose trucking empire stretched to Chicago and who freighted at least fifty percent of the produce to the New York markets. He handed his empty glass to his attentive son for a refill and said, "You're both good boys. I'm proud of you."

Franks felt vaguely discomfited at being patronized so openly and wondered if Nicky did as well. Did having made himself a millionaire match becoming vice president of a Manhattan legal firm? Better, decided Franks. Much better.

"Everything concentrated in England?" said Nicky.

Franks looked directly at the other man, unsure if the question implied insularity. "Not really," he said. "Obviously the companies are headquartered in London, but the businesses extend throughout Europe."

"Good boards?" asked the lawyer.

"Professional boards," qualified Franks, unoffended at the questioning because it provided the opportunity to let them know how successful he was. "Each of the companies is limited; Tina and I control the stock."

Franks saw Enrico's smiling nod of approval and felt the warmth of the unspoken praise that had been so important to him as a child.

"Fortunate position to be in," said Nicky.

There was admiration in the lawyer's voice as well, and Franks' satisfaction increased. He said, "It's the way I always work."

13

"Cautious man," said Nicky.

Franks hesitated again, irritated at the accusation. He said, "There's a very big difference between proper caution and proper risk-taking." It sounded stiffer than he intended; his father had been cautious. Certainly Franks didn't consider himself to be.

"Know what I'd like to see?" said Enrico. "I'd like to see you two together in some sort of business venture. You'd make a great combination."

Before Franks could respond, Nicky said to him, "Ever considered expanding into the North American market?"

"Not really," said Franks, wishing he had a better response.

"You should think about it," urged Nicky. "America is where the really big business is done."

That was definitely a remark designed to minimize what he'd achieved, decided Franks.

That Sunday, after the christening and the inevitable party, Franks predictably read the travel section of *The New York Times,* and when the idea came, studied more carefully the trade journals of the travel industry during the following week. It was definitely worth considering, he decided. He wished to hell it had occurred to him before his first conversation with Nicky and the old man; if he pursued it, the impression would be that he was taking their advice. *Harder, Eddie, try harder,* he thought.

4

Franks' idea was to extend into Caribbean cruising in a specialized way that would make him different from the owners sailing the specially designed, rake-browed vessels he'd read about that Sunday and which his subsequent market research showed to be the accepted way to cruise the area. Franks decided to introduce a complete contrast, promoting the luxury style and class of yesteryear. He inquired into buying one of the oldest ships that Cunard had to sell, a straight-stemmed monolith of high ceilings, handcrafted teak, chandeliers, and crystal glass. The purchase price

14

was cheap, but the conversion costs would be exorbitant. Entire air conditioning was essential for the climate in which he intended to operate, as well as new, cheaper-to-run engines and kitchens and facilities to support a full complement of passengers for three or four weeks instead of the shorter Atlantic-crossing period for which the ship was originally created. There was no possibility of obtaining any sort of government assistance and the banks were unimpressed with the concept, arguing that the conversion was impractical in light of the number of newer, more suitable vessels available.

Franks refused to change his mind, and initially so did they. He commissioned blueprints and estimates from a marine architect and reduced some of the intended expenditure on catering facilities. The banks still refused to advance any more than eight million dollars, leaving him three million dollars short. Quite early in the negotiations the argument was made that he could raise all and more if he went public; the pressure was particularly strong from his main merchant bank, who wanted to broker the offering, but, as always, Franks rejected the suggestion, not wanting to expose himself on any stock market.

He didn't want to stop expanding, either. So he used his own money.

He told Tina before doing it, assuring her that, in absolute control as they were, if the cruise concept failed, they could dispose of the already owned hotels and villas to pay off the bank loans, and his own money was accrued capital. So if the venture failed, their life-style would not be destroyed.

But it didn't fail. "Yesteryear cruising" was an immediate and overwhelming success. Franks' ads blanketed American TV stations in the moneyed states of New York and Texas and Florida and California. This time the champagne in the ad was French, and the models dressed in 1920 flapper style and promoted the message against alternating Dixieland jazz and string orchestras. The demand was sufficient to have justified a second ship, but Franks, attuned to his market, didn't provide one. His ship was unique and had the attraction of rarity; the advertising introduced characters proclaiming a social cachet in actually having to wait for their voyage, disparagingly suggesting that there were other, inferior vessels, but that of course no one with class would consider lowering their standards by actually traveling on one.

The new venture meant that Franks spent even more time away from Tina and the children. The family traveled with him to

America when he planned the promotional campaign, but Tina and the children stayed in Westchester, and this time Franks remained in Manhattan, only getting up on weekends. David caught the measles, so they couldn't travel with him on the maiden voyage. Franks wasn't satisfied with the way the shakedown cruise went, and so he took the second trip as well, which meant he was away a month longer than he intended.

As soon as the Caribbean operation became established and the family returned to England, Franks made a conscious effort to devote more time to them. The Maidenhead house was adequate, but Franks decided upon something bigger. He took whole days off to drive around with Tina and visit estate agents, and let her be the one to decide upon the estate at Henley. It was walled for a large part and covered thirty acres, part sloping down to the Thames, where there was a boathouse. The main house had six bedrooms, and the separate original stabling had been converted into garages with staff accommodations above, and there were two separate staff cottages as well. It meant, for the first time, that the nannies could sleep away from the main house, so although everything was larger, the impression was of greater privacy. There was already a tennis court, but Franks had it enlarged and installed a swimming pool, fenced and gated for safety. He established a routine of not going into the London office until Monday afternoon and always returned by midday on Friday, guaranteeing the tennis weekends they both enjoyed. He registered David for Harrow and entered Gabriella for a prep school in Ascot in preparation for Roedean.

Life, he determined, was very good. The thought came to him sitting with Tina beside the pool. They were wearing the tennis gear from which they hadn't bothered to change, sipping the drinks Franks prepared.

As if aware of his thoughts, she said, "Everything's so wonderful; so safe."

Franks looked beyond the immediate fence, to the distant encircling wall around the estate. He felt safe, too: protected behind that high barrier, invulnerable from everyone and everything. Franks regretted so much that his father hadn't let him do what he'd wanted much earlier. And not just to prove himself, either. His father had earned the security of his own protective stockade. He said, "I'm thinking of extending further. The Caribbean is a hell of a market. We couldn't go wrong with hotels out there."

"Promise me it won't interfere with the way things are now;

I like having a husband who spends so much time with me and who loves me."

Franks stood and leaned across her chair, kissing her. "I promise," he said. "Why don't we all go out? While I'm having a look at the islands you can spend some time with your parents again."

They went two weeks later. Franks stayed in Westchester for the weekend and Nicky came up from New York. At the family meal on Saturday night Nicky introduced the subject.

"Interesting islands in which to start a business," he said. "Ever thought about American finance?"

"No," Franks answered honestly.

"What are the London rates?"

Franks shrugged, unsure he wanted to discuss business in such detail. "Varies," he said. "Lately it's averaged out at about eleven but sometimes it can go as high as fourteen, long term."

"Money's cheaper in New York," assured Nicky.

"Listen to him, Eddie," advised Enrico. "Best corporate and investment lawyer in the city now."

"Why don't we talk about it on Monday?" invited the man.

Nicky was coming to him, seeking the approach, thought Franks. He enjoyed the sensation. "Why not?" he accepted.

5

The sign on the door said "Vice President," and Nicky's suite of rooms justified the title. There were three outer offices, each with its secretary, and a final anteroom for the personal assistant—her desk sign identified her as Maria Spinetti—before Nicky's own corner office, with views along Wall Street on one side, opening into a panoramic picture of the twin towers of the Trade Center, misted in the early morning heat. Wide doors were set into another wall. They were open when the secretary led Franks in, showing a long conference room dominated by a central table around which were at least a dozen chairs. Nicky's desk matched the size and opulence of the room, a massive inlaid affair with a

17

telephone bank at one edge. His seat was high-backed, and buttoned leather, and the same color of leather covered two facing chairs and a couch in an area away from the desk, fronting a small table. Nicky led him there and offered drinks, which Franks refused, taking coffee instead. It was served by Maria, a severely-suited, tightly-coiffeured woman. Franks thought she was very attractive and knew it, and she was vaguely inviting in nearly every movement she made. He gave no reaction; he wasn't interested in her or any other woman apart from Tina.

"Impressive," said Franks, gesturing around the suite as Maria left.

"Room like this adds two zeroes to every contract and the clients expect it," said Nicky boastfully.

By comparison, Franks' office in London was a box, and a pretty small box at that. But it was still Nicky who was making the approach to him. Franks looked at his surrogate brother, thinking how well Nicky fitted into the surroundings. He'd always been heavy, from as long ago as college days, but the immaculate suiting, the material the sort that had a shine to it, reduced the appearance. His hair was thick and curly, without any obvious style, and hair thickly matted the backs of his hands as well. Franks thought passingly of Maria Spinetti in the outside room, guessed there could have been a lot of other Marias, and wondered why Nicky was still a bachelor.

"You said on the weekend that money was cheaper here than in London," said Franks, immediately businesslike.

"You've got a damned good track record," praised Nicky. "Half a dozen banks here in New York would fall over themselves to get you as a customer."

He'd had a pretty damned good track record before he tried to set up the cruising idea, and the English banks had twisted and squirmed, reflected Franks. Guardedly he said, "It might be worth thinking about, after I've had a look to see if I think it's worthwhile. You could arrange the introductions?"

"No problem," assured Nicky at once. "There's always private investors, too."

Franks shook his head. "I've always used bank money and kept the companies private. I told you that."

"Always worth considering something different," pressed Nicky. "This will be a new venture, after all."

"I'm accustomed to running a one-man operation," said Franks. "I don't know that I could work with a board who might oppose me too often."

18

"I'm thinking of financial investors, not active directors," said Nicky.

"Are you talking generally?" asked Franks. "Or do you actually know some financiers who might be available?"

"So you're interested?" demanded Nicky.

"In the most general way," cautioned Franks. "I haven't been to any of the islands yet, to gauge the potential. I haven't decided whether to switch my financing from England. And I haven't decided that I want to change my usual company structuring to include anybody else."

Nicky raised his hands, in retreat. "Okay, okay; I'm not hustling. Just wanted to be sure. To see if there was a deal anywhere."

"There *might* be a deal," said Franks, happy at his control of the meeting.

"How long are you planning to be down there?"

"For as long as it takes," said Franks unhelpfully. "I'm not going to make any commitment about anything until I'm sure." Nicky would be working for him, Franks decided. He liked the idea.

"Mamma will enjoy having Tina and the kids with her for some time," said Nicky.

If he did create anything on the islands—and with the cruise ship already established—they would need a home of their own in America, thought Franks. That would please Tina. He said, "Don't make any approaches until I get back."

Nicky raised his hands between them again. "You're calling the shots."

Franks felt the best satisfaction yet. He said, "It would be good to be able to set something up."

"I'd like that, too," said Nicky. "Remember Poppa said we'd make a hell of a combination?"

Franks expected Enrico to mention the meeting during his last night in Westchester, but the old man didn't, and Franks decided against doing so. He *hadn't* decided anything yet. Nicky and the old man had obviously discussed it, and Franks thought that if he raised the question they might think he was more interested than he was. He spoke to Tina about it, though, when they were alone in their room and he was packing for the following morning's departure.

"What are you going to do?" she said.

"Too early to decide yet," he said.

"I'm not sure about mixing business with family," she said. "What happens if you have a fight?"

Franks turned away from the open suitcase, leaving the packing until the following day, and got into bed beside her. "It's a good point," he admitted. He still liked the idea of Nicky working for him.

"Would it mean spending more time in America?"

Franks smiled at the question, leaning across and kissing her. "Might even buy a house."

"I'd like that," she said at once.

Franks flew first to Bermuda and found he was already known from his businesses in Europe as well as from the success of the cruise liner. From the initial meeting with the tourist minister he was satisfied they would welcome the development. There were subsequent meetings with other officials, particularly with the island's development board. Franks hired a car to explore the island, isolating prospective building sites, aware from the earlier meetings it would not be possible to buy existing properties. He found three possibilities, and from further meetings with the government learned that there would be no possibility of government finance. They wanted his hotels and his reputation but not any financial risk.

Franks telephoned Tina twice and flew to the Bahamas at the end of the week. He scheduled meetings in advance of his arrival, as he had in Bermuda, with ranking officials. This time he hired a small aircraft for several days to visit the outlying islands and realized that here, too, he would have to build. Once again there was a reluctance on the part of the island government to commit itself financially.

At the end of a fortnight Franks was sure he could operate successfully in both places. He would have preferred not to have to build and for the governments to be more willing to involve themselves, but objectively he recognized that the attitude reflected his customary way of working, not a reason for refusing to go ahead. As Nicky Scargo had said, it was a new venture. So maybe new ventures required new approaches. The reflection upon Nicky was a conscious one, the decision to be made there as important as the operation itself. Realistically Franks accepted the attraction: to raise finance through Nicky would establish an employer-to-employee relationship with someone with whom he'd competed throughout his life. And just as realistically, Franks recognized the feeling as stupid and juvenile, and one about which he should feel ashamed, after everything the Scargo family had done for him. Franks knew he would never completely succeed, but he made a conscious effort to subjugate the attitude

20

and to consider instead Nicky's offer simply upon its business attraction. The English banks *had* been difficult over the cruise liner. And sometimes they did charge as high as fourteen percent. So there were sound and proper business reasons for exploring things further with Nicky. And that's all it would be, an exploration. He'd call as soon as he returned to New York. If he didn't like the way things went, he could always withdraw and go back to his traditional sources of finance; it wouldn't hurt, anyway, to let them know he was negotiating with other banks.

His telephone call got routed through the secretaries to the efficient and provocative Maria Spinetti, and Franks was connected to Nicky without any delay.

"How's it look?" demanded Nicky.

"Pretty good," said Franks.

"Interested in my offer?"

"I'd like to go into it further," said Franks guardedly. "See how it compares to anything I could get from England."

"Why don't we lunch tomorrow, so I can set out the options formally? Then talk it through properly back here in the office in the afternoon."

"I'm still only making a comparison at this stage, against anything I might be able to set up back home," qualified Franks.

"No obligation," assured Nicky. "Absolutely no obligation."

6

They ate in a business club off Fulton Street, and Nicky was greeted by an impressive number of people as they entered and made their way to what was obviously a permanently reserved table. They ordered immediately so they could start talking at once, and the lawyer listened without interruption as Franks outlined the trip through the Caribbean.

"So okay," said Nicky when Franks finished, "what's the bottom line, for the complete development?"

"I'd estimate thirty-two million pounds," said Franks. "I'm only interested in a class development. That's always been the keynote."

21

"At a rough conversion, forty-eight million dollars, although there'll obviously be currency fluctuations," said Nicky. "That doesn't seem to be a problem, to me."

"Sure?"

"It's my business to be sure," said the lawyer. He smiled. "I asked around, to test the feeling. Chase Manhattan and Manufacturers Hanover are interested and said the talking could start at twelve percent. Citibank wants to come into any discussion and thought eleven might be the price if the borrowing were over twenty million dollars."

Franks' irritation at the lawyer already having made approaches was only momentary; there would have had to be some discussion in advance of their meeting for Nicky to be able to say whether or not he could broker the deal. He said, "Pretty much in line with English banks."

"They'll do better, now we've got specific figures," insisted Nicky.

"How much better?" demanded Franks.

"Ten," predicted Nicky. "Maybe not for the whole amount but for the majority."

Franks guessed his English financiers would demand a split commitment, too; pegging the development costs but putting a half or maybe a whole point higher on the money necessary until everything was operational. "Why don't we set up some meetings, to see what they'll do?"

Nicky pushed away his plate, hesitating. Then he said, "I've also gone to sources other than banks."

"Private investors prepared for a forty-eight-million-dollar deal?" asked Franks.

"I've known people prepared to invest for a lesser immediate return. And sums greater than forty-eight million dollars," assured Nicky. "People prepared to wait to see their investment mature and stay good. Hotels are bricks and mortar; permanent. Some people are attracted to permanence more than the uncertainty of the stock market."

"No harm in exploring that, too," conceded Franks. What about his unbroken principle? he asked himself at once. It still wasn't a commitment, he thought, in reassurance. And it would all make useful bargaining material when he went to the British banks.

"Took a chance on your saying that," said Nicky. "There are some guys in town I've acted for on previous occasions. Give them my personal guarantee. Two from Chicago and one from

22

Houston. The Chicago guys are going back tonight; they're locked into a meeting there tomorrow. So I've set up a conference this afternoon, back at the office.''

"Thought you weren't hustling," said Franks, unsettled at the speed with which things were moving.

"They couldn't change their plans," repeated Nicky. "It seemed ridiculous to lose the opportunity; we'd arranged to go back after lunch anyway."

Franks tried to avoid the thought but he couldn't; Nicky was very much in the subservient role. He said, "Okay. But just because of the circumstances. From now on let's take things a bit slower; I want to talk things through and make my own decisions how to proceed, not have them made for me."

"You're always going to be the one who calls the shots," reminded Nicky, unoffended by the rebuke.

"You've acted for them before?"

"All of them," assured Nicky. "Like I said, I can personally guarantee them. One, Roberto Pascara, is a friend of my father's, from the early days when he set up the trucking business."

He'd go to the meeting, decided Franks. But from now on he'd insist that Nicky do everything at his pace. He was the one in control, after all; and he was determined to stay that way.

Even before they entered the conference room adjoining Nicky Scargo's office, Franks had strengthened the lunchtime decision and was positively determined against becoming involved with private investors. He'd make the pretense—not just for Nicky's sake but for Enrico as well, as the old man knew one of them—but he'd find a reason to make any business arrangement impossible. He'd always insisted upon personal, unfettered control, and he'd always been successful. So it would be ridiculous to consider changing the pattern.

Franks was not aware of Nicky making any warning telephone calls to Maria Spinetti but she appeared to expect the men, ushering them into the conference room with the same vague seductiveness Franks had noticed before. Franks didn't sit immediately but went instead to the window, gazing out at the twin towers and the nearby Woolworth Building. He looked in the direction of the unseen East River and the Lower East Side, thinking back to the time they had been children together and Enrico had set them the contests in that first apartment, just off East Houston. He'd never dreamed then of being a self-made millionaire—didn't know what a millionaire was—or of one day

23

standing in a high-rise building in the heart of the city's financial district about to discuss, even if in the charade he intended, a forty-eight-million-dollar deal. How much he wished his father had lived to see all this happen.

David Dukes was the first to arrive, precisely on time, a tall, discreetly dressed blond-haired man with a pronounced Texan accent and an even more pronounced Texan courteousness, profusely thanking Franks for making the meeting, as if the Englishman had flown specially from London to keep the appointment. The others arrived within minutes, and Franks was momentarily confused when three instead of the expected two entered. But at the moment of introduction to Roberto Pascara, Franks saw the man offer his hand without direction, and Franks realized that he was blind and that his other hand was resting slightly on the arm of his escort, a younger but very similar man. As if he were conscious of the confusion, Pascara said as they shook hands, "And this is my son, Luigi."

Franks extended the greeting to the younger man and Luigi responded with a firm handshake, cupping his father's grasp to his arm with the other hand while making his gesture.

As Franks completed the ritual with Roland Flamini he thought how similar the three men were. All were darkly saturnine and dressed similarly, in muted greys.

Nicky, who seated himself at the head of the table after making the introductions, retained the role of broker, initiating and guiding the discussion. He spoke at once of the family relationship, to declare his own interest. Briefed from the lunchtime discussion, he was able to detail now the amount of money Franks considered necessary. He talked, too, precisely, factually, of the preliminary discussions with the three U.S. banks. Franks sat attentively, despite his already-made decision, admiring Nicky's presentation. Franks was aware, too, of the attentiveness of everyone else in the room. Only the younger Pascara appeared to be making any notes; the three older financiers sat with head-bent interest toward the lawyer. The blind man seemed completely accustomed now to his surroundings, facing the speaker as if he could see as well as hear. It was the elder Pascara who began the discussion when Nicky stopped talking.

"What's the breakdown of the forty-eight million dollars?" he asked, head moving searchingly, waiting for Franks' response to discern a direction from the sound of a voice.

"For each complex, five complexes in all, 9.6 million," said Franks. "Two in Bermuda, three in the Bahamas. I'm estimating 6.5 million as outright construction cost, for each hotel." The meeting wouldn't be entirely wasted, he thought; it could act as a rehearsal for the approaches he would later make to the banks. He went on: "Into that costing will have to be built commission money. That's always going to remain an uncertain figure, but it's essential that some provision is made. We'll need to spread some money around to maintain schedules."

"Bribes?" said Dukes, determined to understand.

"Bribes," confirmed Franks. "That's the way it is."

The sightless Pascara smiled, and said, "Allowing for that there still seems to be an additional expenditure of 3.1 million."

"The 6.5 million dollars is specifically assigned to the actual construction. The furnishings, fittings . . . everything . . . are planned to the highest specification. The theme is luxury. I'm not interested in hamburgers, and beer served in plastic beakers."

Flamini smiled, an expression without humor, and said, "I'm sure none of us here are either, Mr. Franks."

"So that means budgeting to expensive standards," said Franks. "There also has to be an anticipated operational cost, until there's a cash turnaround. . . ." Franks paused, enjoying himself. It wasn't just a useful rehearsal: it was an opportunity to show Nicky how professional he was. He went on, "This isn't a high-yield investment. This is something that is going to start slowly—maybe with some setbacks—but then come good." The statement might also act as a deterrent if their interest was in a quick-buck return; it might be better for the Scargo family if it were one or more of the financiers who refused to go ahead rather than himself.

"What about the bribes?" persisted Dukes. "It won't stop with the construction. There'll be sweeteners for laundry and garbage collection and for market men—things like that."

"It's a way of life we'll have to go along with," agreed Franks. "The important thing is to let everyone know we will work within the system but that we're not stupid. We'll make a deal and we'll stick to it."

"Don't you object to the system?" asked Pascara unexpectedly.

Franks looked toward the man, wondering if the son ever spoke or merely acted always as his father's eyes. "Of course I object to it," he said. "But it *is* the system." Franks felt a burst of impatience for the meeting to end. He'd indulged himself by meeting these investors and letting Nicky see what sort of negotiator he was. But he'd stay alone; there was little point in extending the playacting any longer.

"We've already heard from Nicky of your considerable success in Europe," said Flamini.

Franks looked up the table toward the man with whom he had been brought up, realizing Nicky had taken the discussion with these men further than he had indicated at lunch. He said pointedly, "All my other companies are strictly limited and private."

"Meaning total independence?" said Flamini.

"Just that," said Franks. He was conscious of the looks that went between Dukes and Flamini and decided that the declaration, coupled with his earlier remark about the slowness of initial profit, would go a long way toward deterring them. Luigi Pascara was hunched over his pad, scribbling hard, the scratch of the pen audible in the silence of the room. Nicky stirred, searching for a way to move the meeting on, but before he could do so the elder Pascara said, "You're telling us that you would expect to retain that independence? Absolute control, in fact?"

"Yes," said Franks. "If whatever company I formed included private investors rather than banks, then of course a board would be correctly constructed and hold proper board meetings. But I would expect the running and administration to be my responsibility."

"Uninterrupted?" pressed Duke.

"Uninterrupted," confirmed Franks. How could he bring everything to an end? he wondered.

"From which it follows that you intend putting up the greater part of the forty-eight million dollars?" said Flamini. "To be a majority shareholder you would expect to make the majority investment?"

Franks paused, uncomfortable with the detailed insistence. "Of course," he said.

"How much do you consider investing and how much would you require from us?" took up Pascara.

"That would depend upon the sort of return you were expecting from your investment," said Franks carelessly, trying to gain time to enable himself to make the calculations.

"Your intended investment doesn't depend upon that," said Dukes, joining in the demands.

"The suggested figure of forty-eight million dollars is a provisional one, an estimate that needs refined calculation after the market study and detailed costing of land purchase and material prices," said Franks, recovering. "I would expect to put in something like twenty million of that myself, with an additional

26

shareholding of five million in my wife's name. That would leave a shortfall of twenty-three million."

"I don't think twenty-three million dollars split in some way between the three of us would be a bad stock holding," said Dukes. "I'd certainly like to consider it further."

"I think I would, too," said Flamini.

"I'm interested," came in Pascara. "I need more detailed costs, development schedules, things like that, of course."

"Naturally," said Franks easily, pleased at seeing an end in sight. "All that would be available." Nicky had set the meeting up so it could be Nicky later to tell them he'd decided to go ahead a different way. He was sure each of them had been involved in abortive business discussions before.

"How soon?" said Dukes.

"I'd guess the market surveys and detailed discussion would take three months," avoided Franks, more relaxed now. "Then there would have to be talks with the landowners, for the site purchases to be costed."

"There should be something in four months then?" said Flamini.

"There should be something by then, certainly," said Franks. He was disinterested now, regretting that he'd agreed at all to such a pointless gathering.

"Can we schedule another meeting?" asked Dukes.

"Of course not," said Franks, letting the feeling show. He gestured to the lawyer at the top of the conference table and said, "Nicky convened this meeting. I'll keep him informed on the progress and when there's something to discuss he'll arrange something further between us."

"That sounds a good enough arrangement," said Pascara, and there were nods from the other men at the table. Luigi Pascara looked up from his pad, stretching the cramp from his fingers, as glad as Franks that it was over.

Nicky insisted on summoning Maria to serve drinks, although it was not yet five o'clock. Dukes and Flamini and the younger Pascara agreed to martinis and whiskey, but the sightless man asked for mineral water. Maintaining the social pretense, Franks took gin as well.

"A toast, to a successful business partnership," proposed Nicky, raising his glass.

"To a successful business partnership," recited the other men in the room.

"A successful business partnership," echoed Franks dutifully.

27

• • •

Within a week of the meeting, Argentina declared a moratorium on foreign debts of forty billion dollars, and Syria and Iraq at the same time demanded the surrender by Israel of the occupied territories on the West Bank with the threat of military intervention if that surrender was not made.

And the money markets of London and New York reacted predictably, going into immediate retreat.

7

Franks had one meeting, with Citibank, before the crisis broke. That meeting concluded with the uncommitted understanding that thirty million dollars might be available—eighteen million at 9.5 percent, the remainder at 11—once there was proper research and costing information available. But when Argentina declared the suspension of its international debt repayments, the reversal was practically immediate: Citibank was heavily involved in a loan consortium at particular risk. Nicky wanted to continue the approaches, to Chase Manhattan and Manufacturers Hanover, but Franks decided the financial markets in Manhattan were too jumpy. Nicky then suggested flying to Chicago to see if Flamini or Pascara might consider an investment beyond their initial general discussion, but Franks rejected that as well.

Franks instead returned to his established financial sources in London. He began with Barclays and Lloyds and National Westminster and went beyond the institutions with which he normally dealt to include two others.

By the time the money-raising talks started there had been sporadic fighting between Israeli and Syrian forces on the Golan, with Jordan joining in, and indications from Iraq—with a hint of support from Saudi Arabia—of a reduction in oil supplies to the West. The clearing banks were involved either directly or through subsidiaries with the Argentinian refusal to meet its debts—a refusal the International Monetary Fund and the World Bank appeared unable to resolve—and while Franks' prospectus was

28

being considered, a national dock strike was declared, further unsettling and tightening the market.

Although he did not have his financing arranged, Franks commissioned the market survey and wrote confirmatory letters to all the officials with whom he had negotiated in both Bermuda and the Bahamas, putting formally in writing his interest to proceed, unwilling for them to read into any delay the difficulties he was having raising cash.

The pressure continued from New York, from Nicky, in a series of telephone calls that finally erupted into an actual argument when Nicky began demanding some sort of timetable, reminiscent of Dukes' attitude at the initial meeting.

"You know the state of the market, for Christ's sake!" protested Franks. "I'm *not* going to be forced into anything until I'm sure. . . ." Franks allowed the pause, seeing another argument. "If Dukes and Pascara and Flamini are so anxious it makes me wonder if I need any sort of association anyway. . . ."

"They're not anxious!" cut off Nicky, from New York.

"They appear to be," said Franks, enjoying as he always did his supremacy. "You know money's tighter than it's been for years. I can't raise sufficient finance here at a price I consider acceptable. Everyone is too nervous and demanding too high a premium."

"Dukes and Flamini and Pascara aren't demanding high premiums," said Nicky. "And you've shown your hand."

"What hand?" demanded Franks.

"What you intend to establish in the two islands; with the possibility of further expansion."

"They wouldn't!" said Franks, immediately recognizing the threat. He had the feeling of being backed into the corner of a particularly small room.

"I'm not predicting what they might do," said Nicky. "I know they were impressed at your presentation. And I know that if I were an American financier with cash to spare and someone fell out of a deal, I'd seriously consider going on by myself. . . ." There was a pause, practically to metronome timing. "Wouldn't you?" Nicky finished.

Yes, thought Franks at once. It was exactly what he would do—what any good businessman would do. Except he wouldn't be the good businessman doing it, he'd be the loser being put down by the winners, and Eddie Franks didn't lose. He hadn't done so yet, and he didn't intend to start now. "They might have the finance but I've got the expertise. What businessman puts his

29

money into an enterprise without some guarantee that it's going to work?''

Nicky exposed the argument at once. "Pascara and Flamini are property developers,'' he said. "Because of what you've already achieved, leisurewise, they wanted you. You're good. But they can always buy expertise.''

Franks had the impression of the particularly small room getting smaller. He said, "You're not just giving me your impressions, are you?''

Nicky didn't respond immediately. Then he said, "Pascara and Flamini came through town last week. When I said nothing seemed to be moving, there were remarks about it being too good an opportunity to fall through their fingers.''

"It isn't falling through anybody's fingers,'' said Franks. "I've written letters of intent to people in the islands and I've commissioned the detailed survey. Everything is going along as it should.''

"You said earlier you didn't have the finance,'' challenged the lawyer.

This wasn't how it was supposed to be, with Nicky in the demanding position, thought Franks. "I told you I didn't have sufficient finance at a price I consider acceptable. There's a big difference.''

"How long?'' persisted Nicky, returning to a time schedule.

"I won't be locked in,'' rejected Franks. Whatever happened, he'd squeeze the bastards out and go it alone. He wasn't going to be treated like some beginner unsure of the profit and loss sides of a balance sheet.

"So what am I going to tell them?'' said Nicky.

To go to hell, thought Franks. He said, "Tell them the truth: that I've confirmed the approaches and commissioned the survey. When it's time to proceed, then I'll proceed.''

"I don't think that will satisfy them,'' said Nicky.

"I don't give a damn about satisfying them,'' said Franks, letting the anger show. "I'm putting together a business proposition in a businesslike way, not setting up a popularity contest. We had exploratory talks, that's all. What gives them the right to imagine they're suddenly running everything?''

"They're not trying to run everything,'' placated Nicky. "And they don't want to. They're just out to seize an opportunity when one presents itself.''

"Tell them nothing is going to happen to diminish the opportunity,'' said Franks. Not much, he thought.

"I'll try," promised Nicky.

There were no further financial approaches Franks could make in England, so he waited for the market to cool. But it didn't. Because oil is priced in dollars, and oil was uncertain as a result of the Middle East tension, there was a switch from the American currency on the world money markets. To halt the slide the Federal Reserve Board raised the prime rate a full point and when that failed to have any effect put it up by another half percent. Although Britain's oil independence gave it an edge, the edge was insufficient for complete confidence, and after three weeks the English interest rate was raised by one percent.

Franks received replies to his letters from both the Bahamas and Bermuda, asking for some indication of the timing he considered possible. Franks replied with stalling letters, promising a further commitment after he'd had time to consider the surveys.

Which were a shock, when they arrived. The detailed estimate was at least fifteen million dollars more than he had calculated. It took less than an hour of talks with the assessors and architects for Franks to discover that during the fine-print conferences both island authorities had insisted that the development provide all the accompanying services, which on four sites meant the provision of full road systems.

Franks flew to the Bahamas and argued the survey figure of an additional nine million down to three million—with the island government contributing the remainder—which he considered quite acceptable. And then, when he contacted the vendors from whom he intended purchasing the land, he was quoted $225 an acre higher than the original figure upon which he had based all his assessments. For the Bahamas alone it increased development costs by twelve million dollars, which more than nullified his success in forcing down the services provision figure.

From the Bahamas he traveled on to Bermuda, where he argued the service provision demand for six million dollars down to 1.5 million. And then found the land price had increased by an average of three hundred dollars an acre, adding nine million to his costing. Franks got the first hint of what he suspected from the Bermuda minister of tourism and took a chance, approaching the minister's principal secretary, conveying the impression he knew more than he did. The secretary didn't name Nicky Scargo as the man acting for other interested developers. He spoke only of "a New York legal firm." Franks actually got the name from one of the property owners and then by suggesting it himself, as if he already knew. Although he didn't need any further confir-

31

mation, Franks returned to the Bahamas. It took him three days to get Scargo's name there. On the fourth he called New York, controlling his anger, not disclosing where he was but suggesting a meeting the following day.

"Where?" asked the lawyer.

"Your office, in the afternoon," said Franks.

"Shall I call the others?"

"No," ordered Franks. "Wait."

Franks was shown into the lawyer's office by the inviting Maria. Nicky rose for the accustomed hand-pumping, shoulder-slapping greeting, and Franks waited until the woman closed the door before stopping the man halfway around his desk.

"Cut the crap," said Franks. "Let's not bother with the friendliness bullshit."

Nicky halted in midstride, hands spread before him in a gesture of confusion. "Eddie! What is it?"

"You know damned well what it is," said Franks. "You set out to screw me. Bastard!"

"I didn't set out to screw anyone."

"You negotiated on their behalf behind my back, trying to cheat me out of my own project."

"Sit down, Eddie," pleaded Nicky. "Please sit down and let's talk about it."

"I don't want to sit down to talk about anything with you," said Franks, shouting and unconcerned that he was doing so. "I'm going to go to another law firm and I'm going to explain what has happened and get you reported for breach of trust to whatever body governs ethics here in New York. You won't fuck me, Nicky!"

"Sit down," repeated the lawyer. "Please sit down."

Franks did so, with reluctance. It was going to create a severe breach in the family; maybe one impossible to repair. He decided it didn't matter.

Nicky retreated behind his desk, sitting and remaining head bent toward it, assembling his thoughts. Then he looked up and said, "Dukes and Pascara and Flamini were my clients before you were: proper business clients, not anything personal, like there is between us. I was acting *for* them when I brought you together. If I'd intended to cheat you, I wouldn't have told you on the telephone how they wanted to go on without you. I was trying to *keep* the project going, involving everyone, by going down as I did to the Bahamas and Bermuda. They're business-men, you know that. Hard, tough businessmen whom you couldn't

32

expect to enter any sort of agreement merely on my say-so and your presentation. Of *course* they wanted a separate, independent analysis. And could have got it, from any of a hundred lawyers or market research specialists. By doing it myself, I kept control of everything: made sure you *weren't* being cheated. Sure I went down. I went down and I saw most of the people and I gave Dukes and Pascara and Flamini the information they wanted when I got back. It was an objective, realistic report. From it they knew I wasn't showing any sort of bias toward your presentation. That they can trust me to remain neutral—professionally neutral—and because of that trust I would have known if they'd decided to go ahead without you." Nicky had been speaking with his body forward over the desk, eager to be understood. Now he sat back, enveloped in his large chair, and said, "If that was failing you then I've failed you. I'm sorry you think I cheated you, and I'm sorry that you think I'm a bastard. I don't honestly think you'd succeed on any breach of trust accusation, but if you feel strongly enough about it, then of course you must go ahead. I don't know how it's going to be on your side but as far as I'm concerned I'll try not to let it spread over, into the family. It won't be easy, but I'll try."

Franks had been angry—in the islands and then here in the office—partly from his belief that he'd been made to look foolish, and that part of his anger increased, but aimed at himself now, for being so hasty. It was a perfectly reasoned and understandable explanation. Acceptable, too. "Do you know what it's achieved?" he said. The effort at continued outrage didn't quite succeed. He continued, "Every single person whom I'd approached to sell me land has jacked up the price, imagining they can run an auction. Because of what you've done the original costing has gone up by twenty-two million dollars at least. And that doesn't include what I've had to concede in extra demands from the governments. That's another 4.5 million dollars."

"The landowners will fall back into line soon enough when they realize there wasn't a contest," said Nicky calmly.

"Isn't there a contest?" demanded Franks, unconvinced.

"Not as far as Pascara and Dukes and Flamini are concerned," assured Nicky. "If you withdraw, then I'm certain now that they intend to go ahead without you. But at the moment they still want to go on *with* you. That's what they've always wanted. What about you?"

"Me?" said Franks.

"Is there a contest from your side?"

Franks felt a further surge of anger, a feeling without direction. If he made it a contest and the financiers decided to oppose him, then the island vendors would have an auction on their hands. And be able to force the whole project up in price. From his efforts over the preceding weeks and months Franks knew he would have difficulty in raising the initial estimated costs. He'd never be able privately to find sufficient capital to meet the additional demands. And if the other three men were determined enough they could bid up the price anyway, poker players with better hands. Franks continued the metaphor. It was a poker game they couldn't lose, either way. If he threw in his hand, they would go on without him. And if he opposed them, they'd still beat him. A good poker player always knew when to quit, to preserve his stake for another game. But Franks didn't want to quit. He didn't want to admit that he had been outmaneuvered or outbid. Franks said, "It never has been a contest, on my side."

"So there doesn't seem to be any cause for us to fall out?"

"You should have warned me what you were doing!" insisted Franks. He was irritated at his own petulance.

"I've explained that!" said Nicky with a trace of irritation of his own. "I was behaving in a proper and professional manner on behalf of contracted clients. I would not have been behaving professionally if I *had* told you."

Nicky had an acceptable answer for every accusation, Franks conceded. "In the future I want to know what's happening. I don't want to have to find it out myself," he said hollowly.

"So there is going to be a future?"

"What?"

"You've raised the money, sufficient for control?" said Nicky.

The price at which it was being offered was still too high, but Franks refused to let the other man know he was bluffing. "Because of what they're asking for the land, it's difficult to know now just how much is needed."

"The vendors will come down," said Nicky confidently. "Let's work on the original figures. Can you come in with the twenty-five million for you and Tina?"

"Yes," said Franks, keeping his cards from being seen.

"And do you want to go on, with Dukes and Pascara and Flamini?"

Franks realized he didn't have any choice. "I think there would be some purpose in a further meeting," he said, still reluctant to make it look too easy for the other man.

34

Nicky got up and came around the desk, not stopping this time. He extended his hand and said, "If I caused any misunderstanding, I apologize. I wasn't trying to cheat you out of anything. I don't want to sour what exists between us."

Momentarily Franks remained seated, looking at the offered hand. Then he stood and accepted the gesture. "Maybe I was too hasty," he said in apology of his own.

8

The second thoughts were almost immediate, the awareness that he'd overcommitted himself and should, if he were sensible, back away. But he didn't. It had become so important for him to be the consummate businessman in the eyes of Nicky and his father that those reflective second thoughts at once clashed with his refusal to appear unsure or hesitant to them, to risk even the suggestion of Enrico's childhood accusation that he wasn't the best. So he flew to Britain to get the necessary finance, although the price was high. He spread the loans through five institutions—four banks and a pension fund—and at varying rates, the lowest eleven and the highest fourteen.

It was three weeks after the confrontation with his brother-in-law before Franks returned to New York. He traveled alone and took a hotel room in the city, at the Plaza, which was his favorite. He flew the Concorde, so there was no jet lag, but he gave himself an intervening day to revise and prepare himself for the encounter. He carried the preparations as far as timing his arrival so that they were assembled and waiting when he entered the conference room. They were seated exactly as they had been on the earlier occasion, Nicky as nominal chairman, Dukes to his right, Flamini to his left, and next to Flamini the blind Pascara and his obedient son.

Nicky guided the meeting, going detail by detail through the professional survey and assessment before Franks spoke up, pointing out that the extra cost came from the landowners' belief they had two prospective buyers. Nicky at once deflated the criticism, suggesting that if they agreed to a proper company formation, he proposed to write to everyone whom he'd approached, officially withdrawing his interest. Dukes improved on the suggestion, saying they should time their approach to coincide with the lawyer's rejection, when the owners would be eager to conclude the original sale rather than risk losing any purchase at all. Franks had the impression of being an onlooker instead of a participant in the discussion.

Pascara introduced the independent assessment that Nicky personally carried out, and for another thirty minutes Nicky dominated the discussion, with more detailed figures going beyond the costing to a forecast of profit. Franks immediately attacked the assessment as overly optimistic. The forecasts were based upon every complex being completed on time and almost at once achieving an occupancy of seventy-five percent. Franks said that if they went ahead they should anticipate minimum building delays of six months beyond whatever finishing date was given, and that in the first year they should consider themselves lucky if they managed fifty percent occupancy. Franks supposed he should have warned the lawyer in advance of his criticism, but he had reached the conclusion only the previous night and he wanted to achieve supremacy in the discussion. "I think we should prepare ourselves for every complex staying in the red for two years," he concluded.

"As long as that!" said Dukes.

"Maybe longer," Franks exaggerated. He wondered if it would work. Nicky's figures were too optimistic, so he was being quite truthful and quite professional. So it still might be possible to frighten them away. If they decided to withdraw because the return was too small in the short term, the company formation would be abandoned and he'd be extricated without losing any face. Being the strong man unable to carry the weaker ones with him, in fact.

"Haven't you been too optimistic?" challenged Pascara. "Your prospectus talks of it having a high profitability potential."

"Nowhere in anything I've said or submitted have I promised quick returns," rejected Franks easily.

"Let's look at the long term," said Dukes. "When everything is established and running, Nicky's estimated five million dollars a year, from each complex. Is that optimistic?"

Shit, thought Franks. As much as he wanted to escape he wouldn't impinge on his own integrity with an outright lie. "No," he said. "When everything is established we could expect something higher, maybe even seven million dollars."

"It's gamblers who expect an instant profit," said Pascara. He spoke as if able to see Dukes.

In reply, the Texan said, "An eventual seven million dollars a unit looks pretty good to me."

Shit, thought Franks again. He said, "That won't be achieved for years."

"If we decide to proceed today, you still want control stock holding?" said Flamini.

"Yes," said Franks. If they tried to override him on that he'd have another acceptable reason for withdrawing.

"So you intend making the success a personal thing?" said Flamini.

Which was how it had always been, reflected Franks. Would a psychiatrist see an inferiority complex in the attitude? Probably. He said, "I think personal control and supervision is important, as you know. That's how I've always operated. I couldn't consider any other arrangement."

"I think the personal involvement is extremely important," said Pascara.

"Is there anything that anyone doesn't consider to have been covered?" prompted Nicky, resuming the chairman's role.

From the assembled men there were various gestures and head shaking.

"Then it would seem to be the time for commitment," encouraged the lawyer.

Pascara was the first to speak. He said, "I accept Franks' controlling stock holding. And I'm prepared to come in for an equal third of the remaining stock."

"That goes for me, too," said Flamini at once.

"I'm happy with that," said Dukes.

"Which leaves you, Eddie," said Nicky.

Franks responded to everyone's attention, rationalizing what had happened. From a true business perspective, it was a good deal; an excellent one in the prevailing economic situation. Fourteen was his top percentage payment, which was just acceptable. Forming the company with them meant he wasn't held up by the current financial tightness. And he was retaining what was always the primary essential: his own control. It was time he succeeded in subjugating completely his ridiculous attitude toward Nicky. Time, too, to lose the sort of inferiority complex that he'd wondered about earlier. He said, "I'd like very much to go forward."

Franks returned to England that same night and the following day called upon the loans he had negotiated. It took only days for the arrangements to be completed and now it became Franks who made the telephone calls to New York, imposing a timetable and belatedly seeking a character reference from each of the financiers. Franks had begrudgingly to concede the response was impressive. Nicky personally vouched for the three men, providing satisfactory details of their previous associations. Franks drafted his own money from London to Manhattan on the same day he received confirmation of the loans, but already Dukes had made his investment. Pascara and Flamini were only three days behind. The only delay came from the legal formalities of incorporation, which would be done in Delaware because of its advantageous tax arrangements. Franks waited until the company became legal before instructing Nicky to send his rejection letters to the island landowners. In each case there was immediate capitulation to the old price, and Franks let them imagine they'd lost a deal by their intransigence until finally they approached him. He drove the price down from their original figure, settling $150 an acre cheaper and saving $375,000.

The bribes he'd predicted were necessary, and Franks went through the formality of calling them commissions and negotiated figures not low enough to cause resentment but not high enough, either, for any of the officials wrongly to imagine there could be additional draining demands.

All the time Franks remained aware that he was operating differently than before and meticulously summoned New York meetings to which he gave complete progress reports. Never once was he seriously questioned.

Franks was busier than he could remember being—even in the early days when he was starting out—and he enjoyed every minute-stretched, hour-packed day of it. The expansion broke the relaxed, long-weekend life-style that he and Tina had enjoyed. There was far less tennis and more long evenings when he isolated himself in the study, maintaining a cent-by-cent check on expenditure and equating it against the day-by-day progression of the building. Franks was very aware of the difficulties that could have arisen between himself and Tina and loved her all the more because she never once complained. There were many times when she had reason. He was in England for the pre-starting Open Day introductions to Harrow, but on the day David actually started at school Franks was unable to leave Bermuda because of a material supply crisis. And he missed Gabriella's birthday, which he had assured her he would attend.

When construction work started simultaneously on every complex, the only way to maintain the supervision he intended was to virtually live permanently in the islands, reducing further his time in England. He decided it was time to fulfill his promise and buy a home in America.

Tina didn't choose to live as close to her parents as he had expected. The Scargo mansion was just outside Pleasantville, with a distant view of the Saw Mill River. The house that Tina selected was quite a lot farther south, on the outskirts of Scarsdale, sufficiently far away from the Scargo house and, conveniently, much nearer to Manhattan. There were about seven acres of land—two of those undeveloped scrub and undergrowth for which he immediately hired a landscape gardener—and the house itself was smaller than the one in England, only four main bedrooms and a small servants apartment over the garages, which meant Elizabeth, who had become Gabriella's permanent nanny, had to live in the main house. It was colonially designed: white clapboard, with front porch pillars and a widow's walk like a hairnet around the roof, although it was a long way from Boston and Portland and Rockland where such high balconies were the traditional lookout points for wives seeking the return of their sea-going husbands. Franks indulged Tina, leaving her entirely in charge of the furnishings and decoration, pleased she had something with which to occupy herself during his long, enforced absences.

He took permanent hotel rooms in Nassau and Hamilton, commuting between the two island capitals in a private aircraft, succeeding by his presence in reducing the building delays to an absolute minimum, the longest being two months in Bermuda. He created an extensive advertising campaign and altered the sailing schedules to enable the cruise liner to offer a combined shore-cruise itinerary. The schedule change succeeded, establishing at once a satisfactory occupancy figure, in advance of the response from the advertising campaign. And when that response came, it exceeded Franks' expectation. It didn't achieve Nicky's estimate, but neither did it reflect the realistically careful figures Franks had advanced.

He made a ceremony out of every opening. Dukes and Flamini attended, but Pascara said business commitments prevented his coming. Dukes' wife was much younger than the Texan, blond and long-legged. Her name was Angela, and Tina said later she liked her. Flamini's wife was quiet and appeared slightly bewildered by everything; she reminded Franks of Mamma Scargo.

Nicky came too, bringing Maria Spinetti with him. Franks was surprised but didn't show it. She behaved impeccably, absolutely confident but never once showing any overfamiliarity because of her working relationship with the board.

The Bahamian ceremonies took ten days, and on the last night, when they were alone in their suite, Tina said excitedly, "Nicky told me tonight he was getting married."

"Who to?" asked Franks obtusely.

"Maria, of course," said the woman. "Isn't that wonderful?"

9

The Caribbean operation became an Eddie Franks success, like everything else. The family was practically domiciled in America, having David brought from England for vacations. Franks divided his time between Manhattan and the islands, commuting weekly and often taking Tina and Gabriella with him. Increasingly there was little to report beyond the profit forecast for the end of the year, but Franks continued to summon monthly board meetings, and Dukes and Flamini and Pascara always attended.

Maria Spinetti left Nicky's firm after their engagement was announced, to be replaced by an upgraded secretary from one of the outer offices, and Franks and Tina became socially involved with the couple. They were living together in advance of the actual wedding ceremony, and Franks and Tina often stayed overnight in Nicky's brownstone in the upper Sixties. On weekends the couple frequently drove up to Scarsdale. Tina had installed a court and there were a lot of tennis parties because it turned out to be Maria's favorite game, too.

As their friendship increased, Franks reflected how fortunate it was that he had not responded stupidly in the early days to the invitation from Maria. He remained convinced there *had* been an invitation. But not any longer. Now her attitude was one of warm but correctly defined friendship. He supposed that she'd actually become Tina's best friend. As the wedding drew nearer the two women spent almost every day together, planning her trousseau and the dresses for the bridesmaids—one of whom was Gabriella—and the changes that Nicky was letting her make to the Manhattan townhouse.

Maria's mother was a widow, with an apartment on Long Island, so the reception was held at the Scargo's Westchester home. There were marquees in the garden again and a band, and the tennis court was floored for dancing. It was in July, during the English school holidays, so David was able to attend. The Scargos invited all their relations, and Nicky included a lot of business acquaintances. Dukes and Flamini and Pascara attended. Apart from the brief period of the opening ceremonies, it was the first time Franks had been involved with them in anything like a social occasion. Angela Dukes wore a tight-fitting suit and a wide-brimmed picture hat, and Flamini's wife still appeared bewildered, although she was more at home here, in a family setting.

It was boisterous and Italian-American. Franks watched Tina dancing with someone he believed was a cousin but wasn't sure and thought how completely happy he was. Contented, too. At last. His fears at taking in outside investors had been misplaced, he accepted honestly. And he finally felt he'd proved himself. *To* himself. And to the Scargo family. He was no longer the refugee with a label in his lapel. He was actually smiling at his own reflections when he felt movement alongside and turned to see Nicky, smiling also.

"Leaving?" said Franks. Nicky and Maria were honeymooning in Europe, two weeks of the trip in one of Franks' villas near the Lido, on the coast near Venice.

"Not yet," said the lawyer. "Poppa wants to see us both."

Enrico was in the drawing room, at the window that overlooked the party. He was standing there gazing out when Franks and Nicky entered. As they did so he held out his arms to both of them, in a welcoming embrace, and when they walked forward put his arms around both of them, pulling them close. Nicky put his arm around his father, and after an embarrassed hesitation Franks did so too. Enrico released them both after a while and said, "This is a wonderful day. Both my sons successful. Now both my sons married to beautiful girls. A wonderful day."

Franks became aware of an ice bucket and wine beside the table from which Nicky usually poured the drinks. Enrico performed the task this time, formally handing them glasses. "I want this to be a very special toast," he said. "Special beyond the rest."

41

Franks smiled back, admiring the man. He had to be seventy, Franks supposed; maybe older. But little seemed to have changed from the day of that dockside arrival, all those years ago. The hair was completely white now but remained very full, and he was still upright and comparatively hard-bodied, apart from the paunch. Franks raised his glass, responding to Enrico's invitation.

"To my son and to a man I regard as my son," said Enrico, thick-voiced. "I want you to know how proud I am. How proud I've always been. I don't think there can be a man as happy as I am with the life he's had."

Franks had the impression that Nicky felt embarrassed now. He said, "Let me make another toast. Let me say thank-you to a wonderful man and a wonderful family who took me in and made me part of it." There was a risk of this becoming maudlin, he thought. But he wanted to say it. None of them would ever know but he'd just made an apology for all his stupidity in the last few years in his attitude toward them.

They drank, and then Enrico proposed again, "To us always being like we are today."

"As we are today," echoed Nicky.

"Get back to the party," instructed Enrico, swallowing heavily. "Get back out there and enjoy the fun."

As they made their way out of the house Nicky said, "David Dukes has a suggestion about the Caribbean operation."

"What?" asked Franks.

"He wasn't specific," said Nicky dismissively.

Franks found the Texan by the dance floor, indulgently watching as Pascara's son swirled around with his flamboyant wife. "Nicky says you've got an idea about the company," he said.

Dukes turned to him. "Only an idea," he said. "Just thought I'd put it forward, to see what everybody thinks."

10

It made practical sense to have preliminary discussions on Dukes' proposal while they were all in New York, despite Nicky's honeymoon absence. They still used his office and conference area—because that was where they always met—the day after the Westchester reception. Franks automatically chaired the meeting, but because the discussions were informal he agreed to Pascara's suggestion that there was no need for formal note-taking or record-making.

"What's the suggestion?" Franks demanded when they were settled.

"Gambling," announced Dukes shortly.

"Gambling?" The question came from Pascara, slightly ahead of Franks.

"Quite separately from our involvement together I've acquired an interest in Las Vegas," expanded Dukes. "I've spent a lot of time there recently. The profit from gaming is astonishing. Some of the larger hotels with casinos, like Caesars Palace and the Sands, think in terms of millions of dollars a week."

"You think we should consider expansion into Las Vegas?" said Pascara, responding to rare prompting from Luigi, beside him.

Dukes shook his head. "My thought was that we should install casinos in our own complexes."

"It goes against our concept," said Franks. "Our whole theme is absolute luxury. Slot machines don't fit in."

"I wasn't suggesting that they did," said Dukes. "Why not make the casinos like the hotels, high class, high stakes, everything discreet and plush? The very fact of *not* having slot machines would be a gimmick that would fit exactly into our mold."

"My feelings are with Franks," said Flamini. "We're doing well with a good image. I'm not sure that gambling fits into it."

"Would the governments of the islands allow it anyway?" said Pascara, hinting opposition.

"We won't know until we've made an approach," said Dukes. "There's already a casino in Nassau so I don't see why they should object to another one."

"Maybe on the grounds that there is already one in existence," said Franks.

"Like I said," reiterated Dukes, "we won't know until we've made an approach."

Franks knew from his French operation how popular the casinos were in places like Cannes and Deauville. Conscious of his mistaken initial attitude toward the men, Franks tried to remain objective. His immediate response was to reject the idea outright, but a more considered reflection was that the sort of casino that Dukes was suggesting might be an advantage. The Bahamas and Bermuda were geared for American vacationers and there was a great limitation to casino gambling in the United States. To Pascara he said, "What do you think?"

"I'm unwilling to come out for or against at this stage," said the blind man. "I'd need some certified accounts to be convinced if it's practicable. And I'd certainly need to know the attitudes of both the island governments."

"Flamini?" invited Franks.

"I like our luxury concept," said the other Italian. "It's worked. At the moment I'm unsure we'd be able to maintain the standard if we go into casinos. There are too many shady areas in gambling."

"Not if it's properly governed and policed," said Dukes. "The sort of security that exists in Vegas is incredible. And it works. They keep files on all the known crooks and gangsters. I'd defy any of them to last longer than an hour before they're identified."

"I don't suppose there would be any harm in exploring it," said Flamini. "This is informal, after all. If we decide against it we haven't really wasted anything."

"I'd like to see something of the actual operation," said Franks with his predictable need to examine everything personally.

"Why don't I take you down and introduce you to my Las Vegas partner? Name's Harry Greenberg. The hotel is the Golden Hat."

"We still need to know the attitude of the islands," reminded Flamini.

"Why don't I go to Las Vegas and then across to the islands?" suggested Franks. "I could get the feel of everything and we could have a complete discussion next time, when Nicky's back."

"It could be a lot of work for nothing," said Flamini.

"Surely you wouldn't consider going on without it!" said Franks, surprised at the apparent reversal of the man's attitude.

"No," said Flamini. "Maybe Nicky's the one to do it, that's all."

"Nicky's not here," said Franks, reluctant to surrender personal supervision.

Franks met Dukes in Nevada at the end of the week. Harry Greenberg was a fleshy, eagerly smiling man who wore a lot of gold jewelry and smoked cigars through a stunted holder. The friendship between him and Dukes was very obvious from the time and trouble the casino director devoted to them. Both were given hospitality suites on the top floor of the hotel and a chauffeured limousine was made available to them throughout their stay. Greenberg personally escorted them through the security and monitoring rooms, producing the criminal files about which Dukes had spoken in New York. Greenberg explained the intricacies of the various games and their profit margins, and did not confine himself to his own hotel but took them on varying tours through the rest of the hotels on the strip. Everywhere they were personally greeted by other directors and shown the facilities.

Franks didn't like Las Vegas in any way. The supposedly luxury hotels seemed to him plasticized and surface smart, the halter-topped and check-shirted clientele raucous and herdlike, and the casinos garishly offensive. Throughout, however, he remained utterly objective, refusing any judgment on initial impressions and letting everyone fully explain the benefits.

He refused, too, to commit any opinion to Dukes, although he did in Dukes' suite go fully through the figures that Greenberg made available. From those figures, incomplete though they were, the profit of which Dukes was so enthusiastic was undeniable.

From Las Vegas Franks flew directly to Bermuda where in less than a week he encountered opposition from almost every government minister and official to whom he talked. Franks went to the Bahamas prepared for the same response, but found the attitude quite different.

He raised the question with William Snarsbrook, the tourist minister with whom Franks had first made contact when he arrived on the island to investigate the possibility of hotels and with whom he had remained in social and business contact ever since. Snarsbrook was a refined, educated Bahamian—with a degree in economics from the London School of Economics—and one of the few officials during those early negotiations who had not sought what was now disguised in the audited returns as "commission." A tall, bespectacled, quiet man, Snarsbrook had only ever accepted the hospitality at the various hotel openings, and although it had been made clear he could dine and stay as a guest of the company at any of the hotels, Franks knew the man had never taken advantage of the offer.

They met on the second day of Franks' visit, at the hotel across the round-backed bridge leading to Paradise Island. Of the three complexes on the island the one nearest the capital had unofficially become the leader of the chain, and in the early part of their discussion Franks let the other man infer his visit was like so many of the others before it, the sort of personal check they had come to recognize and expect from him. It was only when they were well into the discussion, agreeing how successful the investment had been, that Franks mentioned the possibility of installing a casino.

"You'd like me to test the water?"

Franks hesitated at the man's expression. Surely at this late stage Snarsbrook wasn't maneuvering for a bribe? Cautiously Franks said, "I'd welcome some indication of how an approach might be received. . . ." He paused further, and then to give the man the opportunity for a demand if he intended one, said, "Would it be difficult?"

"It shouldn't be too much of a problem to gauge a reaction," said the minister.

Snarsbrook wasn't going to ask for any commission, Franks decided. He was relieved. He liked the man, and his opinion would have been diminished if there'd been any sort of approach. "How long?" he said.

"Soon," promised Snarsbrook. It was a promise he kept, making contact within two days. Following the success and prestige of the existing hotels, the Bahamian government would favorably consider a casino providing it was an improvement over that which already existed.

"This is an official reaction?" pressed Franks, determined against any misunderstanding.

"Absolutely," guaranteed Snarsbrook. "Your company—but more importantly you, personally—have got a very good name here on the island. An established reputation."

"That's very flattering," said Franks.

"There's no reason why it should be," said Snarsbrook. "What's been achieved here on the island is a personal thing . . . personal to you."

Franks was warmed by the praise, happy that other people were aware of how things always were for him. "This is a preliminary discussion," he said.

"I understand that," reassured Snarsbrook. "If you decide to go ahead, the government will be receptive to any proposals you'd like to make."

Franks returned to New York the following day. He summoned a meeting for the upcoming week, which meant Nicky would be back in time to attend, and managed a long weekend in Scarsdale with Tina and Gabriella. They played a lot of tennis, and on Sunday Franks took Gabriella riding, although he was uncomfortable on a horse.

The casino meeting was a long one. The suntanned Nicky, who briefly seemed vaguely distracted or disinterested, was brought up to date from their initial informal discussion, and then Dukes and Franks reported on the Las Vegas visit. Dukes gave the financial details, and when the Texan finished and invited questions it was Flamini who responded, putting them not to Dukes but to Franks.

"What did you think?" asked the Chicago developer.

"From the figures we have I don't think there can be any doubt about the profitability," said Franks. "It's huge compared to any other hotel-related operation. But I thought the casinos were appalling. There's no way what I saw in Las Vegas could merge successfully with what we've established; each would destroy the other."

"That seems a pretty formidable condemnation," said the son-escorted Pascara.

"I think before we start discussing the idea we should hear fully what happened in Bermuda and the Bahamas," said Dukes.

Franks dismissed Bermuda because of the clear opposition, but concentrated upon the more responsive Bahamas, setting out everything of his discussions with Snarsbrook.

At the end of the account, Pascara said, "So they're prepared to have us there?"

"No," said Franks, regretting the sigh of condescension as it came. "What's there now is a much diluted version of Las Vegas. They don't want another. They're prepared to consider a gambling situation on the same level as the existing hotels."

"Is there sufficient profit in something on the same level to make the whole thing worthwhile?" asked Pascara.

"The concept has worked in the hotels," reminded Franks.

"But will it work with casinos?" persisted Pascara.

Dukes intruded before Franks could reply. He said, "The Bahamas have worked brilliantly because of the efforts and the expertise of our chairman. But that success forecasts, in the next two years, a profitability upon the three complexes of only two million dollars each." The Texan hesitated. "Consider the figures from Las Vegas. If we were able to establish some sort of gambling situation in the Bahamas and keep it properly exclusive we could jack up that profitability to eight million dollars, over the course of a year. . . ." Dukes waved his sheet of figures. "And that's a *minimal* expectation."

"Each would destroy the other," echoed Flamini.

Everyone looked at him, and Nicky entered the discussion for the first time. "What does that mean?" he said.

"That was Eddie's remark," reminded Flamini. "I know he was talking about trying to link the Las Vegas concept with what we've already established. And that we're going beyond the Las Vegas concept. But I think there's an underlying point that applies. I don't think we should risk uniting the present corporation with any gambling enterprise, even if we decide to proceed. I think there should be a separate company. Same stockholders, if everyone here feels like coming in. But I think the hotel company should be in a position to shed the casinos if they don't work. And, I suppose, the casino group ought to be able to distance itself from the hotels, if the need or wish arose."

That was sensible company structuring, Franks recognized. If separate holdings were established it would mean the operations in both islands would remain safe.

"If one—or any of us—didn't feel like continuing then I'm pretty sure Harry Greenberg would want in," said Dukes.

"If he thinks it's a good investment, he obviously thinks it would work," said Pascara.

"On Las Vegas terms," came in Franks at once, "which are cheap, nasty, and nothing whatsoever to do with the sort of hotels we've established . . ." He paused to emphasize the objection, which would nullify the sort of operation that Greenberg would install. "And which we already know the Bahamian government won't allow."

"What about a specialized, exclusive casino operation?" demanded Flamini.

Franks paused momentarily. Then he said, "I am in favor, on the condition the gambling operation is under a separate company. I'd like ease of severance, if it became necessary."

"I'm prepared to proceed, on the same understanding," said

48

Pascara. "It's a good proposal but I don't think we should consider it if it risks putting in danger something that is already proving successful. I want separate companies; if that's not the majority feeling, then I'm not interested in continuing any further."

Franks was surprised at the forcefulness. Pleased, as well. He had control, so independent support was unnecessary, but he still welcomed the backing of the other man.

"If it's a separate company it's going to mean separate development costs," pointed out Flamini, always concerned with finance. "Have we got any costing for a casino?"

"None," said Franks. "It hasn't got to that stage yet."

Flamini nodded, a man in private agreement with himself. He said, "I'll want figures, before a positive commitment. I'd expect all of us will. But in principle, I'm happy to proceed."

"And everyone knows how I feel," said Dukes. "What about Greenberg?"

"We've got a good working board," said Pascara. "I don't see the need for any outside involvement."

"He's got casino expertise," persisted the Texan.

"Of the sort of casinos we've already decided we don't want," rejected Flamini. "I don't think we should consider any change from what exists now."

"I propose Eddie Franks remain as chairman of the new company," said Pascara. "I don't like switching bets from winning horses."

"Would you be prepared to be chairman?" asked Nicky formally.

"Yes," said Franks. "If, at the end of all the inquiries and negotiations, we decide to go on, then I'd be very pleased to act as chairman."

The appointment formally occurred three months later, after the Bahamian goverment agreed and the first casino opened. This time Pascara and his son traveled to the island for the official opening, with all the other directors of the new company. The profit return began after six months, doubling the prediction from the earlier financial forecasts. There was an attempt to repay Harry Greenberg's help and Las Vegas hospitality by inviting him to the Bahamian opening. His suggestion came shortly after the profits began, and was delivered through Dukes: why not set up lines of credit between the Golden Hat and the Bahamas, enabling gamblers at one location to gamble on money—or winnings—deposited at the other? With the standards established and strictly monitored on the islands, Franks did not see the linkup being detrimental to their casino, and accepted Dukes' argument that the appeal at the Las Vegas end would be limited to the high rollers from the few large-stakes tables at the Golden Hat.

Franks personally involved himself in the early weeks as he always did, concentrating upon the security installation that had been copied from Las Vegas and using their financial linkup with the Golden Hat to obtain access to their criminal file. He explained the system to the Bahamian authorities and agreed with the island police to add to the list people they considered undesirable.

He and Tina were able to return to their neglected English home in time for David's summer holiday. Franks did so with a feeling of relief, looking upon the homecoming as an opportunity to rest. This feeling surprised him, because rest had never been an object before. But it was now. Before, he had always known that there would be something else for him to do; another mountain to climb. But it wasn't there anymore. He'd established himself internationally. Remembering his thoughts at Nicky's wedding, Franks realized, further surprised, that for the first time in his life he was truly, properly satisfied.

At the end of the summer, Nicky and Maria came for an extended stay, using the Thameside estate as a base from which to tour England, and remaining there all the time for the last three weeks.

There were boat trips on the river and the inevitable tennis and a lot of swimming, and Franks oversaw it all with a feeling of continued contentment. There was a faint but perceptible deference toward him in Nicky's demeanor and Franks decided, amused at the thought, that he was becoming patriarchal, like Enrico.

Maria came close to saying it openly. She and Franks were alone by the pool. Tina was in the house supervising an evening meal, and Nicky was there with her, waiting for a call from New York.

"Nicky admires you," said Maria unexpectedly.

"I admire him," said Franks. "He's a good corporate lawyer."

"I didn't mean like that," said the woman. "He looks up to you, like an elder brother. Respects you."

They were side by side, on loungers. Franks swung off, sitting on one edge and looking directly at her. She smiled at him and momentarily he imagined the long-ago invitation. He couldn't see her eyes, hidden behind dark glasses.

"I'm younger than him, by a year and a half," Franks said lightly.

"Ouch!" said the woman archly. "Hurt pride!" She pouted at him coquettishly.

Franks laughed with her, knowing his own eyes would be hidden by the sunglasses. Not having had any children, she was tighter-bodied than Tina, smooth-stomached and heavy-busted, the nipples obvious through the brief bikini. She seemed aware of the examination, drawing herself in slightly, and Franks grew irritated at himself for comparing her against his wife and for responding to her mild flirtation. "Enrico certainly regards us as brothers," he said, trying to reestablish the barrier.

"Don't you?"

"I guess so," said Franks easily. As close as he and Nicky had become—and since the business involvement their relationship had become far closer than it had been when he was just part of the family—he knew he'd never be able to regard Nicky as a brother. Why, he thought, was there always difficulty with relationships? Thank whatever God existed that he'd succeeded in establishing one with Tina. He was right to feel ashamed of himself, ogling Maria's body.

"Want to know something?" she said.

Franks lay back upon the lounger, to avoid looking at her. "What?" he said.

"I thought you were very forbidding, at first."

"Forbidding!"

"Nicky had given me the buildup about this big business tycoon from England with whom he had some kind of relationship, and when I saw you that first day in the office I thought you looked exactly like one. Why don't you ever smile?"

"I do smile."

"Maybe just now. But you don't often. For a long time that was how I thought of you, always stern-faced."

Franks was uncomfortable with the conversation, embarrassed by it. "Now you know differently," he said.

"Do I?" she said. "I still think you're frightened of showing any emotion."

He might have been mistaken about the invitations on other occasions but he couldn't be now, Franks decided. He said, "I can show emotion, when there's emotion to show."

"Maybe I've just been unlucky, in not seeing it."

51

Franks sat up again, wanting to stop the stupidity. "Something wrong between you and Nicky?" he asked directly, purposely wanting to off-balance her.

It didn't succeed. "No," she smiled up at him. "What makes you think that?"

"Just the impression you're conveying."

"Maybe you misunderstood."

"You're making some things pretty obvious."

"So?"

"So stop it."

She laughed at him again. "Stern Mr. Franks, always taking himself so seriously!"

"I take Tina and me very seriously."

"Lucky Tina."

"And it's going to stay that way."

"Sure?"

"Quite sure."

"Haven't you ever been wrong, Eddie?"

"Not on anything important." What about his reservations about forming a company with investment directors? Nobody knew that he had been wrong, which was the important consideration.

"It's going to hurt when it happens," she said.

"It isn't going to," he said.

11

Eddie Franks welcomed the return of the sort of patterned, settled life that he enjoyed before his entry into American business. He did not become complacent and neither did he truly relax; both would have been impossible for him. Rather, the inner need to strive and succeed lessened. He tried to revert, as much as possible, to the Friday-afternoon-to-Monday-afternoon weekends and to a large part succeeded, certainly as far as the European operations were concerned, because there was nowhere too distant for him not to visit and monitor in the intervening three full days. He maintained the same discipline with the islands and the ship, but he was able to plan well in advance, and for the longer visits he usually took Tina and Gabriella with him.

During the American trips they invariably spent a lot of time with Nicky and Maria, and Franks was always conscious of an atmosphere between himself and Maria. At times it seemed so obvious that he expected Tina to remark upon it. He considered raising it with Tina himself but always stopped short and finally decided against it. He'd recognized long ago that the women were close—best friends. Why spoil it for nothing? And it would have been nothing. There was no harm or danger in Maria playing her games providing he didn't join in. And Franks had no intention whatsoever of joining in.

David did exceptionally well at school, never falling below the top four in any subject, and in mathematics and English usually achieving first place. With time to adjust to anything now, Franks was able to respond personally to the headmaster's invitation, a year before examinations, and sat proudly in the man's study, sipping the overwarm supermarket sherry, to hear the suggestion that David's ability was such that he should be considered for scholarship entrance. Franks reflected how pleased his father would have been at a similar interview. Just as he was pleased and proud. His father would probably have accepted the invitation, Franks guessed. But he didn't. And he didn't because of his father, remembering the old man's disappointment at his having to complete his education at an American rather than an English university. He thanked the headmaster for his confidence in David's ability but said that if that ability were such, then there was little danger of the boy failing entry at Common Entrance. He was more than able financially to support the boy throughout any education. So wouldn't it be better to offer the chance of a free education to a less privileged child?

There was another glass of unwanted sherry in gratitude for his response and in the car on the way home a kiss from Tina, who said she never stopped thinking that he was the most wonderful man in the world.

Franks often thought of the perpetual testing that Enrico Scargo had imposed between himself and Nicky, knowing of course that the old man had always set the tasks for their benefit. But he found it impossible to lose the feeling that such constant testing had established in him the inferiority complex that had taken him so long to acknowledge. If that had been the result of the prodding, then he supposed it had caused him more benefit than harm. But he was determined against either of his children inheriting the attitude. And for that reason never set David against Gabriella in anything.

It proved unnecessary anyway, as an incentive to try. Gabriella's progress at the Ascot prep school was as encouraging as David's. Gabriella was stopped from being precocious by Franks' determination not to spoil her—just as he was equally determined not to spoil David—but there *was* precocity about her aptitude for learning. The school responded to it, urging instead of stifling, letting her jump whole forms until she was in classes a year and sometimes more ahead of her age and still able to find the curriculum untaxing.

It became a time when Franks concentrated upon the children, whom he adored, a man to whom security had increasingly become more important, deciding that he should do more to ensure their future. He created trust funds for both David and Gabriella of one million pounds. Franks drew up the governing clauses himself, insistent upon absolute protection, and then had them legally incorporated with only minor, unimpeding adjustments. The most essential provisions were that the capital sum remained untouchable by either child until each was twenty-one and until that time should be invested in gilt-edged bonds attracting the highest compound interest. It meant that by the time David and Gabriella reached maturity, each would have a fortune at least double and likely even more than his original gift to them. He was as careful about the appointment of trustees as he was about the rules of the trust. It was an impulse to think of Nicky, and when he talked it through with Tina she said she couldn't think of anyone better with whom to place the children's welfare than her brother. Franks asked the lawyer on the next visit to New York, and Nicky said he would consider it an honor. Thoroughly fulfilling his duties, Nicky asked to examine the trust documents, seeking flaws he didn't find, and said afterward, "They're damned lucky kids."

Franks by now shared Tina's confidence in Nicky and was glad he'd thought of asking the man. It was visible proof of his feelings—not just to Nicky but to the Scargo family as well—but it was also an expiation of them, an atonement for his personal benefit for the wrong and unjust way he had regarded the American for too many years.

It was after their return from America where Nicky agreed to the principal trusteeship that Tina raised positively between them for the first time how different his life had become in the immediately preceding months.

54

"You're not running anymore," she said.

"Is that how you thought of it?" he asked. "As me running all the time?"

"That's how it seemed," she said.

Franks supposed it was a good enough description. "Maybe I'm just getting my second breath."

"Are you?" she demanded pointedly.

"Complaining?" he said, putting a question of his own because he didn't know the answer to hers.

"You know I'm not," she said. "You know I adore the amount of time we're able to spend together. I just want to make sure it's likely to continue, that's all."

"I don't see any reason why it shouldn't," he said.

Tina stared across the living room of the Thameside house, the disbelief obvious. "No more expansion?" she said.

"I'm not planning any."

"Which just means you haven't thought of anything, not yet?"

"I haven't thought of anything," Franks admitted. "And I'm not trying very hard, either."

"That makes me very happy," she said simply.

"Why?"

"You know why," she said. "We've had enough for a long time now. I'm greedy. I want you all to myself."

"So now you've got me," he said.

"So now I'm happy," she repeated.

It was a sudden, unconsidered decision to visit his father's grave, something he hadn't done for years. The provision for maintenance was made by bankers' draft and the site was immaculate, the surroundings neatly clipped and the flowers fresh and the stone only a little less white than it had been before David's birth, when he'd stood before it with Tina and wondered where the emotion was. It was a freak day in September, a warning of the winter that was to come, the sky greyly overcast with scudding clouds, herded by a sharp, thrusting wind. Franks hadn't brought a coat and regretted it, shivering before the resting place of his father.

"I've stopped now," said Franks, aloud, embarrassed at the sentimentality. "I've achieved what I wanted, just like you achieved what you wanted. I'm sorry that I didn't understand." Inexplicably the tears came that hadn't been there when they should have been. Franks swallowed against them and when that failed hurried a handkerchief from his pocket and wiped his eyes. "Beloved father of Edmund" said the inscription. Franks had felt hypocritical about it before, but he didn't now. The old man *had* been beloved and Franks was glad that at last—after too long—he'd finally recognized it.

The reflection about his real father led naturally to thoughts of the surrogate one, settling without reason on the embarrassing toasting scene after Nicky's wedding. What was it Enrico had said? No man could be happier with the life he had. Something like that. Enrico—the constant challenger—had a challenger of his own now, thought Franks. He was sure that he was personally happier and more content than the old man in Westchester.

Franks was still in a reflective, subdued mood when he arrived back at the house, grateful that Tina was involved with the nanny and Gabriella. He was in the study when the telephone rang and he answered it himself, ahead of the staff.

"Hello," he said, recognizing Nicky's voice at once. "This is unexpected."

"We've got problems," announced the American. "Big problems."

"What are you talking about?" demanded Franks.

"Not on the telephone."

Franks was aware for the first time of the wavering uncertainty in the other man's voice.

"You want me to come across?"

"As soon as possible," said the lawyer. "Tonight if you can."

PART TWO

Revenge is a kind of wild justice,
which the more man's nature
runs to, the more ought law to
weed it out.

Francis Bacon
OF REVENGE

12

That night was not possible because all the flights had gone. Franks went the following day, by the Concorde as usual, so he was in Manhattan by early morning, New York time. Nicky was already in the office, waiting, when he arrived. His brother-in-law was crumpled, as if he had slept in the suit he was wearing, and his face was drawn and badly shaved, tufted with missed stubble. There was no hand-pumping greeting. Instead Nicky remained sitting at the desk, actually appearing shrunken behind it, and when he used the telephone console to tell the secretaries outside to hold all calls Franks saw that the man's hand was shaking.

"What the hell's the matter?" demanded Franks.

Nicky looked away, refusing to meet Franks' look. His hand twitched in a palm-upward gesture of helplessness, and he said, "I don't know how to begin. I haven't slept at all and I've thought about it a hundred different ways and I still don't know how to begin."

Franks leaned forward over the desk, so that only feet separated them, and said, "Nicky! For God's sake what is it?"

The lawyer looked at him at last, blinking red-eyed. "We're being investigated," he said.

"Investigated!"

Nicky nodded. "I'm sorry, Eddie," he said. "Really, I'm very sorry."

"Investigated by whom?" demanded Franks. There couldn't be anything wrong with the books. He supervised the accounts with the care that he controlled everything else, and they were properly audited and the returns made promptly on time.

"The FBI," said Nicky.

"The FBI!" Franks backed away from the desk, going to his chair. "Why should the FBI investigate us?"

Instead of replying directly, Nicky said, "They used you, Eddie. I swear to God I didn't know how they were going to do it

59

when I set everything up. I thought it was a good deal. Safe. Honestly I did!''

"Nicky," said Franks, forcing the calmness in his voice, "you're not making sense. You put in a trans-Atlantic telephone call to get me here, you look like hell, and you're rambling about the FBI and they—whoever *they* are—using me. If we've got a problem then I've got to understand it to solve it and at the moment I don't know what you're talking about. From the beginning. Tell me everything from the very beginning.''

Nicky made a conscious effort to recover, grasping one hand with the other and trying to straighten out of the slumped, collapsed way he was sitting. "It was a favor," he said. "A repayment of a debt, I suppose. Although I didn't realize it, not at the beginning. Pascara set it up. He helped Poppa, years ago. Loaned him stake money to set up the trucking business and then made sure there were no union problems. . . .'' Nicky shook his head disbelievingly. "Poppa always knew how it was. *What* Pascara was. Things weren't easy in those days. You used your friends. Pascara's family came from Bagheria: that's very close to Palermo, and Grandfather knew· them. Pascara helped, when they asked him, and saw that stuff was put Poppa's way when the business started. The stake money was paid back, of course. All settled. They practically lost touch, for years. . . .'' Nicky looked around the office, as if he were seeing it for the first time. "It was Pascara who made contact, about a year after I got taken on here. Made an appointment and came here with Luigi and said how pleased he was that I'd done so well, that he'd heard about me joining the firm through some friends in New York and liked doing things the old way, arranging business through people he knew and trusted rather than through strangers. He wanted investment opportunities. Nothing high flying. Steady, sensible investment. I put him into a lot of things. Real estate, here in Manhattan and then outside, on the Connecticut border. Down in Florida, too; it was a good deal, Florida. Hit a development boom there. Lumber, in Oregon. Construction company, in Kansas . . .''

Franks sat bent forward, attentive to everything. There were a lot of questions he needed to ask but he didn't, not wanting to stop the other man despite the account being disjointed and his inability still to fully appreciate what the problem was.

"Then Flamini came, recommended by Pascara. Dukes, too. It was good business for me. Made my name, in fact. There· was always money available, and if things went wrong—which they did occasionally, natural that they should—there was never a

60

big complaint. . . ." The man looked up directly at Franks, shaking his head again. "Talked to Poppa about it, of course. He only knew Pascara, not the other two. That's how I learned what Pascara was; what he had been, at least. . . ."

"What?" demanded Franks, risking the interruption.

"Rackets," disclosed Nicky. "Controlled a lot of shipping out of Chicago. Not just Chicago, either. Milwaukee, and across the state into Michigan, to cover Detroit . . ."

"You mean Pascara's a gangster!" erupted Franks, uncaring now whether he stopped the other man.

Nicky sniggered, showing his uncertain control. "I always thought that was a word in movies," he said.

"It's a word that means what it says," insisted Franks. "Does Pascara's money come from crime?"

Nicky nodded reluctantly. "Poppa only knew about how it was in his time. Didn't know about now, of course. Thought Pascara might have gone legitimate. . . ."

"Didn't you try to find out?" said Franks. "You're a lawyer, for Christ's sake! Maybe not a criminal one, okay. But a lawyer. Couldn't you have made some inquiries?"

"I wasn't being asked to do anything illegal," said Nicky. "Everything was out in the open."

"Crap!" rejected Franks, remembering the man's earlier remark. " 'Made my name,' you said. You knew what he was and where the money came from, but it was business that made you look good and so you went along with it!" Franks swept his arm out, gesturing around the office. "You wanted all this. You wanted all this and the title on the door and a load of secretaries who jumped when you said jump."

"So maybe I did," fought back the other man. "Maybe I was sick and tired of having you held up to me as the big tycoon, an example to be followed. Just as I was sick and tired of having to be as good as you when we were kids and as good as you when we were at college. . . ." Nicky broke off, his voice blocked.

He scrubbed his hand across his eyes, and Franks wondered if he was going to cry openly. All these years and he had never known—never guessed—that it had been for Nicky just as it had been for him. Worse, in fact, from the blurted, near tearful admission. Franks didn't give a damn, not now. All that mattered was understanding about the investigation, and at the moment he didn't understand. "How does this involve me?" he said.

"It became an agreement between us that if ever I heard about something that looked good I should talk to them about it.

61

The hotel idea seemed good. I knew that the money would be available. Better than banks. . . ."

"Wait!" stopped Franks, actually holding up his hands. "Just wait. By the time I talked to you about expanding into Bermuda and the Bahamas, you knew what Pascara was. And because they came to you through him you knew—guessed at least—what Dukes and Flamini were."

Nicky nodded dumbly.

"Say it!" yelled Franks.

"I knew it," said the lawyer.

"Bastard!"

"I've said I was sorry."

"Sorry!" said Franks, still shouting. "You set me up. Trapped me into God knows what!"

"I didn't think there was any risk. I honestly didn't think there was any danger at all."

"Everything," insisted Franks. "I want to know every single thing that happened."

"I approached the banks first—you know I did—and found out how much the money would cost. And then I let them know. All three said at once they wanted in."

"Did you tell them what the banks' rates were?"

"Yes," said Nicky.

"So they could undercut?"

"I suppose so."

Christ how easy it had been for them, thought Franks. He said, "What about when I held back? When you went down to the islands yourself? Did they ever intend to go it alone?"

Nicky swallowed awkwardly. "Christ, Eddie. I'm sorry."

"Tell me!" shouted Franks again.

Nicky made an uncertain shaking gesture with his head. "I said I didn't want to do it, that it was stupid. That's when Pascara said he was calling in the debts, for the help he'd given Poppa, all those years ago, and for everything he'd put my way."

"You didn't have to do it!"

"He threatened to take his money out of everything I'd set up for him. Dukes and Flamini, too. They said they'd get another firm to do it and spread the word that I'd fouled up for them. You know how small Wall Street is; what rumors can do. It would have broken me, Eddie. It didn't matter that it wasn't true. We're talking about a lot of money. Millions. Suddenly shifting that, all at once, would have registered."

"Bloody fool!"

62

"Don't you think I realize that now!"

"So what was the point of going down?"

"To force you along."

Franks felt physically sick and swallowed against the sensation. A puppet, he thought. A puppet jerking and dancing to whatever string they chose to pull. "They never wanted control?"

"Never," said Nicky. "They always wanted the public impression to be that it was your company."

Franks burned with humiliation as he remembered all the discussions and talk at the board meetings. It had all been a charade, every bit of it. He'd imagined they were giving way to his pressure and all the time he'd been doing exactly what they wanted, creating the shield behind which they could hide. "What about the gambling?" he said in abrupt recollection.

"That was the eventual aim," disclosed Nicky.

"I don't understand."

"The FBI came here yesterday. Two guys. I don't know what they've found but they said they've been investigating for months. They know about the credit linkup between Las Vegas and Nassau. Said it was the classic way these guys get money out. All they do is make the deposit in Las Vegas and draw it from us, in the Bahamas. Gamble a little, to make it appear genuine, cash up the rest, and put it into an offshore account."

The feeling of sickness came to Franks again, at a further realization. The discussion about installing the casino had occurred when Nicky was away on his honeymoon. Informal, they'd said. No reason to keep any notes. So any investigation would show the initiative to the Bahamas government to be his, with the formal company discussion only occurring afterward. Franks' mind stayed on records. He said, "What documentation is there that I haven't seen? Stuff beween you and Pascara? With any of them?"

Nicky licked his lips, not moving.

"Give it to me!" yelled Franks.

Hesitantly the lawyer took a slim folder from a desk drawer, sliding it across the table toward the other man. "I wasn't keeping it from you," he said.

"Liar," said Franks. "You *have* kept it from me. What's here?"

"Dukes' bank transfer, for the original company creation. Came from an offshore account in the Netherlands Antilles. Instructions from Pascara, for dividend payments. That's offshore, too. An account in the Bahamas . . ."

"Into which goes the casino money?"

"I don't know," said Nicky. "There's also my own notes, about the formation. What I was asked to do. Some stuff about Pascara's other investments, too."

Franks looked down at the folder and then back up to Nicky. "Didn't the FBI ask for this?"

"They probably would have done if they'd known about it. They just wanted the company books; said if I refused they'd get them by subpoena."

Franks sat back in his chair, trying to analyze everything. It was a mess. An embarrassing, humiliating mess that was going to tarnish his reputation badly and probably destroy Nicky's. Which the bloody man deserved anyway; he felt no sympathy for him. Thank God he'd kept the companies separate from everything in Europe.

"How were things left with the investigators?"

"They told me not to get in touch with Pascara, Dukes, or Flamini. Said they'd want to talk to you and wanted to know when you'd next be in America."

"We'll cooperate," decided Franks. He lifted the unopened folder. "Make this available and anything else they might want. It'll wreck the company, of course. We'll get some sort of price for the hotels but we won't cover ourselves. We'll need lawyers, naturally. The best. You must be able to get the names. Do that this afternoon."

"I'm not sure," said Nicky.

"Not sure about what?"

"Cooperating."

"What are you talking about! We've been suckered—I have, at least. I don't like it and I like even less the thought of it becoming public knowledge. But it's going to become public knowledge. There's nothing we can do about it. The important thing now is to salvage what little we can."

"There's nothing wrong with the public affairs of the company," said Nicky. "Nor the hotel company or the casino holding. We took an investment in good faith and operated strictly according to the law."

"You know—and now I know—that it was crooked money! We've been set up, as a front, for criminals to operate," protested Franks. "Are you suggesting we become criminals too?"

"There's been nothing criminal in the operation of the company," insisted the lawyer.

"Surely in American law it's criminal to withhold information in a criminal investigation?"

"I'm not a criminal lawyer, as you said," agreed Nicky. "But my understanding is that we comply with the law if we respond to the requests that are made of us. But no more."

"What are you saying?"

"Just that," said Nicky. "We comply, but we don't offer any more than what's asked of us."

"You mean there might not be any prosecution?"

"I've no idea if there's going to be any sort of prosecution. Certainly, from what was said yesterday, they seem to know a lot, but it's a lot about Pascara and Dukes and Flamini. It's not about this company. And that's our only involvement. The hotels and the subsidiary casino operation."

"Through which they've washed their money!"

"Is it provable?" asked Nicky.

Franks waved the folder at the other man. "The offshore accounts listed here would probably make it so."

"We haven't been asked for that."

"Are you suggesting we go on fronting for a bunch of gangsters?"

"No," said Nicky. "I'm suggesting that we try to protect ourselves. In every way. If there's no prosecution, then we quietly withdraw and divest ourselves of the holding."

"What if there is a prosecution?"

"Then we're innocent victims. Stupid maybe, but still people who were cheated."

Franks shook his head. "That won't work."

"Why not?"

"Are you prepared to lie on oath?"

"Yes," said Nicky, without any hesitation. "I don't give a damn about perjury if I'm thinking about survival; I went to church to get christened, confirmed, and married."

He didn't have any religion, thought Franks. So did perjury matter if it meant minimizing the damage that was likely? "What would you say?"

"Nothing," said Nicky. "That I only knew them as business investors with whom every dealing was absolutely satisfactory."

"That sounds like a character reference."

"To me it sounds like common sense."

"I asked for anything that wasn't in the official company records. Because it seemed obvious that there *would* be something. What happens if the investigators ask as well?"

Nicky spread his hands. "I don't have it anymore."

"Don't be glib," said Franks.

"Let's destroy it, while we've got the chance," said Nicky, suddenly urgent.

"I haven't looked at it yet."

"Take my word for what's there."

"I took your word. And got trapped because of it. Don't be fucking stupid."

"You're not in England now, Eddie. Here things are different. Pascara and Flamini and Dukes aren't small time. They're important, *really* important. We're not talking of bicycle thefts and parking tickets."

"What are we talking about?"

"We're talking about getting killed."

"Don't be ridiculous!" Franks' rejection was automatic but there was an immediate feeling of chill. He'd read about gangland assassinations, in newspapers and magazines. Read about them in fictionalized books, too, and seen the films. But that's what it was. Newspaper stories about other people. And fiction. Not something that happened to him.

"I'm not being ridiculous, Eddie. I'm being desperately serious."

"Are you telling me that you won't testify against them if a case is made?"

"Exactly that."

"How can you!"

"Easy," said Nicky. "I acted for clients believing they were reputable businessmen. I'm shocked and dismayed to find that they're not. Embarrassed, too. But as I know nothing about any criminality, I can't give evidence about it."

"What about me?" demanded Franks. "What about my being the majority stockholder in both companies. The man who negotiated the casino agreement?"

"You thought they were reputable businessmen too. You *did*, until today."

"Not anymore I don't."

"Because I chose to tell you. Because I owed it to you."

"It's lying."

"It's living."

"I still think that's ridiculous."

"I don't want my sister to be a widow. Or David and Gabriella to be orphans."

"Isn't it a bit late to think like that?"

"I deserve anything you feel like saying," capitulated the lawyer.

66

Franks was engulfed in a fresh wave of anger, a feeling of impotence. He wanted physically to hit the man but guessed he wouldn't fight back that way, either. "You're a shit!" he said. "A complete, lying shit. I hope you get everything that's coming."

"All those things," agreed Nicky. "I wanted to be like you and I couldn't, not in a million years. Now it's atonement time. I'm not asking for forgiveness. Don't expect it. But I am sorry. Once it started, I couldn't stop. Okay, I admit it. I didn't want it to stop. It was a ladder to climb and I got to the top."

"You didn't have to involve me," said Franks bitterly.

"I didn't think there could ever be any risk," repeated the lawyer. "Everything else before had been so smooth and so easy. . . ." There was a pause. "I wanted you to see me as a big-time fixit lawyer with a big office, able to pluck millions out of the air with a phone call. There wasn't any maybe about it," he concluded, completely prostrating himself.

Franks supposed the man was being honest and genuine now, but he still couldn't find any compassion or forgiveness. Nicky wasn't sorry for entrapping him. The weak, vacillating bastard was sorry that it had been discovered and there was a risk of everything coming out. If the FBI hadn't come the previous day, Nicky would have gone on being the shoulder-slapping, bonhomie-filled brother figure who would have always kept the private file in his bottom drawer and laughed to himself all the time how easy it had been to con the supposedly big-time operator.

And it had been easy. It had been easy because despite all the bullshit about personal control and attention to every detail that Franks boasted about, he'd taken Nicky's word and accepted Pascara and Dukes and Flamini as business partners. He hadn't run any sort of independent check—the sort of independent check they'd clearly run on him and which he should have run on them if he purported to be half as good a businessman as he thought he was—which might have warned him. A credit survey would have been enough, because credit surveys threw up criminal convictions. He wouldn't have considered tying himself to anyone with a criminal conviction, no matter how many years ago it had occurred.

The anger now wasn't so much directed toward the lawyer as to himself. Maybe Nicky had set him up, but Franks recognized that he only had himself to blame. He could have backed out from the preliminary meeting. And he could have backed out after the charade that they'd staged in the islands, even though he hadn't known what sort of charade it was at the time. The anger

67

wasn't just at recognizing how ineptly he'd behaved. It was at remembering that he'd actually *known*, at the time, that he wasn't being properly businesslike. And still going on! He was physically hot, flushed, and didn't care that Nicky would see it. Weak, vacillating bastard, he thought again.

But he wasn't. He hadn't shown himself to be much of a businessman so far in his involvement with them, but now was the time to start; *the* way to start if he was to minimize the damage. He'd been stupid, but so had they, in their eagerness to make him a puppet. He knew the way the strings worked now. So they could dance to his manipulation.

"I'm the controlling stockholder," he said, making it an announcement.

"Yes," agreed Nicky, doubtful at Franks' sudden forcefulness.

"So I'm going to summon a board meeting."

"What!" demanded the lawyer.

"I want to dissolve both companies," said Franks. "There's a formation clause about impropriety?"

"It's standard," agreed Nicky.

"I'm not satisfied about the propriety of my fellow directors—and I'm going to find out more that will make me become even more dissatisfied—and I have the power as controlling stockholder, with Tina's vote, to dissolve the companies. Which is what I intend to do."

"The investigators said . . ."

"I don't give a damn what the investigators said! At the moment I'm provably fronting for men involved in God knows what. If there is a prosecution and we've disposed of the companies, then we've shown some responsibility. Distanced ourselves."

"Eddie," said Nicky, empty-voiced, "I don't want to confront Pascara and the others."

"You don't have to," said Franks. "I do."

68

13

Having made the decision—and fueled by anger at his own stupidity and their use of him—Franks' impulse was to summon the meeting immediately to get rid of them. It was the same anger that enabled him to control the impulse. An investigation was just that, an inquiry that might prove nothing, leaving only the suspicion. Recognizing that he needed more, Franks initiated the sort of credit surveys he should have commissioned at the beginning. Through a separate legal firm in Chicago and another in Houston he asked for personal checks on all three men. When he faced them, he was determined there would be no way they could rebut the propriety clause.

There was an inexplicable discomfort at Tina being so far away. The same night as his disclosure meeting with Nicky, Franks booked into the Plaza—impatient at the commuting delays that would have arisen if he'd opened up the Scarsdale house—and called Tina in England. As reluctant as Nicky had been during his telephone conversation, Franks refused to go into any details. He said there was a serious problem—the most serious that he'd ever had to confront—but he thought that there might be a way to limit the damage. It meant her vote and he wanted her with him, not thousands of miles away. She agreed to fly out the following day and asked whether she should bring Gabriella. Franks hesitated, and then said the child should remain at home in the care of Elizabeth.

He met Tina at Kennedy Airport but refused to talk in the car, within the hearing of the driver, so by the time they reached their suite Tina was positively irritated, imagining Franks was being overly dramatic. The attitude leaked away as he told her what had happened. When he finished she said, "Oh, God! Oh my God!"

"We haven't done anything wrong," insisted Franks. "I've been tricked, and I was stupid, but stupidity isn't a crime."

"You think the courts will see it that way?"

69

"I don't know how American courts work," said Franks. "I don't know how English courts work, for that matter. What I do know is that going ahead as I am now shows proper business responsibility."

"Nicky trapped you?" she demanded, working through what Franks had said.

"Yes."

"The little bastard."

"I've said it all."

"Have you spoken to Poppa? He knew, as well."

"There hasn't been time."

"Aren't you going to?"

Franks had avoided thinking about it. He could hardly wait for the confrontation with Pascara and Dukes and Flamini. But not with Enrico. Franks despised Nicky because Nicky had actively, knowingly involved him. But Enrico hadn't. Franks supposed Enrico had some guilt, but it was guilt of omission—of omitting to warn him—not his true son's guilt of commission. He would face the old man, but he didn't think it would be in anger, even though he might try to indicate the feeling. Toward Enrico he felt only disappointment. Despite all the bombast and the bullying and the competition-setting, Franks had trusted the old man. Trusted and respected and admired him. Loved him, Franks supposed, forcing the admission from himself. But Enrico couldn't have loved him, to let happen what had happened. To Tina, Franks said, "Of course I'm going to talk to him. But not yet. There's too much to do here yet."

"I want to see Nicky," she demanded.

"I've got to see him," said Franks. "I've left him setting up the inquiries, in Chicago and Houston."

"I want to come, too."

Tina actually entered her brother's office suite ahead of Franks when they got there, in the afternoon, stopping in the middle of the big room with her hands on her hips and yelling, "What the fuck do you think you've done!"

"We've been through it all," said Nicky wearily, nodding beyond his sister to Franks. "There isn't anything else left to say."

"Oh yes there is," insisted the woman. "I want to hear you tell me, personally, why you thought nothing of getting us involved with mobsters. In the middle of some fucking FBI investigation. Don't you know what you've done?"

"Of course I know what I've done. And I'm sorry." Nicky

70

was as disheveled as he had been the previous day, pouch-eyed with fatigue.

"Sorry!"

"Tina," intruded Franks from behind, "we've had the recriminations. I want to know what the other lawyers have said; how long they think things will take."

"Not yet." Tina went farther toward her brother. She stopped at the edge of the huge desk, staring down at the man. "I think you're a bastard," she said. "I think you're scum. You used us. Not just in the business. You cheated us in that, but you cheated us as friends as well. How the hell could you and Maria get as close to us as you did when you still knew what you were doing!"

"Maria didn't know; doesn't know. I haven't told her anything."

"You don't care who you cheat and lie to, do you!"

Nicky shrugged, with no defense.

"You've broken up the family, Nicky," she said. "We're going to be together in the next few days because that's how it's got to be, to try to salvage something. But when it's over— however it finishes—I never want to see you again. I never want to speak to you or hear from you. I hope you rot in hell. And I don't know how I feel about Poppa, either. He knew; maybe not everything, but he knew and he could have prevented it if he'd wanted to. I don't think I want to see or speak to him again, either."

The lawyer sat with his head cupped in his hands under the onslaught, refusing to look up at his sister. Tina was right, thought Franks. Whatever the outcome, things were going to be very much different for all of them. He supposed Tina would suffer more from the break than he would; Maria had been her closest friend, and any continuing relationship between the two women would be difficult now. Did Tina really mean that she never wanted to see her father again? Whether or not she meant it, Franks realized he wouldn't want to spend any more time in the old man's company. Not just the end of a close relationship, then. The end of the Westchester visits and the wet-eyed sentimentality. Would they even need the Scarsdale house, now that the companies were being dissolved? There had been as much family as business reason for buying, and neither were going to exist anymore. Certainly the running of the cruise liner didn't necessitate a place here. Franks stopped the reflection. He was running ahead of himself, far ahead of himself. He reached out,

71

pulling the furious Tina away from the desk, feeling the anger vibrating through her, and seated her in the same chair into which he'd slumped in the first moment of shock the previous day. Turning back to the lawyer, Franks said, "Okay, so what about the surveys and the checks?"

Nicky brought his head up, appearing reluctant to look at anyone. "They didn't think it would take too long," he said.

"*How* long?" insisted Franks. Common sense dictated that he didn't go into any meeting with the three men inadequately prepared, but he was reluctant to allow too much time. Getting out was the only consideration now.

Nicky turned away once more, awkwardly. "Seems Pascara's quite well known. By reputation at least. They thought some sort of preliminary report might be available in a couple of days."

"You made it clear what we want? Something provable! Recorded!"

Nicky sighed at the unremitting pressure. "You set it all out last night! Sat here while I wrote it out!"

And I'm glad I did, thought Franks. He was worried—was worried to hell—but he wasn't giving up. He was fighting back and he was going to win, although he wasn't precisely sure what winning was going to be. Nicky seemed to have given up at the very first indication of trouble. Franks said, "I don't want any mistakes." He paused and added, "Any more mistakes."

"I still don't think we should do this," said Nicky.

"Do what?" demanded Tina, coming into the conversation.

"Face them down."

"Jesus, Nicky. You make me sick!" she said.

"You should know what it's like, better than Eddie," said the lawyer.

"I told you he thinks it might be physically dangerous," Franks reminded his wife.

"Do you *really* think that?" said Tina.

"It could be a possibility."

"I think we should talk to Poppa about it," said Tina. "He's involved, after all. Knew Pascara a long time ago, according to what you say. He'd know if there was any danger."

Franks supposed there would have to be a meeting between them sometime. It might as well be now—almost immediately—as later. And Tina was right. Enrico had known Pascara in the early days. So he might know something that he could use against the man at the dissolution meeting. He said, "Don't you think Maria should hear about it, too?"

"Yes," said Tina, in immediate agreement. "I think that's exactly what we should have. A family meeting. The last."

Nicky nodded uncertainly. "I suppose we should," he said. Seemingly reminded, he looked to Franks and said, "Have you finished with the folder?"

"What folder?" interrupted Tina again.

"I told you about it," said Franks. "The records that Nicky kept, of the offshore accounts and some of the formation details." It hadn't taken him very long to read, the previous night at the Plaza. According to the file, Pascara had separate investments totaling nearly two million dollars, spread throughout America, in addition to the hotels and casino stock.

"I'd like it back," Nicky said.

"So you could destroy it?" Franks asked at once. Because he'd gone out to meet Tina's Concorde flight there had not been time to go to a bank, so at the moment Franks had it in a safe-deposit box at the hotel. But he *would* put it into the bank, he decided, staring at the sweating lawyer and remembering his earlier thoughts about the man's collapse. Nicky didn't think there should be any confrontation, and he was already running scared. Franks wasn't sure there was any protective value in what little documentation Nicky had retained, but he was damned sure he didn't want it burned or shredded. Just as he was damned sure that's exactly what Nicky would do if he returned it.

"It's my property!" insisted the lawyer desperately.

"It's company property," Franks said, the argument already prepared. "The property of a company which belongs to me and of which you're a servant, as secretary. I've every right to it; I had every right to it a long time ago."

"Please!" Nicky's desperation was worsening. "You're being stupid!"

"Not anymore," said Franks. "I have been, for far too long. But not anymore. If we're going to survive this, we're going to need evidence, not throw it away."

"Is that what you think we should do?" Tina asked her brother. "Get rid of something that could help us prove we weren't part of all this!"

"It isn't proof like that," said Nicky. "It's only stuff about investments. Bank records."

"Which we'll keep," said Tina. "You make me sick, Nicky. Sick to my stomach!"

Franks decided there wasn't any point in continuing the personal abuse. Friendship—any relationship—was over, and they

73

all recognized it. The only consideration now was getting out with as little damage as possible. And as quickly as possible. To Nicky he said, "Why not make a meeting with your father? Tonight?"

"What if he says do nothing?" said the lawyer, in sudden urgency. "He's our father, Eddie. As much yours as he is mine. We've always done what he said. . . ." The man looked to his sister. "You, too."

"No," rejected Franks at once. "Maybe once. For a long time. But not anymore. We'll talk it through. Because we should. Poppa could have stopped it happening, but he didn't. I don't have to respect him anymore, don't have to do what he says." All the relationships over, he thought again. Despite everything— despite the anger at their cynicism and their betrayal—Franks still felt sadness.

"I feel like Eddie," said Tina, declaring herself.

"Wrong," said Nicky emptily. "You're wrong."

"Make the calls, Nicky," ordered Tina. "Call Poppa and call Maria."

The lawyer did, stumbling and rambling, speaking first to his father, who agreed at once, and then to Maria, with whom he attempted to sound more forceful but didn't really succeed. They could have gone immediately, but Franks was increasingly conscious of the importance of the file, and so he delayed, arranging to travel out in convoy at three o'clock.

From the hotel Franks telephoned his bank on Third Avenue so that the officials were waiting when he and Tina arrived. As well as a business account Franks maintained a joint private account, because it had always been his practice to give his wife access to all his various holdings, including current deposits, and, although he hadn't considered it until they were actually going through the formalities, he made her a joint signatory to the safe-deposit box as well.

The agreement with Nicky was that the lawyer and his wife should meet them at the Plaza. Nicky was on time and there was an immediate, difficult embarrassment when Maria got from their car expecting the normal sort of greeting and encountered instead a wall of reserve, which was impossible for either of them to avoid showing, although each was aware of her innocence of anything that had happened. Franks insisted they set out at once, glad they were traveling in separate limousines. Franks and Tina remained silent as the car negotiated the difficult Manhattan streets, but after they'd cleared the traffic-clogged city and reached the Saw Mill River Parkway, Tina reached across for his hand and said abruptly, "I want to tell you something."

"What?"

"That I'm very proud of you. All the time when we were with Nicky today and I saw how he was behaving, I kept thinking how strong you are. And how weak he is. I don't know what the outcome of all this is going to be, but I want you to understand that I'm with you, all the way. I trust you, Eddie. Trust you to do everything right."

Briefly Franks did not know how to respond. Then he said, "I will always look after you; keep you safe."

"I know, my darling. I think you're wonderful. My family's screwed you: fucked you—fucked us both—completely."

"It's bad," said Franks. "As bad as it could be. But I'll get us out of it. I'll get us and the kids out of it. There'll be a period when it'll be nasty, with a lot of exposure and embarrassing things like that. We'll have to ride it all. You prepared for that?"

"I don't think that's a fair question, after what I've just said."

"No," said Franks, immediately contrite. "I'm sorry."

"I'm very lucky," said Tina. "I know that well enough."

"We both are," said Franks. "I'm sorry for what it's going to do to the family."

"You know how I feel about the family."

"Now maybe," said Franks sensibly. "You'll feel differently later."

"I won't," said Tina positively. "Later it will be like it is now, about all of them. I hate them, Eddie, for what they've done. I hate Poppa and I hate Nicky. For what they've done I'll always hate them, and I'll never forgive them."

"Shush, Tina," he said. "You mustn't hate. Maybe now, but not later."

"I will," she said. "I'll always hate them."

"I can get us out of it," said Franks, equally positive.

"Which is why I said I'm lucky."

The arrival in Westchester was unlike any moment before with the family; more difficult, Franks was sure, than his wartime arrival. Then only he was uncertain, but now they all were. Not at once, of course. Initially there was the waiting-on-the-porch, open-front-door normality, despite Tina's unannounced arrival from England. But Tina held back from any embrace—something she'd never done before—and he did, too. The stumbling change in Nicky was more obvious than anything, so there was a disordered, confused entry into the house.

Enrico *did* see himself as the patriarch, Franks recognized. That was obvious from the way the old, still upright, white-maned man conducted himself in those early, obviously uncertain moments. But then, thought Franks in retrospect, it might not have been too difficult for him to guess, because always at the back of his mind must have been the thought of somehow, some day, *something* happening.

Franks hadn't been aware of it until now, but it was always traditional for them to separate within the house, the women going with the children, the men going with the men. Today that didn't happen, although not by any announcement. Mamma Scargo instinctively led on, actually going toward the kitchen, but Tina stopped, refusing to follow her, and so Maria—already confused from the chill in the city—stopped too, so there was a swirl of uncertainty in the hallway. Franks moved for control, determined at last to achieve it. He announced, "This isn't exactly a social visit. I think we should meet as a family. All of us."

Enrico Scargo looked at him, immediately irritated at someone making declarations in his house. "What?"

"We're going to talk." Franks refused to acknowledge the intimidation he felt at once. Wanting to establish himself, he said, "We're going to talk about my being cheated and conned and thrown aside by this family."

Enrico and Maria and Mamma Scargo had been milling about in the entrance, but now they stopped, matching the stillness of those who knew.

It was Enrico, naturally, again, who reacted ahead of the women, rising to the challenge within his own household. "What?" he demanded again, his voice a rising roar.

"Stop it!" said Franks, opposing the old man for the first time but convinced against any pretense. "You heard what I said and just in case you didn't I'll repeat it. I've come here tonight—with Tina, who flew in this morning from London, and who hasn't slept and wanted this meeting because she's as devastated—no, that's a pompous-sounding word. She's as broken up, even though that's not much better, at what's happened to both of us. Because we trusted this family—" Franks stopped awkwardly. He'd been about to refer to Enrico but he didn't know how. Always, verbally, it had been Poppa, although he'd always thought of him as Enrico. Now neither fitted. He wasn't Poppa and he wasn't Enrico. Another change. "She had the right to trust you. You're her father. Children should be able to trust their father. I trusted you because although you weren't my father—although

76

this wasn't my true family—you made yourself so and I accepted it. So we both made mistakes."

"I will not be spoken to—have this sort of conversation—in my house!" shouted Enrico, confronting the challenge.

Franks met it with the same determination. "You will," he said. "Because you deserve it. Here in the hall, if you like. Anywhere. But you're going to hear what's happened. How this family's been wrecked."

Franks thought at once that the word sounded dramatic, although he supposed it fitted. It registered with Mamma Scargo, who gave a strangely muted cry, almost a screech. She broke it off almost as quickly as it came, and said to her daughter, "Tina! What is it? What's happened?"

Franks strode into the large drawing room, the others trailing behind him. Enrico was the last to enter, puce-faced at losing control in his own house. The whiteness of his hair accentuated the coloring. Franks didn't start to talk at once. He looked instead around the room, remembering the times he'd spent there, the weekends away from Harvard, the parties and the weddings, thinking last of the emotional scene with Enrico after Nicky's marriage to Maria. So much was ending. Franks looked to the lawyer: "You tell them, Nicky," he ordered. "You tell them what it's all about."

The man looked up at him imploringly, but Franks felt no sympathy. *"Tell them!"* he yelled, the anger bursting from him.

It was a pitiful performance. Nicky mumbled, head down toward the floor, and Franks shouted at him to speak up, and when he did, the account was still disjointed and confusing, so that Franks constantly had to intrude to ensure some coherence. Toward the end Nicky's shoulders began to heave, and he struggled a handkerchief from his pocket and held it to his face, so that the words were even more muffled. Despite the need to prompt, Franks remained attentive to the reactions of everyone in the room. Tina, who knew it all, was stone-faced, an expression of contempt gradually forming as Nicky groped on. Maria stared unbroken at Nicky, too, her face showing a mixture of emotions, shock and bewilderment and, toward the end, perhaps contempt as well. Mamma Scargo's was the quickest and most open response, the tears coming almost at once, but even these controlled in male surroundings, so that she sat with a handkerchief bunched in front of her mouth, weeping quite silently. Enrico's aggression stayed for some time, but at the end it was an attitude he couldn't sustain. There was no weeping breakdown, of course. Instead the

77

man sagged, as if some inner support had collapsed, and in Franks' eyes he looked for the first time what he was: an old, paunchy, white-haired man.

It was Maria who spoke when Nicky finally finished, and her reflex was ironically the same as Tina's had been that morning in the hotel room. "Dear God!" she said, swallowing in an effort for complete comprehension. "Oh, God." The woman looked toward Enrico, instinctively seeking the strength that had always been there, and her face registered the shock when she realized that the slumped old man didn't have it anymore. Desperately she looked around, so relieved when she saw how Franks was standing that she actually smiled, an automatic expression of relief. "What are we going to do?" she said.

"Get out of it," said Franks at once. "Save what we can, abandon what we can't, but get out of it."

"What do you mean?" The question croaked out of Enrico, and Franks thought fleetingly that even the man's voice seemed old now.

Franks didn't reply at once. Where was the apology! he thought in another flush of anger. Where was the explanation from the man who could have prevented it by one simple, easy warning? Franks actually opened his mouth, forming the demand. But then he stopped, conscious how quickly a man who had known unquestioned obedience and respect from his family throughout his life had been humiliated. Franks didn't want to further that humiliation. Enrico had constantly bullied him, but he didn't want to bully in return. He didn't want revenge, even. To think of revenge—consider the word—was stupid. Franks answered the older man finally, setting out how he intended to dissolve the company, and although he was looking directly at Enrico he was aware of another fleeting smile of admiration from Maria.

"No," said Enrico simply.

"Why not?" demanded Tina. "They can't stop us doing it, because they made the mistake of vesting control in Eddie and me. It's a brilliant idea."

Now it was Enrico who talked, gazing down at the carpet, for the first time humble in his own household. "Pascara is an important man," he said. "A big man. He tells; he doesn't *get* told."

"How important?" said Franks.

Enrico looked up, actually meeting Franks' eyes. "Bigger than us, to confront," he said, still simply. "Bigger than the law, always."

78

"Nonsense!" erupted Franks. "This is an FBI investigation!"

Enrico smiled sadly. "There have been others. I don't know how many, but a lot of others. They've all failed."

Maria's hopeful expression faltered. "You mean Mafia?"

"I'm not going to use words like Mafia or La Cosa Nostra or organized crime. I'm just saying that we don't try to fight Pascara or Flamini or Dukes."

"Which means doing the alternative," said Franks. "It means sitting back and getting caught up in God knows what and seeing perhaps not just these two companies but my other companies as well dragged down and maybe destroyed."

"I've just told you that there have been other investigations that have been started and failed."

"You're being ridiculous," said Franks. "Are you suggesting that if this investigation fails, like the others, that we just go on like nothing has ever happened? That we *knowingly* front for them?"

"Yes," said Enrico.

"No!" shouted Franks. "Do you know what you're saying?"

"I know exactly what I'm saying."

"I've told him, Poppa," said Nicky, like Maria earlier, seeking strength from someone he'd always known to have it. "I told him, but he didn't believe me."

"Believe what?" said Maria.

"That someone could be killed," said Enrico, answering for his son.

"This isn't a movie!" rejected Franks contemptuously. Who was it who had said something like that? Nicky, he remembered. During the office confrontation. Why was everything so unbelievable?

"No," said Enrico, regaining a little of his chipped control. "This isn't a movie. This is reality; hard, actual reality. And that reality is that Pascara is capable of having someone killed if he wants it done. They all are."

"Do you *know* that he's had anyone killed?" persisted Franks.

"Of course I don't."

"So it's just a story—a story spread about to make Pascara seem more important than he is and frighten people prepared to be frightened into doing what he says and never daring to challenge him."

Enrico spread out his hands toward the still-standing man, an imploring gesture, and Franks' feeling was one of embarrass-

79

ment. "I'm sorry," said Enrico, the final concession. "I'm sorry
I let it happen. That you think I trapped you. That I let Nicky trap
you. Okay, so maybe we did. It's the way the system works,
favors given, favors repaid. I had—we had—no right to involve
you. I was wrong and I apologize and ask you to forgive me. . . ."
The man paused, appearing physically choked at making the
admission and worse, having to make it in front of his family.
"Now I ask you one thing more. I know you've no reason to
listen to me anymore—to trust me. But about this you must trust
me. I know these people. What they're capable of. Stonewall the
investigation; let it happen and don't help any more than is
absolutely necessary. That way Pascara and Flamini and Dukes
will respect you, know that they can trust you. When it's over,
you can ask to dissolve the companies. That's the way things are
settled. Quietly. No fuss."

"*Ask!*" said Franks. "It's my bloody company. Ask permission to do something about a company which I created and I
control?"

"Yes, you have to," said Enrico.

Franks raised his hands and let them drop again, frustrated
and feeling impotent in his effort to penetrate the old man's
stupid attitude. Trying again, he said, "What if this investigation
doesn't fail, like the rest! You expect me to appear in court—be
stained by guilt of association maybe?"

"I told you, it won't happen," said Enrico. "But if it does,
then yes, that's what I expect you to do. What they expect you to
do."

"You're preposterous," Franks said. "All of you. Preposterous."

"Okay," said Enrico gently. "So maybe these things don't
happen in England. Not in those countries of Europe that you
know, although I would have expected you to have some idea of
how things are in parts of Italy. But you read the newspapers.
See TV. You *know* it happens here, in America."

"Please, Eddie. Please believe him; do as he says."

There was a moment of surprised silence in the room as
Mamma Scargo spoke, intruding for the first time in her life into
business where she traditionally had no part. The old lady looked
apprehensively toward her husband, as if for a rebuke. Nothing
came. She said, emboldened, "He knows. No more damage;
don't let there be any more damage than has been caused to us
by what's already done."

Illogically, thoughts of his real father came into Franks'

80

mind. His father had run from gangsters. At once Franks felt a surge of irritation. It was the cliché of history to talk of Nazis as gangsters. They might have been, but they were a party and a government, and his father had been a Jew who had been right to run. It had been the sensible, honorable way to survive. There wasn't any comparison between the sort of running that his father did and the sort of running that was being demanded of him now. For his father to run—to do what he did—had been courageous. For him to do it would be cowardly. Franks said, "I won't give in."

Mamma Scargo began to cry, quietly, as before. Beside her, Enrico said, "You're a fool."

"I know," Franks spat back. "You made me one."

"Don't be glib," said the old man. "Don't you have a family to think of?"

"This one!" sneered Franks.

"No," said Enrico. "I know how that's got to be from now on. I meant Tina and David and Gabriella."

Franks stopped, remembering his earlier decision not to bully and realizing he'd been attempting exactly that. "It's because of Tina and David and Gabriella that I'm doing what I am," he insisted. "I don't want them tainted: exposed to the sort of public embarrassment that could happen if I did what you want me to."

"You're wrong, Eddie," said Enrico helplessly. "You're wrong and you're going to regret it."

"I regret a lot of things, sure," said Franks. "But I'm not wrong. You're living in the past; *exactly* like a movie."

On the way out to Westchester, Tina had been tensed with anger, but on the ride back to Manhattan, Franks was conscious of her being more subdued and reflective.

"Changed your mind?" he said.

"They seemed very sure."

"They're frightened."

"If they're right, they're frightened with good reason."

"I don't think they're right."

"Things *are* different here from Europe."

"You want me to do what they ask?"

Tina didn't reply at once. Then she said, "I want what I said before. For you to do what you think is right."

Franks had retained the plasticized entry key to his suite, so there was no need to stop at the porters' desk when they got back to the Plaza. He was actually at the elevator with Tina beside him when the challenge came.

81

"Edmund Franks?"

Franks turned. The man was fat to the point of obesity. His shirt collar was undone, the tie pulled down, and the concertinaed jacket of his fawn suit hung awkwardly from his shoulders, falling backward as if in some retreat from the embarrassment of being there at all.

"Yes," frowned Franks. He saw that behind the fat man there was another: neat, thin, and bespectacled. They looked like the before-and-after part of some diet advertisement.

"Name's Waldo, Harry Waldo. . . ." The fat man jerked his head sideways. "This is my partner, John Schultz. Thought you might have made contact."

"Why should I have made contact?"

"FBI, Mr. Franks. Didn't Mr. Scargo tell you we'd seen him?"

"Of course he told me; that's why I'm here. From what he said I expected you to contact me."

"That's what we're doing right now, Mr. Franks. It's time to talk, don't you think?"

14

The crush in the elevator separated them, the FBI agents facing Franks and his wife, all with their backs against the paneled walls. Franks had the bizarre thought of their lining up in some sort of battle formation, one to oppose the other. The investigators fell deferentially behind him as they approached the suite, and immediately inside, Waldo gazed around in an attitude that Franks defined as something like mocking admiration.

"Wow!" said the FBI man. "Must be more than a thousand bucks a day."

"Probably something like that," said Franks, unsettled by the man's demeanor but determined against letting it show. He indicated the bar and said, "Would either of you like something?"

"No, thank you," said Schultz, answering for both of them. "But please go ahead, yourself."

"If I feel like it, I will," said Franks, annoyed at the condescension. At once he tried to curb the attitude, wondering if they weren't attempting to off-balance him.

"Why?" said Waldo, turning theatrically in the center of the main room, with its views not just of the avenue but of the zoo and Central Park as well.

"Why what?" said Tina, coming in on her husband's side.

"Why pay thousands of dollars for a suite when you've got that lovely place in Scarsdale?" said Waldo. "Now that's what I call a property!"

He was letting the encounter get away from him, Franks recognized. And he wasn't going to survive if he allowed anything—and certainly not this initial meeting—to get away from him. He said, "Who are you?"

"We told you downstairs, sir," said Schultz politely. "FBI."

"I know what you told me," said Franks. "So if you're FBI you have identification?"

"Sure," said Waldo. Neither FBI man moved, and neither did Franks.

"Let me see it," demanded Franks.

Waldo looked at Schultz, as if unsure whether to obey or refuse, and then said, "That's your right."

Both men pulled wallets from their pockets. There was another hesitation, and then Waldo waddled forward, offering the shields. Franks, who had no idea what an FBI identification badge looked like, made the pretense of examining both and then said, "Thank you."

"In fact," said Schultz, "you've got further rights. You aware of American law, Mr. Franks?"

"No," said Franks.

"You, Mrs. Franks?" Waldo asked Tina.

"What's my wife got to do with these inquiries?" Franks asked at once.

"We don't know yet, sir," said Waldo, maintaining the stiff politeness. "But it's only right that she should know her rights and privileges under American law, wouldn't you say?"

"My wife hasn't got anything to do with any of it," said Franks.

"Any of what, sir?" said Schultz.

Franks realized he was sweating, disoriented by this comedy act. Except that it wasn't a comedy. He desperately wanted a drink, which was rare for him, but realized that if he moved to get one they would discern it as a sign of weakness. He remained instead where he was. "Why would I need to invoke the rights and privileges available under American law?"

"Like I said," reminded Waldo, "we don't know, not yet."

His impression in the elevator of their lining up in some sort of battle formation hadn't been bizarre at all, Franks realized. It had been entirely appropriate. Further, these two apparently incompatible men seemed formidable opponents. He asked, "If our rights are important, shouldn't you set them out?"

"You have the right to remain silent," Schultz recited formally. "Anything you say can and will be used against you in a court of law. You have the right to talk to a lawyer, and to have him present during any questioning. If you cannot afford to hire a lawyer"—Schultz paused and looked around the suite—"one will be appointed to represent you before any questioning if you wish one. If you decide to answer questions without a lawyer present, you have the right to stop answering questions at any time you so choose."

Franks experienced the numbness of incredulity. And nervousness, too. He'd gone through two meetings—the first with Nicky, the second with Enrico—and felt nothing but disbelieving contempt for the suggestions of killing. He'd spent a lot of time considering the damage that was possible to all the businesses. But never had he imagined that the investigators would seriously consider him implicated, a knowing and willingly involved participant in whatever crime they were probing. But that's what they clearly thought, from the way the conversation was going: they thought he was an active partner in some sort of criminality. He'd already decided—*almost* decided—not to give in to any pressure that Pascara or Flamini or Dukes might attempt. And he wouldn't give in to any pressure here, he decided, equally determined. He was innocent of any wrongdoing. So there was no way he *could* be coerced. "I've committed no crime, so I've not got any fear of incrimination," he said.

"Let's get a lawyer," said Tina, suddenly urgent.

"That's your right, quite independent of your husband," said Schultz, maintaining absolute formality.

"My husband decides," said Tina loyally. She attempted to sound forceful, but there was a waver in her voice.

"I have—we have—nothing whatsoever to fear or to hide in talking to you," said Franks. "I understand from Scargo that you're making investigations into the Bahamian and Bermudan hotel company and also of the separate casino corporation involved in the Bahamas. Both are entirely properly run, bona fide companies that can withstand any sort of investigation or inquiry. You have the company records. From your examination of those you will know what I'm saying is the truth."

His throat felt dry, and his anxiousness for a drink worsened. Uninvited, Waldo eased himself into a chair, sitting awkwardly because he overflowed from it. From a briefcase as bulging and untidy as he was, Waldo took a file. Franks thought immediately how thick it looked. Waldo took a long time finding what he wanted, grinning up at last in satisfaction. "We've got problems," said the FBI agent. "Big problems."

Franks looked uncertainly at the American, frowning. Then he remembered Nicky Scargo's panicked telephone call—could it only really have been two nights before?—and said, outraged, "You've tapped my telephone!"

"No," said Waldo, clearly unimpressed by Franks' anger. "You were in England when that call was made. We've got a wire on Nicky Scargo."

"But why?" demanded Franks, instantly aware of the stupidity of the question.

"You're fronting for gangsters, Mr. Franks. You've set up a perfect company—two perfect companies, each relying on the other—through which mobsters like Pascara and Flamini and Dukes are cleaning their money." Waldo paused, enjoying himself. "You've got the biggest car wash in town, Mr. Franks. You're cleaning up millions of dollars from numbers and from loan sharking and from prostitution and from drugs and from protection and from larceny. From where we're sitting, Mr. Franks, you seem a pretty important guy to an awful lot of people. . . ." Waldo stopped once more, looking toward Tina. "You, and your wife," he finished.

"No!" said Franks, holding out his hand like a man trying to ward off something unpleasant. "No, wait! I can explain it. Everything can be explained."

Waldo laughed openly, and Schultz joined in, sharing the same joke. "We had a bet," said Waldo. "Johnnie and I. Just how long it would take one of you to say you could explain it. Everyone always says it, you know? Everyone always says something like that."

"I won," said Schultz. "I said fifteen minutes and you said twelve."

Despite his fear of what they might construe from it, Franks went to the bar and poured himself a brandy, indicating the bottle to Tina. She shook her head. Able to look directly at her for the first time since they entered the apartment, Franks saw that she was white-faced, lips pinched together in a tight line of uncertainty. She stared at him pleadingly. Franks broke away from her, still not turning to the two men. They'd perfected a very good act, he conceded; an act calculated to irritate and offend and off-balance, so that an interviewee would become completely enmeshed in the sticky web of his own half answers and evasions. A very good act. He'd damned near become enmeshed himself. For no reason, because there was no reason for him to feel the guilt that he had felt only minutes before. He turned back to them, drink in his hand, and said with forced control, "Why don't you tell me what you want?"

"We want to know everything," said Waldo, an expert in the game.

"About what?" came back Franks, who was learning to play himself now.

Waldo went back to his file again. "You are the managing director, holding also the position of chairman, of a company running three hotels in the Bahamas and two in Bermuda?"

Franks hesitated, recalling the lecture on their rights at the beginning of the interview. Would it have been better to have insisted upon the presence of a lawyer? Nothing to hide, he told himself: entirely innocent. "Yes," he said.

"A company of which, with the portfolio of your wife, you are the controlling stockholder?"

"Yes," said Franks again.

"You are managing director, holding also the position of chairman, of a company owning a casino in Nassau, in the Bahamas?"

If he was entirely innocent, with nothing to hide or be frightened about, why did he feel so unsettled? Franks asked himself. He said, "Yes."

"A company of which, with the portfolio of your wife, you are the controlling stockholder?"

"There is nothing wrong with either of the two companies," said Franks. "Neither is there anything wrong or particularly unusual about the share construction of either company."

"You, with the portfolio of your wife, are the controlling stockholder of the casino company operating in Nassau, in the Bahamas?" persisted Waldo.

"Yes," said Franks. He drank from his brandy glass, needing it.

Waldo flicked through the documents in front of him, appar-

86

ently seeking something. He glanced briefly up, smiling his pleased-at-discovery smile. "Do you know Peter Armitrage, Winston Graham, and Richard Blackstaff?" he asked.

Franks hesitated. Three of the development and tourist officials with whom he'd negotiated in Bermuda. "I am acquainted with them," he admitted.

Waldo turned a page. "And Herbert Wilkinson, James Partridge, and Eric de Falco?"

Wilkinson and Partridge were in the Bahamas development office. De Falco was a deputy in the tourist section. "Those are men with whom I dealt in the establishment of the hotels in Nassau and elsewhere," said Franks.

"Men who helped you in establishing your hotels in Bermuda and the Bahamas?" It was Schultz, coming into the questioning for the first time.

"Government officials whom I met in the course of establishing hotels in Bermuda and the Bahamas," said Franks, responding to pedantry with pedantry, hoping his unease wasn't showing and waiting for the inevitable question.

It came at once. "Men whom you bribed, for permission to set up your company?" said Waldo, back at his files. "Peter Armitrage, twenty thousand dollars, Winston Graham, a total of fifteen thousand dollars, and Richard Blackstaff three payments, a total of ten thousand dollars?"

Did the FBI have jurisdiction in the Bahamas? thought Franks worriedly. Surely that was a British possession? He said, "The audited and publicly available accounts of the company record those figures as commission payments."

"Did you pay twenty-five thousand dollars to Herbert Wilkinson, fifteen thousand dollars to James Partridge, and make two separate payments of ten thousand dollars to Eric de Falco?"

"Those sums are also listed in the audited and publicly available accounts of the company as commission," said Franks.

"We know they are, Mr. Franks," came in Schultz again. "We've checked. Carried out our own audit in fact. As far as we've been able. We know the sums are listed as commission but the beneficiaries of that commission, either in the Bahamas or Bermuda, are not named."

"The companies are incorporated in Delaware," said Franks. "There's no requirement under the state law of Delaware for commission payments to be itemized to named recipients."

Poppa Scargo had made him and Nicky go climbing, during that pup-tent trip to the Catskill mountains when they were

87

children, challenging them to reach a certain promontory. Nicky had won because Franks had tried to take a shortcut across a shale slurry that began to move and shift with him, so badly that at one stage he actually felt that it was going to overwhelm and engulf him. He'd experienced the feeling of choking suffocation and he felt it now, the sensation of nothing firm or steady being underfoot.

"We've done a lot of reading of the company records," took up Waldo. "Are you familiar with a man named William Snarsbrook?"

"If you've done a lot of reading of the company records you know full well that I am," said Franks, irritated despite himself at the mocking condescension. "He was the Bahamian official with whom I negotiated the setting up of the casino."

"Yes," smiled Waldo. "He was. The first reference to that casino idea was entered into the company records on August sixteenth, according to what we've discovered."

"Yes," said Franks shortly. A problem he'd already isolated, he thought.

"Yet according to our information from William Snarsbrook, you visited the Bahamas to discuss the establishment of such a casino on June tenth. There were, in fact, three meetings. June tenth, eleventh, and again on the fourteenth. There were also visits, from what we've been able to discover, to Bermuda. Discussions with officials there, as well."

"Yes," conceded Franks. The slurry was still shifting, and the feeling of suffocation was worsening.

"Is it your normal practice to make such inquiries in advance of any board discussion?" said Schultz, giving his partner a rest.

"There was board discussion," insisted Franks.

"We couldn't find any record of it," said Schultz.

"Informal discussion," said Franks.

"Ah!" said Waldo in exaggerated awareness. "Informal discussion it was not thought necessary to file in company records?"

"That was exactly how it happened," he said. Franks heard movement to his right and saw Tina at the bar. He held out his empty glass toward her. He didn't give a damn whether they construed it as nervousness or not. With that thought came another. The demanding, unasked request was *exactly* the sort of gesture he had found so offensive from Poppa Scargo. "Please," he said hurriedly to his wife.

Waldo sat forward, on the edge of his already difficult seat,

88

so that he could reach across the distance separating him from Franks. From the strained briefcase he took a bundle of photographs, shuffling them into the order he wanted. "Do you recognize these men?"

Franks looked down at the publicity shots taken at the opening of the Bahamian and Bermuda hotels, clearly showing him with Dukes and Flamini. "Of course I do!" he said.

"Whom do you recognize them to be?" insisted Schultz.

"Dukes and Flamini."

"And these?" continued Waldo, dealing out a fresh print.

The photograph had been taken at Nicky's wedding, and this time he was captured not just with Dukes and Flamini, but with Pascara as well. "Dukes, Flamini, and Pascara," acknowledged Franks dully.

"And these?"

Franks hadn't been aware of any photography during his visit to Las Vegas to examine the viability of a casino operation, but there were a lot, of him alone by various tables and games and then with Dukes and Harry Greenberg. "I went to Las Vegas to see the sort of gambling setups that exist there."

"And these?"

It was the opening of the Nassau casino. He was with everyone again, including Harry Greenberg this time. Tina was pictured, too, he saw. "I'm not amused by all this," he said.

"We're not doing it for your amusement, Mr. Franks," replied Schultz.

"Who is this man, Mr. Franks?" demanded Waldo.

Franks breathed deeply, feeling engulfed, looking at the person whom the FBI agent was indicating in a photograph taken at Nicky's wedding. "David Dukes," he said.

"What do you know of him?"

"He's a financial investor. Made a lot of money in oil. Has interests in Las Vegas, too. It was he who set up the trip that I made . . . where the other photographs were taken," said Franks.

"Just that?" said Waldo.

"Just that."

"Who is Tony Alberi?"

"I don't know anyone of that name."

"Georgio Alcante?"

"I do not know a Georgio Alcante."

"Who is this man?" asked Waldo, moving his finger.

"Roland Flamini."

"What about Frederick Dialcano?"

89

"I don't know anyone named Frederick Dialcano."

"Emanuel Calvo?"

"No."

"This man?" The finger moved again.

"Roberto Pascara."

"What about Arno Pellacio?"

"I do not know any Arno Pellacio."

"Roberto Longurno?"

"No."

"Luigi del Angelo?"

"No." Franks was sweating openly, knowing that they could see his reaction to the pressure. Not guilty, he thought, repeating the litany through his mind. No matter what all this meant and however bad it looked—and he didn't know yet whether it looked bad or not—he *wasn't* guilty, and if he wasn't guilty of anything then he didn't have anything to fear.

"This man?" Waldo pressed on.

"Harry Greenberg."

"Sam D'Amato?"

"No."

"Marty Tannenbaum?"

"No."

Waldo sat back, easing himself as much as he could into his chair. On cue, Schultz relieved him, taking up the questioning. "Do you consider yourself a good businessman, Mr. Franks?"

Once, thought Franks, replying honestly to himself. Now he wasn't so sure. "Yes," he said.

"You've businesses in Spain, France, and Italy? And you run a Caribbean cruise liner?"

"Yes."

"Successful, then?"

"Yes."

Schultz held out his hand to his partner and Waldo passed across the briefcase. The neat man fumbled through, once pulling out a sheet of paper and then replacing it, walking his fingers on through the file. He searched unhurriedly, and Franks decided it was all part of the questioning technique. Schultz found at last what he was apparently looking for. He looked at Franks and said, "According to our information, you made several pro-tracted visits to the Bahamas and to Bermuda before the forma-tion date of the hotel company."

"Yes," replied Franks.

"Why?"

"I thought that would have been obvious," said Franks. "Before setting up a business I always make sure that it will be viable."

"*Always?*" demanded Schultz.

"Always."

Schultz went briefly to his sheet of paper. "That's why you visited Las Vegas before the official formation date of the casino company?"

"Yes."

"And satisfied yourself from all those prior visits that both the hotels and the casino would be profitable, money-making enterprises?"

"If I hadn't been satisfied, I wouldn't have proceeded."

"Tell us how you proceeded, after satisfying yourself on the islands?" It was Waldo, coming back into the questioning.

"I'm not sure I know what you mean," said Franks. He heard Tina moving, slightly behind him. He looked to her, imagining she wanted his attention, but she was staring down fixedly at the floor, almost as if she weren't listening to what was going on.

"Tell us how you went about setting up the company."

"All my European enterprises are private companies, with boards composed—"

"Of accountant and lawyer nonvoting directors," interrupted Schultz, wanting him to know the depth of their inquiries. "We know, Mr. Franks!"

"I intended the corporation in the Bahamas and Bermuda to be the same. I discussed it with my brother-in-law, Scargo. He told me there could be cheaper finance in New York than there was in England." Franks paused, wondering if he were putting Nicky at risk. At once a rush of anger swept the reservation aside. Nicky had put him at risk, for Christ's sake! All he was doing was telling the truth. "We made inquiries. I actually had meetings with bankers here in New York and with my normal financiers in London."

"Who were prepared to advance the capital necessary?" demanded Schultz.

"Yes," said Franks. "But the markets were unsettled. Money was very dear. Scargo then said he could introduce me to some private investors who might be interested in putting up the money."

"Why are all your other companies privately controlled?" asked Waldo.

91

"Because I prefer it that way."

"But on this occasion you were prepared to change the system: take in outside stockholders?"

"The holding was strictly agreed," said Franks. "You know that, from the formation documents. You've already talked about it; with my wife's holding, I retain control."

"Why did you change, just like that?" asked Waldo, snapping his fingers.

"Because it was a sound business proposition; I was able to raise finance to set up a perfectly bona fide corporation with money costing less—far less—than the banks were offering, either here or in England." Franks glanced sideways again to where Tina was still staring down, deep in thought. How would she react if he confessed how much he'd wanted Nicky in a position subservient to himself?

"A sound business proposition?" echoed Schultz.

"That's what I said," replied Franks.

"Like the sound business propositions that already exist in Spain and France and Italy?"

"Yes."

"Established by careful attention to the market? Commissioning market surveys and financial forecasts?" said Waldo.

There didn't seem to be anything they didn't know about him, Franks thought. He said, "Yes, that's exactly how I go about setting up a business."

"Carefully?" pressed Schultz.

"Properly," qualified Franks. "Making every inquiry before I commit myself."

Franks was conscious of the smiles of satisfaction that passed between the two FBI men, and sat waiting apprehensively.

"So!" pounced Waldo. "Here you are, a successful, established businessman who always, quite properly, makes every inquiry before committing himself, committing himself in this case to a company formation different from any in which you'd ever before been involved, taking on investing stockholders. So tell us about the inquiries you made about David Dukes, Roland Flamini, and Roberto Pascara?"

Franks remained silent. He'd fallen headlong into yet another trap. How bad it appeared! "I made no inquiries," he admitted. Until now, he thought; when it seemed too late. He hoped to God it wasn't.

"You made no inquiries!" said Schultz with forced incredulity. "You've just told us what a careful, proper businessman you are, Mr. Franks. We know from our investigations of the surveys and the reports that you *always* commission . . ." The man allowed a theatrical pause. "Or always have commissioned until now . . ." There was another gap. "Shall I tell you something, Mr. Franks?"

"What?" said Franks.

"We find it very difficult to understand—to believe—that someone who behaves as you always behave would on this occasion not have bothered about even a casual inquiry concerning the background of men upon whom your company depended."

So did he, thought Franks. It was inconceivable—incomprehensible—that he could have done anything so stupid. Damn Nicky Scargo to every sort of hell that existed. He said, "My brother-in-law, Scargo, vouched for them. They were investors with whom he had done business in the past. He said they were reputable."

"On his say-so—just on his word—you were prepared to go ahead?" said Waldo.

"Yes."

"That doesn't seem like the action of a careful, responsible businessman. A good businessman," said Schultz.

"No," said Franks. "It doesn't, does it? Now I bitterly regret it." It seemed to be the day for everyone to be humiliated, he thought.

"Why?" Schultz asked at once.

"Because I now know them to be what they are," said Franks. "Because I now know how stupidly and easily I was tricked into creating a front for them."

"From your meeting tonight in Westchester with the Scargo family?" said Waldo.

"You followed me?"

"Yes, sir," said Schultz. "We've been following you ever since our surveillance picked you up entering Nicky Scargo's offices."

Franks felt a physical irritation—an itching discomfort on his back and across his shoulders—at the awareness that for more than forty-eight hours everything he had done had been witnessed and noted. He said, "I learned about it first yesterday, from my meeting with Nicky Scargo, here in New York."

Waldo took up one of his prompt files, not from the briefcase this time but from the floor, where he'd neatly arranged the papers to which he'd already referred in the earlier questioning. "So you know that David Dukes is also known by the name

93

Tony Alberi? And that Georgio Alcante is another Dukes alias, the one under which he has convictions for illegal gambling, loansharking, and organizing the passage of women across the state line, in the pursuance of prostitution?"

Franks swallowed and for the briefest moment experienced dizziness, so that he had to squeeze his eyes tightly closed to clear his vision. "No," he said hollowly.

"And that Roland Flamini is also known by the aliases of Frederick Dialcano and Emanuel Calvo, and under all three names has been charged—but acquitted—of running illegal gambling operations and the organization of protection rackets?"

"No," said Franks, "I did not know that."

"Or that Roberto Pascara, whose real name is Pascaralino, is also known as Arno Pellacio and Roberto Longurno and Luigi del Angelo, a man who has five times been arrested on charges of extortion, illegal gambling, prostitution, and loansharking?" persisted Waldo relentlessly.

Franks sat shaking his head, punch-drunk with the facts that were being thrown at him. "No," he said.

"Or that Harry Greenberg is also Sam D'Amato and Marty Tannenbaum, and graduated into Las Vegas gambling after serving as a lieutenant in the Mafia family of Santos Trafficante in Florida. And under the name of Sam D'Amato was arraigned on a charge of first-degree murder, the prosecution of which could not proceed because of the disappearance of an eyewitness to the killing?"

Franks held out his hands, beseechingly, as Enrico Scargo had beseeched him earlier that evening. "You know I don't!" he said.

"No, Mr. Franks," said Schultz. "We don't know that at all." He nodded toward his partner. "Like Harry said a while back, it seems to us you set up the perfect washing operation knowing damned well what you were doing and who you were doing it for."

"That's nonsense!" erupted Franks. "I told you I was tricked. Trapped by Nicky Scargo into going along with something without any idea what it was to be used for. I was stupid. Okay, I've admitted that. But I'm not a criminal. I haven't done anything wrong."

"You control a hotel company and a casino company in the Bahamas and Bermuda?" demanded Schultz.

"What sort of question is that?" said Franks. "That's what we've been talking about for the past hour!"

"We've evidence that through that casino operation, through the credit linkup you approved—your signature is on the agreement—at least four million dollars has been moved, undeclared on any income tax return from Dukes, Flamini, Pascara, or Greenberg. We are satisfied—and we're sure any grand jury and any court will be satisfied—that the actual figure is several times higher than that," said Schultz. "The four-million-dollar figure is merely a sample, to list on the actual charges. . . ."

"Charges!" cried Franks, but Schultz overrode him. "You controlled the companies through which those illegal transactions took place, Mr. Franks. Your name—your signature—is on the credit agreement. You did all the negotiations for the establishment, first of the hotels and then of the very necessary casino. Those negotiations were conducted in advance of any contractual agreement between yourself and any of the people we've been talking about here tonight. You expect us to believe you haven't done anything wrong?"

"Yes," said Franks.

"Mrs. Franks," said Waldo, "we've been talking for a long time and you've said very little. Practically nothing. Is there anything you'd like to say?"

"I've told you of my wife's involvement," said Franks protectively, before Tina could reply. "My wife's holdings in these and every other company I control are little more than nominee structures, devices to ensure that the control remains with me."

"I invited your wife to comment, Mr. Franks," said Waldo.

"You reminded us before all this began of certain rights," said Tina, her voice distant. "I don't think I have anything to say except in the presence of a lawyer."

That's what she'd wanted at the start, Franks remembered. He wished now that he'd listened.

"Like I told you," said Waldo, "those are your rights."

The unkempt man started collecting the documents from the floor beside him, patting them into some order and then stacking them back into the briefcase.

Schultz said, "You told us earlier that you're not familiar with American law, Mr. Franks. So let me tell you about a part of it. On the statute books there is legislation known by the acronym RICO. It stands for the Racketeer Influenced and Corrupt Organization Law. There's also another appropriate piece of legislation, the Continuing Criminal Enterprise Law. From our inquiries we consider there are charges sufficient to bring you before a grand jury, for that jury to determine whether a case can be brought against you in a court of law. This material has already been placed before a district attorney in the state of New York, for such charges to be prepared against you. . . ."

"No, wait!" said Franks desperately, once more feeling the sweep of dizziness. "You haven't let me explain."

"There'll be adequate occasion for you to explain, sir," said Waldo, the condescension gone now, replaced by polite formality. "There will be the need for further interviews between us. . . ." The man paused, holding out his hand invitingly. "It is your right to refuse, but I am going to request that you hand over your passport to us tonight."

"Go to hell!" said Franks. He *had* been punch-drunk, overwhelmed by the enormity of his entrapment. But not any longer. He'd told the Scargo family that night that he was going to fight and win, and he was going to fight and win against these two supercilious cabaret performers. Everything of which they had accused him was perfectly explainable. And he would explain it. Before any grand jury or court they chose. Explain it and be proven innocent. "I'm not going anywhere," he said. "I'm going to stay here in New York and I'm going to prove myself not guilty of every accusation you make. Or think of making!"

He had Nicky's file. That was going to save him. He'd thought the account records were the important pieces of evidence, but there was also the formation notes, proving that everything he said was the truth. That—and the evidence that Nicky himself would be forced to give on oath—would clear him completely, Franks knew. He actually smiled, knowing that he wasn't vulnerable. He wouldn't tell them about it, though. Technically it was evidence, and they could insist he hand it over. They could wait until he'd divested himself of Dukes and Flamini and Pascara and discussed everything with the best criminal lawyer that money could buy and then sit in court and hear their whole circumstantial case collapse to the ground. How condescending would they be then?

"Then I must formally ask you not to leave the city," said Waldo.

"I've already told you I've no intention of doing that!"

"So you don't intend to go up to Scarsdale?" said Schultz.

Franks frowned, surprised that they literally meant to restrict him to Manhattan. "No," he said, unwilling to make any small request of them, like extending his boundaries.

"Get a lawyer, Mr. Franks," said Schultz. "You're going to need a lawyer."

"I intend to."

When Franks returned from letting them out into the corridor, Tina was still in the chair she had occupied throughout most of the encounter, staring down as she had all the time. "Tina?" he said.

She looked up at him, blank-faced momentarily, as if she did not recognize him.

"Tina?" he said again.

"You're going to jail!" she said, jagged-voiced. "Everything they said makes you look like an accomplice; a criminal, like the others."

"No!" said Franks. "I know it looks bad. Terrible. But I can win."

"For Christ's sake, stop saying all the time that you can win!" she burst out, angry in her despair. "They've got you, every way you turn!"

Franks went over and knelt before her, trying to pull her to him. She came, but stiffly, as if she was reluctant for any physical contact between them. "You said tonight that you trusted me always to do the right thing," he reminded her quietly.

She nodded.

"So go on trusting me," he said. "Trust me when I say it's all going to turn out all right. It's going to be nasty, but then I told you that it would be. But in the end it's going to be all right."

She remained looking at him for several moments, their faces only inches apart. Then she said, "You didn't, did you?"

"Didn't what?" he asked, hoping she didn't mean what he thought.

"Know."

Now he stared at her for a long time, not speaking because he wasn't able to, not at once. The anger flickered and died, sadness overcoming it. "You really feel you've got to ask me that!"

"Yes," she said. "If you want the trust that you've always had, then I've got to be told."

"I didn't know," said Franks, still sad. Of all the shocks and revelations of the past two days, the greatest was this: that they weren't as close—Tina to him, at least—as he'd always imagined them to be. Nothing ever the same again, he thought, recognizing the now familiar reflection.

97

15

Franks' instinctive, automatic reaction after his meeting with the
FBI agents was to abandon Nicky Scargo completely: to divest
himself of the lawyer as quickly as he intended to divest himself
of the others, as further proof of his innocence. And then he
remembered how important Nicky's corroborative evidence would
be, when he produced the file of formation notes and bank
records, and decided that he couldn't alienate the man; not yet.
Because he remembered Nicky's reaction—the very words—when
he asked him if he was prepared to lie on oath. *"Yes. I don't give
a damn about perjury if I'm thinking about survival."* Nicky was
a liar and a cheat. Franks wasn't going to have the little bastard
running out on him. Nicky had used him, decided Franks. So
now he would use Nicky. He'd use him, each and every way he
considered necessary, and then he'd dump the man, like Nicky
had been willing to dump him—*had,* in fact, dumped him. Based
on what they knew—thought they knew—he supposed the two
FBI agents were justified in sneering at him, as a businessman.
But they were going to see just what sort of hard, ruthless
businessman he could be, long before the eventual collapse of
their court case.

The next day Nicky was waiting in the office when he and
Tina arrived. She'd intended to come before he'd actually asked
her. Franks wanted her to be with him because, although he had
some vague recollection of the difficulty of wives giving evidence either in support of or against their husbands, or vice
versa, he still considered it important now to have a witness at all
times. Tina was the only one he felt he could trust, even though
her trust in him had needed reassurance.

Nicky looked better than he had: his suit and shirt were fresh
and appeared newly pressed, and the sag appeared to have lessened, both in his face and in the way he held himself. The
lawyer smiled as they entered the suite, and said, "I'm glad the
family knows now."

Nicky didn't mean the family, Franks realized. He meant Enrico. Now that everything was in the open with his father, Nicky considered the responsibility shifted; himself no longer solely to blame. "Yes," said Franks.

"They were very upset after you left." As if he still found it difficult to believe, the lawyer added, "Poppa cried."

"What about?" asked Tina, her voice hard and unsympathetic.

"What do you think?"

"After the way the family has treated Eddie and me, it's difficult to imagine," she said harshly.

"About what's happened, of course," said her brother.

"I thought we decided last night that everything was too late for that."

"He still cried. Mamma too."

"You trying to make a point?" asked Tina, the bridge between them impassable now.

"Don't cooperate," said Nicky. "For God's sake, realize what you are up against and don't cooperate."

"I know what I'm up against," said Franks.

"What do you mean?"

"Two FBI agents were waiting for us when we got back to the Plaza last night. In fact, they weren't really waiting. They—or other agents at least—followed us out of Manhattan and up to Westchester and then back again. They know everything about my business dealings, right back from the very start. They've photographs of me with Dukes and Flamini and Pascara and my signature on every incriminating document imaginable." He stopped, indicating the impressive console he'd noticed the first time he'd entered the office. "Incidentally," continued Franks, "they've got a tap on your telephone. Quoted the conversation we had when you called to get me here."

Nicky jerked back from the telephone bank as if it were hot and he were frightened of being burned. "Fuck me!" he said.

"Someone's going to get fucked, Nicky," said Franks, picking up the other man's word. "But it isn't going to be me."

"What can we do?" pleaded Nicky, the new, fragile confidence crumbling at the first indication of pressure.

"What I've always intended we should do," said Franks. "Protect ourselves. I want a name, Nicky. The name of the best criminal lawyer in the city." Franks paused, looking to Tina to give her the credit. "I made a mistake last night. I agreed to the meeting without a lawyer being present. It's a mistake I won't make again."

99

"Rosenberg," said the other lawyer at once. "Ruben Rosenberg." There was the slightest hesitation, and then Nicky said, "He's a Jew, of course."

"I'd never have guessed," said Franks. "My father was a Jew, too. Remember?"

"I'm sorry," apologized Nicky in the now familiar stumbling way. "I didn't mean—"

"It doesn't matter what you meant," Franks said impatiently. "Do you know this man?"

"You've seen him, when we've lunched at the club," said Nicky. "Bald-headed guy with glasses who has the permanent booth second from the door."

"Do you *know* him?" persisted Franks.

"We used to play squash together, in the club on Sixtieth."

"Call him," ordered Franks. "Set up a meeting. I want to meet him right away. Today."

Nicky looked nervously toward the monitored telephone bank.

"It's the FBI's idea that I *get* a lawyer," said Franks, still impatient. Tying Nicky in—even on something so apparently inconsequential as an interview with another lawyer—might help later in some way, thought Franks. As Nicky got a line and dialed, Franks felt across for Tina's hand. She let him take it and smiled back wanly, but it was a minimal response. Just as there had been the minimal response the previous night when he'd moved to make love and she'd turned away and asked him how he could think of doing that after what they'd been through. Maybe he shouldn't be too critical of her reaction, thought Franks. Maybe he *had* been unreasonable. He'd actually felt relieved—confident the safe-deposited folder was their salvation—but perhaps it had been unrealistic to expect Tina to understand everything as clearly as he did now.

Nicky sat beyond the huge desk, head forward and his free hand against his forehead, creating a cowl, so that it was difficult to hear every word, but even before he replaced the receiver Franks knew that a meeting wasn't possible that day.

"Friday," announced Nicky. "Ten o'clock."

"That's three days away," protested Franks.

"You wanted the best," said Nicky. "The best are busy. Because they're the best."

Franks knew he'd been unrealistic, but he'd wanted the meeting at once; that day. There was something else that didn't have to be delayed any longer. "I want the dissolution meeting called," he announced.

"You're still determined to go ahead?"

"Even more so."

"I don't want to be involved," said the man.

"You *are* involved, whether you want to be or not," said Franks dismissively. "You'll not achieve anything by not being at the meeting."

"You'll say it was you? Just you?"

Franks sighed at the plea, and beside him Tina said, "Oh Christ, Nicky! Stop it!"

"I'll say it's all my idea," said Franks, disgusted at the man's hesitation. "Everything will be my fault. Now for God's sake make the calls. Let's get something started instead of sitting around wetting ourselves."

Nicky looked again at the bugged telephones. "From here?" he said.

This time Franks hesitated. He didn't know anything about telephone monitoring but he presumed that it was practically simultaneous, so that Waldo and Schultz or whoever else were bothering would know very quickly of the contact. He didn't mind their knowing—was anxious for them to know about it and be aware of the reason—but not *before* he'd put the dissolution into effect. He couldn't foresee any reason for them to intervene, but he knew he'd made one mistake by speaking too openly to them and he didn't intend making another. "You've got a telephone credit card?" he said.

"Yes," nodded Nicky.

"Make it from a phone booth then."

"When?" Nicky sat with his hands against the desk, as if it were a positive barrier, something to protect him against any sort of attack.

"Is there a pay phone in the building?"

"I guess so."

"So what's wrong with right now?"

"What shall I say?"

"Give me a piece of paper," instructed Franks, not immediately replying. Franks wrote out not just the names of Dukes, Flamini, and Pascara but beside them the aliases that had been listed to him the previous night by Harry Waldo. He pushed the yellow legal pad back across the desk and said, "Tell them I want to talk to them about those names as well."

"Who are they?" asked Nicky.

"Just tell them," said Franks.

Nicky stared down at the paper, unwilling to move. He rose

at last, but stopped at the door and looked back into the room. "You sure?" he said.

"Make the call, Nicky," said Franks. He looked across to Tina as her brother left the room, and said, "You okay?"

"I guess so," she said.

"I want to make you a promise," said Franks.

"What?"

"When this is all over, I'm going to quit. The islands operation will be over anyway. There's bound to be a lot of bad publicity, so I'll have to stay in some sort of control in Europe, but as soon as I think it's safe to do so—that the companies won't be affected—I'll get somebody else in to run them. We can live where you like, here or in England. Or anywhere else if you like. Both the kids will be at boarding school by then so it'll just be the two of us."

"That would be nice," said Tina.

Franks frowned at the lack of interest in her voice. "It'll be like it was before, when I was taking the long weekends. Only better."

"Yes," she said, her voice still empty.

Franks decided he couldn't expect any other attitude from her, not at the moment. Later it would be better.

She looked directly at him, and said, "Maybe we should have the children here, with us."

"Why?"

Tina shrugged. "I don't know. I'd just like to have them with me."

"Call David's headmaster if you like, and have them brought over."

"I might," she said. "It wouldn't mean taking David away for too much of the term. And I don't think it matters too much if Gabby misses school at her age."

"Whatever you want," agreed Franks. It would probably be a good thing, give Tina something else to think about.

Nicky came back hurriedly into his office, almost as if he were being pursued. Before he sat down, he said, "They don't like it, Eddie. I knew they wouldn't like it."

"They're going to like it a damned sight less before I'm through."

"Pascara told me to tell you something."

"What?"

"Not to do anything silly. Those were his words, 'Tell Eddie not to do anything silly.' "

"When?"

102

"They're flying in tonight, all of them. I said eleven tomorrow morning."

"What did you tell them?"

"That you wanted to talk about the future of the companies."

"That the FBI were investigating?"

"I had to, Eddie! You must see that I had to!"

"I'm not saying that you shouldn't have done so."

"That's when Pascara told me to tell you not to do anything silly."

"I think I will get the children brought across," said Tina.

"What?" frowned her brother.

"Something we were talking about while you were telephoning," said Franks. She was becoming infected with the nervousness of everyone else, he thought.

"It means you'll have to meet them without the reports, either from Chicago or Houston," said the lawyer.

"I don't think I need them, after last night," said Franks.

But the reports did arrive from both sets of lawyers, by the special delivery that afternoon that Nicky had requested when he commissioned the inquiries. They were addressed to the lawyer, but he had them sent unopened across to the Plaza, wanting to separate himself from everything as much as possible. Franks was glad to have something upon which to concentrate, although he didn't imagine there would be much beyond what Waldo and Schultz had told him. A challenging atmosphere arose in the suite between himself and Tina, so that she snapped rather than talked to him, and Franks consciously had to hold back to avoid an argument. Imagining the cause to be her concern over the children, he encouraged her to call England to make arrangements to fly them both out to New York. Harrow agreed to David's premature release, and Franks had his London secretary make the Concorde reservations for the children and Elizabeth.

"Why not take them directly up to Scarsdale?" he suggested.

"I thought we were restricted to Manhattan," she said aggressively.

"I am," said Franks. "I don't think you are; certainly the children aren't. You could meet the flight in tomorrow morning and go straight on up."

"That means I couldn't come to the meeting."

Franks looked curiously at her. "I hadn't thought you'd want to attend."

"Shouldn't I?"

"Your official proxy would be sufficient for the vote."

She smiled, a fleeting expression, and Franks got the impression that she was relieved. "Sure you don't need any support? I can't imagine Nicky being much use."

"It would probably be better if I did it alone." Was he being affected by everyone else's uncertainty? he wondered.

"I'm prepared to come, if you want me."

Franks shook his head. "Get the house opened up this afternoon and get the kids up when they arrive. I'll call you there, to tell you how the meeting went."

"Why not get the lawyer—" She hesitated, trying to remember the name. "Rosenberg," she managed. "Why not get Rosenberg to arrange with the FBI that you could come up for the weekend?"

Franks felt a resurgence of last night's irritation at the restrictions that had been imposed upon him. "I will," he said positively.

Tina telephoned the Scarsdale housekeeper, to talk about opening up the house, while Franks settled down with the investigation package. The Chicago file was biggest, involving both Pascara and Flamini, and Franks went through that first. Pascara's full name—Pascaralino—wasn't listed, and they'd missed the Luigi del Angelo pseudonym, but the charges that had been made against the man were itemized. The extortion indictment claimed that three men had died in Pascara's campaign to extract protection money from Chicago freight-ship operators. Three of the charges alleging the running of brothels accused Pascara of dope peddling from the premises and there was a lawyer's note with the gambling indictment to say that it had failed because the two major witnesses had disappeared between the time of the grand jury hearing and the trial. Franks looked up from the documents. Tina was deep in her conversation with the housekeeper. He wouldn't tell her, he decided. She was becoming increasingly nervous as it was. From the extortion indictments against Flamini—made in the name of Frederick Dialcano—it was clear to Franks that the man and Pascara had attempted to divide the waterfront up between them, wharf by wharf. Flamini had been jointly charged with Pascara in one of the gambling indictments in which the witnesses had disappeared.

From the Houston report it seemed that Dukes was better known as Georgio Alcante. It was in that name that he had been indicted and later convicted for taking women across the state line for the purpose of prostitution and also for illegal gambling. There was another prostitution conviction in the name of Tony Alberi.

Determined to prepare himself as carefully as possible for the confrontation, Franks read and reread everything several times, absorbing the details of all the indictments and then reading all the newspaper clippings that the lawyers in both towns had managed to assemble. All the indictments and the media coverage that stemmed from them dated from at least ten years earlier. In the covering letter from Chicago, the lawyers said that the businesses in which Flamini and Pascara had involved themselves since that time appeared reputable and bona fide. It provided no reassurance for Franks. He decided that he deserved the sneers and the suspicions of the FBI agents for blundering into the situation as he had. And Nicky and his father weren't entirely to blame. Predominantly, certainly, but he was at fault, too. He could have—should have—initiated just this sort of character search, but he'd been too eager to win a race and create the situation of Nicky working for him. Whatever happened, Franks knew that he would always suffer self-recrimination for that infantile attitude. He deserved, in fact, to suffer it.

Although Franks was confident he'd memorized all the pertinent facts, he made notes to prompt himself for the confrontation. He worked oblivious to the time, only vaguely aware of Tina calling England and moving around the suite, surprised when he finally looked up that it was already dark beyond the windows and that she'd put the lights on in the suite.

"Must be good stuff," she said.

"Just more detail to what the FBI people said last night."

"No difficulty in invoking the propriety clause then?"

"None whatsoever," said Franks. He hoped she didn't ask to see the material. "Everything fixed at the house?"

She nodded. "It's the early Concorde tomorrow, nine A.M. We should be up there long before lunch."

Franks put the papers back into their envelopes and then put the envelopes into his briefcase. He said, "Hope David doesn't suffer too much at school when all this becomes public. Children can be cruel little bastards."

"*Will* it become public?"

"I think we've got to accept the fact that they'll try to bring charges, from the attitude of those two last night."

"But it's not like in England, not here," she said. "Grand jury hearings are usually private. If the charges are dismissed at that stage, then there won't be much publicity. Certainly not enough to get over to England and cause David any embarrassment."

Maybe only minimally as far as the businesses were concerned, he thought. "We'll see what Rosenberg says."

105

They ate dinner out, more to escape the restricting walls of the hotel suite than through hunger, at Keane's just off Sixth Avenue. Franks could rarely remember their having difficulty talking before, but tonight there was, each making concerted efforts to find something other than the current crisis and each failing. He was relieved when, finally realizing it, she actually burst out laughing and said, "This is bloody ridiculous, isn't it?"

He laughed with her and predicted, "This is what we'll do when it's over. Laugh about it."

"I hope so," she said.

"I know so," he said confidently.

That night it was Tina who wanted to make love, and they did, relaxed and enjoying each other, climaxing together like they always did, and then staying together and he grew hard again, and they made love again, very quickly.

"You're a good fuck," said Tina.

"So are you," said Franks, who knew Tina got pleasure from talking dirty when they made love.

"Don't ever fuck anybody else."

"I haven't. And I won't."

"I'd cut your balls off if I found out you had."

"Sadist."

"Be one. Hurt me. Squeeze my tits."

He did, hard, pinching the nipples, and she screamed and bucked beneath him, and said, "I came, without you."

"I love you," said Franks.

"I love you, too," said Tina. "I'm sorry I was shitty and wouldn't do it last night."

"You weren't shitty."

"I was," she said. "I know I was. Those men frightened me. I hadn't been frightened, not until then. They made everything look so bad. I couldn't make love after that."

"You made up for it tonight," said Franks, moving away from her at last.

"I think it would be nice," she said.

"What?"

"You quitting when it's over. The kids at school and us together all the time." She turned to him in the darkness and said, "Do you know that's something about us? We're never bored with each other's company, are we?"

"No," said Franks. "Lucky, I guess."

"I don't think luck has got anything to do with it." She was silent for several moments and then she said, "Poor Maria."

"Why poor Maria?"

"Didn't you see how she was, up at the house?" demanded Tina. "Bewildered. Disgusted, too. How can she have any more respect—love—for Nicky after this? It must have been awful for her, watching him cringe and crawl. I just can't believe anymore that he's my brother."

"Maybe you could still stay friends with Maria," said Franks. "It's going to be difficult for anyone else to stay close, but I don't see why you couldn't keep in contact with her. She wasn't involved in any of it, after all."

Tina shifted beside him in the bed, folding herself into his body. "She was Nicky's personal assistant when it began. She must have known something."

"I don't see why," said Franks, trying to be objective.

"Maybe I'll try to keep something going," said Tina. "Let's get the immediate problems over and start again from there."

Tina had to leave early the following morning to meet the incoming flight from England. They breakfasted in the suite, not speaking a lot, and there was a hesitation, a reluctance at the actual moment of parting, when the call came from the lobby that her car was waiting.

"Be careful," she said.

"And you."

"I'm just going out to an airport."

"And I'm just going to a business meeting."

"Good luck."

"It'll be fine. Don't worry."

"Call me?"

"As soon as I can."

"Sure you don't want me to-come? Elizabeth could take the kids up to Scarsdale by herself. She's done it before."

"You go," said Franks. "I've got your proxy vote. That's enough."

"It's going to be nasty, isn't it?"

"Maybe."

"Careful," she said again.

"You know I'll be."

"I love you, Eddie Franks."

"I love you, Tina Franks."

He kissed her and she held on to him, reluctant to let him go, as well. He said, "Kiss the kids for me."

"Okay."

"I'll get up on the weekend. I promise. They can't make me stay here."

107

"Call me after the meeting with Rosenberg, too? I want to know everything that's going on."

"Of course I will."

"I love you."

"You've said that already."

"I just wanted to make sure you understood."

"You'll be late for the flight."

Tina stood away, looking at him intently. Abruptly she stretched up, kissed him again, and then she was gone.

Franks felt a lonely emptiness after she left; briefly he wished he'd accepted her offer to come with him to the meeting, something he had never wanted and she had never done before. He shook himself, like a dog sloughing off water, at the reflection. It wouldn't be so bad after the confrontation. Franks showered and shaved leisurely, and, still in his robe, went again through all the documentation that he'd read the previous day, making the final, absolute check. There was no necessity to add anything to his notes or to his intended presentation, Franks decided.

Franks went early to Nicky's office, wanting to be there waiting when they arrived. The lawyer looked awful, wax-faced and sweating, his suit crumpled and damp around him.

"For God's sake, get hold of yourself!" Franks said to the other man.

"I'm sorry," Nicky said. "I'm scared, Eddie. Really scared."

Franks curbed his irritation. "It won't take long," he said. "There's nothing to discuss. It'll be over very quickly."

"Maria's moved out," announced Nicky.

"Left you?"

Nicky shrugged. "I don't know. She said she wanted to go back to her mother's place for a while, to think things out."

Franks supposed he should express some regret, but he didn't; it would have been hypocritical. Nicky's problems were of his own creation, every one of them.

"You'll run the meeting?" urged Nicky.

"Of course."

"What did the reports say, from Houston and Chicago?"

"Nothing that we didn't already know; just more detail, that's all."

"I wondered if Tina might come?"

"She wanted to. I told her to go to Scarsdale instead."

"She going to see the family this weekend?" asked Nicky carelessly.

"No," said Franks.

108

"Course not," mumbled Nicky in immediate retreat. "Stupid question." He looked unnecessarily at his watch and said, "Ten forty-five."

"Yes."

"They'll be here soon."

"Take a drink or something, Nicky."

"Maybe I will. You want one?"

"No."

Franks watched while the man he'd once thought of as a brother went to a cocktail cabinet concealed in a floor-to-ceiling bookcase and gushed liquor into a glass. There were no identifying bottles, everything in cut glass decanters, but the liquid was amber and so Franks guessed it was some sort of whiskey. Nicky gulped at it and coughed awkwardly. "Sure?" said the lawyer, holding up the glass.

"Sure."

Embarrassed, despite his contempt now for the man, Franks walked from the office into the conference chamber. Where it began and where it was going to end, he thought. It was strange that they'd never changed the venue, to the Madison Avenue office suite from which the island businesses were run. The two office floors were only rented, Franks remembered, his mind straying to practicalities. With the demand for office space in Manhattan as high as it was, it would be easy enough to get out of the lease, might even make a profit. It would be the only part of the businesses that stood any possibility of doing so.

He took the chair at the head of the table and spread out his prepared material. Should he feel scared, like everyone else? He didn't. He knew now—had proof—what sort of men Dukes and Flamini and Pascara were, but he didn't feel scared of them. If he felt anything, he supposed it was contempt again. Anger, too. Anger at their imagining they could cheat him. He qualified the thought. They *had* cheated him. And would have gone on cheating him, but for the FBI investigation. Maybe they had reason to be contemptuous of him. Of his naivety, at least. They wouldn't be contemptuous, not after today.

Nicky must have had some warning of their arrival because before the men appeared the lawyer hurried in and came close to where Franks was sitting, like a child seeking the protection of a bigger brother at the threat from the school bullies.

They all entered together, and Franks wondered if they'd met elsewhere first; they might have considered it a good idea. Dukes led, blank-faced, gazing around the conference area as if

109

he expected there to be more people than just Scargo and Franks present. Pascara followed with the caution of his blindness, Luigi attentively by his side, and Flamini came last. They grouped inside the door and Franks decided at once that their controlled apprehension was in his favor.

"Shall we sit down?" he said.

Their hesitation lasted a few more seconds, and then they moved around the table, Dukes still leading, taking their customary chairs.

"What about you?" Franks said to Nicky, who'd remained standing nervously at his side.

The lawyer physically started at being addressed, hurrying to a seat next to Franks, not the one he normally occupied at the far end.

"What's the reason for this?" demanded Pascara, his head moving searchingly as he tried to establish where Franks was sitting.

"The dissolution, under the propriety clause that exists in each and every contract, of the companies holding the hotels in Bermuda and the Bahamas and of the separate company running the casino in Nassau," announced Franks with strict formality.

"Why?" demanded Flamini.

Franks already had a bookmark in the record of the company deeds, so he found the place easily. "Clause Fourteen, to which all of you are signatories, in the case of Roberto Pascara by the hand of Luigi Pascara, vested with power of attorney, reads as follows," said Franks, still formal, " 'All agreements, understandings and contractual agreements understood and agreed by the directors of this company shall be deemed null and void if, in the opinion of the controlling stockholders, each or any of those directors commits any act or conducts himself in any way so as to endanger the public propriety of this company. If such impropriety having occurred or been discovered, it shall be the duty of the chairman to summon a full meeting of the board to decide upon the action to be taken, such a meeting not to be later than fourteen full working days after the date of any such occurrence or discovery. . . .' " Franks looked up. "My first awareness that there could be some transgression of this clause came less than five days ago," he said. "Therefore this meeting is called well within the understood and accepted regulations governing the conduct of the companies concerned."

"What are you talking about?" said Dukes.

"I'm talking about mobs," said Franks, abandoning formal-

110

ity. "I'm talking about extortion and illegal gambling and drug peddling and usury. I'm talking about being tricked into the formation of these companies—particularly the casino corporation—for the movement and channeling of money from those activities beyond the jurisdiction and tax legislation of this country. And I'm talking about the respectability—and acceptability to me, as controlling stockholder—of members of this board. As controlling stockholder—with the proxy vote of my wife—" Franks took Tina's attested vote from his briefcase and slid it across the table toward them. "I intend today dissolving the companies, in their entirety. The real estate will be placed upon the open market and after the payment of all mortgage liens and any other debts, an equitable division will be made among members of this board, by a firm of independent auditors."

No one moved to check the validity of Tina's proxy vote. Nicky sat, hands cupping his head, hiding, childlike.

"You know what I think?" said Pascara. "I think you're talking bullshit."

"Do you know what I think, Mr. Pascara?" said Franks. "I think you're a crook. I think you're a two-bit gangster with an inflated reputation, who's so far been lucky in avoiding the indictments made out against him, who should be very careful about a current, ongoing FBI investigation."

Pascara had felt out, as if for reassurance, for his son. Luigi took his father's hand without looking at it, staring instead at the table, his face a mask of fixed intensity.

"I think someone should be careful," said Dukes in his rolling Texan accent.

"You're right," said Franks. "I should have been, a long time ago. Had I been careful then, I might have known what I know now." He looked away from the men gazing across the table at him, consulting his carefully made prompt notes. Franks started with Pascara, setting out the aliases—and the true name—and then all the indictments and accusations. From Pascara he went to Flamini and from Flamini to Dukes, itemizing everything and then, for good measure, he disclosed what he knew about Greenberg, in Las Vegas. Franks came up at last from the documents, looking for a reaction. There wasn't one, from any of them; they were as expressionless as they had been when he looked away from them minutes before. And when they had entered.

"There are two ways that these companies can be terminated," lectured Franks. "Either here, today, by agreement of

111

this board. Or by a court, before which all the facts and evidence can be put and which can be invited to dissolve them, upon my application. I would prefer it to be done by the first method, here today. But I'm quite prepared to go to court. In fact, I would welcome the opportunity of publicly clearing my name of any slur that might now be attached to it by association with you.''

The court idea had come to Franks as he spoke. He wasn't sure of the validity of what he said but he knew it applied in England and guessed there were similar provisions in company law in America.

"I can't make up my mind whether you're very brave or very stupid," said Flamini.

"You prepared to put it to the test?" demanded Franks. He *wasn't* scared, he realized proudly. They were trying to make him so, with their artificial, theatrical composure, but they weren't succeeding.

"How do you know there is an FBI investigation?" said Pascara.

"Because I've undergone some hours of interrogation by FBI agents who've got a dossier on the affairs of this company that must have taken months to create. They've got samples of how much money has been moved through the credit agreement with Vegas and the identities of everyone who we bribed to set up the hotels and the casino," said Franks.

There was a reaction at last, frowns between Dukes and Flamini and something whispered from Pascara to his son.

"They got the company books?"

The question came from Dukes, and Franks concentrated upon the Texan, guessing that he was the most worried of the three. "Yes," said Franks. "They've got everything they asked for."

"Why the hell did you give them the books!" shouted Flamini.

"Why shouldn't I have done?" Franks yelled back. He hadn't done it, he realized. Nicky had. The qualification didn't seem to matter.

"What did they say?" demanded the Texan. "Tell us everything they said."

"They accused me of knowingly setting up a laundering operation—referred to it as a car wash—for money you got from the rackets. Knew everything about you. Everything. Listed the formation dates and the meetings. They've got photographs in the Bahamas and in Bermuda and in Las Vegas. And like I said, they know the money that's been going through."

112

"You?" seized Flamini.

"What?" said Franks, not understanding.

"They accused you of setting up the operation?"

"I did, didn't I?" said Franks. "Stupidly and unknowingly. That's why I intend to dissolve it."

Flamini smiled at Dukes and then looked back across the table. "So the investigation isn't into us. It's into your activities?"

Franks looked briefly at Nicky, still hand-hidden, remembering the meeting in Westchester and Enrico saying openly that they would expect him to go to jail on their behalf. He looked back to the grouped men and said, "Activities carried out upon your behalf. Activities which, if it ever gets to court, I shall set out in chapter and verse."

"Do you think that would be wise, Mr. Franks?" asked Pascara conversationally.

"I think it would be essential if it's going to keep me out of jail and put you in it," said Franks.

"All the evidence must surely point to you if that's the way their investigation is going," said Dukes.

"All the evidence they've got so far," said Franks.

There was complete silence in the room. It lasted for a long time—so long that Nicky actually looked up—and then Pascara said, "What does that remark mean?"

"It means I have the recorded numbers of the offshore island accounts held by you, Mr. Pascara. And those in the Netherlands Antilles held by you, Dukes. It means I've also got details and records of the formation discussions that occurred without my knowledge, proving my complete innocence of any knowing involvement in what was being set up."

"Scargo!"

Nicky cringed at Pascara's demand, blinking up at last like someone emerging from darkness into sudden light. "I didn't make them available when the FBI came here. Honest I didn't."

"Where are they?" said Flamini.

"Safe," said Franks. "Very safe. And they're going to stay that way, unless anything happens to me or to any member of my family. And then they will be automatically released. Released to the FBI, who I guess would like very much to get hold of them."

Like the earlier threat of a civil court hearing, this use of the records as a protection was an improvisation. Which still didn't mean he was scared, thought Franks in private reassurance. It just let these bastards know how helpless they were to do anything at all to him.

113

"I want them," said Pascara softly. "I want everything that the FBI doesn't have, handed over to me today."

"Go to hell," said Franks. "I'm neither impressed nor am I frightened of you, Pascara. Of any of you. You conned me and I'm going to be made to look a fool. I accept that. But I'm not going to appear in court or go to jail on your behalf. If any charges are made they are going to be made against the guilty people. And that isn't me."

"You been asked to cooperate?" said Dukes.

"Not yet."

"I don't think we should lose our heads over this," said the Texan. He smiled, a brief on-off expression. "You got every right to be sore, Eddie. Sore as hell. But let's think it through. Where's the benefit in giving the FBI any more than they've got?"

"I'm not giving them any more than they've got."

"Good," said the Texan, smiling longer this time, his tone that of a patient teacher to a dull child. "That's good."

"But I will if they try to make a case against me."

Dukes' smile went off, as quickly as it had come.

"How much do you want?" said Flamini.

Franks laughed at the man, prolonging the laugh as long as he could. "I'm a millionaire, too. Remember?" he said. "The difference between us is that I got my money honestly. You think you can buy me off to say nothing? Now who's being stupid?"

"I sent you a message," said Pascara. "I told Scargo to give you a message."

"He gave it to me," said Franks. "Something about being silly."

"I think you're being silly," said Pascara.

"And I think we're wasting time," said Franks impatiently. "I'm formally moving the dissolution of the companies, as already set out. I have the power and sufficient stock holding to do that. You—either together or separately—have the right under the formation agreement to challenge in court any major decision you consider would be to the detriment of the company. Dissolution could be so considered. Do any of you intend challenging me in court?"

He looked slowly around them, from face to face. When was the last time these men had been put down, as they had been today? Franks said, "It needs to be formally recorded in the minutes of the meeting that there is to be no challenge. Dukes?"

"No," said the Texan.

"Flamini?"

"No."

"Pascara?"

"No."

"I'll issue all the formal declarations. Put the properties on the market. You'll each get separate, certified accounts," said Franks. "There'll be no need for us to meet again, as a board."

"I'm not accustomed to being treated discourteously, Mr. Franks," said Pascara.

"I'm not accustomed to being used, as I have been used," said Franks. He stood, the gesture intentionally dismissive. "This meeting is over," he said. "So is any association between us."

Briefly the men across the table remained sitting as they were. Luigi Pascara was the first to rise, helping his father up with him. Dukes and Flamini stood at the same time.

"Remember what I said about not doing anything silly," said Pascara at the door.

"Remember what I said about not appearing in court or going to jail on your behalf," said Franks.

Nicky stayed as he was, hunched over his legal pad. Franks said, "You can look up now. They've gone."

He regretted it at once. That was bullying, like Enrico. Still, Franks felt euphoric. It had gone far easier than he had expected. Realistically he knew there was nothing they could have done to oppose him, but their acquiescence had still been quick, with little or no argument. He wished Tina had been with him, to have witnessed how much in control he had been, of everything. To Nicky he said, "I wasn't aware of you making many notes."

"It wasn't necessary to take many notes."

"I want the dissolution notice filed today, with whatever authority has the jurisdiction. Delaware, I suppose. Can we do that, today?"

"I can telex the decision and promise the formal notices by express mail tomorrow."

"Do that," instructed Franks.

"Why the hurry?"

"I would have thought that was obvious," said Franks. He added: "How did you think it went?"

"I don't know," shrugged Nicky.

"What do you mean, you don't know?"

"I thought they would have said more."

"There wasn't a lot they could say."

"Where is the file? The one with the bank account details and the formation stuff?"

"Safe, like I said."

"Not anywhere they could get hold of it?"

"No."

Nicky sighed, relieved. "Keep it that way," he said.

"Bang! Bang!" jeered Franks.

"It isn't a joke," said Nicky. "Stop thinking that it is."

"It's all over, Nicky," said Franks. "You're out, free. You don't deserve to be, but you are."

Nicky smiled, briefly. "I hope you're right," he said.

Franks remained in the lawyer's office, determined to see that the dissolution procedure was followed. The Delaware registration authority acknowledged Nicky's telex, and Franks waited until one of the outer office secretaries returned with the post office receipt for the overnight delivery. Nicky offered him a drink from the recessed cabinet, appearing to think some sort of celebration was in order, but Franks rejected it, making it clear to the other man that the association was over here, too.

Tina had been at the Scarsdale house for two hours when he telephoned. First David and then Gabriella clamored to the telephone to speak to him and it was easier to go through conversations with them before he talked to Tina. He said he loved them both and would be up on the weekend, but until then they were to do what their mommy and the nanny told them. Tina came on the line at last, the anxiety obvious in her voice. He told her everything that had happened, knowing that he was boasting, wishing again that she had been there.

"Sounds as if you were very tough on them," she said.

"You're damned right I was tough. Haven't I the right to be, after what they did?"

"Still seems to have gone quite easily, though."

"I told you I'd sort everything out, didn't I?" said Franks, boasting still. "Believe me, everything is going to be fine."

16

Franks could not remember encountering Ruben Rosenberg during any of his visits to the businessmen's club with Nicky. The man's baldness, only a hedge of hair remaining around his head, prematurely aged him, because Franks guessed he was not much more than forty years old. He had an unlined, pinkly shaved face and was slight and unobtrusive. In fact, everything about the man was discreetly unremarkable. The suit was muted grey, with a muted grey tie over a white shirt. The office was comparatively small and unostentatious: an uncluttered desk, functional working bookcase full of law books, and filing cabinets actually in the room, not outside as in Nicky's chambers. Franks found a marked contrast between the two men. Rosenberg gave him a firm handshake and an offer of coffee, which Franks declined.

"I know Nicky Scargo only slightly. Socially at that," said Rosenberg. "The appointment message said just that there was a criminal problem. You'll have to take me completely through everything."

Franks hesitated, unsure whether to begin with the apparently innocent linkup through Nicky with the three men or with the FBI interview. He decided upon the very beginning, to maintain the chronology, setting out the establishment of the companies step by step from the initial finance search to the island visits, the eventual formations, and then the Las Vegas and casino progression. Rosenberg had started a small tape recorder at the commencement of the account but still occasionally made notes on a pad in front of him, never once intruding a question as Franks talked. The note-taking increased when Franks reached the FBI meeting, and when Franks spoke of the previous day's dissolution conference the lawyer looked up, momentarily frowning. It took over an hour for Franks to complete the account, and when he finished he said, "I think I will take that coffee now."

Rosenberg ordered it through the intercom on his desk,

continuing to stare down at the notepad while the secretary appeared briefly to deliver it. After she left, Rosenberg looked up. "I must first ask you an important question—the most important question. Were you at any time prior to the FBI interview aware that the companies you formed were being used for any criminal enterprise?"

"No!" said Franks at once. Just as quickly he qualified it, for absolute accuracy. "Nicky told me first," he said. "He telephoned me in England and said I should come, because of a problem. When I got here we had a meeting, which was before I saw the FBI people. It was at the meeting with Nicky that I learned, for the first time."

"Thank you for being so precise," said Rosenberg. "What I must establish is that you were in no way aware prior to this current visit?"

"No, I was not," insisted Franks.

Rosenberg went back to studying his notes. He looked up at last and said, "All right, Mr. Franks, I'll represent you. I'll represent you in every respect, which includes any court appearances. But if at any time it becomes clear to me that the assurance you've just given was untrue then I shall immediately withdraw from the case. I will only act for people on the basis that there be complete honesty between us, whether that honesty involves an admission of guilt or a declaration of innocence."

"I am innocent," insisted Franks again. "Completely and utterly innocent."

"I offer the same honesty that I demand," said Rosenberg. "And quite honestly, Mr. Franks, I don't think it is going to be an easy job proving that, either to the satisfaction of the FBI or to a court."

Franks hadn't expected such an opinion from the man and he felt a sinking feeling of uncertainty. "What about the file that Nicky maintained? With the account numbers and the real formation details?"

"Without that I wouldn't think you stood a hope in Hell's chance," said the lawyer. "That's still in safe-deposit?"

"Yes."

"I think it better stay there. I'll come with you to the safe-deposit room, read it, and then it can be returned without it having to be taken from the bank premises."

"You think Pascara or somebody might try to get it from us?"

Rosenberg looked at him quizzically. "Wouldn't you, if you were them?"

"So it is proof!" seized Franks hopefully.

"I won't know until I've had the opportunity of examining it," said Rosenberg. "The real question is whether it's sufficient proof. Would Nicky Scargo give evidence on your behalf?"

"I don't know," said Franks.

"He'd need to, to convince any court that it was material he'd prepared and kept. He'd need to be the man to testify that you were duped. And if he did that in a court of law then he would be committing professional suicide; he'd have to be debarred."

I don't give a damn about perjury if I'm thinking about survival, remembered Franks, feeling another sinking feeling of uncertainty. "I don't know if he'd do that," he said again.

"It's something we need to establish," said Rosenberg. "And not just about the file he kept. According to what you've told me, Scargo was the man who trapped you. Any jury will hear how it was with you, being taken in as part of the family when you were a child, during the war. Being treated like the guy's brother. Unless they hear from Scargo's own mouth that he did what he did to you, then they're not going to believe that someone with a relationship like you had would behave in such a way."

"But he did!" protested Franks.

"It's not me you have to convince, Mr. Franks. Your record, up to now, has been that of a successful businessman. Entrepreneurial, certainly. Innovative, from what you've told me. But also, from what you've told me, someone who has always shown proper care and caution. How does that character reconcile with linking yourself up with mobsters, without so much as a basic character check?" The lawyer indicated the material that had come from Chicago and Houston and which Franks had provided as he told his story.

"I know! I know!" said Franks desperately. "I trusted Nicky Scargo."

"Then Nicky Scargo's got to say so. He's got to flagellate himself in the witness box and admit to some sort of biblical deception."

"What about the dissolution of the company!" demanded Franks. "The moment I discovered who they were I got rid of them. Doesn't that prove my innocence?"

"No," said Rosenberg shortly.

"What?"

"The FBI advised you of your rights, before the interview began? That you could have had a lawyer present?"

"Yes."

"Why didn't you?"

"Okay," said Franks, raising his hand. "Another mistake. I accept that. But I'm not *guilty* of anything! What have I got to be afraid of if I'm not guilty?"

"A very great deal," said the lawyer. "You didn't know of me when the FBI got to you, but you did before the dissolution meeting. I want another undertaking from you, Mr. Franks. And that is that from now on you'll do nothing, absolutely nothing at all, without first discussing it fully with me."

"But what's wrong with dissolving the company?"

"Shall I tell you how any prosecutor would present that to a jury?" said Rosenberg. "Not as proof of innocence. As proof of guilt. In little more than a day, gentlemen of the jury, of Mr. Franks knowing that the FBI had discovered what he was doing, he tried to divest himself of his criminal colleagues, people he was happy and content to front for while they washed millions of illegal dollars but from whom he tried to run when they got found out."

"That's a travesty!" protested Franks.

"It's the obvious prosecution," said Rosenberg. "You should have done absolutely nothing. You /should have come to me. We should have waited for any prosecution to be launched and then subpoenaed Dukes and Flamini and Pascara and Greenberg and everyone else we could have thought of. Courts are theaters, Mr. Franks. Juries are impressed by the actors, so impressions are important." Rosenberg gestured again to the material that had come from Houston and Chicago. "They look like mobsters. You don't."

"You can still subpoena them, can't you?"

"Of course I can. And I will, if the need arises. They won't talk, of course. They'll invoke the Fifth Amendment. Which again would have been in our favor if you hadn't closed up the company. While the company existed there was the chance of your appearing the dupe. Dissolved looks like you were running."

"I haven't handled anything very well, have I?"

"No," said the relentlessly honest lawyer. "Which for me is something actually in your favor. I've told you how a prosecution will present it, and I've told you how it could be viewed by a jury, but I think you've behaved exactly like an honest man." He smiled apologetically. "Please don't be offended, but if you'd been crooked I would have expected you to be cleverer than you have been."

Franks laughed humorlessly. "Thanks!" he said. "Until now I've thought of myself as a pretty smart businessman. It's not going to look much like that in court, is it?"

"I've given you the bottom line, in everything," said Rosenberg. "It's the way I work, never promising anything I don't think I can deliver. It's bad, but it's a very long way from being hopeless. Scargo's file is an ace. He'll be another, if he's prepared to testify. Even if he's not, that won't mean that everything is lost. Don't forget what I said about courts being theater. The Fifth Amendment prevents people incriminating themselves out of their own mouths. I've never known a jury yet who haven't believed the point that was being put to a witness who invokes his rights. If it gets to a court and I get Scargo in the box, I can make him confirm that file to the jury by just letting him hide behind the law. The Cain and Abel bit might be more difficult, particularly as you're married to his sister. Is there any evidence we could bring to prove that it was a split, feuding family?"

"None," said Franks. "Until now it's always been close; incredibly close."

"So why did he do it?"

Franks hesitated. Wasn't it precisely a Cain and Abel situation between him and Nicky? "Competition," he said.

"What?"

Franks told the other man of the perpetual contests that Enrico had set them when they were children, the constant demands that one should excel over the other, and then he recounted Nicky's outburst at their confrontation after the summons from England.

"Wait!" stopped Rosenberg. "This is important. The exact words, as far as you can remember them. I want the exact words!"

Franks frowned, recollecting. "He said he was 'sick and tired,' " he groped. "Something about being sick and tired of having me held up to him as a big tycoon. Just as he had been sick and tired of having to be as good as me when we were kids and at school."

"Jealousy?" said Rosenberg.

"I suppose so."

"I wonder if he'd admit that in court?" said Rosenberg, more to himself than to the other man.

"Would it be important?"

"It's the motive, isn't it? Trying to involve himself with you; be as big an operator?"

121

"I suppose it is," agreed Franks.

"A jury could accept that. Understand it," said Rosenberg, still reflective. He came back up to Franks. "What about you?" he said.

"Me?"

"How do you feel about Nicky Scargo?"

Rosenberg was very good, conceded Franks. But then that was why he'd come to the man in the first place. Complete honesty, the lawyer had demanded. And he was going to have to be completely honest in everything if he were to extricate himself. "It's never been a feeling of jealousy," he said. "Not a conscious feeling, anyway. But there's always been competition, the need to prove ourselves better."

"*Yourself* better?" persisted Rosenberg.

"I suppose so," admitted Franks reluctantly.

"Nicky was working for you, setting up the companies?"

"Yes," said Franks in further admission. He was aware that he was coloring.

"Was that how it was? Why you went into it so openly? To get Nicky Scargo working for you?"

"I trusted him to set up an honest deal."

"We've talked about that," said Rosenberg, refusing to be deflected. "Were you eager—overeager to the point of ignoring business practices you would normally have followed—to set yourself up with Nicky Scargo so that you would be his boss?"

"Yes," said Franks, his voice hardly audible.

Rosenberg sat back, appearing satisfied. "If this comes to court I'll have to bring it out," he said. "You understand that, don't you? It provides the rationale. It doesn't detract from the fact that you were incredibly stupid, but it makes explainable, partially at least, how it could have happened."

What was he going to have left at the end of all this? wondered Franks. He said wearily, "Yes, I understand."

"Okay. Is there anything else that I don't know that you think maybe I should?"

Franks considered and then shook his head. "No, I don't think so." Then he said, "Yes, one thing. Waldo, the FBI man, said he wanted me to remain here, in Manhattan. I don't know if he meant the actual city or what. My wife and family are up in Scarsdale and I want to go up there too. Is there any reason why I shouldn't?"

Rosenberg shook his head. "You were bullied, weren't you?" he said.

"I guess so."

"Did Waldo or the other guy say where they were working from? New York office or the Washington headquarters?"

"No," said Franks.

Rosenberg told his secretary to get him a number, and said, "The New York office will know, even if he isn't attached to them. I'll enter an undertaking as your counselor, guaranteeing your cooperation and appearance whenever requested. They can't impose the sort of restrictions they were trying, not at this stage."

The telephone rang and Rosenberg lifted it, frowning across the desk as soon as he identified himself and said whom he was representing and asking to be connected to Waldo.

"They are looking for you," he said to Franks, hand cupped over the receiver.

Waldo apparently came on to the line. Rosenberg said, "What!" and then, "Yes, of course. Yes. I understand. Of course we'll come. Right away!"

The lawyer replaced the receiver and looked across the desk, momentarily unspeaking. "Nicky Scargo's been shot," he announced. "He's dead."

17

They went in Rosenberg's car, Franks hunched behind the driver, head bent. He thought they went by a park but he was only vaguely aware and didn't know—wasn't interested—whether it was Central Park or one of the other oases in the city. When was he going to stop being wrong! When, dear God, whoever He was, was he going to be able to see six inches beyond the end of his own nose, appreciate what he was involved in and do something right instead of wrong, for a change! He'd been wrong about the establishment of the companies and he'd been wrong about cooperating with the FBI interview and he'd been wrong in confronting the mobsters and dissolving the companies and he'd been wrong in dismissing—laughing as if it were absurd—the

123

possibility of someone being killed. And now it had happened. Nicky was dead. Franks found it difficult to comprehend; no, not comprehend. The lawyer had spoken to the FBI and the FBI had said Nicky was dead, so he had to comprehend that. Assimilate, then. That was the word. Difficult to assimilate. He'd accepted—they'd all accepted—that the family was destroyed figuratively. But this was literally. Shot, Rosenberg had said. Dead. What would that mean? Franks asked himself, striving to understand; striving to understand *properly*. It would devastate Mamma and Poppa Scargo; destroy them as effectively as the bullet or bullets had destroyed their son. Maria, too. She might have gone back to her mother on Long Island, but Franks couldn't believe that she'd ceased loving Nicky, not completely. Any more than he believed Tina had, despite everything. Both of them—Maria and Tina—were reacting to events, not to their hearts. What about himself? The question settled, giving some coherence at last to his thoughts. Nothing, he realized. Nothing, just as there'd been nothing all those years ago in the English graveyard when he'd stood over his father's grave and tried to feel something. Not grief, at least. His awareness of what Nicky's death meant revolved around the just-ended interview with the lawyer. *'Nicky Scargo's got to say so.'* That's what Rosenberg had said: Nicky's evidence—even if the man hid behind the Fifth Amendment—could have saved him in front of a jury. Now Nicky wasn't alive anymore, either to speak or to hide. Did that mean he couldn't be saved?

Franks wasn't aware of the car stopping. Rosenberg had to nudge him into something like wakefulness, and Franks tried to recover, staring around, startled. There were police cars lined in an orderly fashion and a squarely solid, red brick building, which in the first few seconds Franks thought was actually Nicky's brownstone and then immediately knew was not, because it was too square and squat.

"It's the precinct building," said Rosenberg, providing the identification. "There's a mortuary at the back. That's where I've arranged to meet the FBI people."

Franks let the lawyer leave the car first, trailing docilely behind, wanting very much to follow and not to lead. They entered through the main door, into a bedlam of a receiving area. It appeared to be crowded with people, all shouting and arguing. There was a high, commanding desk behind which sat a sergeant and two assistants, who seemed—illogically—to be unaware of the movement and cacophony and jostling parading before them. There were uniformed officers shouting for attention and ordinary

124

people shouting for attention and telephones ringing, demanding attention. On a bench along one wall three men sat, handcuffed, bent forward to look down at the floor; one had a bloodstained cloth around his head but didn't seem in any pain. Franks would have thought the man should have been in a hospital. Rosenberg didn't become one of the assembled people demanding attention: He paused, taking Franks' arm so that the man could not be intercepted, and set off confidently along a corridor beside the reception desk. The challenge came as they drew level and were about to pass. Rosenberg's reaction was as quick as the challenge, shouting Waldo's name and a telephone extension number and then saying, "FBI." The identification roused the sergeant, who focused upon them, demanded their names, and then nodded them through. Still with his hand cupping Franks' elbow, Rosenberg continued on. It was a heaving labyrinth of a place, interlocked corridors jostled with people, all of whom appeared unaware or unconcerned of everyone around them. Rosenberg and Franks ebbed and flowed with the human wash until Rosenberg located office numbers running in the sequence he wanted. He hurried down the minor corridor, head moving as he counted off the numbers, and when he found the door he wanted thrust in without knocking.

It looked more like a storeroom than a place in which people worked. The window faced out onto a blank wall only a few feet away, so there was little natural light, the main illumination coming from a chipped and stained fixture in the middle of the ceiling. Waldo was at an empty steel desk, sitting doing nothing, and Schultz was by a filing cabinet wedged into the corner of a wall against which was a calendar showing January, 1982. Someone had started crossing off the days but stopped at the sixteenth. The place smelled dusty and unused, like a rarely opened cupboard.

"You Rosenberg?" demanded the obese FBI agent.

"Waldo?"

"Yes."

"Yes."

"Been waiting for you," said Waldo.

"Crosstown traffic was bad," said Rosenberg.

Franks stood just inside the door, offended by the exchange. Somebody had been killed—all right, somebody about whom he found it difficult to arouse any feeling, but that was a personal problem. But still, a human being. And these two men were discussing the difficulty of driving in Manhattan.

"Mr. Franks," greeted Waldo, nodding.

125

"What's happened?" demanded Franks, impatient with the artificial politeness.

"Scargo's dead," said Waldo.

"I know that," said Franks, still impatient. "What *happened?*"

"They got him—it was two men—in the garage." The man paused. "You know the brownstone, on Sixty-second?"

"Yes," said Franks. How long ago had it been that he and Tina had stayed there and enjoyed Nicky's and Maria's company and considered themselves friends?

"Scargo used to park his car opposite, in the basement garage of the apartment house. Got him there this morning. Shotguns. It's a hell of a mess. Janitor heard the blast, but by the time he got there—he didn't hurry, who would?—it was all over. No one there, of course."

Franks came farther into the room, angered by the laconic account. "It's Pascara," he said. "Or Dukes or Flamini. All of them. It's got to be. Have you arrested them?"

Franks was conscious of Schultz actually shaking his head, a gesture of sadness. "Mr. Franks," said the FBI man, "from what the janitor says, Nicky was shot down around eight forty-five this morning. At eight forty-five this morning, Pascara and Flamini were publicly identified breakfasting at the Continental Plaza on Michigan Avenue, Chicago. David Dukes was photographed at Caesars Palace, part of a welcoming delegation to Las Vegas for the Los Angeles Lions Club. Dukes is very big in charities. The Lions are one of his favorites."

"You believe they weren't involved?"

"Of course we don't believe they weren't involved," said Waldo. "You know something we don't that could tie them into it?"

Franks shook his head helplessly.

"That's the way it's done, Mr. Franks," said Waldo. "You think Pascara and Flamini went to the Continental Plaza for its waffles? Or Dukes to Caesars just to be a public benefactor?"

"Why?" said Franks. It was an empty question, really to himself, but Schultz responded to it.

"Why don't you tell us, Mr. Franks?" said Schultz. "Why not tell us what happened at the meeting yesterday that you had with them at Scargo's office?"

"You picked them up?" said Franks.

"We picked up the telephone calls, off Scargo's credit card," said Waldo. "Got them at the airport. Wanted to see where they went."

"I'm Mr. Franks' attorney," intruded Rosenberg. "Is he under investigation for possible criminal proceedings?"

"Yes, sir," said Waldo.

"Then I shall limit his answers."

"Something secret enough at that meeting to cause a man to be murdered?" demanded Schultz.

"I can tell you the point of that meeting was to dissolve the companies running the hotels and casino in the Bahamas and Bermuda," said Rosenberg.

"Jesus!" said Waldo, amazed. Despite the legally imposed restriction, he said to Franks, "You told them about the investigation? About our meeting with you?"

"Yes," said Franks.

"Why did you stop there?" said the overflowing man contemptuously. "Why didn't you wait in the garage this morning and pull the trigger yourself? You killed him anyway!"

"That's improper!" protested Rosenberg.

"It's true," said Waldo. "Don't you think that's true, Mr. Rosenberg?"

"You asked us to come down to assist in your inquiries," reminded Rosenberg stiffly.

"I think you just did," said Waldo, world weary. "Jesus!"

Schultz said, "Didn't Scargo tell you what we'd told him? Not to approach them?"

"Yes," admitted Franks, dry-throated.

"But you decided you knew best!"

"My client doesn't have to debate the matter with you," said Rosenberg.

Schultz sighed. "Do you have any idea, Mr. Franks, where Scargo's wife might be? She was last seen leaving the brownstone two days ago and she hasn't been seen since."

"Long Island," replied Franks at once. "Her mother has an apartment near Fort Salonga. I don't know the address but I guess it would be in the book. The name is Spinetti."

"How do you know she's there?"

"Nicky told me yesterday. Said Maria wanted to get away for a few days."

"That her name—Maria?" asked Schultz, who was using the top of the filing cabinet to rest a pad upon.

"Yes," said Franks. The thought engulfed him, as he spoke, and he said, "Do you think she's in danger? Anyone else? My wife and family are alone in Scarsdale!"

"Mr. Franks," said Waldo easily, "your wife and two

127

children have been under FBI and U.S. Marshals protection since eleven o'clock this morning. We've known where she's been from the time she left the Plaza to collect them at the airport."

Franks remembered Waldo's early boast about surveillance. He said, "If you followed her, then you would have followed me to Mr. Rosenberg's. And if your surveillance was that good, then you'd have been outside Nicky's house today!"

Waldo shifted, uncomfortable. "Crosstown traffic," he said, nodding toward the lawyer. "We lost you. We had a man outside Scargo's brownstone. Saw him leave this morning and stayed in the car, ready for him to come up from his parking spot and drive to the office. Our man never heard the shooting."

"And you expect me to be satisfied with the protection you've got at Scarsdale!" said Franks.

"No," said Waldo. "I don't expect you to be satisfied at all. It's just the best shot you've got, that's all."

"I want to go there, right away," said Franks.

"At this stage you can't enforce any sort of boundary restriction," said Rosenberg.

The telephone in the makeshift office was lodged on the windowsill. Schultz turned away from it and bent toward Waldo, so that neither of the other two men could overhear the conversation. Waldo nodded and looked up to Franks. "You know Scargo very well?" he said. "Were brought up with him?"

"Yes," agreed Franks doubtfully, not sure of the questioning.

"We need a formal identification of the body," said Schultz. "We've got people going out to get Mrs. Scargo now, but it's going to take a while to get her back in from Long Island. Salonga's way out."

"And he's a mess," said Waldo.

"You can refuse," said Rosenberg hurriedly.

Franks frowned at his lawyer. "Why should I refuse?" he said. Looking back to Waldo, he said, "Of course."

They emerged from the cramped room back into the human flow, going against the tide toward the rear of the building. Nearer the attached mortuary the throng lessened and they were able to walk abreast. Franks said to Waldo, "Do you think they'll try to kill me? Or my family?"

"Your wife know anything?"

"She held the proxy vote that enabled me to dissolve the company."

"Does she know anything?"

"I suppose she does," said Franks.

128

"She could be hit, if she's a threat," said Waldo.

Franks stopped, confronting the man. "Doesn't anything move you?" he demanded. "You're talking about killing with about the same emotion as you'd talk about a sandwich filling for lunch!"

Waldo stared back at him patiently. "If I thought getting outraged and upset would help, Mr. Franks, I'd get outraged and upset. Emotion gets in the way of my job."

Franks felt Rosenberg's hand upon his arm. "Let's get on with it, shall we?" said the lawyer.

Waldo thrust through the rubber-buffered doors of the mortuary. Franks paused momentarily, and then followed. To the immediate left were other doors, topped by an "enter—do not enter" lighting arrangement—some sort of autopsy theater? Waldo went straight past, farther along the corridor, and then turned left, through a door. There was a mixed odor of antiseptic and formaldehyde, and it was cold. Directly inside the door a man sat at a desk. He was reading the *Daily News,* and there was a thermos flask near an adjustable lamp. The attendant was unscrewing it when they entered, but he resealed it when he saw them.

"Mort," greeted the FBI man.

"Hi, Harry," said the attendant.

"Scargo," requested Waldo.

The man looked briefly at Franks and Rosenberg, as if he were trying to isolate the relative, and then led them to a bank of what appeared to be huge filing cabinets. He stopped at the third from the left and pulled at it. The tray emerged on smoothly oiled runners, and Franks stood just to one side, gazing in.

Nicky's body was encased in plastic, and Franks' impression, absurdly, was that Nicky looked as if he were wrapped up like lettuce in a supermarket. The attendant jerked back the cover, and although he had nerved himself, Franks winced at the sight, unable to stop the grunt of shock either. Nicky was completely naked, his body appearing unnaturally white. The back of his head was almost completely blown away, a tangled mass of hair and bone and blood and visceral threads. His face was almost entirely untouched, just one small pellet indentation on his chin, and there was no grimace of pain or distortion, or sudden shock. The right arm had been severed just above the elbow and what remained of it was wrapped in a separate plastic container and laid where it properly belonged, to the right side of the body. There was a massive chest wound on the left, so there was just a hole where the breast and the shoulder should have been. As

Franks backed away he saw that they really did tie identification tags on the toes. Nicky's was to the right and he saw that the name had already been neatly inscribed in block capitals.

"Yes," he said, "that's Nicky." Had he been responsible for that? For that mutilated butchery?

Franks backed farther away from the mortuary cabinet, swallowing against the acid that rose in the back of his throat. "Christ!" he said. He felt a hand on his arm and turned to see it was Rosenberg, guiding him away. The attendant thrust the drawer back into the wall and made some notation on the identification panel attached to the front.

"Thank you," said Schultz. "Now you see why I asked you to do it and not Mrs. Scargo."

Franks nodded, unable to speak. As they went out through the door the attendant had regained his desk and was opening the thermos top.

They walked unspeaking back to the temporary office. By the time they got there the immediate sensation of sickness had gone, and Franks said, "I'd like to speak to my wife. Can I use that telephone?"

"Go ahead," said Waldo.

Franks dialed the number and Tina answered at once, the stored-up words jumbling from her when she recognized his voice. "Eddie, what the hell's happening! There are men here; FBI men and marshals. They say it's to protect me and the children, but they won't say why."

"Nicky's dead," he said abruptly, cutting her off.

There was complete silence. Franks waited, but when there was no response, he said, "Tina?"

"I'm here." Her voice sounded quite strong. "How?"

"Shot," said Franks. "A shotgun."

"Oh," she said, all emotion drained from her voice, even shock.

"I'm at the police station. With the people who came to the hotel. Maria's being brought in from Long Island. I suppose I should stay until she gets here."

"Yes," said Tina, sounding quite controlled. "You should do that."

"Maybe she should come back to the house?"

"Is it bad?"

"Awful."

"She won't have to see?"

"No."

130

"Poor Maria."

"Yes."

"Who's going to tell Mamma and Poppa?"

Franks hadn't thought about it. Holding the telephone away, he said to Waldo, "Are there people with the Scargo family, up in Westchester?"

Waldo nodded. "Same time as we put a guard on your wife."

Going back to the telephone, Franks said, "There are people looking after them. I suppose I'll have to tell them."

Her hold went at last. He heard the sound of sobbing and then her obvious attempt to control it. "Oh, Eddie," she said, "what are we going to do?"

"I don't know, not yet," admitted Franks. "Don't worry. You're safe."

"I don't feel safe, Eddie. Not anymore. I want it to stop. Everything to stop."

"It will," he said. "I promise it will."

"I want you with me."

"I'll come as soon as Maria gets here."

"Please hurry."

Franks replaced the telephone and thanked Schultz.

"What caused that death, Mr. Franks?" insisted Waldo. "What went on at that meeting yesterday?"

"My client doesn't choose to answer that question, not at this time," Rosenberg said at once.

"When?" demanded Waldo, speaking to the lawyer this time.

"Is there going to be any prosecution of my client?" demanded Rosenberg.

"I don't decide that, do I?" said Waldo.

"Do you intend holding him?"

Franks blinked. It had never occurred to him that he might be physically detained: locked up. A criminal. He stared around the decaying, chipped building and wondered if the cells were somewhere here. Of course they were.

"Not at this time," said Waldo.

"Has the district attorney involved in the case been told of the killing? "

"Yes," said Schultz.

"I'll make contact tomorrow," said Rosenberg. "Who is it?"

"Walter Ronan," said Schultz. "You know him?"

131

"Yes," nodded Rosenberg.

Everything was back to their idea of normality, thought Franks; sandwich-filling conversation. He forced his thoughts on, trying to go beyond these casual, unemotional men, the circle turning to his reflections in the car on the way here. All the fears had been justified. He'd despised Nicky and accused everyone of Hollywood fantasies, and they'd been right and he'd been wrong. And now Nicky—poor, frightened, cringing Nicky—was dead. Would Nicky be dead if he hadn't forced the dissolution meeting? Of course not, decided Franks. So Waldo was right; he'd pressed the trigger. And done more than kill Nicky. Taken away the corroboration for his own defense against the charges that had been prepared so carefully and were now to be deliberated upon by some district attorney named Walter Ronan. Did he lunch at the same club, off Fulton?

Franks looked helplessly toward Rosenberg, and said, "What's going to happen?"

The lawyer responded curiously, caught by the tone of Franks' voice. "You can go home to Scarsdale. Tonight. Tomorrow we'll meet at my office. Noon. By then I'll have made contact with the district attorney."

There was the sound of movement from beyond the door and then a knock. It opened at once, and Franks saw Maria between two plainclothesmen. She walked sedately into the room, looking at him without any recognition. The place was too small to accommodate the agents who had escorted her from Long Island; they shuffled unsurely at the entrance and withdrew into the corridor.

"Mrs. Scargo?" said Waldo.

She nodded, looking at Franks. "It's Nicky, isn't it?" she said. "I thought it might be you, but now I know it's Nicky."

"I'm sorry," said Franks. Why weren't there better words!

"How?" she asked.

"Shot," said Franks. "Leaving home this morning."

"He said it would happen. You didn't believe him."

"No."

"Do I see him?"

"It's better you don't," said Franks. When was she going to collapse?

Maria looked at Waldo, seated behind the desk. "You a detective?"

"FBI."

"What do I have to do?"

132

"Nothing now," said Waldo. "There'll be protection."
"Tina's at Scarsdale, with the children," said Franks.
"Come and stay there with us."
"Do Mamma and Poppa Scargo know?" she said.
"I've got to tell them."
"I think I should go to them. They'll need someone."
"Come with me, then," said Franks.
"He said it would happen," she repeated. "He said that if it
happened to him he hoped there wouldn't be any pain because he
couldn't stand pain. He was a coward, you see. He knew it,
which made it worse. . . ." She looked around to each of them
as she talked, as if she wanted them all to understand. "He said it
was going to happen and I didn't believe him, either." And then
she burst into tears.

18

The two agents who had brought Maria in from Long Island
drove escort in a backup car. Schultz drove their vehicle, with
Waldo in the front passenger seat. Franks was behind the driver,
his arm around Maria. She had her head against his chest and
reached across, as soon as the car began to move, taking his other
hand in both of hers, needing the additional reassurance. Occasionally, unconsciously, she stroked his fingers. The dry sobbing—
all the tears used up in the outburst of grief in the cramped
office—was less now, but still shuddered through her every so
often. The traffic that had occupied part of the earlier conversation was easier now, at dusk. Schultz drove hurriedly, both men
constantly looking around them; the neon reflections of unseen,
passing advertisements kaleidoscoped into the vehicle, tattooing
them in strange colors. The car had a radio system, turned down
so that the dispatcher's voice was a blurred, indistinct mumble.
They had to stop at a light on Second and Franks heard Schultz
say, "Shit!" Waldo snatched at the microphone and said "close
up" and Franks glanced over his shoulder to see the second
protective car drive right up behind them, so close he thought

133

there was going to be a collision. They were able to go faster on the FDR Drive, and Franks supposed there was some identification on the vehicles to prevent their being stopped by traffic police. They crossed the bridge and picked up the Bruckner Expressway, and Maria settled tighter against him. Beneath his arm her breathing became more even and he wondered if she was asleep. It seemed absurd, but she was in shock and people behaved strangely—absurdly—in shock. He looked down and in a brief illumination he saw that her eyes were closed, but as he looked she opened them briefly, then closed them again. Waldo and Schultz spoke only rarely to each other, their voices low so Franks couldn't hear, and they never tried to talk to him during the drive. Waldo seemed to be making timed transmissions on the radio, and Franks guessed it was locked onto an agreed frequency, because the man never appeared to adjust it.

Franks was being gripped by a feeling of unreality and concentrated on fighting it because what was happening wasn't unreal. To think it was—to allow himself to think that it was a dream from which he would soon wake up—was trying to run away and hide. And Franks wasn't going to run away and hide. He wasn't going to do anything on his own anymore, because he'd promised Rosenberg that he wouldn't, and he knew he needed the lawyer; needed him like hell. But he wasn't going to let the bastards win by terrorizing him. He hadn't been frightened of them at the misguided dissolution conference, and he wasn't frightened of them now. He was frightened for Tina and the kids and Maria and the Scargos, but he wasn't frightened for himself. Even though he had seen the mutilated, blasted body of Nicky Scargo, Franks couldn't believe that anything like that could ever happen to him. Which was allowing the unreality he'd determined to resist, Franks recognized.

At last Waldo turned to the back of the car, and said, "You want to stop at Scarsdale first, to see your wife?"

"Please," said Franks.

"The two guys in the car behind will stay over tonight," said Waldo. "Come in to town with you tomorrow."

"Thanks," said Franks. Would Rosenberg manage to find out what the district attorney intended doing by then?

Waldo turned back to his radio, and when they approached the house Franks imagined it had been to warn the people already guarding it that they were approaching. As they swept in through the gates, Franks briefly saw a marked police car in addition to the undesignated vehicles at the entrance. The warned agents appeared to have alerted Tina, too. A man opened the door, squinting out to assure himself who they were, but Tina was waiting just inside. Maria got hesitatingly from the car, as if she was unsure where she was, and Franks had to guide her across the porchway. Tina held out her hands, wordlessly. The two women clutched each other in a silent embrace, and then Tina led Maria off to the main sitting room, to the right. Only Waldo and Schultz came into the house. Franks said, "Can I get you a drink?"

"Yes," said Waldo.

There was a tray in the smaller sitting room, where the main television was and where he and Tina sat in the evenings when they were alone. Franks poured scotch for them and brandy for himself, and said, "How long?"

"How long what?"

"All this?" said Franks, gesturing to the guarded grounds outside the window.

Waldo shrugged. "As long as it takes."

"I can't believe that they'd try to kill me," said Franks, remembering the reflections in the car.

"People never can," said Schultz.

Franks thought back to their consideration at the precinct house, where they'd withdrawn from the room to let Maria cry out her grief just to him. He gave another enveloping gesture and said, "Thanks, for all this."

"It's the job, Mr. Franks."

"Did you mean what you said back there in the city? That there isn't a chance of connecting Pascara and Flamini and Dukes with Nicky's killing?"

"Not one in a million, I wouldn't think," said Schultz matter-of-factly. "Even if we picked up the guys who did it. They probably wouldn't know of Pascara or anyone else, you see. It's not done that way. The contract comes down through middlemen to other middlemen. They're clean."

"Why the public breakfast and the charity photographs, then?"

"Pascara and Flamini and Dukes are where they are—and have survived for so long and beaten a lot of raps—because they don't take chances. Any chances at all."

The three men turned as Tina came into the room. She wasn't wearing any makeup and her eyes were wetly red. Franks wondered if Maria had cried any more. "She wants to go to the family," said Tina. "I asked her to stay but she said she wants to go there."

135

"I know," said Franks. "We already talked about it. You okay?"

Tina humped her shoulders. "I don't know."

"What about the children?"

"I told them that all the men were people who worked for you; that you were having a meeting. It's all I could think of. There've been several police cars and David's seen them. He couldn't understand that." She shuddered. "He kept asking to see the policemen's guns."

"You coming with us?" asked Franks.

Tina looked toward Waldo and Schultz, as if expecting some guidance. She said, "It would mean leaving the children."

"They'd be quite safe."

Tina shook her head doubtfully. "I think I'll stay. Will you be long?"

"I don't know," said Franks.

"It isn't going to be easy, is it?"

"Nothing is, not anymore," said Franks.

"Do you mind if we set out, Mr. Franks?" said Schultz. "After this we've got to get back to New York."

"Sure," said Franks. "Where's Maria?"

"Waiting," said Tina. "She's ready."

The change in Maria was very marked. She didn't appear to have cried, like Tina. She emerged from the larger room into the hallway quite composed, looking alertly around her, and said, strong-voiced, "Shall we go?"

She didn't sit against him in the car this time. Instead she pulled away, into the corner of the car, staring out at the vehicles and the darkened figures of the patroling guards as they went down the drive and out onto the highway. As they started north-ward, she said, "There'll be the funeral to arrange."

"I'll do it," said Franks.

"I can manage," she said positively.

The shock had swung the pendulum in the other direction, Franks decided, from vulnerable to independent. "We'll talk about it later," he said.

She didn't reply.

Franks twisted, looking over his shoulder. The escort car was tightly in position, and Waldo was back on the radio, maintaining his links. Franks supposed they were trained for situations like this. He was conscious of Waldo talking at greater length on the radio than he had before. The road directly outside the Scargo house was secured by roadblocks, as it had been in

Scarsdale, so that no vehicle could pass without check. But this time Schultz stopped the car and Waldo got out. The huge man stood, head bent, in the lights of their own and another car, nodding to whatever was being said to him by a man whose features Franks could not properly see. The car actually moved when Waldo got back in, going down slightly under his weight. He looked over the seat at Franks and said, "Old man Scargo's causing trouble. He's ordered everyone off his property; says he doesn't want any police around."

"Does he know why they're here?"

"It was left for you to tell them."

"Then I'd better do it, hadn't I?" said Franks.

The old man was visible in the porchlights before they actually reached the house, standing in the doorway and gesticulating to the officers who were grouped around, refusing to move.

Enrico started forward when he saw Franks and Maria get out of the car, his mouth open to continue the protest, and then it registered that it *was* Maria with Franks, not Tina, and he stopped.

"Let's go inside," said Franks.

The old man remained where he was for a few moments and then looked hurriedly around him, toward the men with whom he had been arguing, appearing suddenly embarrassed. He turned, obediently, and went slump-shouldered into the house. Mamma Scargo was just beyond the front door and her eyes went from Franks to Maria and then back again and her face closed, in the same sort of immediate awareness that her husband had shown in the porchway. Enrico didn't stop, but went directly into the large room overlooking the tennis courts where they seemed to have had all the family meetings. He went heavily to a chair and sat bent forward, his arms against his knees, gazing downward. Maria reached out to the old woman, offering comfort as Tina had done to her earlier, and Mamma Scargo came forward into the embrace. The two women, old and young, went to a couch and sat. It was to Enrico they looked, not Franks.

"I asked them why they'd come," said Enrico distantly. "Asked why there was the need, but they lied to me. They said there wasn't anything wrong; that it was just a precaution. They should have told me. I would not have argued if I'd known." He looked up at Franks. "When?"

"This morning."

"He's dead, of course?"

"Yes."

137

"Yes," accepted Enrico. "Of course."

"You should let them stay here," said Franks. "They're guarding Tina and the children. Maria, too."

"Did he suffer?"

"No," said Franks definitely. Having come all this way, there didn't seem enough to say.

"That's good," said Enrico. "It's good he didn't suffer."

The old lady was still looking across at her husband, seeking guidance, but both appeared calm and resigned to what had happened. Why were tears so easy when they were happy, but difficult in grief? wondered Franks. He tried to think of different words—better words—but there weren't any, so he said, "I'm very sorry."

The old man stared steadily at Franks for a long time without speaking, and Franks stood, waiting for the inevitable accusation. Instead the old man said, "I wish it had been you."

"I suppose you do," said Franks. He didn't feel any anger or outrage at the honesty. Whatever happened, he didn't intend getting into any sort of argument or shouting match with the old man. Like Enrico, Franks felt a strange resignation about everything. He supposed that was a better reaction than trying to imagine it was all unreal and not happening at all.

"I'd like to stay here," said Maria from beside the old lady.

"Yes," said Enrico. He looked past Franks toward the gardens in which the FBI men were assembled. "They should stay. For the moment they should stay. While Maria's here."

"It's only a precaution," said Franks. "No one thinks they'll make a move against you. Or Maria." Did he know enough to say that? Franks asked himself. It seemed important to offer them some sort of reassurance.

"How do they know what's going to happen!" said Enrico contemptuously.

"I should get back to Tina," said Franks.

Enrico shrugged dismissively.

"Is there anything you'd like me to do?"

There was another long look, but still no accusation at the end of it. Enrico said simply, "No."

Franks looked across to Maria, and said, "I'll call you tomorrow, about the funeral."

"I said I'd do it."

"There might be something."

"There won't be."

Waldo and Schultz were still in the porchway, talking to the

138

other officers. They looked at Franks as he emerged, and Waldo said, "Well?"

"He agrees they should stay."

"They would have done anyway," said Waldo.

Franks settled into the back of the car, engulfed in a sudden fatigue that spread through his entire body. So much so quickly, he thought. Dear God, what was still to come?

Franks leaned back with his head against the seat, his eyes closed. From the movement of the vehicle Franks knew when they regained the highway, on the way back to Scarsdale, but he didn't open his eyes, too disinterested to confirm it. Not disinterested in getting back to Scarsdale, but in the constant movement and traveling. Did he still feel like fighting, like he'd determined on the ride up with Maria; fighting in such a way to keep the bastards from winning? The resignation he'd felt at the Scargo's became entwined with the bone-aching weariness, and Franks decided he wasn't sure anymore. He forced his eyes open, not to concentrate upon the drive but upon the way his mind was drifting. Of course he was going to fight. Make them pay for what they'd tried to do to him and what they had done to Nicky. Just tired, that's all. All he needed was some sleep and another detailed meeting with Rosenberg and then they'd work out a way to settle everything.

At the Scarsdale house Waldo stopped long enough to check all the precautions and said maybe he'd see him tomorrow, and Franks said sure, and then they left. He was conscious of the sag of his own shoulders as he closed the door behind them, remaining for a moment where he was, not wanting to move.

"You all right?" said Tina from behind him.

He turned slowly toward her. She was in the small room, where the drinks were, and he went in and sank gratefully into a chair, leaning back and closing his eyes. "Exhausted," he said.

"Do you want a drink?"

He shook his head, eyes still closed, not replying.

"How was it at the house?"

"Not how I expected it to be. I thought there were going to be tears and screaming, but there wasn't. Almost as if they expected it."

"How about Maria?"

"I thought she was going back, inside herself. Shock, I guess."

"Do you know what's going to happen, Eddie? How everything is going to work out?"

139

"No," said Franks honestly.

"Don't get killed, Eddie. Please don't get killed."

"I don't intend to," said Franks too quickly.

"Neither did Nicky," she said just as quickly. "Don't do anything else to cause any trouble."

"Give in to Pascara and Flamini and Dukes, you mean?"

"If that's what it takes, then yes, that's what I mean," said Tina urgently. "I want you alive, Eddie. To go on living. I don't want to be a widow, like Maria. I'm not brave enough."

19

Franks hadn't considered the children; their reaction at least. It had been a bad night. Despite his tiredness, it had been difficult to sleep at first, and then his mind was blocked by half-awake dreams of Nicky's mutilated body that became Tina's mutilated body and then Maria's—but never his own—and a repeated sound, which he identified as a bell but then changed his mind and thought it was the clanging of some heavy metal door being slammed behind him. He woke fully before it was light, lying still to avoid waking Tina, wishing that he didn't feel so exhausted and that he was able to think clearer. He was going to need to be able to think very clearly today. Tina stirred at last and said, "You didn't sleep very well, did you?"

"Did I disturb you?"

"Yes."

"Sorry."

She was about to go on when David and Gabriella burst giggling into the room, still in their nightclothes, Elizabeth helplessly behind. Tina said, "It's all right. We're awake. You can leave them, Elizabeth."

"Daddy! Daddy!" said the boy. "Who are all these men with guns?"

Franks lifted David onto the bed, so that the child sat astride his stomach, and Tina hauled Gabriella in on her side, in the same pose.

"Men who've got to be here for a while," said Franks. "And hello. Don't boys who fly all the way from England and who've not seen their daddy for more than two months say hello and maybe manage a kiss?"

"Hello," said David. "Kissing's stupid."

Franks smiled up at the boy. He realized—guiltily—how little lately he'd actually looked at his son; really looked to see how tall or short or fat or thin he was or whether he had pimples or whatever else it was that kids got growing up. David was beautiful, Franks thought, guessing at the outrage with which the child who'd just dismissed kissing would respond to the word. His hair was lustrously black, and the long-lashed eyes were deeply brown, almost black, too. The fingers of the hands he held were long and tapered and he guessed the boy was going to be tall, taller than he was. Franks supposed David inherited his coloring from Tina, although the boy reminded him of someone else, and then he realized the resemblance was to Nicky. He swallowed, wishing it hadn't occurred to him. He looked sideways to Gabriella, thinking how Tina's influence was obvious in the girl, too. They both looked like her children, not his. "I love you," he said to Gabriella.

"David says that's stupid, too," the child reported.

"Okay," said Franks. "You and I can love each other and David and I can be friends. . . ." He looked back to the boy. "That all right?"

David looked at his father suspiciously. "What's the difference?"

"You tell me," said Franks. "You're the one who says kissing and love is stupid."

"*Best* friends?" asked the boy, seeking a guarantee.

"The best friends there ever were," promised Franks.

"All right," accepted David. At once he said, "Can you have one of them shoot his gun, so I can see it? Can I hold it, see what it's like? Can I? Please?"

"No!" The rejection came from Tina, too loud and too quick. The children looked at her, surprised; Gabriella's bottom lip trembled briefly.

"I won't ask them to fire their guns. Or let you hold one," said Franks, better controlled. "Guns are more stupid than kissing or love; much more stupid."

"Why have they got them, then?" demanded David belligerently.

141

"They're guarding something very precious," said Franks, not wanting the conversation to go on.

"Treasure!" demanded Gabriella, infected by her brother's romantic enthusiasm.

"Yes," said Franks. "Treasure."

"Here? Where?" said the boy, staring around the bedroom. Gabriella gazed around, too, following her brother.

"It's locked up," said Franks.

"Can we see it? Please can we see the treasure?"

"No," said Franks.

"Why not?"

"Because I say so," groped Franks helplessly.

"That's not a reason," protested the boy, with childlike logic.

Tina tried to come to the rescue. "If Daddy says you can't see it, you can't see it."

"That isn't fair," pouted Gabriella.

"It's only something that grown-ups can see, at the moment," said Franks. "Maybe later."

"When?" insisted David.

"When I say so."

Beside him Franks was aware of Tina dialing one of the internal extension numbers, to get the nanny to come to collect them. Elizabeth arrived immediately and apologized again, and Tina said it didn't matter but to get them ready for breakfast.

As the children were led reluctantly from the room, Franks said, "I wish I could have managed something better."

"I don't want them getting some sort of psychosis, believing their parents could be killed."

"What are we going to tell them about Nicky?"

"Nothing," said Tina at once. "They didn't see him that much; there's no need to say anything. Not yet."

"It might be all right with Gabby, but I don't think we can keep putting David off."

"Not yet!" shouted Tina, angry. "We've got things more important to worry about at the moment than satisfying children's curiosity. The important thing is that they're here, safe. Everything else can wait."

"I didn't tell you about Rosenberg," said Franks.

"There wasn't a lot of time, was there?"

"He said I shouldn't have dissolved the companies. And that Nicky was an important witness about the truth of everything I say."

142

"*Would* have been an important witness," corrected Tina.

"Yes," said Franks. "He's making some sort of contact with the prosecutor today; I'm due to meet him at noon."

"You're going back into New York?"

"Yes."

"I thought you'd stay here, with us. I *want* you to stay with me."

"I've told you how it's going to be," said Franks. "When it's over, we'll be together all the time. But first I've got to get it all over. Which means doing whatever Rosenberg advises."

"Have you forgotten what I said last night?"

"No."

"Don't," insisted Tina. "I meant it."

"I won't do anything silly," promised Franks. "Nothing wrong."

The children tried to persist when Franks and Tina went downstairs, but Tina had them taken from the breakfast room, disregarding Gabriella when she started to cry at the abruptness of the dismissal. Neither ate; Franks had difficulty even drinking coffee.

"How long will you be?" asked Tina as Franks prepared to leave.

"I don't know."

"Call if you can?"

"If I can."

"Thought I'd call Poppa today; speak to Maria, as well."

"See if she's changed her mind about the funeral. Arranging it herself."

"What should I do about all these men? Feeding them, I mean. They're using the bathroom by the tennis court, but I suppose we should feed them."

"I suppose so," Franks agreed. "Ask them."

"Drinks, too? Booze, I mean?"

"It's hardly a party," said Franks. "Let's cut out the booze."

"I feel self-conscious," said Tina. "It's like doing something in front of an audience."

"Try not to let the kids get too close."

"How the hell am I suppose to stop that!" demanded Tina, her control fragile. "If I send them out for the day on a trip they'll have to have a guard, won't they?"

"Yes," agreed Franks. It was like some strange form of imprisonment, he thought.

"Try not to be too late."

"I'll come back as quickly as I can."

"Do you know what I've got to stop myself thinking?"

"What?"

"That it isn't your fault. That it was Nicky's and Poppa's. Isn't that strange? Last night, before you got back with Maria, I actually found myself blaming you." She smiled, embarrassed. "I'm sorry, I wanted you to know. And to know that I'm sorry. And that I realize it wasn't your fault."

"Thanks," said Franks. There was movement in the vestibule and Franks recognized one of the two men who had escorted him home the previous night. "Time to go," he said.

"Be careful."

"I'm well protected," he said needlessly.

She held on to him when they kissed, and he almost had to force himself away from her. The FBI man didn't attempt to move and Franks thought back to Tina's remark: doing things in front of an audience. He followed the agent out into the driveway, conscious of the children far away, using the tennis court for their own form of softball. He supposed he should go over to them before he left, but he hesitated, unwilling to repeat the bedroom scene. To Tina, who followed him to the doorway, Franks said, "Tell them I said good-bye and I'll try to be back early, so we can spend some time together."

"Okay," said Tina. "Be careful," she repeated.

"I will be."

"And don't forget what I said."

Franks sat behind the driver, as he had the previous night. The agent who escorted him from the house smiled back from the passenger seat. "Tomkiss. Mike Tomkiss. My partner is Roger Sheridan."

"Hello," said Franks.

"Nice morning," said Tomkiss chattily.

"It's difficult to think so," said Franks.

"Guess it would be for you," said Tomkiss, undeterred.

The curve of the drive took the vehicle near to the tennis courts and Franks hoped the children didn't look up to see him. Tomkiss said, "They're nice kids."

"It's difficult for them to understand, too," said Franks.

"It always is, for kids," said Tomkiss.

"You been involved in this sort of thing before?" asked Franks.

Tomkiss was looking out through the front window. He

144

twisted in his seat, so that it was more comfortable for him to look into the back of the car. "Couple of times," he admitted.

"What happened?"

"What do you mean, Mr. Franks?—'what happened?' "

"How long did it last? All this protection? Everything?"

"It's still covered by restrictions," said the FBI man. "Quite a while. Everything worked out okay."

"What do you mean?" asked Franks. " 'Everything worked out okay'?"

"No one got killed," Tomkiss said succinctly. "We didn't lose a defendant or a witness."

Franks turned away from the conversation, glad they were on the end of the Bruckner Expressway and would soon be getting into the city. As they crossed the bridge Franks gazed intently to his left, to the smog-veiled skyscraper fingers, and wondered why the hell it had been so important for him to involve himself in America. Why hadn't he been content with what he had and stayed in Europe? Which he shouldn't forget, whatever the pressures, he thought suddenly. Nicky's murder would have been reported by now; probably reached the British newspapers. It was important he call the London managers to put them into the picture as fully as possible; he didn't want any uncertainty.

The FBI driver ignored all the parking restrictions and pulled up directly outside Rosenberg's office. But as Franks reached for the door handle Tomkiss stopped him, saying, "Don't!" Tomkiss got out, actually shielding the door immediately adjacent to the pavement with his own body. The driver got out, too. It was several minutes before they appeared satisfied. Tomkiss quickly jerked the door open and said, "Okay." Franks hurried across the sidewalk, tight between the two men, feeling self-conscious. They were dissatisfied with the crowding in the first elevator, gesturing it on, and in the second backed him into the wedge of the corner and positioned themselves solidly in front. Franks stood staring at their joined shoulders only inches from his nose, his embarrassment increasing.

In Rosenberg's office, Tomkiss said, "We'll be waiting, when you're through."

Franks was still hot with discomfort when he went into the lawyer's room. He explained how he'd journeyed in from Scarsdale and said, "It's like being under arrest, for Christ's sake!"

"That's probably how they regard it," said Rosenberg.

"What's that mean?"

145

"I've spoken to Ronan. Had a long talk. It doesn't look good."

"I still don't understand," protested Franks.

"I told you yesterday how your explanation for everything could be regarded by a prosecutor. It looks as if that's how Ronan *is* regarding it."

"You mean he's going to prosecute me?"

"I think so."

"I'm innocent!" said Franks, uncaring that the protest groaned out of him like a plea.

"With Nicky dead, it isn't going to be easy for us to prove it."

"Is that why they killed him?"

The lawyer shrugged. "Maybe. Who knows? They knew about the file?"

"I said so, yesterday."

"Maybe it was a warning not to use it."

"How good is it, without Nicky to testify to its authenticity?"

"I won't know that until I've seen it," said Rosenberg. "Nicky's murder still diminishes it."

"I want to know something," said Franks urgently. "Could I go to jail? Although I haven't done anything wrong and I'm absolutely innocent, could I still go to jail?"

"From what I know so far—and you must realize that I know virtually nothing of the prosecution case—I'd say it was a strong possibility. A very strong possibility."

"That can't happen," said Franks, incredulous.

"It can," said Rosenberg. "You must believe me that it can."

"Help me," said Franks, still pleading and knowing it. "Help me so that it doesn't." How long ago had it been that he'd despised Nicky for weakly showing his fear?

"We're meeting Ronan this afternoon. The fact that we are seeing him together—at all—is curious. I don't understand that yet. Before then I want to examine what's in the safe-deposit."

"You going to tell Ronan about it? Or the FBI?"

"Why?"

"I had an FBI escort in from Scarsdale today. One of them—Tomkiss—is waiting outside, like I said."

Rosenberg sat considering the difficulty. "Is there anything else in the box, apart from the file?"

"No," said Franks.

"People keep all sorts of things in safe-deposit boxes,"

146

said Rosenberg. "We can refuse them access to the actual vaults. They can think and suspect what they like, but I don't see it's a problem, at the moment. The problem is avoiding any sort of prosecution in the first place."

The lawyer called Tomkiss into his office and announced where they were going, adding the client-lawyer relationship precluded the man's admission to the safe-deposit section. Tomkiss accepted the announcement without the argument that Franks expected and actually suggested that the two of them travel to the bank in the FBI car, to make his job easier. Rosenberg said it seemed like a good idea. The agents showed the same care getting him from the building as they had entering; Rosenberg was part of it this time and appeared quite unembarrassed. They rode uptown unspeaking and Tomkiss escorted them into the bank building, only leaving them a few yards from the safe-deposit section. Rosenberg produced identification, and Franks signed an entry permission, attesting that the lawyer was examining his box with his full permission, and then they filed behind the bank official to the air-conditioned, muted vault. The official produced his key and Franks his, releasing the box, and then Franks stood waiting while the official withdrew. Franks took the box completely from its recess and offered it to Rosenberg. Although he'd read everything before, Franks studied the notes and the bank details again, taking each sheet as Rosenberg finished with it. Rosenberg read more slowly than Franks, with a lawyer's precision, and Franks tried to concentrate upon what he was reading with growing impatience, anxious for the man to finish and give an opinion. It was an hour before Rosenberg looked up. He smiled, bleakly, and with precision replaced everything in the box.

"Well?" demanded Franks.

"Interesting," said Rosenberg.

"Is that all? Interesting?"

"I would have liked more," said the lawyer. "And like I said, it would have been better with Nicky alive, to support it."

"You're telling me we've got a weak case?"

Rosenberg looked down into the box as if seeking something he had overlooked. Then he looked up and said, "I told you when we met yesterday that everything would be on the basis of complete honesty." He ruffled his fingers through the safe-deposit box. "There could be a contest about the admissibility of this. Could be I won't be allowed to produce it at all in front of a jury. *With* it I've got a defensible case. Just. But only just.

Without it we're on weak ground. Weaker ground than I like and that's not yet knowing the prosecution case. I can subpoena Pascara and Flamini and Dukes, and I can try to discredit them with details of their criminal records. But if I get a tough trial judge, I won't get away with much of that. And don't forget that Pascara hasn't got convictions; he's beaten every accusation. And there's something else. Just how much good will it do our case to prove they're the worst gangsters since Al Capone with the apparent proof that the prosecution has against you that you were acting for them? That just makes it worse for you."

Franks felt a wash of helplessness, another of the dizzy sensations, so that momentarily the metal-lined, barred room misted and he had to blink to concentrate again. "Surely Nicky's murder proves something?"

"Sure it does," said Rosenberg. "It proves involvement and association with mobsters. It doesn't prove your innocence."

"You think a jury would believe that I was involved with the murder of someone I was brought up to regard as my brother?"

"You're asking a jury to believe that someone you were brought up to regard as your brother knowingly and without any compunction tricked, cheated, and trapped you into involvement with mobsters," reminded Rosenberg.

Franks shook his head, bewilderment growing. "You know something?" he said to the lawyer. "I always believed in the law. I always believed in the law and in justice."

"So do I, Mr. Franks," said Rosenberg. "If I didn't, I wouldn't be trying to do the job I do. Ninety percent of the time, it works like it's supposed to."

"And about the other ten percent?"

"That's where we are now," said Rosenberg. He offered the box to Franks, who stood, ringing the bell for the official. The official completed his part of the operation and led them back into the main hall of the bank, where Tomkiss was patiently waiting.

"What now?" asked the FBI man.

"I don't suppose you feel like lunching at the club?" the lawyer said to Franks.

"I don't feel like lunching at all," said Franks. "Certainly not there."

"We'd better eat something," said Rosenberg practically.

They went to a pseudo-Italian restaurant near Rosenberg's office, where Franks ordered automatically and forgot what he ate the moment the plates were cleared. Tomkiss and Sheridan

148

ate two tables away, from where they could watch both the entrance and the kitchen swing doors. In anticipation of that afternoon's encounter with the district attorney Rosenberg went again through everything that Franks had told him at the first interview, elaborating upon points where he was uncertain. He did so entirely without notes and Franks was impressed by the man's recall of detail; not once did he have to correct the man on any fact. Although he had been totally disinterested in the food Franks agreed to a second cup of coffee, recognizing the reason as he did so. He was reluctant to move; to get up from the table and into the waiting car and go to see the district attorney to hear what the man intended, just like Nicky had been reluctant to make contact with the three men to summon the dissolution meeting.

"It's time," urged Rosenberg.

"Yes."

"Ready?"

"I suppose so."

"Remember," warned the lawyer as he settled the check, "everything goes through me. I do the talking."

"You say this sort of meeting is unusual?"

"Very," said Rosenberg, rising from the table.

"Maybe it's something in our favor," said Franks anxiously. "Maybe the case isn't so strong, after all."

Rosenberg looked down sympathetically at the other man, waiting for him to stand. "From what I know already it's strong enough," he said. "Let's actually see the straws before we start to clutch at them, shall we?"

There was no delay when they reached the justice building. Tomkiss traveled up with them from the reception area, and when they emerged on the district attorney's floor Franks saw that Waldo was already there. Waldo nodded a greeting and Franks nodded back. Tomkiss went at once to the FBI man, who cupped an arm around Tomkiss and propelled him out of the waiting area and back along the corridor so that they could talk without being overheard. It meant that the man had to hurry back and arrived in the district attorney's office after Rosenberg and Franks had already been admitted and offered seats by the prosecutor.

Ronan was a large, thrusting man, constrained by the necessity of a business suit. Behind his desk, among the legal diplomas, there were several sports pennants displayed and four photographs of what Franks thought were football teams in which he guessed Ronan featured. There was another person with Ronan

149

in the office when they entered: a tall, bespectacled man whose easy movements contrasted with those of the prosecutor. He rose as Franks and Rosenberg entered the room, and Ronan said, "I'd like you to meet Joseph Knap."

The man offered his hand and Franks waited to follow Rosenberg's lead. The lawyer accepted the gesture and so did Franks.

"Sorry," apologized Waldo, the late arrival. "Something came up."

Franks and Rosenberg took the seats that Ronan suggested, and the district attorney said, "Thank you for coming."

Rosenberg looked around the office, apparently seeking something, and said, "No recording?"

"No," said Ronan.

"Shouldn't we establish some ground rules?"

"Of course."

"This is entirely privileged?" said Rosenberg.

"Absolutely," agreed the other lawyer.

"With no prejudice at all to my client?"

"None," guaranteed Ronan. "And it can be suspended the moment you decide."

Rosenberg looked away from Ronan to the other men in the room. "I know whom Mr. Waldo represents," he said. "We met last night. Is Mr. Knap on your staff?"

"Mr. Knap is a senior investigator for the Internal Revenue Service."

"This is a tax investigation, as well?"

"It's every sort of investigation," said Ronan.

"Would you like to explain that further?"

"That's exactly what I intend doing," said Ronan.

Rosenberg looked directly toward Waldo. "This meeting forms no part of any investigation of my client?" he insisted.

"No," assured Waldo. Franks wondered if he heard a reluctance in the man's voice.

Rosenberg smiled toward the athletic man. "Then I guess we'd better hear you out, like you suggest," he said.

There were a lot of papers and files on Ronan's desk; the contents of Waldo's briefcase at the hotel meeting, guessed Franks. Ronan arranged them in front of him, like a barricade. Looking over the top and not bothering initially to consult them, he said, "You'll be aware of the task forces formally established by President Reagan to combat organized crime. Even before their establishment, the FBI had ongoing investigations into the affairs of three men who operate under various pseudonyms but who, for the sake of this discussion, I shall refer to as David Dukes, Roberto Pascara, and Roland Flamini.''

Ronan paused, going to the first file. "Because of that monitoring,'' he took up, "the bureau was quite quickly aware of their involvement as apparent investors in the hotel chain established in the Bahamas and Bermuda by Mr. Franks. For the last nine months, there has been a squad assigned specifically to those enterprises; every transaction has been followed, every involvement checked.''

Ronan looked over his barricade directly at Franks. "Three months ago the papers were submitted to me for a decision upon taking the case before a grand jury. The file was very complete. I have details of the Delaware incorporation, from which it is quite obvious that Mr. Franks—with the holding of his wife—controls the companies. I have sworn affidavits from officials in the Bahamas and Bermuda admitting the payment of bribes to facilitate the building of the hotels on both islands. The Bahamian and Bermudan authorities have prosecutions pending against each of them, depending upon the results of our investigations and decisions. There is also prosecution pending against William Snarsbrook, a Bahamian minister who has fully confessed to being personally paid three hundred thousand dollars through an offshore account to facilitate the establishment of a casino attached to Franks' main hotel, in Nassau; part of the Bahamian evidence—'' Ronan took a slip of paper from one file. "Here's a photostat, a note that says, 'Thanks for all your help and assistance, Eddie.' ''

Rosenberg jerked in Franks' direction. Franks shook his head desperately.

"I have documentary and photographic evidence of Mr. Franks' presence in Las Vegas, not only with Dukes, but with another known gangster. There is also proof of Mr. Franks with Dukes and Flamini in Bermuda and the Bahamas and on other social occasions with Pascara.'' Ronan nodded in the direction of the Revenue investigator. "Mr. Knap has been a senior member of the specially assigned squad. During the last nine months he has traced the movement through the credit link that again was personally established by Mr. Franks between Las Vegas and the Bahamas of some eighteen million dollars, which his inquiries suggest were not gambling winnings. The money was moved from the United States mainland into the Bahamas along the credit link created by Mr. Franks; of that sum, Mr. Knap has provided me with sample charges in the sum of four million

151

dollars, and I am satisfied that the evidence with which he has accompanied those suggested charges is sufficient for a prosecution against Mr. Franks."

Franks felt crushed under the weight of the further accusations, trying to assimilate what was being said but not completely grasping it all. Only one thing was obvious to him. He was lost; utterly lost beneath a welter of false evidence that it was going to be impossible to prove to be false. Because to these people it *wasn't* false. Everything was there, documented, photostated and photographed. Lost, he thought again; utterly lost.

Ronan held up a file that looked less worn and used than everything else upon his desk. "This contains a total of twelve charges, which I intend to lay before a grand jury to obtain indictments against Mr. Franks. They are variously brought under the Racketeer Influenced and Corrupt Organization Law, the Continuing Criminal Enterprise Law and the Tax Reform Act of 1976, as amended by the legislation of 1982."

He offered it to Rosenberg, who accepted it, opened the folder, and looked at the material inside. There was complete silence in the room, interrupted only by the occasional rustle of the pages. Franks found it difficult to concentrate upon what was going on around him. Instead he thought of Tina and of David sitting on his chest that morning and Gabriella looking trustingly at him. Be careful, Tina had said. Franks was too confused to be sure any longer just what it was that he had to be careful about.

"My client denies each and every one of these charges, of course," said Rosenberg.

Franks tried to bring himself back inside the room. How was it so easy for Rosenberg to remain calm?

"Of course," said Ronan, just as controlled.

"You asked us to hear you out fully," prompted Rosenberg.

"The proposed charges name only Mr. Franks," pointed out Ronan. "I intend further charges, bringing in Dukes and Flamini and Pascara on indictments of conspiracy. But I think they can be defeated."

"You want us to become a prosecution witness?" anticipated Rosenberg.

Franks jerked his head between the two men like a spectator at a tennis tournament, trying to comprehend what was happening.

"Yes," said Ronan. "If you are prepared to cooperate in every way, if you enable indictments to be handed down against Dukes, Flamini, and Pascara, I am prepared to offer you complete immunity against prosecution."

"I wouldn't be prosecuted!" burst out Franks, forgetting his promise to Rosenberg.

"No," confirmed Ronan shortly.

Why wasn't Rosenberg showing more enthusiasm! thought Franks. They were being offered everything!

"Yesterday Nicky Scargo, who introduced my client to these men in a manner which we say was criminal deception, was shot dead," reminded Rosenberg.

"We are further prepared to offer your client and his family complete protection throughout the duration of the grand jury hearing and trial," said Ronan.

"And afterward?" persisted the other lawyer.

"He and his family will be admitted to the Witnesses Protection Program," said Ronan.

"What's that?" asked Franks.

Rosenberg looked sideways at him. "An entirely new life," he said.

PART THREE

PART THREE

De Duobus malis minus est semper aligendum.
(Of the two evils the lesser is always to be chosen.)
                              Thomas à Kempis

20

Franks looked warily around the chambers, stopping finally at his own lawyer. Let's actually see the straws before we start to clutch at them, Rosenberg had advised. Franks recognized the straw but wasn't sure how to reach out for it. Looking at Rosenberg, Franks said, "I want to know what an entirely new life means."

"Exactly that," said Rosenberg. The lawyer looked beyond, to Waldo. "Would you like to explain it?"

The FBI agent tried and failed to straighten in the chair, pulling his huge bulk forward on to its edge. "Like the district attorney has already explained," he said, "in return for your cooperation—your complete cooperation in providing us with all the evidence you might have and testifying in court against them—we will provide you and your family with guaranteed twenty-four-hour protection, until the conclusion of the trial. That means you, your wife, and your children . . ."

Waldo hesitated, looking deferentially toward Ronan. The district attorney nodded, and said, "You're doing fine."

"At the conclusion of all the hearings you—and your family—will enter a program that has been evolved to protect absolutely the identities and safety of those who help us convict recognized criminals and racketeers. The government will move you and your family anywhere in the country that you choose. You will be provided with new Social Security numbers, new bank accounts, new names. You'll be guarded, until the FBI and the United States Marshals Service is satisfied that you have adjusted completely. And then you'll be safe."

Franks remained staring at the man, sure he'd misunderstood. He purposely waited, expected Waldo to continue and correct the ridiculous inference but Waldo didn't. Franks said, "Let's just wait a minute. Are you proposing—saying—that at the end of the grand jury hearings and whatever trial follows I—and my family—will just disappear? I shall cease to be Eddie

157

Franks and my wife will cease to be Tina Franks and my children will have to have different names, as well?"

"Yes," said Ronan, answering for the FBI agent.

Franks laughed disbelievingly. "You can't be serious!"

"Oh, we're very serious, Mr. Franks. There are a large number of people living safe, contented lives under the protection program. It's proven extremely successful in persuading criminals to testify against their superiors."

"I am not a criminal, and Dukes and Flamini and Pascara are *not* my superiors!"

Ronan and the two investigators stared at him steadily, making no response to the protest. "What if I say no?" demanded Franks.

"I shall convene a grand jury and present the evidence before them and invite them to find that a case is justified," said Ronan simply.

"But that's . . . that's . . . that's . . ."

"What, Mr. Franks?" asked Ronan politely.

"What about the businesses in Europe?" said Franks, not responding to the other man's question. "How could they be run?"

"You have a legal advisor, Mr. Franks," said the district attorney, nodding toward Rosenberg. "I suggest you take his advice."

"Why couldn't I just go back to England?" demanded Franks. "There's nothing left for me here anyway. Why can't I just go back there?"

"It's my obligation to make the facts clear to you," said Ronan. "By cooperate we mean precisely that. Your agreement can't be obtained under any sort of duress or misunderstanding. The Witnesses Protection Program has been designed to serve just that purpose: to protect witnesses."

"Are you telling me that I wouldn't be safe—I wouldn't be safe, or my wife and children—if I remained here to give evidence and then, at the conclusion of any hearing, returned to Europe?"

"As your own counsel has already pointed out, Mr. Franks, one person involved in this affair has already been murdered. Before any legal proceedings have been instituted."

"Here!" protested Franks. "In America. I'm talking about Europe."

"I know what you're talking about, Mr. Franks."

"You're telling me I've got to lose everything!" said Franks,

158

aghast. "You're telling me that I've got to abandon everything I've built up throughout my life! Become somebody else!"

"Yes," said Ronan.

"That's not a choice! That's blackmail!"

"It *is* a choice," argued Ronan. "It's a choice that I would advise you to talk through with your advisor."

Franks shook his head. The lawyer responded, looking first to Franks and then to the district attorney. "Is there somewhere I can talk to my client alone?"

"Of course," said Ronan, rising and leading the way to a small anteroom. Rosenberg went first, with Franks trailing behind him. There were more pennants on the wall and a small cot, covered with a blanket. There was no desk, but two easy chairs, and Rosenberg gestured Franks toward the one with its back to the window so that he sat looking into the room. Rosenberg remained standing, to see the other lawyer from the room. He securely closed the door behind the man and then came back to the other chair, moving it so that he was directly in front of Franks.

"Well?" he said.

"No!" refused Franks. "It's preposterous."

"I know it seems that way," said Rosenberg. "And I guess it is, but not to them. They can't really lose, either way."

"But I can!"

"I'd already warned you about that."

"No," said Franks again, shaking his head, more to clear it than as a gesture of refusal. "They're expecting me to give up everything."

"Except your freedom," said Rosenberg. "If you want me to, then I shall refuse this offer and let the case proceed. But I've already told you what I think the chances are of getting an acquittal. And that was *before* I had any idea of the degree and extent of their investigation. We talked earlier about percentages, so let's go on talking about them. In my honest opinion, from what I've heard here today and from what I've heard from you earlier—and taking into account what I read in that safe-deposit vault—I wouldn't assess my chances of an acquittal higher than five percent."

"Five percent!"

Rosenberg held up his hands, halting the outburst. "Let me finish," said the lawyer. "I repeat, five percent. To try to achieve that acquittal I would, as I've already told you, call Flamini and Pascara and Dukes and do everything, in addition-to whatever Ronan would attempt with his conspiracy charges, to convict them and save you.'' The lawyer hesitated, to make his point. "Five percent," he repeated. "And if I failed you'd go to jail—I guess on the charges that Ronan has let me see—for a minimum of eight years. Maybe five. To a jail where Pascara and Flamini and Dukes have more power and control than they have outside.''

"You telling me that I would be killed there?''

"Yes," said Rosenberg. "I'm saying that you'd be subject to constant attack and assault and that the person who succeeded would probably have enough money to set himself up for life when he got out.''

"You recommending that I should do what Ronan wants? Cooperate and then run and change my name?''

"I think it's your only way out of an impossible situation. Certainly I don't imagine you could expect to go back to Europe and live safely there. Whether there was a successful conviction or not.''

The analogy came suddenly to Eddie Franks, so forcefully that momentarily it silenced him. It was the complete circle. Not identical, in every respect, but similar enough. His father had run to survive and had abandoned Isaac Frankovich, and now he was expected to run to survive and abandon Eddie Franks. But there *were* differences; important differences. Would his father have run from Liberec and Warsaw and Frankfurt and Berlin and Hamburg if he'd had successful and thriving businesses, businesses he had no reason nor cause to leave? And Franks couldn't convince himself that he did have cause; maybe here, in New York, or even beyond, in America, he had cause for fear, but surely not in safe, respectable London! The confidence grew, and then he remembered the blown-apart body of Nicky Scargo with his arm in its own plastic container lying where it should have been and the gaping head and chest.

"All this is only your opinion!'' said Franks in sudden belligerence.

"Of course it is," said Rosenberg, unoffended. "If you'd like to transfer the case then I shall do everything to help whatever new counsel you bring in. I'll even help you find someone else; someone I think would try as hard as I would.''

"Why?" demanded Franks, suddenly suspicious. "Why would you do that?''

Rosenberg smiled at the hostility. "For a number of reasons, actually, Mr. Franks. I've made a reputation out of taking on difficult—seemingly impossible—cases and winning. I don't believe I can win in this case. Not if we fight it. Which is not saying that I wouldn't try everything I know to get your acquittal, if we *do* fight. So, personally, I don't want to get involved in a case that is going to attract quite a lot of publicity and fail. It's not an attitude in which I feel any particular pride. In fact, I'm ashamed to admit it. I'd try to do my best to find you another equally good lawyer because I would owe it to you, because of my own attitude. Cowardice, if you like." The man stopped, thinking. "And there's another reason. I'd do everything I could to get you the best man available and brief him as completely as possible because I feel desperately sorry for you. I *believe* that you're innocent; I told you during that first interview that I believed you. I think you're entirely innocent, but you're caught up in a situation from which you can't possibly escape. I feel as sorry as hell for you."

"I'm not sure that I want you to be so honest."

"That was the agreement we made when we started," reminded Rosenberg.

"I can't make a decision right now," protested Franks. "I need to talk it over with my wife. Have time to consider all the implications."

"I think that's reasonable," said Rosenberg.

"I want to go back to Scarsdale."

"I'll be available at any time. Come up there to you, if you like."

"Thank you," said Franks. "Something else."

"What?"

"I don't want another lawyer. Whatever I decide to do, I want to stay with you."

"I meant what I said," reminded Rosenberg. "I will work for you to the very best and absolute of my ability. All the time."

"Which is why I want things to stay as they are," said Franks.

Rosenberg led the way back into the larger room. Ronan had organized coffee in their absence and offered it to them. Rosenberg accepted, but Franks declined. Rosenberg explained that Franks wanted time to think; Ronan agreed, saying that of course he understood. They had no intention of risking such an in-depth investigation by haste, and Franks could have as long as he wanted. Rosenberg thanked him and said he thought two or three days would be sufficient; a week at the outside. A week was quite acceptable, Ronan agreed.

161

"We've also had the opportunity of talking while you were out of the room," said the district attorney.

"About what?" said Rosenberg.

"We reached an understanding at the beginning of this meeting," said Ronan. "I've no intention at this stage of trying to change that understanding." He nodded toward Waldo. "But I've heard from the FBI of your visit to the safe-deposit vault. I thought it might indicate an advantage of our working together."

"I've no intention whatsoever of entering into any sort of discussion about what might or might not form part of my client's defense, should this proceed to trial," said Rosenberg, reverting to formality.

"I didn't expect you to, not for a moment," assured Ronan smoothly. "I just considered it a point worth making."

"I'm quite aware of all the points worth making," said Rosenberg. "The full protection of my client remains?"

"Of course," said Ronan.

Rosenberg rose to leave and Franks followed. As Franks stood, Ronan said to him, "Please think very deeply about everything I've said."

"I'm hardly likely to forget," said Franks.

They left the building with Tomkiss and his partner and the same sort of elaborate security precaution. Just before the car reached Rosenberg's office, the lawyer said, "Anything you're not sure about?"

"No," said Franks.

Rosenberg handed him a card and said, "That's my home number; call me there if anything suddenly occurs to you."

Franks took it and put it in his breast pocket. "I'll probably call you tomorrow."

"Take your time."

"And thanks."

"I haven't done anything yet," said the lawyer.

"Thanks anyway."

The FBI men let Rosenberg leave the vehicle unescorted, spurting the car away from the curb as soon as the man slammed the door. The clogged Manhattan traffic, constantly stopping them, worried both the agents. Franks stayed hunched in the back, uncaring. He tried to consider everything that had been said that afternoon, to create the necessary balance in his mind and prepare himself for the discussion that would be necessary with Tina, because it was important that he talk everything through with her, but persistently one remark kept presenting itself. *You're*

caught up in a situation from which you can't possibly escape.
Only days before—or was it hours?—he'd been considering a
defense against any charges, and now he was confronting the
reality of there being no defense; just situations from which he
couldn't escape. How much—dear God, how much—he wanted to
imagine it was all a dream, a nightmare, something from which
he was going to awaken and find his life as settled and safe and
organized as it had been such a very short time ago. Franks
strained against the temptation, like he'd strained against it before
and for the same reason. But it was a recurring reflection, he
recognized. Was a lawyer enough for him to face what he was
going to have to face, whatever his decision? Shouldn't he seek
the help of a doctor as well? Franks blinked against the thought,
angry at another weakness. Definitely not a doctor. He wasn't
going to become dependent on pills, and he wasn't going to
become dependent on booze. Maybe he'd never known pressure
like this—never conceived pressure like this was possible—but
he was still strong enough to handle it without the need for any
sort of artificial crutch.

The men in front relaxed when they reached the FDR Drive
and more speed was possible. Tomkiss attempted conversation,
but Franks only grunted, uninterested in small talk, and the FBI
agent quickly abandoned the effort. It was still daylight when
they reached Scarsdale, and Franks appreciated for the first time
just how absolute the protection was around the house. There was
actually a helicopter fluttering overhead when they approached,
and there was a wedge-shaped formation of four vehicles in the
immediate entrance, making any entry impossible. He counted
six figures on the grounds on the way up to the main house,
where there were three more cars that didn't belong to him or the
staff, and a man he hadn't seen before opened the door at their
arrival.

The children ran out, ahead of Tina, and David said triumphantly, "I saw one! I saw a gun. A man in a police car showed
me. There was a shotgun in a rack in between the front seats,
too. He says I can have a picture to take back to school."

Franks picked up Gabriella, looking back painfully at Tomkiss.
"I don't want that to happen."

"Sure," agreed the FBI man. "I'll fix it."

"Why not, Daddy! Why not!" wailed the boy. "He
promised."

"Because," said Franks.

"That's not fair!"

163

"There's a lot that's not fair," said Franks.

"Can we see the treasure, Daddy? Can we please?" said the girl. She had her arm around his neck and tugged, at every question, so that Franks had to lean back against her.

"Stop it, Gabby," he said. "Not yet. I'll tell you when."

At the door Tina frowned at how he looked, and said, "Hello."

"Hello," said Franks. "Get someone to take the children, will you?"

Her frown deepened but she said nothing, turning back into the house and calling to the hovering Elizabeth.

"I want my picture taken with a gun!" insisted David defiantly.

"No," said Franks.

"Yes!" said the boy.

Franks hit him, harder than he intended, although the rudeness justified the slap on the leg, irrespective of what it was about. David stared up at his father in shocked surprise and then burst into screaming tears. Franks saw that where he'd hit the child, just above the knee, he'd left a white imprint. Gabriella began crying too, in support. Franks looked angrily at the approaching nanny and said, "For God's sake, take them away!"

"Come in," said Tina tightly, pulling him toward the door of the smaller sitting room, where the drinks were.

Franks looked awkwardly at the unspeaking and unknown FBI man and then at the accusing face of Elizabeth and followed his wife into the room. Tina pointedly closed the door behind him and said, "You need a drink."

Franks thought about artificial crutches, and said, "Yes. Gin."

He sat, staring directly ahead. He took the drink without looking at her or thanking her, drinking deeply at it. It *wasn't* an artificial crutch! Millions of people had a drink, like this. How many people had the choice of going to jail to be killed, or adopting a new identity to prevent being killed?

"You look awful."

"I feel awful."

"Shouldn't I know about it?"

"I want you to," said Franks.

It took a long time for him to recount the day: several times he ran ahead of himself and had to backtrack, and then he forgot the point he'd reached and Tina had to remind him. Twice she got up, freshening his glass; not a crutch, he convinced himself. His

164

glass was empty when he finished, and this time he got up to help himself. Behind him Tina said, "I don't believe what you've just told me!"

"I still can't."

"It's . . . it's . . . not fair."

Franks turned back toward his wife, thinking as he looked at her just how much he loved her and remembering, too, the promises he'd made always to keep her safe. That hadn't meant keeping her safe behind a protective ring of men who thought there was nothing wrong in letting children pose for school photographs holding guns. With his mind on the boy, Franks said, "That's what David said."

"Stop it!"

"I'm sorry."

"Tell me again," she insisted. "Not what happened; I understood that. Tell me what it would mean."

"All these people around us, for I don't know how long. I guess that's got to happen anyway, for some time. Then we'd get new identities; go somewhere else to live."

"Why!" exclaimed Tina. "Who are the gangsters, who kill and cheat and rob, for Christ's sake! We haven't done anything wrong!"

"I know," said Franks.

"Then solve it. Do something to make it all work out right. You're the man I trust. Do you seriously mean that I've got to tell Gabby that she isn't Gabriella Franks? And David that he isn't David Franks? That we're not going to live here anymore? Or in England? That they're not going to go to the schools they go to now and that at whatever school they *do* go to they've got to pretend to be somebody else—and always remember who that somebody else is—and that we're not the mommy and daddy they always thought and trusted us to be but some other people—" Tina ran out of breath, staring at him across the room. She gulped, dragging the air into her, and said, "Tell me, Eddie! You've always been the one with the answers! So what are the answers to all that! Let's go from there, for starters!"

Franks stared down into his empty glass, wanting another drink but not wanting another drink either, at that crux of drunkenness when he knew absolutely that he could handle another drink—quite a few other drinks—and knew absolutely that if he had one more he'd become stupidly drunk. "I know what we're going to do," he said.

Tina gazed at him, anger and frustration and incomprehension gone. "I knew you would," she said.

"I'm going to cooperate, like I always intended to do," said Franks. "Like I told Nicky we should do, from the moment I knew what had happened. I'm going to see that Dukes and Flamini and Pascara go to jail. Go to jail *for* killing Nicky, whatever he did to me; to us. The conviction won't be for that, of course. But it will be the same. Mean the same as far as we're concerned. We'll take the protection—we've got to take the protection, intrusive and unpleasant as it is—and I'll go through whatever charade they think is necessary, about names and things like that." Franks hesitated, still looking into the empty glass. God, he wanted another drink. "And we'll go into the program. *Actually* go into it. But only for a while. And when everything blows over and is forgotten we'll go back to England and start all over again and do exactly what I promised we would. I'll take only a token interest in the businesses and I'll be with you all the time and the kids can pick up whatever education they've lost— we'll cram them if necessary—and it'll all be over."

"I thought you told me that would be dangerous?" said Tina.

"Dangerous if we tried to go back immediately after the trial. But we wouldn't. We'll go into the program for a few weeks. Maybe a few months. Until everything calms down."

"I want so much for everything to calm down," said Tina.

So did he, thought Franks.

21

Franks didn't take another drink. He had coffee, consciously sobering up to make the calls to England, to the London managers. Reports of Nicky's murder had reached London. When he heard that, Franks telephoned the lawyer and accountant nonvoting directors, too, to satisfy any concern they might have, and then set about the plan that had occurred to him as he'd sat waiting for the effect of the alcohol to wear off. The final call was to the principal lawyer-director, Nigel Kenham. Franks explained he was going to establish a holding company into which all his and Tina's shares from the various groups were to be transferred and protected. Kenham was to start the necessary formalities at once and have everything ready for him by the time he got back to London. He wasn't sure when that was going to be, he apologized; maybe a week, maybe a little longer.

Franks was completely sober when he finished making the calls, buoyed by the activity and confident because of it. He'd come very close to collapse; to giving everything up in despair. Which was hardly surprising, considering all the circumstances. But he'd managed to pull back. Now he was behaving like the businessman he'd always been—apart from the one appalling lapse—and he was going to prove, to himself and he supposed to Tina, just how much he'd learned from that appalling lapse. Franks actually felt excited at what he was doing. Certainly he didn't want the interruption of eating, so Tina ate with the children while he remained on the telephone. After London he called Rosenberg, glad the lawyer had thoughtfully provided a home number, and said that having talked everything through with his wife he'd decided to cooperate and enter the protection program. But there were things he wanted—guarantees to be established—and so he needed further meetings. Rosenberg promised to arrange them and they fixed an appointment for the following day. When Tina joined him again, Franks told her what he'd already done and what he intended doing, and Tina asked if he was sure it would work.

"It's got to work," insisted Franks. "I've made enough sacrifices, and I guess we're going to have to make some more. I'm sure as hell not going to lose everything."

That night they made love, although Franks half suspected that Tina didn't want to, and afterward she said, "We'll always have each other, won't we? No matter what happens, we'll always have each other?"

"And a lot more," assured Franks.

"I don't think I want a lot more," said the woman.

It wasn't until the following morning that they discussed Nicky's funeral. Tina said that during the previous day's telephone conversation Maria insisted she wanted to organize it herself. Tina had promised that day to drive up to her parents' anyway, wanting to be with them.

"I thought I'd take the kids; it's getting claustrophobic with all these men around."

"I didn't think you wanted them to know yet about Nicky's death?"

"I don't mean them to be in on any talk or grieving," said Tina irritably. "They can play in the garden; Elizabeth can come to look after them."

"I suppose that will be okay," said Franks.

Franks spoke to Tomkiss, repeating that he didn't want David posing with any guns, and Tomkiss assured him he'd spread the word and that they were sorry. Franks saw the children just before he left the house. There wasn't any talk of guns or treasure and Franks was glad. In the car on the way into the city, Franks wondered if he could convince the children it was some sort of grown-up game they were being invited to play when they went through the formalities of the protection program. Almost at once he decided against it. The story couldn't be sustained for however long it was going to take, and they'd realize he'd lied to them. Better to tell them some sort of truth, though he'd hold back from frightening them. Franks knew he'd think of something when the time came. Which wasn't yet. Just like he'd have to think of how to handle their schooling. Could he risk some sort of interregnum: ask both places to agree to a period of suspension on the understanding that the children would eventually return? Something else to discuss with Tina; he'd always felt things like that were more her responsibility than his. The kids would be all right, whatever; kids were adaptable. Into his mind, for no apparent reason, came a remark that Rosenberg had made the previous day. There'd be a lot of publicity, the man had said. Perhaps the schools wouldn't accept David and Gabriella back if the notoriety became too much. Okay, he was escaping prosecution, but some of the evidence might indicate that he'd been a knowing partner; he guessed that would certainly be what the defense lawyers for Dukes and Flamini and Pascara would try to establish. To discredit him as completely as possible, in fact. What was it going to be like? *Really* like? The grand jury hearing and the trial itself? He supposed Rosenberg was the person to ask; he was the ace trial lawyer, after all.

"I think you've made the right decision," said Rosenberg as Franks seated himself in the lawyer's office.

"I thought we already decided it wasn't much of a choice."

"Still, better than trying to mount a defense."

"I want some undertakings, beyond the protection," warned Franks.

"Like what?"

"I've already got my people in London setting up a holding company for the European groups; I'm not going to just abandon them. I'll need to go back, to put it into operation. Arrange a capital transfer, too."

"They won't like that."

"I don't care whether they like it or not," said Franks. "That's the way I want it to be."

"They'll probably say they can't guarantee protection."

"I don't want them to," said Franks. "I'm quite prepared to go back on my own."

"It won't be your safety they'll be worried about," said Rosenberg. "It'll be losing their star witness."

"I must go back," insisted Franks. "I'm not going to go into this leaving the European operations as they are at present." He hesitated. "As it's the word of the moment, I'm not leaving them unprotected."

"I thought you understood how the program worked," said Rosenberg cautiously. "You can't go back to anything that existed before."

"Which is why I'm making the arrangements that I am," said Franks. "I'm going to set up a sideways holding company. Do you know what an omnibus account is, in a Swiss bank?"

"What?" said Rosenberg.

"Something guaranteeing complete anonymity," said Franks. "I'm going to transfer all my working capital into an omnibus account that will be in the name of a company, not a personal name. The holding company for the European groups will be activated in Switzerland but formed in Liechtenstein. It's called an *actiengesellschaft*. That will form complete but independent anonymity, too."

"You seem to know a lot about how to move money around the world, Mr. Franks," remarked the lawyer steadily.

"You making a point?"

"I'm not," said Rosenberg. "But a defense lawyer for Pascara or Flamini or Dukes could make a lot of it—particularly in the apparent payment to the Bahamian minister from an offshore account."

"How are they going to know?"

"I hope they don't," said Rosenberg. "Ronan still isn't going to be happy with the idea; he might refuse."

"Can't we bargain?"

"The file is all we've really got," said Rosenberg. "I'm hoping there will be something in that payment to Snarsbrook in the Bahamas that ties in with the account we now know Pascara holds."

169

"Have you spoken to Ronan?"

"He suggested another meeting, this afternoon. I didn't see any reason to say no."

"With the file?"

"After we've copied it," said Rosenberg.

"Why the precaution?"

"Why not? I thought taking precautions was the name of the game now."

"I'm sorry," said Franks. "It was a stupid question. A lot are."

Tomkiss and Sheridan provided the same escort as before, and when they took the file from the safe-deposit box Franks supposed he should feel grateful; he didn't. Despite everything he remained embarrassed at the theatricality of pavement and door-way and elevator checks. It would be good to get away to Europe. Tina was right; it felt claustrophobic. He guessed it was going to become a problem later.

The gathering in Ronan's office was the same as before, but when they entered this time the district attorney offered his hand first to Franks, and said, "Thank you. I'm sure it's going to work. That everything will come out all right."

The previous day Franks had been bewildered and unsure and knew it must have showed. He didn't like the knowledge and moved immediately to correct the impression he must have made. He said, "I know it might be difficult—even impossible at this stage—for any of you to believe that I am innocent. Maybe you will, later. At the moment it's not important. I know, too, that although everyone's going through the motions, it'll never be possible for Scargo's murder to be proven against any of them. Having made the decision to cooperate, my commitment will be absolute; I'll do anything and everything to ensure that they're jailed for as long as possible, on whatever charges are formulated against them."

"There have been prosecutions that have failed before," said Ronan. "This time they won't."

"Perhaps whatever it was you brought today from the safe-deposit box might help?" asked Waldo, the unremitting professional.

"Mr. Franks has something further to say," prompted Rosenberg.

Recalling Rosenberg's reaction in their earlier meeting, Franks did not go into detail about the holding company and hidden accounts he intended to set up. Instead he said simply that he knew the hearings would take time, making it impossible for him to involve himself in his businesses, but that he was refusing to abandon them altogether and wanted the opportunity to make arrangements.

"Mr. Franks," set out Ronan as the other lawyer had earlier, "you must understand what is involved in cooperating—"

"I understand completely," cut off Franks, overly forceful in his need to recover from the previous day. He looked toward the tax investigator. "You're familiar with the protection afforded by Switzerland and Liechtenstein?"

"Yes," said Knap.

"*Is* their banking secure?"

"An investigatory understanding exists between the United States and Switzerland in the pursuit of criminal enterprise," said Knap pedantically. "But taking the question on the level that you've posed it, yes, the anonymity provision of the banking laws of both countries is extensive. If we are thinking—as we must be thinking—of the chances of organized crime later getting to Mr. Franks through any Swiss or Liechtenstein source, then I must say I consider that extremely unlikely."

"So it's safe?" persisted Franks.

"My objection wasn't so much at your being traced through any such system after the trial. It was at their discovering your going there now—going anywhere—and their removing you as a prosecution witness," said the district attorney bluntly.

"Have they any indication that there is going to be a prosecution?" said Franks.

"No, I suppose not," conceded Ronan. "But they had no indication when they hit Scargo, did they?" Ronan permitted a small gap, and then added, "Although I gather from the preliminary meeting you had with Mr. Waldo, you told them about an incriminating file. If they felt the details of that file were sufficiently important to take Scargo out, then wouldn't they be sufficiently important to justify an attempt upon you, as well?"

"Aren't we being introverted about this?" said Franks. "I'm not attempting for a moment to diminish the importance of any case you try to make; I've already made it clear what I intend to do and how seriously I regard it. But are you seriously suggesting—really *seriously* suggesting—that their influence and power extend as far as that?"

"I only suggest it as a possibility of which you should be aware," said Ronan.

"I want to go to Europe," said Franks insistently. "I've agreed to cooperate fully with you. I'm asking you to cooperate with me."

"*After* the trial?" suggested Ronan.

"No."

"After the grand jury hearings, then?"

"No."

Ronan looked to Waldo and then to the tax inspector and then down at his desk. Finally he looked up and said, "Don't you think you're being a little too confident, Mr. Franks? You sure you can impose such conditions?"

"You tell me," Franks said at once. "You approached me. . . ." He looked at Rosenberg. "Us," he qualified. "We didn't approach you. So you tell me. Do you want to prosecute me and let Pascara and Flamini and Dukes get away again? Or is there going to be the sort of cooperation you've been talking about, ever since these discussions began?"

"You're telling me that our working together is dependent upon my agreeing to your going to Europe?"

"Yes," said Franks shortly.

"Do you think I am completely stupid, Mr. Franks?"

"I don't understand that question."

"The moment you leave America you leave my jurisdiction," said Ronan. "At the moment—with you here—I've got a cast iron case against you with the possibility—remote, I agree, but nevertheless a possibility—of proceeding in some way against the others. Do you seriously imagine that I'm going to let you fly away somewhere where I'd never be able to touch you?" The D.A. looked sadly at Rosenberg. "Please!" he said.

In turn Rosenberg looked to Waldo, and said, "I've already made it clear, as far as movement restrictions are concerned, that I am accepting full responsibility for my client. That pledge remains for what Mr. Franks is suggesting."

Franks looked appreciatively at the other man, realizing for the first time just how completely Rosenberg believed him.

"No," said Ronan. "You can't expect me to accept that."

"I'm prepared for that to be a financial pledge," said Rosenberg.

"Still no," said Ronan. "You're a lawyer, for God's sake! You know the impossibility of what you're asking."

"What about being escorted?" said Rosenberg.

"No," insisted Ronan. "Your client's misfortune—and appreciate I'm being generous—is of his own making. His problem. I'm prepared to go so far, but not as far as this. You know I can't."

Rosenberg looked toward the door leading into the smaller

172

office, and said, "I'd like the opportunity to talk privately to my client again."

"That won't be necessary," said Franks, ahead of Ronan. He stood, moving toward the opposite door leading into the outer offices. "I'm sorry we weren't able to reach any agreement," he said. "I was prepared to, on my part."

Rosenberg was standing now, shifting uncertainly. As he moved to follow Franks, the district attorney said, "Wait!"

Both men stopped at the door.

"Escorted at all times?" said Ronan.

"I've already suggested that," said Rosenberg.

The district attorney made to speak and then stopped, rearranging the words. "And Mrs. Franks and the children remain here, in America."

Franks realized, discomforted, that the idea of taking Tina and the children had never occurred to him.

"That's taking hostages," said Rosenberg contemptuously.

"Yes," admitted Ronan. "That's exactly what it is."

Would Tina be expecting to go with him? Probably, thought Franks. But she'd readily enough accept the alternative. He was doing it for the benefit of her and the children, after all. Wasn't he? The question presented itself abruptly. Was it for Tina and the children, to ensure their future financial well-being? Or was it for him, unable as he'd always been to face the thought of not having any money? It *was* a fear—deep-rooted like all the other secret feelings—although he'd never known what it was like not to have money. Or access to it. He couldn't conceive—had never been able to conceive—how his father had been able to survive, journeying across Europe with *no* money. Or the ability to get it. He said, "I have no intention of running away; I've nothing to run from. I'm quite prepared for my wife and children to remain here, as surety for my return. Although I think the insistence upon it—the thought of it being necessary—is obscene."

"I'm not in the morality business, Mr. Franks," said Ronan. "I'm in the immorality business. It sours you."

"Then I'm glad I'm not in it," said Franks.

"Shall we go on?" invited Ronan, gesturing them back toward their chairs. Franks led the way, as he had led the walkout.

As the two men resumed their seats, Ronan went on, "We've got an agreement, but I'm not sure exactly *what* we've agreed upon. Isn't it about time you showed how closely you're prepared to cooperate by making available whatever you recovered from the safe-deposit?"

173

Rosenberg looked to Franks, who nodded permission. The lawyer took the folder from his briefcase and offered it across the table. Ronan practically snatched at it in his eagerness, beckoning Waldo and Knap to join him at the desk so that they could examine it at the same time. Franks and Rosenberg sat watching them, momentarily forgotten. It was Knap who reacted, stabbing his finger at something. Ronan went immediately to the file that the FBI had created, hurrying from it the photostat that he'd produced the previous day, when he'd talked about Snarsbrook. Waldo said, "It's the same branch."

"And the same account code," identified Knap more expertly, pointing again.

Ronan smiled across at Franks. "This is identified as being the bank account in Nassau from which Pascara transferred his original investment capital?"

"Yes," said Franks.

"You're prepared to testify to that effect?"

"Of course," said Franks, surprised at the question.

"And we can positively link it with a three-hundred-thousand-dollar bribe paid to a Bahamian government minister," said the district attorney, talking more to himself than to anyone else.

Knap was away from the desk, fumbling excitedly through the briefcase that he'd left beside his chair. He pulled out a sheaf of paper, stapled together, and then Franks realized it wasn't paper but checks. "I've got it!" said Knap, exultantly. "I thought so! I've got it!"

"What?" demanded Ronan.

"Some of the money drawn from the casino was in bearer checks, no identity, you understand. Just bearer checks. But after payment and clearance they were returned to the casino account for audit cancellation. It's the customary procedure. Look," he said. "Here . . . here . . . and again here. And here." The tax inspector looked up, his face suffused with a smile of satisfaction. "There'll be more. I know there'll be more because I'm going to run every check that's ever been issued from the casino through a computer and stand over it myself, to make sure it doesn't make any mistake. But here already we've got four checks, totaling some 850 thousand dollars, endorsed into the account that we now know to be Pascara's. We've got him! We've got him on income tax evasion. . . ." The man giggled. "That's the mistake they always make. It's classic."

Ronan looked seriously across the table at Franks, refusing to be affected by Knap's euphoria. "The Bahamian authorities made available to me a note that they discovered during their investigation of Snarsbrook."

"You showed it to me yesterday," said Franks.

"So now I'm going to ask you a question. You've produced documentation linking Pascara into the account. Is it his? Or is it a joint holding?"

"I have no interest or control whatsoever in that account. Or access to it," said Franks. "The bank will authenticate that."

"They're going to have to," said Ronan. He looked sideways to Knap, and said, "You're right. I think we've got him. I wanted something criminal but tax is good enough for me."

"Doesn't this prove something?" suggested Rosenberg.

Ronan frowned toward him. "What?"

"The innocence of my client? An always proclaimed innocence?"

"It's a point," conceded Ronan reluctantly.

"One I would expect to be brought out in court," said Rosenberg.

"If it checks out, upon inquiries, then of course."

Knap was back at the district attorney's elbow, hurrying through the new material and snatching up the second set of bank records, those of Dukes. "I can do it again," said Knap, another man in private conversation with himself. "There's no declaration in any Dukes return of any offshore account in the Netherlands Antilles."

Ronan spoke to Franks across the desk. "I told you this prosecution wouldn't fail," he said. "And it isn't going to. We've got them; I'm sure we've got them."

The meeting continued for another hour, with the district attorney's positive agreement that Franks would be allowed to travel to Europe under the conditions already decided upon—Waldo actually being deputed as the escort—and promises for further contact when Ronan and the rest of the investigatory unit had been fully able to study the material that Franks and Rosenberg had provided.

On the way back to Rosenberg's office, the lawyer said, "You worried the hell out of me back there."

"Sorry."

"Were you really prepared to walk out? Upset everything and go for trial, instead?"

"Yes," said Franks. It was a lie. In the office he hadn't thought it through, but he'd won the bluff, and so now he could afford to make it seem intentional.

175

"Why?"

"I'm fed up with being told what to do and how to do it; being pushed around," said Franks. He put his hand up against his chin. "Fed up to here."

"I want to come," Tina insisted when he told her about going to Europe.

"You can't."

"Why not?"

Franks told her, and she sat staring at him, disbelievingly. "You agreed to that?"

"I didn't have any choice."

"Bastard!" she erupted. "Who do you think I am?"

"Someone I'm trying to look after. You and the kids." Why couldn't she understand?

"You'd better be," she said. "Christ, you'd better be!"

Tina and Maria walked on either side of Mamma Scargo, holding her arms supportively, but from the upright way she held herself, Franks didn't think the old lady needed any assistance. All three women were heavily veiled, so it wasn't possible to see if any of them were crying. He didn't think they were. Tina was quite controlled. Maria as well. They all wore black and Enrico, too, keeping close behind his wife.

Enrico had acknowledged their arrival at the church with nothing more than a curt head movement, not attempting any conversation. Franks and Tina had stood, without any conversation of their own, and Franks hoped the old man imagined the silence between himself and his wife was because of the ceremony. All the relations whom Franks saw at weddings and christenings but at no other time appeared to be there, but there was a division between them and the intimate family, an actual distancing. Franks was unsure if it was out of respect or out of fear that there might be more violence here today.

The FBI and the police remained outside on the steps. Franks saw two men using cameras, movie as well as still; he supposed Schultz and Waldo were around somewhere, but he couldn't see them; Tomkiss seemed to be their permanent guard of the moment.

The priest delivered the customary eulogy, praising Nicky for his uprightness and public spirit and for being a credit to one of the county's foremost families. Franks stood beside his rigid wife and remembered Nicky planning perjury. Did priests ever

176

feel hypocritical? Why should they? Usually they didn't know; certainly this man wouldn't. After the oration the cortege filed out to the graveyard behind the draped coffin, between banks of elaborate wreaths and flower arrangements. Tina was responsible for their floral tribute, and Franks was disinterested in seeing it. He was conscious of other people looking intently as they passed along the avenue; seeking their own to decide if they'd won the contest for the most ostentatious, he thought. The priest continued the service from the grave side. At last Mamma Scargo's shoulders began to move and Maria and Tina put their arms around her. Enrico stared into the open grave at the coffin, but didn't break down.

The last funeral he'd known had been that of his father, Franks remembered. Six years ago. Or was it seven? He could date it from David's birth, because Tina had been pregnant. Almost ten, then. He was embarrassed at having forgotten. He should have a better idea when his father died. A lot had happened in that time; toward the end, too much.

The trowel was offered and the immediate family began the ritual of casting earth in upon the coffin. Franks took the tool when it was offered to him, made his token gesture, and thought, who's being hypocritical now? The priest escorted them to the waiting cars and there was the delay of farewell, and then the line crocodiled out of the cemetery and back to the main highway. The FBI photographers kept shooting right up to the moment of departure, and, looking more closely, Franks realized that there were some newspeople with cameras, as well.

At the house Franks formed part of the family receiving line, touching hands with people he didn't know and accepting mumbled commiserations he didn't hear. People assembled in family ghettos: tight, unmixing groups—protection again? he wondered. He followed Tina's lead, moving with her among them, parroting the words and wishing it would end. Franks had never been able to understand the need for a gathering after a burial: tears and tea, crying and cake.

Extra caterers had in fact been brought in, and waitresses moved among them; there were drinks as well as tea and coffee, and during the tour Franks took two gins. As he reached for the third, when they'd almost completed the circuit, Tina said, "Is that really necessary?"

"We're not here to fight."

"Or to get drunk."

Franks didn't bother to reply, but took the drink anyway.

177

Booze had never been a problem for him and it wouldn't become one now. He'd taken too much after the first meeting with the district attorney, but he didn't think he had any reason to feel guilt about that; most people would have drunk far more, and he'd sobered up quickly enough to initiate the changes he wanted in Europe. So maybe he did average three at night; sometimes more since the crisis had arisen. It was well within his capability. A lot of people drank a damned sight more than that. Tina wasn't concerned at his drinking; she couldn't forgive him for making the arrangement he had to get to Europe. Which was stupid and something he hadn't expected from her. The tension; that's what it had to be. Europe had just become the object, something she could focus on, for all the other feelings and fears.

"You should say something to Mamma and Poppa," said Tina.

"They didn't seem keen on any conversation when we arrived."

"Haven't you got any feelings, for anything?"

"What shall I say?"

Tina had thrown the veil back, so he could see the abrupt tightening of her face. "Just something. I don't care what it is. Just something to show you're human."

"What's that supposed to mean?"

"It isn't supposed to mean anything," she sighed.

The Scargos were by the door of the main room. Maria was with them, protective still, standing behind the chair in which the old lady was sitting. All three watched him as he crossed the room, still unsure what sympathy to offer. He wondered if he should kiss the two women but decided against it. He didn't think they would want the gesture and it seemed too late anyway; he should have done it when he arrived. Instead, he indicated the roomful of mourners and said, "He was very much loved," hating the words. They sounded like something out of a television soap opera.

"Yes," said Enrico, seeming to make a point. "He was."

"I know the investigation is going on," said Franks, trying to recover.

Enrico snorted a laugh. "Taking photographs of those who come to pay their last respects!"

"Other things," said Franks.

"They know who did it!" demanded Maria. She looked quite composed and dry-eyed.

"I don't know the details," avoided Franks. "Just that

178

they're hopeful." Would they be grateful for what he was going to do; the risks he was going to run? He wasn't doing it for their gratitude. He was doing it for what Pascara and Dukes and Flamini did to him. Until this moment he hadn't so clearly defined it in his mind as personal revenge. He was going to enjoy it, Franks decided. He was going to enjoy being in court and seeing those unemotional, supercilious bastards who'd sneered at him behind his back have their crooked little worlds crumble around them, like they'd been prepared to see his world crumble about him. That moment was going to justify a lot of worry and a lot of irritation and a lot of inconvenience. Even the widening gap between him and Tina. That was only temporary, he determined.

"No one will be brought to justice for Nicky's death," insisted Enrico, resigned.

"I think they will," said Franks, wondering how much personal guilt Enrico felt. Should he tell them more? There was a temptation to do so—they deserved it, after all—but he held back. Enrico had been the original link to Pascara, the *cause* of it, if anyone bothered to analyze the entire sequence. The old man must hate Pascara now. But Franks remained unsure. Better—safer—to wait until the indictments had been handed down and the arrests made. To tell them today would be premature. Boastful. Why did he need to boast to Mamma and Poppa Scargo? Contest time was over, forever. Would it be to them he would be boasting? There was also Maria. Franks frowned curiously toward the woman, intrigued by the sudden question. Why on earth would he want to boast to Nicky's widow, on the very day of her husband's funeral? Seeing his expression, Maria frowned back and said, "What is it?"

"Nothing," said Franks, disconcerted. A drinks tray passed nearby and Franks wanted one but he held back, sure that Tina would be watching from somewhere in the room and reluctant to provide her with any more ammunition. "They're keeping in touch with me. The FBI, I mean. I'll let you know as soon as I hear anything."

"Yes," said Enrico dully.

Throughout the encounter Franks realized that Mamma Scargo had remained absolutely unmoving, arms stretched along the chair rests, staring up at him. He felt uncomfortable, not knowing what she was expecting. To Maria, Franks said, "You staying on here?"

"I haven't thought about it," said the woman. "I haven't thought about anything."

179

"Of course not," said Franks. "Anything I can do to help . . ." Quickly he added, "Tina or me."

"I know."

"Tina will keep in touch."

"I'd like her to."

Franks looked around for his wife and moved toward her, glad to leave one tense situation although possibly entering another; it would be a relief to get away to Europe. Franks supposed he should feel guilty at the thought, but he didn't. He felt like a stranger here: a casual acquaintance rather than a member of the family.

"I've done the rounds," said Tina.

"And I've done my duty."

"Is that how you regarded it—a duty?"

"That's how they made it seem."

"They're burying their son, for Christ's sake!"

Tina seemed to have forgotten who was responsible for everything, thought Franks. It didn't seem important to remind her. "Shouldn't we get back to the children?"

"We're *family*," she said, angrily. "We can't leave ahead of everyone else. What's wrong with you?"

"Actually there's nothing wrong with me," he said.

"What's that supposed to mean?"

"Let it mean whatever you want," said Franks. He moved away from her. A waitress passed conveniently and he took the drink he'd earlier denied himself. Fuck Tina! All he was trying to do was work things out in the best possible way—the best possible way for her and the kids—and he didn't deserve the hard time. So he'd left them hostage, which was theatrical, like so much else. But she should understand why he was doing it. She wasn't stupid. He tempered the thought; she hadn't been until now. He was aware of Maria looking at him. He smiled, briefly, and briefly she smiled back. He looked away, moving near the window with its garden view, so he was able to see the assembly of cars when departures began after a little while. Inside the room a vague line had formed, to file out past the family with further, parting condolences. Tina didn't move, to re-form the original receiving line, so Franks remained gratefully by the window, glad to be spared the empty repetition. At least, he thought, looking out, the FBI appeared to have stopped taking photographs. He wondered if the newspeople had gone. Around him the caterers began clearing the debris and he moved out of their way. His glass was empty and he looked hopefully for a

180

refill, but service was finished. He placed the glass on a table. A lot of other people here today would have had more than he had, Franks knew. He moved back, trailing the final line of departing guests, until he reached Tina, and then the immediate family.

"We'll be getting back," said Tina.

"Yes," said her mother.

"Maybe I'll come up tomorrow. With the children," said Tina, filling in the abrupt silence.

"Yes," said the old lady again.

"Or would you like to come down to us; get out of the house for a while?"

"No," said Enrico. "You come here."

"Good-bye," said Franks.

"Good-bye," said Maria, the only one bothering to reply.

"I'll let you know anything that happens," he promised again.

"Thank you."

To kiss them—the old lady, at least—would be appropriate now, but Franks couldn't bring himself to do it. Outward emotion had always been easy for them, but never for him. Now it seemed difficult for them as well. Tina did it instead, hugging her father first and then her mother, and then kissing Maria.

Franks and Tina had come in their own car from Scarsdale, with the FBI escort in a following vehicle, and that was how they returned. For a long time they traveled in heavy silence, and then Tina said, "I wonder what Maria will do?"

"I got the impression she'd stay on there for a while," said Franks, not understanding.

"I didn't mean that. I meant now that Nicky's dead. Maria never seemed to have many friends of her own."

"I always thought you were her closest friend."

Franks was aware of his wife looking at him across the car. "Did you tell her about the trial?"

"No," said Franks.

"Why not?"

"We don't know if there's going to be one yet," he said. "Nothing has been presented to a grand jury."

"When are you going to England? To Europe?" demanded Tina, coming to the point of tension between them.

"As soon as everything is settled with the prosecution, I suppose."

"You didn't say how long for?"

"I don't know how long for," said Franks. "All the prelim-

181

inary work is already being done. I've only got to do the final signing and the Swiss arrangements. It shouldn't take long."

"How long?" she demanded.

"A week," he said, not wanting to resurrect the argument between them. "Not more than a fortnight."

"I'm beginning to find all this very difficult," she blurted suddenly. "All of it."

And it had hardly started yet, thought Franks. "Me, too," said Franks, trying to ease things between them.

"I couldn't live like this forever," she said.

Seeing the opportunity, Franks said, "That's why I am doing what I am: to ensure that you won't have to."

"I liked the way things were before," said Tina. "When it was a proper life."

"It'll be like that again," promised Franks, hoping he sounded convincing.

"It'll have to be," said Tina. "I don't think I could live any other way."

22

Franks had the impression that he and Tina were circling each other, seeking an opening, like prizefighters or matadors. His own affairs had entered an abrupt lull. He maintained daily telephone contact with Rosenberg—eager to go into the city to escape from the restrictions of the house, however slender the excuse—but the trial lawyer kept insisting there was no reason and that they should await the next move from Ronan and his investigators. Franks pressed for permission to take the promised European trip, but Rosenberg said they should wait until Ronan was prepared to present what he had to a grand jury.

Toward the end of the week Franks gave in and let David have his photograph taken with the police gun—the pump-action shotgun as well as a pistol. Tina seized upon it when she heard, ranting at him for hypocrisy and stupidity, and Franks made only a token defense, conscious that she was right and that he was wrong and had let the pictures be taken because he couldn't be bothered to refuse the child anymore. Several times she ate with the children, early, to avoid dinner with him. Franks was grateful rather than annoyed because he didn't particularly want to share the meal with her, either.

Rosenberg insisted that Franks stay out of disposing of the Bahamian and Bermuda hotels, denying a further excuse for Franks to go into town, but at least it provided a reason for some telephone conversations, giving the impression of work. Anxious to have something further to do—to make the large hand on the clock move from one marker to the next—Franks maintained twice-a-day contact with London, checking on the arrangements he had initiated there.

Tina sought her escape in visits to her parents. She started making the journey almost every morning and not returning until late evening. Franks rigidly controlled his drinking, always conscious—confident—that there was no problem but equally aware that with so much time on his hands the habit could grow insidiously. He allowed two—but positively only two—at lunchtime and two each evening and possibly a final one—but not always—after his usually solitary supper. Nothing wrong with five drinks, spread over the course of the entire day; and he didn't have a single glass of wine with any of his meals. When he did, Franks was always careful to ensure that there was wine left in the decanter until the following day, yet further proof that he was in absolute control. At all times. And going to stay that way.

During one of his days alone—in the second week—Franks recognized that, temporary though it might be, the erosion between himself and Tina was ridiculous and moved to stop it. She ate with him that night, providing the opportunity. Franks refused all her challenges, deflecting every one of her attempts to exacerbate their differences, instead remaining courteous and considerate, which seemed to annoy her further. When the meal was over, there was still wine left, as he made sure she noticed. He poured brandy for them both and said, "This has got to stop, hasn't it?"

"What?"

"Don't pretend you don't know, Tina. That's ridiculous. Us. Warring all the time."

"Do we war?"

"You know we do. It was never difficult for us to be alone; we actually *wanted* it that way."

"Alone!" she said. "Surrounded by an army!"

"You know it's not going to last."

"I don't know anything of the sort."

"We've gone through it, all of it. We've just got to endure it and wait until it passes and then start living like we did before."

"I don't think it's possible for anything ever to be like it was before."

"It won't be if we go on like this," continued Franks gently. "If we go on like this then we're going to end up hating each other. Is that how you want it to be?"

"You know the answer to that."

"Do I?" he said. "Recently I've not been so sure that I do."

"It's so . . . it's so . . ." tried Tina, waving her arms. "Oh, I don't know what it is."

"It's unreal," provided Franks. "You said it a long time ago: doing everything in front of an audience. I hate it, too. I'm doing what I'm doing to avoid going to jail and every day is like being in jail. We're not trying, either of us. We're giving up, like people do give up when they go to jail."

Tina remained for a long time gazing down into her brandy. "I know you're right," she admitted finally. "And I haven't been helping. Didn't want to help . . ." She looked up at him, wet-eyed. "Do you know what I thought when you told me that you were going back to England and we had to stay here?"

"What?"

"That you were running away. That you were running away somewhere and weren't going to come back for us."

Franks stared at her. "You thought *that?*"

"I'm sorry."

"But why? You've never had any cause to think like that."

"I know. Now that I've said it, I feel stupid."

They'd taken their drinks into the small sitting room and were sitting on opposite couches. Now Franks got up, setting his drink on a side table, and knelt down in front of her. "I didn't know it had got that bad for you," he said. "I honestly didn't."

"Neither did I. Not really."

Franks tried to kiss her but she only half responded.

"I don't believe what they said, whoever it was; Ronan or Waldo or whoever. I can't believe people can live like this."

"Do you want to get away somewhere with the kids?" said Franks.

"But isn't that just the point?" she demanded. "We can't go away just like that. Which is what makes it worse. We used to be able to. We could go anywhere we wanted, when we wanted. All we had to do was buy an airplane ticket and we could always afford that, too. Now we can't go anywhere without cars in front and behind and people checking doorways and alleys. . . ." She looked directly at him. "Last night Gabby wet the bed," she said. "She's five years old, for God's sake. She hasn't wet the bed for years. I think it's because of what's going on here."

Franks swallowed. "I meant, go away somewhere by yourself, with the kids," he said. "There'll have to be somebody with you, of course; just to be sure. But it's me they'll try to hit, if they try it at all. Are you frightened of being around me?"

"No!" shouted Tina desperately. "Being *without* you is what I'm frightened of. Not having you, like Maria hasn't got Nicky anymore. I'm not going anywhere without you; that's why it hurt—why I started to think stupidly—when you said you had to go to London by yourself."

"I've explained that."

"I know," she said. "I know that now."

"What are you going to do about Gabby?"

"Nothing," said Tina practically. "I'm not even letting her know that I'm aware it happened. If I draw attention to it then it will be a big thing. I might be wrong, after all. There might be no connection."

"What if it happens again?"

"Let's wait *until* it happens again," she said, still practical.

"It won't seem so bad," said Franks. "Not when we're back in England and the kids are back at school and we're living like we were before."

"Is that ever going to be possible?" asked Tina. "Don't lie to me; don't say something just because you're trying to make everything seem better. Do you believe—honestly, sincerely believe—that we're going to be able to go back?"

Franks stared up at her, his knees beginning to ache from the unaccustomed position, but not moving because if he did she'd imagine he felt some awkwardness about her demand. And he was feeling an awkwardness beyond any physical discomfort. Don't lie, she'd said. "I've agreed to testify and to cooperate because it's right—necessary—that I should. It's necessary, too, that I take us all into this protection program. I still don't believe that they'd try to kill me, but because of you and because of the

185

kids I can't take that risk. But you know I don't intend staying in. *That's* why I'm going to London. And why I'm going to set up the situations in Switzerland. When the time comes we can opt out."

"With the children at the schools they were before?" persisted Tina.

"I've thought about that," said Franks. "It's something that I'm going to sort out, when I go back."

"And we still can be in this house?" she pressed on.

Franks frowned. "No," he said. "I don't think in this house. I didn't imagine you'd want to, anyway."

"What about the house at Henley?"

"I don't know. Maybe," he said. "Maybe we'll have to go somewhere else."

"Using what names? Are the kids going to leave one term with one name and go back again with another?"

"I don't *know!*" said Franks. His legs were hurting, so he had to stand; it had been a silly gesture anyway.

"I do," said Tina evenly. "It isn't going to be the same. None of it. Not ever again."

"We'll be together," said Franks. "I won't be behind bars somewhere, serving a sentence for offenses I had no part of."

"Yes," she said. "We'll be together."

"A little while ago you were telling me that's all that mattered."

"Yes," said Tina, flat-voiced. "I was, wasn't I?"

That night they tried to make love, which they hadn't for a long time, not since the previous failed attempt. This time it didn't work either, although she tried to pretend, like she had before.

"Sorry," she said openly.

"It doesn't matter."

"Thanks!"

"You know what I mean."

"I just can't . . . it's . . . I keep thinking of those men outside and imagining they're watching. They probably are. David says they've got devices on rifles that enable them to see in the dark."

"He seems to be becoming quite an expert on weapons."

"It's hardly surprising, is it?"

"We mustn't let this break us up, Tina," said Franks. "We mustn't let that happen."

"I know. I just hope I'm strong enough to prevent it happening."

The following morning Rosenberg called; Ronan wanted another meeting. Franks set the appointment for that afternoon, eager to get away from Scarsdale and into the city. In the car Franks gazed around him at the familiar landscape as if seeing it for the first time. It was like freedom from imprisonment, he thought, and then immediately wished he hadn't.

He met Rosenberg at the district attorney's office. The usual group was assembled. There was a handshake from Ronan and a smile of greeting from Knap. Waldo nodded without any facial expression.

"We're ready," announced Ronan at once.

"Against Pascara, Flamini, *and* Dukes?" said Rosenberg.

"All three," confirmed the district attorney.

"What are the charges?"

"Conspiracy, against all three. We're seeking five separate indictments; objectively I think we'll get three. Against Dukes and Pascara, willful evasion of taxes . . ." Ronan smiled toward Knap. "That's strictly an IRS prosecution."

"We're very confident," said the tax investigator. "We haven't been able to penetrate either offshore account, obviously. But in Pascara's case we've racked up a total of 3.5 million dollars in canceled checks that have not been declared on any return. In Dukes' case we're alleging 2.5 million dollars. . . ."

"We're also proceeding against Dukes and Flamini for entering a business arrangement without declaring previous felonious convictions. . . ." The district attorney smiled toward Franks. "You prepared to testify that no such declaration was ever made?"

"You've got to be joking!" said Franks at once. "And even without my testimony you've got the company minutes, *proving* that there was no such declaration."

"Which is why we've included it," said Ronan. "I have to hear everything from you, in the form of a deposition, to enable me finally to go forward. You're the pivot to any prosecution we bring, Mr. Franks. So I don't want anything—no matter how inconsequential—overlooked. If we can complete the deposition today, then fine. But I don't want it rushed. We're this close." Ronan held up a hand with the thumb and forefinger narrowed, closing an imperceptible space. "So I'm not going to blow it. If it takes a week—two weeks—to get everything right, then I don't care."

"It won't," assured Franks at once. "We can do it this afternoon."

"I'd like to think you're right," said Ronan. "But let's not be overeager, okay?"

187

They achieved it in one sitting. But it took much longer than Franks anticipated. By the time he finished, aching as if he'd been engaged in some form of physical labor, there were five completed spools lying beside the tape machine on Ronan's desk and a further, final tape still in the machine. Waldo led the interrogation throughout, showing by his questioning a still better knowledge of the case than the district attorney. It was dark when the account was finished; looking around the room, Franks knew that everyone else was as physically strained as he was. Ronan summoned a secretary and handed her the tapes for transcription, smiling first to Waldo and then to Knap. "Well?" he said.

"We've got a case," judged Knap at once. "A damned good one."

"It'll do," said Waldo, less enthusiastic.

"When?" said Rosenberg.

"From now on it's largely a matter of mechanics," said the district attorney. "Impaneling a jury. Formulating the charges."

"What about my going to London?" demanded Franks.

"Yes," agreed Ronan. "It'll have to be before the hearings start. Right away then." The man looked at Waldo. "No problem with you?"

"No problem," said the FBI supervisor. "Whenever."

"How long do you want?" said Ronan, coming back to Franks.

"Two weeks?" said Franks.

"Right away," said the district attorney. To Waldo he said, "By yourself?"

Waldo shook his head. "Thought I'd take my partner."

Franks was glad there would be the other man. He didn't like the idea of having Waldo's unrelieved company for so long. He said, "When we last met there was some discussion about my family remaining here?"

"Yes," Ronan said.

"I'd like to be able to take my wife."

Franks was aware of the look that went between Waldo and the district attorney.

"No," said Ronan.

23

Franks told Tina at once that he was going, hoping it might lessen the problem between them, but it didn't. Not that they argued; maybe it would have been better if they had. Instead they became overly polite and considerate—matadors not wanting to tarnish their suits of lights, he thought—each conceding to the other, each deferring to that concession. Franks endured it *because* there was a time limit, virtually only hours before he was due to catch the plane. He devoted the final full day to the children, trying to bridge the gap between himself and Tina through them and despising himself for doing it. He'd always been critical of adults who used children to get at each other, for anything. It didn't work, because she didn't respond.

He let David beat him at tennis and then had a picnic prepared and walked with them away from the house, to a woodsy area he'd never had cleared. Tina came too, perfunctorily, and so did four FBI men, led by Tomkiss; halfway through the meal Gabby ran screaming from a sound in the trees and one of the bureau bodyguards emerged shamefaced from peeing to say he was sorry. David developed a rash from poison ivy, which none of them saw, and Franks was sorry there was no gin packed in the hamper. He drank most of the wine, instead, and wished there had been a second bottle. As they trailed back to the house, far earlier than Franks intended, Tina said that Gabby had again wet the bed. He asked what she intended doing and Tina said still nothing, not yet. Any more than she intended to correct David for swearing. Franks said he didn't know about any swearing and Tina said she and the nanny were both aware of the boy cursing—"shit" seemed the favorite, but they'd both heard "fuck"—and thought he'd picked it up from the guards.

"Or us," said Franks.

"Us?"

"They're words we've been using a lot lately."

"You mean I have!"

189

Franks couldn't be bothered to withdraw anymore; at least they were being honest, arguing outright. "Okay," he said, "you have."

"So now I'm guilty of everything since the death of Jesus."

"It doesn't suit you."

"What doesn't suit me!"

"That sort of brittleness."

"You anxious to get away tomorrow?"

She'd asked him not to lie, before, Franks remembered. "Yes," he said.

"I knew," she said.

"I'm coming back."

"You told me before."

"And I meant it before. And I mean it now." She wouldn't believe he'd asked Ronan to allow her to go with him, so there wasn't any purpose in telling her.

"Maria's coming," said Tina in a sudden switch.

"Coming where?" said Franks, not immediately following her.

"To the house. For dinner tonight. And to stay. I said you were going away and asked her to keep me company. She called up this morning."

"You told her I was going away?"

"Not *where*," said Tina. "Stop panicking. I just said you had to be away for a few days."

"I wasn't panicking," said Franks. Christ, let this night pass and bring another day so I can leave, he thought. "I would have thought you'd have kept the last night free, before I went away."

"Is it the last night?" she seized at once.

"I didn't mean like that! And you know it!" Franks was uncaring that his voice was loud until he saw the children turn back just before the house to stare at them. He waved. They responded halfheartedly.

"Well done!" she said.

"Shut up, for God's sake!"

"We invited Maria whenever she felt like coming. So today she called. Did you expect me to put her off?"

Franks thought briefly. "Yes, why not? Why couldn't she have come tomorrow?"

"Okay, so I made a mistake. Is that such a big deal?"

Franks turned and looked behind him. The FBI men were

190

following four abreast. Two were talking to each other and they all appeared sufficiently far away not to have heard. "I'm glad she's coming anyway," he said, trying to defuse the mood worsening between them. "It's good you'll have company."

"What about you?"

"What's the matter with you?" he said. "I told you Waldo and Schultz were coming with me."

"Sure!"

"You're being ridiculous!"

At the house Franks announced that he was going to pack—not needing to yet, but to separate himself from her—and David asked if he could help and Franks said of course. Franks made a game out of it, sending the boy to drawers and cupboards and then letting him pack the things, actually enjoying the child's company. They'd almost completed one suitcase when David said, "Why do you and Mommy shout at each other so much?"

"We don't," said Franks.

"Yes, you do. Since I came back from England you've always been arguing."

"Everyone has arguments."

"You didn't used to. Not you and Mommy."

"Mommy's worried about something," said Franks. Realizing it seemed as if he were shifting the guilt to Tina, he added, "I've been worried, too."

"Is that why these men are here, with guns?"

Franks winced, glad he had his back to the boy and was bending over a suitcase. He said, "They're looking after us, for a while."

"I don't understand," protested David. "Why do they need to look after us?"

"There are some bad people who don't want Daddy to do something; something I've got to do. The men are here to stop those bad people coming here and telling me not to do it." Franks was hot with discomfort; he would have liked the explanation to have been better but decided it wasn't too bad.

"What must you do?"

"Tell some other people—a judge—just how bad they are."

"You going to be in a court, like on television?"

"Yes," said Franks.

"Can I come to watch?"

"No," said Franks.

"Why not! Please let me!"

191

"Children aren't allowed in courts."

"I think that's shitty."

"Those are the rules," Franks said, refusing to respond to the language.

"Is it in England?"

Franks turned, frowning. "What?"

"The court?"

"No."

"Why are you going to England then?"

"There's some business I have to do there; I go back and forth all the time. You know that."

"You *are* coming back, aren't you?" said the boy. "You're not leaving us?"

Franks sat on the edge of the bed, holding his arms out to the boy. David hesitated and then fell forward into the embrace, clutching at Franks.

"Of course I'm coming back," he said. Damn the argument with Tina after the picnic.

His voice muffled in Franks' shoulder, David said, "There are boys at school whose parents aren't together. I always want you and Mommy to be together."

"Mommy and I will always be together," said Franks. "We love each other, don't we?"

"Promise?"

"Have I ever broken a promise to you?"

"I don't know," said David. "I don't think so."

"I haven't," assured Franks. "And I'm promising you now that Mommy and I will always stay together." He held the boy away from him, conscious of the effort David was making not to cry. "Okay?" he said.

"Okay."

Remembering the bed-wetting, Franks said, "Do you and Gabby talk about it?"

"Sometimes."

"Is Gabby worried?"

"I think so."

"Think we should get her in on this conversation?"

"I don't know," said David.

"Or would it be better if you told her we had a kind of grown-up talk, and let her know what I said?"

"Maybe better if I told her," said the boy. "If we call her in she'll think I've been splitting on her: telling tales."

"Aunty Maria is coming tonight. Going to stay with us a while," said Franks.

"And Uncle Nicky?" asked the child.

Damn, thought Franks again. "No," he said, "not Uncle Nicky."

"Why not? Aren't they together anymore?"

Franks pulled the child into his shoulder once more, unable to go on facing the trusting stare. "He's had to go away on business, like me," said Franks. Was it right not to have told him? One uncertainty prompted another. Should he have brought Gabby in, to tell her everything was all right between himself and Tina? He'd avoided—run away from—both questions, and he shouldn't have done, Franks decided. It was too late now to go back on either.

"Perhaps he'll come later," said the boy.

Franks stood abruptly, looking at the suitcases. "Didn't we come here to do a job?" he said. Still running, he thought.

Franks was relieved when the nanny came to take David away for his bath. He prolonged the packing, not wanting to go down to Tina. But at last he did. He saw she'd changed, which meant she'd visited the dressing room next door to the bedroom, and wondered if she'd heard any of the conversation between himself and David. She made no reference to it. He supposed he'd have to tell her, but not yet; later, so there'd be less time for any dispute. Tina said she didn't want anything to drink. Franks was finishing his second when Maria arrived. Maybe it was a good idea after all that she'd come tonight instead of tomorrow, thought Franks; it might cut down the bickering between himself and Tina. Then again, it might not. Franks carried her suitcases, and Tina kissed her sister-in-law and took the children up for their baths, promising them they could come back for a visit with their aunt. Tina remained upstairs, to help the nanny with the baths, which left Franks and Maria alone in the small sitting room. She chose a martini and Franks had another one, too.

"How are things?" he asked.

"Kind of suspended, in limbo," she said. She smiled and added, "Know what I thought on the way here?"

"What?"

"How I wouldn't like to be a president or a world statesman or something like that, surrounded by bodyguards all the time."

"I guess you get used to it," said Franks. She looked far more relaxed than Tina. The grey dress was silk and tightly cut. Franks thought back to his poolside comparison between Maria and his wife and this time didn't feel embarrassed.

"I'm not sure I would," said Maria. "How are things with you?"

"Okay," said Franks.

"There didn't seem a lot of reassurance in that."

Franks could have turned the remark aside, but he decided he didn't want to. He said, "I wasn't just making small talk at the funeral. Something's moving, against Pascara and Flamini and Dukes."

Maria had been sitting with that faint, mocking smile playing at the corners of her mouth but at once she became serious. "For Nicky's murder!"

Franks shook his head. "In the strictest confidence, right?"

"Of course," she said.

"I don't think Enrico should know, not until it starts," insisted Franks.

Maria hesitated and said, "Doesn't he deserve to?"

"His was the original association."

"Do you think that matters, now?"

"I can't take the risk," said Franks.

"*You?*"

"Yes," said Franks. "It's all to do with the company."

"Will they be jailed?"

"Yes," said Franks.

"How can you be sure?"

"Everyone's very confident."

"Will Nicky's murder be involved?"

"It's bound to be part of the evidence, I would have thought."

"You'll be a witness?"

"Naturally."

"So it's going to be dangerous for you?"

How completely would they be removed from everyone they knew when they entered the protection program? The separation couldn't be absolute. He said, "Yes, it'll be dangerous."

The smile came back, an admiring expression, he thought. Maria said, "Aren't you frightened, after what happened to Nicky?"

Franks realized that he was enjoying impressing her, but thought that to say he wasn't frightened—which he genuinely wasn't—would sound too boastful. He said, "Let's say I'm aware of what it could mean."

"Are you?" she said. "Fully aware?"

"I think so."

Maria made a sweeping gesture, to encompass the grounds and the unseen protectors. "It's going to mean this goes on for some time, surely?"

194

"For quite a while," agreed Franks.

"Don't you find it difficult?"

"Quite a lot," admitted Franks. "I think it's getting to Tina more than me."

"I thought she looked tired," said Maria.

He saw her glass was empty. She surrendered it to be refilled, their hands touching when he took it from her. With his back toward the woman while he made the drinks, Franks decided that he wouldn't let the conversation settle upon his wife. He said, "How are things up there?"

"Suspended, like I said. I think Mamma still expects Nicky to walk in, at any time. Enrico, too. They still talk about him in the present tense, like he isn't dead."

Franks returned with her drink, careful this time there was no contact between them. She smiled up at him. "That can't make things easy for you," he said.

"I've sort of turned myself off from it," she said. "I must say I'm glad to come here for a while."

"What about later? You're welcome to stay here for as long as you like. You know that. And I guess with all the protection they'd like us to remain fairly stable, in one or two places. But it'll have to end, sometime. What are you going to do then?"

"I don't want to keep the brownstone in New York," she said, positively. "It's too big, and anyway I don't think I want to stay on there. Not sure about Manhattan at all. I don't think there'll be the need to work, but I don't think I can go on doing nothing. If I'm going to work then the city's the best place to be. Which will mean an apartment there, I guess." She looked toward the windows and the unseen guards. "How long *will* this go on?"

"I'd say for you, only until immediately after the trial."

"When will that be?"

"I don't know, not yet. Everything seems to be moving quite quickly."

"Nicky and I were having problems, you know," she confessed abruptly.

"No," said Franks. "I didn't know."

Maria was looking down into her drink. "Personal things; stuff like that. Even talked of a divorce. . . ." She brought her eyes up to him. "I want you to know," she said.

"Sure," said Franks.

"It's important, you see. Because I want you to understand. Although I don't think that I *loved* him, not like I should have

195

done, I still thought a lot of him. Which is why I hope somebody is going to be tried and jailed for his killing. I *want*
somebody to be punished for it. I'd do anything to see that
happen.''
"I told you everyone seems very confident," said Franks.
"But you said it was the company," reminded Maria. "Not
for the killing. That's what I want. Someone punished for the
actual murder.''
"They'll be in jail," said Franks. "I think I can understand
the way you feel. But they'll be in jail for something, even
though the conviction won't be for murder.''
"Will it be for a long time?''
"I don't know that," said Franks. "I still know very little
about American law. Certainly that's the impression I get.''
"Thank you," said Maria.
"What for?''
"Being brave enough to confront them.''
"You don't feel like Enrico then? Or like Nicky did?''
"I've never liked weakness, Eddie. I discovered it in Nicky
a long time before you did. I only wish I had realized it before
we got married. So no, I don't think you should back away.''
They heard the children approaching and turned toward the
door. Franks remembered the suitcase-packing conversation with
David and waited apprehensively for a question about Nicky. But
it didn't come. Instead the boy produced the photograph of
himself with the guns and showed his poison ivy rash, and Gabby
sat tightly on Maria's lap and demanded, when Franks announced
the visit over, that Maria put them to bed, which she agreed to
do.
"We're drinking martinis," Franks said to Tina when Maria
left the room with the children.
"Thanks." A skein of hair had fallen away from her chignon
while she was helping the nanny, and there was a damp patch
from the bath on the sleeve of her dress.
"I've told Maria," Franks announced, "about there being a
trial. I didn't go into detail.''
"I didn't think anybody was supposed to be told.''
"I thought she deserved it. I've asked her not to tell your
mother and father.''
Tina took her drink. "What did she say?''
"That she wanted somebody to go to jail for Nicky's killing.''
Maria had walked back into the room as Franks was speak-
ing. "I also said that I thought it was a brave thing to do.''

"Seems a long time ago that I thought the same thing," said Tina.

"Don't you now?" said Maria. She looked around expectantly for her drink and Franks refilled the glass she'd left empty. He still felt completely in control but wondered about Maria; she had sounded to him quite barbed.

"I'd like to be able to think objectively about anything," said Tina.

"Maybe it would be a good thing if you did remain objective," said Maria. "I'm not sure what it is you've lost; at the moment, I've lost a husband." She hesitated, looking to Franks and then back to Tina. "You weren't here when I told Eddie that things weren't good between Nicky and me. What I didn't tell Eddie was that I didn't know—and now I never will—whether it would have ended in divorce or in something different. I'd have liked to know."

"Meaning?" demanded Tina, responding to the challenge.

"Meaning don't fall backward into a trough of self-pity until you've got good and proper reason."

"Thanks!" said Tina.

Maria purposely misunderstood the sarcasm. "If it helps, I'm glad," she said.

Tina's glass was certainly empty and his could have done with topping up, but Franks held back, not wanting to contribute anything that might exacerbate a situation he hadn't expected. Nor wanted. He actually looked at his watch, calculating the time before the plane took off the following morning.

Tina saw the gesture, and said, "You got an appointment? Or expecting a call?"

"No," said Franks. Tina and Maria were sitting side by side on a facing couch, as if they were inviting comparison. Franks began to make it because it was so obvious and then determinedly stopped. Too much was being eroded too quickly, he thought.

"Eddie's anxious to leave tomorrow. He's told me so," said Tina with childlike petulance.

"Can you tell me where you're going?" asked Maria.

"You're not supposed to know," said Tina.

"Europe," said Franks.

"There!" said Tina. "See how secret everything is?"

"I don't mind Maria knowing," said Franks. "Why should I?"

"You made the rules," reminded Tina. "I didn't."

"Shall I tell you something?" asked Maria.

197

"What?" said Tina.

"I can close my eyes listening to you both and hear Nicky and me."

"Except you didn't have the pressure," said Franks at once.

"Not your pressure," said Maria. She made an embarrassed shrug and said, "I'm not proving myself to be the ideal houseguest, am I?"

"I'm not sure we're proving ourselves ideal hosts."

"You might, if you gave me another drink," said Maria.

Franks took the pitcher to Maria but Tina shook her head against a refill. He added to his own glass.

A loud silence settled in the room, no one knowing whether to speak or remain silent to make way for someone else. As he replaced the martini pitcher, Franks realized there was less than one glass left. To make more would give him some activity, putting the responsibility for conversation upon the women. But it might also provoke Tina into a fresh assault, perhaps with good reason. How many was it he had drunk already? Franks thought it was five, but conceded it might have been more. Not more than seven. Seven martinis—strong ones, too—and he was still in absolute control, thinking good, speaking good, behaving good. It was good to know how well he could hold his drink. Why was good a recurring word? Why couldn't he think of another one? Not important. Didn't indicate anything. It *was* good. Proper word then.

Dinner was announced. The women made a more determined effort in the dining room, and Franks responded to it. Recognizing it was fatuous to attempt anything but the one conversation between them, he talked further—but still generally, so that Tina remained the knowledgeable one of the two—giving Maria only a broad indication of how the case was to be made against Pascara and Flamini and Dukes. When Maria asked outright what Europe had to do with it and why he was going, Franks still remained vague, talking about how long he'd been away and how it was necessary to remain in some sort of control. By the end of the meal Franks decided again that it was good that Maria had come, although he'd been uncertain immediately before dinner. They had two bottles of wine and Franks set himself a private challenge, knowing he'd passed because at the end of the meal he was sure he was still sober. As they left the table he was thinking how glad he was that Maria would be with Tina during his absence. Franks didn't have any doubts that had she stayed in the house alone, with only the children and staff and the

198

constant FBI protectors, her unhappiness would have deepened. They went back to the small drawing room, where Maria refused anything more to drink. Franks nursed a brandy, more to prove that he could still manage it without difficulty than because he needed it, happy to hear them talking eagerly to each other, all antagonism gone. It was practically like it had been before, he thought, when Nicky had been alive and they had spent so much time together.

When they finally went to bed Franks remembered the earlier bedroom conversation with David—surely another indication that booze didn't cause any impairment to his control?—and told Tina about it.

"You should have talked to Gabby, as well as David," she said at once.

"I didn't want to make it seem more of an issue—a big deal—than it really is," he said. "You're not talking to her about the bed-wetting; you're pretending it isn't happening."

Ignoring the logic—and truth—of his response, Tina said, "They're obviously aware of more that's going on around them than we thought they were."

"Maybe that'll make it easier later."

"How?"

"We're still going to have to go through this false identity piece."

"Are you sure that's absolutely necessary?" she said.

"I'm not sure," said Franks. "They are: Ronan and Rosenberg and the FBI people."

"It's going to seem so ridiculous."

Franks hoped so. The alternative—for them to be convinced it was necessary to protect their lives—would be far worse than ridiculous. "I thought you should know about the kids," he said. "There might be a right moment when you could talk to her about it; reassure her."

Tina looked at him sharply and Franks waited for some accusation, but it didn't come. Instead she said, "Something registered with me tonight about what Maria said."

"What?"

"That I was wallowing in self-pity; that I hadn't lost a husband."

"I keep trying to convince you of that."

"All those people outside, with their stupid guns, protecting us from some outside attack. We're destroying ourselves, aren't we?"

Franks tried to think of the precise moment when he'd

199

decided to stop and mentally examine every word and sentence—tasting them before speaking. It seemed like a long time ago but he knew it couldn't be. "Yes, we are," he said. "Surely—by knowing it—we can stop it happening."

Later they lay side by side, and Franks knew that Tina expected him to make the first move, to make love. He didn't. Before all this she'd initiated their lovemaking as much as he had; he'd enjoyed her being the aggressor—far better than the sort of aggressor she was now—finding it an exciting part of the act. Beside him Tina stayed rigid in the same attitude of stubborn refusal. She went to sleep before he did. Franks found himself thinking of Maria, farther along the corridor, and wished that he didn't.

24

Waldo and Schultz weren't as extreme as Tomkiss, but they were still protective. Franks realized that the departure for England was his first outing in anything like public for days—weeks. His feeling was one of acute, head-down embarrassment; the way he was surrounded made him feel like a criminal and he supposed averting his face from public scrutiny made him look just that. The departure from Kennedy was a full FBI operation, a front and back car escort to the airport and all the departure formalities carried out in a private room outside of which two men were posted. The same men made up the escort onto the plane, in advance of the normal passenger embarkation. Their seats backed against the bulkhead, so that it was impossible for anyone to sit behind them; it also meant that the seats would not recline and that for the entire flight they had to sit stiffly upright. That wasn't the only discomfort. Franks had no difficulty from the slim, neatly compact Schultz to his left, but Waldo overflowed from the other bordering seat, legs apart, reducing Franks' space. Franks refused the in-flight food but maintained a steady supply of drinks from the attentive cabin staff to whom he knew he was the object of curiosity. Because of the drinks Franks needed to use the lavatory before they landed and Schultz insisted upon going with him there and remaining outside; Franks emerged, face blazing, to find everyone in the first-class section staring at him. Before the London arrival every one of the flight crew had come out to look, and the captain asked if everything was all right. Waldo said it was fine.

The London arrival was similar. The Americans had enlisted embassy police and immigration help and Franks was led off ahead of all the other passengers, through side corridors to a small office where the formalities were completed; when he emerged to the waiting line of cars assembled in a strictly no-waiting area, Franks saw that their luggage was already loaded.

"This is bloody ridiculous!" he protested as the car picked up the motorway for the trip into London.

"I think so, too," said Waldo, who was sitting in the front. "I don't think you should have been allowed to come."

"That wasn't what I meant and you know it!" said Franks, further angered. "And who the hell could say if I'd be *allowed* or not!"

"We could, Mr. Franks," said Schultz. "You're a material witness in a major crime trial."

"A material witness," said Franks. "Not a bloody criminal! Did you see what it was like on that plane?"

"We didn't enjoy it any more than you did."

"It was preposterous."

"Do you know something, Mr. Franks? Organized crime has got more control and influence at Kennedy Airport than the New York Port Authority, who is supposed to run it. Already Pascara and Flamini and Dukes know what flight you caught, what seat number you occupied, and probably how much gin you drank on the way over," said Waldo.

"Am I supposed to be impressed?" said Franks.

"No," said Schultz. "You're supposed to understand why we imposed the sort of cover on you that we did."

"That was New York," said Franks. "This is England."

"Where we're still going to be as careful as we think is necessary," said Waldo. "Before we came here today our embassy had several discussions with the Home Office. The British have assigned members of the antiterrorist police as additional backup."

Franks twisted in his seat and saw two cars in tight formation behind them. He slumped back in his corner of the vehicle, trying to control the anger, because he knew it was pointless. It

201

was still difficult. They should have given him some indication of what it was going to be like, not waited for him to be paraded like some freak. It was fortunate that Tina hadn't come with him. It had been difficult to judge this morning, but his impression had been that Tina and Maria were maintaining the truce of the previous night's dinner. It *was* a good thing that Maria was there, beyond the obvious advantage of companionship while he was away. Maria had adjusted more quickly and far better than Tina to the constant surveillance. It bothered her, but not to the degree of paranoia that Tina seemed to be developing. Franks wondered what Maria had meant by the personal difficulties that she and Nicky had experienced. Perhaps it was better that he didn't wonder; didn't think of her at all.

Franks had designated the Dorchester, where the precautions continued. He entered through a side door, bypassed the reception completely, and found a man already in position outside the door of his suite. It was a corner set of rooms, which meant there was only one adjoining suite. Schultz occupied that, and Waldo's rooms were opposite.

"I don't know what you planned to do about eating," said Waldo. "We'd like you to use room service."

At least the man appeared to be asking rather than insisting, thought Franks. He said, "Do you actually think I want the embarrassment of being the performing bear in a restaurant?" He still wasn't hungry, anyway. He called room service, though, and made arrangements for a mobile bar to be installed. He saw Waldo and Schultz exchange looks and he thought, fuck them.

As soon as he unpacked, Franks made contact with his London offices, arranging meetings with the managers the following day. He then telephoned the accountants and lawyers who held the nonvoting directorships of his companies. He'd warned them of his arrival, and found they were all waiting; seeing no purpose in delaying, he arranged a conference for that afternoon. Still with time to spare before the meeting, he called David's and Gabby's schools. The headmaster and headmistress both agreed to the appointments he suggested.

All his arrangements made, Franks poured himself a drink and sat back, feeling more contented than he had for a long time. It was because he was working again, he knew at once; involved in some positive activity instead of atrophying in a prisonlike house. He looked down at his reminder pad, upon which the school appointments were the last listing. How long *would* it be before everything was finally settled and he could get rid of all the nonsense? Maria and Tina's question, as well as his. Still unanswerable. Not more than months, Franks decided positively. He didn't give a damn what the FBI or Rosenberg or Ronan said or thought, he wasn't going to go on like this for more than a few months. Already it was doing things he didn't want to the kids and to Tina and to himself. Only temporary, he reassured himself. Everything would sort itself out once things became normal again.

Although he hadn't slept at all on the plane, Franks didn't feel any jet lag. He showered and changed and was actually making for the door when he remembered the man outside and supposed he should tell Waldo and Schultz. He telephoned both their rooms and they insisted on going with him, which meant he had to wait fifteen minutes. He had another drink to fill in the time.

The companies' main office was a tower block bordering the Thames, with a view of the river on one side and the City and St. Paul's Cathedral from the other. Franks had meant to be there ahead of everyone else, but once the agents were ready the traffic was bad, and two of the six directors were already waiting. The Americans came right to the door of the conference room with him and arranged themselves on chairs directly outside. The two waiting directors, James Podmore, who was a City solicitor, and William Hunter, a lawyer, looked curiously from Franks to the FBI agents and then back again.

"Sorry I'm late," apologized Franks, coloring with embarrassment. Responding to their curiosity, he said, "It's a long and rather unfortunate story. I think we'd better wait until the others get here."

They arrived almost at once. Anthony Dore was an accountant who sat with Podmore on the boards of the French and Italian companies. Nigel Kenham—who, with Hunter, sat on three boards—was a solicitor and the overall company secretary whom Franks had instructed to make the Swiss arrangements. Donald Wise and Thomas Phillips were, respectively, an accountant and a solicitor, who completed the necessary nonvoting directorships. Franks greeted them individually. They were all staid, respectable professional men, chosen specifically for that reason, the necessarily solid balance to his own entrepreneurial attitude. They were going to be shocked, Franks decided. For the first time he wondered if what he was going to tell them would make them unwilling to continue with him.

To the men who came after him, Franks said, "You saw those two men outside, when you came in?"

Kenham, who was plump—although not as fat as Waldo—wore glasses and looked owlish because of them, said, "Who were they?"

"FBI," announced Franks. He'd spent weeks sneering at theatricality and was now indulging in it himself, he thought.

"What?" said Dore.

Indicating Podmore and Hunter, Franks said, "I've already referred to it as a long story." He paused. "And an unfortunate one. Just how unfortunate I fully intend to explain to you. I'm going to need your help and support. For how long I don't know."

Franks sat back, preparing the account in his mind. It was going to take a long time, he realized; he wished he'd thought of arranging some drinks. It was too late now. Franks didn't spare himself, didn't try to make himself appear less naive and foolish in the eyes of a group of men who checked everything a dozen different ways and then started all over again. He withheld only one thing—the reason, which he'd confessed to no one except Rosenberg in New York, exactly *why* he'd gone along with it. Knowing there had to be an explanation, he said it was because he'd implicitly—he now realized stupidly—trusted Nicky, because of the relationship between them. At the beginning of his speech there had been shifts and movements from the assembled group—Hunter and Phillips actually started making notes—but very quickly it all stopped; they sat regarding him with expressions that Franks decided went through the whole gamut from disbelief to astonishment to amazement to horror. The varying expressions remained when he finished. For a long time the stillness stayed, too.

It was Dore—astonished—who spoke first. "Good God!" he managed.

"This man was shot down—killed—because of what he knew!" said the horrified Hunter.

"That's not going to be one of the charges, but yes, unquestionably so."

Wise—disbelieving—said, "But you're going to give evidence against them!"

"Which is why those two men are waiting outside the door," said Franks. "It's very embarrassing—almost laughably so—but they insist it's necessary. It's something I've got to endure."

The reactions were subsiding and they were becoming the professional men again. "As a board—in fact as a composite of several boards—I think we should try to think beyond the immediate personal and embarrassing difficulties of our controlling chairman and managing director," said Podmore. "I think we should consider the possible repercussions of all this upon the companies when it becomes more public than it already has."

"I've already tried to anticipate that," said Franks at once. Indicating Kenham he told them of his instructions to create the Swiss and Liechtenstein holding companies, effectively to remove his name from the shareholders' register in London and in Spain, France and Italy, aware as he concluded that Podmore was shaking his head.

"The City doesn't like shell companies and nominee holdings," said the lawyer.

"The City is full of them!" Franks had anticipated the argument. "Any hesitation in any case is over investments. I'm not—we're not—seeking investment. The only confidence we've got to maintain and worry about is that of the people who book our holidays and our villas and our cruises. As far as they are concerned, I will no longer be involved."

"How long will you have to remain under this rather peculiar protection program before you can expect properly and fully to resume control?" asked Wise.

Franks paused. "The protection program isn't particularly peculiar," he said. "A similar system has been in operation for some years now involving witnesses and events in Northern Ireland."

"They're called supergrasses," said the persistent Podmore. "They're criminals who've chosen to give evidence against their former criminal colleagues to avoid prosecution themselves."

Franks sighed, supposing he should have expected the suspicion. "I've made it quite clear to you—honestly clear to you—how my involvement arose. Just as I've made it quite clear that I faced prosecution. We have been involved for many years now. Professionally involved. You've had those many years to come to know me. I hope you do, all of you. I know of some of the publicity in the past: the stupidity about being a pirate and a high flier. And you know how that was not ever—has not ever—been the case. At most I might be guilty—if in fact it is a crime—of being unconventional. But behind that unconventionality you all know, every one of you, how I have worked. The manner in which I've worked. And the honesty with which I've worked. I have been stupid, a fool. I've already made that abundantly clear, in what I've said—but I am not nor have I ever been a crook."

205

There was another period of silence in the room as each man considered.

Podmore said, "It is not us you have to convince, is it?"

"Oh yes, it is!" said Franks at once. "You, most importantly. There are going to be several months when—although there'll be some telephone contact between us—you will effectively be running the companies. That's what I meant about seeking your support."

"Is that how long it will be?" asked Wise. "Months?"

"That's all I intend it to be," said Franks.

"Will you be the one to decide?" said Phillips.

"The interest of the authorities is in the grand jury hearings and the trial," said Franks. "I don't consider the need for protection will remain long after that."

"What happens if you are assassinated?" Hunter asked. He smiled, embarrassed. "I know it sounds ridiculous, but from what we've heard today it isn't. If the holding company is formulated in Switzerland and then established in Liechtenstein—and you were to die—what access would we have? We'd have legal responsibilities to discharge. We couldn't discharge them if we couldn't find out where the parent was."

It was a good point and one he hadn't considered, realized Franks. He said at once, "There will be a properly drawn agreement—copies of which will be deposited with each company secretary, as well as the establishing lawyer in Switzerland—ordering that all the details should be made available to you for the disposal or any other action necessary involving the companies in the event of my death."

"It's still all extremely irregular and unusual," objected the doubtful Podmore. "I'm not sure that I like it—like it at all."

"Mr. Podmore," said Franks, curbing his irritation. "Let me assure you that I like it a damned sight less. I'm caught up in a situation I'm still not sure I completely understand. What I'm doing here today—and what I'm going to be doing in the subsequent days—is to salvage and sustain something, a great deal, in fact, from an unfortunate and regrettable situation. A situation which is causing me—and I'm sure will continue to cause me—very great embarrassment."

"I can't understand how you allowed it to occur in the first place," said Phillips.

"Neither can I, not now," said Franks. "The approaches I had in New York seemed very good at the time. The best—and obvious—ones to take. All I can say—utterly inadequate though I

206

know it to be—is that I'm sorry." There was a time, he thought, not so very long ago, when to have made such an abject admission would have been difficult for him. It didn't seem to be, not any longer.

"I don't think the confidence of our customers is the only ˿sideration," said Kenham. "What about our suppliers? I ˾w there's not a lot—not like, for instance, a service industry as such—but we're involved with office staff and airlines and printers and tourist organizations in other countries. What if they start to withdraw because of any nervousness in becoming associated with some sort of crime syndicate?"

"We get other suppliers," said Franks.

"Just like that?" said Kenham.

"What other way is there?"

"Normally, quite a few," agreed the solicitor. "In this case I don't think there would be."

"There are always suppliers, for a price," said Franks.

"Which we're prepared to pay?" demanded Podmore, alert to everything.

"Which *I'm* prepared to pay," said Franks. "I remain the controlling shareholder, don't forget."

"You've got your wife's vote, recording that?" said Phillips.

Thank God he'd remembered it, thought Franks; he hadn't expected an easy meeting but he hadn't quite imagined such obvious opposition, either. From his briefcase he produced the notarized proxy. He offered it first to Phillips, the questioner, and there was another gap in the discussion while it was passed around the table and each man—none willing to trust the examination of his partner—steadily read through everything to ensure that it was satisfactory. Franks waited until the proxy had gone completely around the table and then demanded, careless of showing his irritation, "Well?"

"It seems to be in order," said Phillips.

"Of course it's in order," said Franks, still irritated. "Just as it will be in order to pay higher prices to alternative suppliers if those that already exist withdraw. The essential exercise now— the essential, vital necessity—is to protect what is after all the major part of our business. . . ." When nobody responded, Franks said, "And that is why I've summoned this conference here today. I repeat: I'm seeking your support. Now!" He was pleading again, Franks realized, unconcerned.

Once more silence settled upon the room, each of the gathered directors looking around, but each appearing reluctant actu-

207

ally to meet another's gaze. It was Podmore, the perpetual doubter, who spoke first. The solicitor said, "I take completely the point that has been so eloquently made by our chairman and managing director: of his unblemished character and reputation in every dealing with me, from the moment of our first association. While it has a direct and important bearing upon the affairs of the various companies with which we are professionally associated, what occurred in the Bahamas and in Bermuda *did* occur with separate, completely unconnected companies, apart from the extremely peripheral linkup between the hotels and the visiting of the cruise ship. . . ."

Got them! thought Franks, acknowledging for the first time how uncertain he had become during the meeting. Podmore was the overcautious obstacle. Once he committed himself—which was what he was doing now—the rest would obediently follow, like sheep after the bellwether.

"I therefore propose a motion in complete support of our chairman and managing director," continued Podmore. He stopped, not for agreement from the others but to reinforce his next point; it came to Franks like a punch. "But not unconditionally," went on Podmore. "Professionally I—all of us—have an obligation to work for the good of the companies. I do not think we can work in that capacity for an indeterminate time. I am prepared to agree to everything that has been suggested here today on the condition that it is for a period not exceeding six months from the date of this meeting. And further, that company managers are elevated— not necessarily in any voting capacity—onto the reconstituted boards of the operating companies to enable us properly to monitor the week by week, month by month, working of those companies. I will only agree to continue on those understandings; understandings which guarantee a complete and open scrutiny of each and every company if in the opinion of any of their working boards such scrutiny becomes necessary."

The bastard didn't believe him, Franks realized at once. All the crap about unblemished character and reputation was exactly that: so much crap. Franks worked at controlling himself. Podmore was a man who existed within the square mile of the city of London and who depended upon his own reputation within that stiflingly enclosed environment remaining absolutely unquestioned. Considering it objectively—which it was essential that he do— Podmore was merely suggesting insurance to protect that reputation. It would be wrong to become annoyed—offended even—at a man doing in effect no more than he was attempting to do

208

himself. He couldn't argue against anything except the time limit, but he had to argue with that. Franks waited, too experienced a negotiator to rush in with offers and arguments before he'd heard all the opinions.

"I think those observations have a lot to commend them," said Hunter. At once Phillips and Wise nodded agreement. "I think so, too," said the first man, and the second added, "My feelings, exactly."

Kenham refused to commit himself, for the same reason as Franks. The solicitor said, "I'd like to hear the reaction from our chairman and managing director."

Shit, thought Franks. He said, "The reason I've come back here today"—he gestured beyond the doors, to where Waldo and Schultz were waiting—"at considerable awkwardness and inconvenience is, as I've already attempted to make clear, to protect what is controlled from here and what exists in Spain and France and in Italy and in the Caribbean, with the cruise ship. If it is the feeling of these assembled boards that such protection is best provided by what Podmore has suggested—and I acknowledge and commend the sound business logic of those suggestions—then of course I would agree to them. Agree to them formally, upon a properly recorded vote and with the proxy of my wife committed also."

"It would seem that there is no disagreement among us, then?" said Kenham. "I'm personally in favor of Podmore's proposals."

"I hadn't finished the point I was making," said Franks quietly.

There had been a discernible relaxation in the room, but now the six men came abruptly back to him. "What?" demanded Podmore, the leader.

"The time limit," said Franks. "I agree entirely that I cannot expect you to carry on with the arrangement I have suggested today for an indeterminate time. I never intended that it should be for an unlimited period; that would have been unrealistic. Equally, I think it is unrealistic for you, today, to expect me to commit myself to a schedule as *tight* as six months from today's date. I've told you I have to appear before a grand jury. After that there has to be a trial. And the protection in the immediate aftermath that I've already spoken to you about."

"How long?" insisted Podmore. "I will not agree to anything open-ended."

Franks realized he'd been backed into a corner, with little

room to maneuver or escape. He said, "Six months from the conclusion of the trial."

The men all deferred to Podmore, the emerging leader and spokesman. Podmore said, "I had a further point to make, as well."

"What?" asked Franks apprehensively.

"Although they are not public, the companies have public responsibilities. There are a great number of employees, both English and foreign nationals. There is the crew of the cruise liner. Our contracted suppliers, to which reference has already been made. And the many thousands of holiday makers and tourists who have relied upon us in the past and rely upon us for the future."

"What's the point?" pressed Franks. The damned man was posturing, playing to a suddenly unexpected audience.

"That any agreement we reach today allows the newly constituted boards to offer the companies to public subscription and public directorship to continue their running and the obligations that I believe all of us recognize."

Franks knew the visual impression was a misleading one, but the grouping around the conference table made it appear to him that he was alone, confronting an opposing force led by Podmore. The response came to him automatically—instinctively— because it was in direct contradiction to the basic principle by which he'd always worked. It took a great effort of will to hold back the rejection, but he managed it. Instead he said, his voice surprisingly even, "You, all of you, know how I feel about opening the companies to any sort of public subscription or involvement." He paused and added bitterly, "And after the American experience, I feel that way even more strongly. I can, however, see and appreciate the argument that is being advanced. I have a question. What would your reaction be if I refused the condition of going public, as I have always refused it in the past?"

It was a demand to all of them but Franks spoke directly to Podmore.

"We are hypothesizing extremes," said Podmore. "Your demise—which all of us here obviously and sincerely hope doesn't occur—or your inability to return here to pick up the running of the companies. We've already decided upon a formula for access to their affairs in the event of your assassination. Without you, the companies would *have* to go public, to ensure their continuance. Just as they would if you were unable, for whatever reason,

210

to come back here. I imposed a time limit—and concede it from the conclusion of the trial—because I am not prepared to make the commitment necessary for me to be involved in the full-time running of the companies in your absence. You insist upon private companies; I don't. Unless we have an agreement here today, including the public offering, then I do not consider myself able to continue in the directorial capacity that I hold. I would today have to tender my resignation, from each and every company.''

Bastard, thought Franks again. With the controlling shareholding provided by Tina's proxy he didn't need any of their agreements to form the holding company and do what he intended to do. But he did need them—desperately needed them—to continue running the companies in his absence. There had to be board control over the managers, and there wasn't anyone else who understood the companies like these men did. And they knew it; at least Podmore did. Franks said, ''We've had the benefit of Podmore's views. What about the rest of the directors?''

''We're considering an unusual situation,'' said Kenham. ''Bizarre. I don't think I'd be prepared to continue without the agreements that Podmore has set out.''

''Or me,'' came in Hunter.

''I think they're precautions we've got to take,'' said Dore.

''The last thing we can sustain—if we can even sustain what's going to happen when the American situation becomes public—is split boards,'' said Phillips. ''I agree with the rest.''

''So do I,'' concluded Wise.

He was trapped, Franks realized, desperation churning through him. Just like he'd been trapped by the FBI investigation and then by the ultimatum presented by the district attorney. Which was exactly what it was: an ultimatum, not a choice. All he wanted was a fucking choice that didn't involve him risking everything! He might have promised Tina that he intended to get out—maintain only a token presence—when everything had been resolved, but he'd wanted it to be on his terms; in his way. Not dismissed by these grey-suited, grey-faced, grey-existing upstart clerks whose biggest risk was trying a second glass of punch at the office Christmas party. Jesus, he'd have liked a drink of his own! Franks determined against letting them see how bitterly he felt their insistence. He said, his voice still controlled and even, ''I repeat once more what I've already made clear: the continuance of the companies is of paramount importance. For me to agree to what you've demanded amounts to a concession. I feel justified, then, in seeking undertakings from each of you. We've already talked of the period when I am going to be absent. My managers and their managers run efficient enterprises; if they didn't, they wouldn't be my managers. But I've always—until the last few moments—insisted on the tightest final control; not interference. Control. I am aware of your other interests. I would ask you today to enter with me into the same sort of contractual agreement you are seeking from me—written, binding contracts— that for the period under discussion you are prepared to relegate your other interests so that these companies can become your primary consideration.''

It didn't amount to much of a demand; it was the sort of posturing of which he'd earlier considered Podmore guilty. But it would be something, if they agreed. And he *did* want the tight control to be retained in his absence.

"We're salaried directors," reminded Podmore quietly.

The man *was* a bastard, decided Franks. When he was back in control he'd sack the man and replace him with somebody who didn't peck and pull like some vulture trying to strip clean a carcass. "Ten percent of whatever increase is shown over the previous year's comparable period," he said, in further unavoidable concession.

"I'm prepared to enter into such an undertaking on that condition," accepted Podmore at once, which further upset Franks; the quickness indicated that the man would have done it for less. There was a follow-my-leader acceptance from everyone else in the room.

Headed by Kenham in his role as company secretary, the four lawyers drew up the provisional documentation for immediate agreement while they sat in the conference room, and when Franks gave that, they promised the properly prepared contracts within two days. Franks realized it would mean his having to return from Switzerland to London on his way back to America, but did not consider that a major detour. After he'd initialed the draft agreements, Podmore said, "How are we going to be able to get into contact with you?"

Franks nodded toward the head-bent Kenham. "He's made the Swiss arrangements. He's got all the details. . . ." He hesitated as the thought came to him. "And you will have the name of my attorney in New York," he added. Would it have been an idea to bring Rosenberg with him? The idea hadn't occurred until now, but Franks wished he'd thought of it earlier. He didn't know how Rosenberg would have confronted the demands—

212

there wasn't anything with which he could logically have resisted them—but Franks would have liked to have had someone on his side. He'd expected more support from Kenham. Why was it—in practically everything he did—he felt increasingly isolated?

Franks made an appointment to see Kenham after the meeting the following day with the managers, and the six men assured him they would be immediately available upon his return from Switzerland.

It was already dark when Franks emerged once more into the embarrassing protective custody of Waldo and Schultz. Franks realized he'd kept the FBI men waiting for more than four hours, and although he knew the feeling to be juvenile Franks hoped they were annoyed at the length of time. Neither gave any indication of being so.

By the time Franks reached the hotel he was at last feeling the tiredness of the journey, so he would have eaten in his rooms anyway. He delayed ordering, first putting in a call to Tina. He asked her how she was, and she said fine and asked him how he was, and he said fine and asked her how the children were, and she said fine. Franks hesitated and decided it would appear strange if he didn't mention Maria, so he asked how things were working out with her and Tina said that was fine, too. He told her that he'd met the nonvoting directors, and she asked how it had gone, and Franks hesitated once more. The honest answer was that it had gone badly, but there was no point in her knowing that, not yet.

"There have had to be some changes in the arrangements," he said.

"Like what?"

"Provisions for them to run things more actively when I'm unable to," said Franks. They were hardly nonvoting directors anymore, he thought. Damn them!

"You don't intend to be as active in any case," said Tina, seizing an immediate point. "That's what you've promised. So the changes would have had to be made."

"You're right," conceded Franks, too weary to get into any sort of dispute. Podmore was definitely a change that was going to be made, he thought.

"So everything's all right, then?" she pressed.

"Sure. Everything's fine." Except for a guard outside in the corridor and another next door and another opposite and a contingent of antiterrorist police God knows where, and a perpetual feeling of being a criminal. Franks supposed he should tell her of

213

his appointments with the schools but couldn't be bothered. Better to wait until after the meetings, when he'd have something positive to talk about. He gave her his suite number in case she needed to contact him, and promised to call again, and put the telephone down gratefully.

Franks poured another drink, looked at the menu, and decided he wasn't really hungry. When was the last time he'd eaten? Last night, with Tina and Maria. It was too much trouble to calculate in hours just when that had been. What would Maria be doing now? He frowned, concentrating more fully on the menu. Hungry or not, he should eat something. He decided, disinterested, upon steak, paying more attention to the wine list. He picked at the meal and drank the wine and when he went to bed he slept the deep sleep of drunken exhaustion.

Waldo and Schultz were waiting for his call the following morning. Franks emerged from the hotel, blinking in the strong sunlight, regretting the previous day's intake and hoping the headache would soon go. He was sure it wasn't just the booze; there was the jet lag to consider, too. They'd conceded to his demands about the hotel; he should have insisted upon the Concorde as well.

There was a following car and Waldo was as attentive as ever, gazing around, never still. As he looked from the front seat into the rear of the vehicle the American said, "I know, Mr. Franks, that you consider all this to be a fatuous waste of time, but do you really think it was such a good idea to give your wife your room number? She knew the hotel, didn't she?"

"You listened to my call?" demanded Franks, outraged.

"I told you we were going to be as careful as we considered necessary," said Waldo. "I suggested it to the British, because it's their responsibility, and they agreed."

Franks came forward on his seat, so that he was very close to the FBI man. "Stop it!" he insisted, red-faced with anger. "I want an assurance—not from you but from Ronan himself—that I will not be spied upon. I *will* not continue any sort of cooperation— any sort whatsoever—unless I have his assurance that I'm going to be properly treated. You got that?"

"It's my job to protect you," said Waldo. "You got that?"

Franks wanted to hit the man, to knock the supercilious expression off his face. "As a material witness," he said, remembering the previous day's dispute. "Everything will already have been started by now against Pascara and Flamini and Dukes. And without me, you haven't got a case. That's why you *are* protecting me. Stop the spying or I withdraw. Your choice."

214

Waldo seemed unmoved, but Franks was sure Schultz shifted in his seat, worried by the threat.

"We're doing our job, Mr. Franks," argued Waldo.

"You're overdoing your job," said Franks. "Any listening device will be removed from my hotel telephone before I return, today." And he knew a way to guarantee it, Franks decided.

He allowed them to escort him to the conference room, as they had the previous day, and as they had the previous day Waldo and Schultz settled themselves outside the room. Inside Franks used the internal telephone to delay the managers' meeting by fifteen minutes and then called Rosenberg, in New York, glad of the man's home telephone number and careless of waking him because of the time difference. He was surprised that the American lawyer did not regard it as much of an intrusion.

"They're just nervous, that's all," said Rosenberg sleepily.

"I'm not," said Franks. "I want you to get on to Ronan and tell him. I'm being treated like shit instead of someone who's helping them. If the tap doesn't come off, then everything else is off—literally—as far as I am concerned. Tell him that."

"What if they revert to the prosecution of you?"

It would mean there would be no immediate grand jury hearing—not against Pascara or anyone else at least—and so the six-month time limit to which he'd agreed yesterday wouldn't apply. But Podmore and those who'd followed him had realized their strength; they'd insist upon six months from some other starting point, if they agreed to remain at all with an actual prosecution against him. Fuck it! thought Franks. He'd got away with the bluff once and he could get away with it again. "We know now how their evidence ties in with the file Nicky left, how it points toward my innocence. If they want to prosecute me, then let them go ahead and lose everything."

"I'll tell him," promised Rosenberg, fully awake now. "How's it going there?"

"Could be better," said Franks.

"Big problems?" asked the lawyer.

"Nothing I can't solve," said Franks. I hope, he thought.

"Call if you think I can help."

Franks thought again how much he would have liked the man alongside him the previous day. "I will," he said.

Franks was still hot with annoyance over the tap, but he tried to put the attitude aside for his meeting with the managers and their immediate subordinates. It was easier than the previous day, but Franks still felt uncomfortable. Franks rigidly main-

215

tained the employer-to-employee relationship and this time greatly abbreviated the circumstances of his entrapment, not wanting to diminish himself in their eyes. He devoted more discussion to the company changes, announcing the elevation of the managers to their respective boards and offering his congratulations. Remembering his promise to Tina—and her reminder the previous night—he said that although much of what he had talked about was temporary, their appointment would not be. Determined to prove that he was still absolutely in control and wanting to show it to the awkward bastards who'd backed him into a corner, he said further that their directors' fees would be five thousand pounds a year but that there would be additional emoluments representing a commission based upon five percent of whatever increase was shown over the previous year's trading. The decision would irritate Podmore and the others, but there was not a damned thing they would be able to do to reverse it.

The managers' meeting went on longer than he had anticipated because of the salary increases upon which he'd suddenly decided, which meant the second meeting with Kenham was delayed. Franks welcomed the delay and then indulged himself, actually protracting it. He had never used his office in the building regularly. It was simply a place to be—like a bus shelter was a place to wait for a bus—when he was required to work from the company building. Which hadn't been often because of his constant involvement in setting up the new enterprises. But the office was there, actually adjoining the conference chamber. Franks was surprised—worried, because it was so inexplicable—that it hadn't occurred to him to go into it the previous day, but now he did. It was a reasonably expansive room—although, he remembered, not as flamboyant as Nicky's; but he felt no association or even attachment to it. A plush bus shelter. It was dusted and neat. He sat in the chair—again not as high-backed or chariotlike as Nicky's—and swiveled left and right and tried to feel some attachment. Nothing came. Deciding he could do with a drink, Franks looked around the room and realized there wasn't a refrigerator or hospitality bar. Had he needed to look around— this theatricality was becoming ridiculous as well as infectious—to realize that? It was his office, for Christ's sake. He'd approved the fittings and the design and he knew damned well he hadn't decreed any sort of booze cabinet. So why was he looking for one now?

Remembering the headachy legacy from last night, Franks welcomed the way he was feeling now. The discomfort had gone

216

and the meeting with the impressed managers—maybe wrongly impressed but nevertheless impressed, some even unashamedly open-mouthed—gave Franks a renewed feeling of confidence. He'd needed—looked for—that sort of confidence for weeks. He realized further that despite every attempt at self-analysis, until now he hadn't been prepared to accept something that was essential to his survival. So much had happened so quickly—at least something he'd already accepted—that his personal confidence was gone. The awareness worried him; he'd lost too much—how much he didn't yet know—to lose that. Everything he had achieved had been because of his own unshakable, unassailable confidence. If he couldn't sustain the belief in himself, then he couldn't sustain anything. Franks sat at the unaccustomed desk, surveyed the unaccustomed office, and was glad he'd come here because the visit crystallized more empty apprehensions and more positive realities than he'd so far been able—or prepared—to confront. He'd fight, because he was a fighter. A survivor, like his father. In fights people sometimes got beaten—a misstep or a misjudgment—but the champion was the person who recovered from those mistakes to go on to win. He was going to go on to win; to win against the bastards who thought they could manipulate him in America and the bastards who thought they could manipulate him in England. He looked again, reluctantly, around the office, wishing he'd installed some sort of hospitality arrangement; winning was going to be better than the best drink he'd ever imagined.

Franks summoned Kenham at last, remaining behind his desk and not bothering with anything but the most perfunctory greeting when the lawyer entered. His association with the business professionals who comprised his boards had never become social—not that they had a particularly social life—but of them all Franks had hoped there might have been something different between himself and Kenham. The owlish lawyer had been a junior partner to a financial solicitor who had been one of the men with whom his father had forged wartime links, and Kenham had been the man whom his father—and then, very quickly Franks—had drawn forward after the original friend died. Because of their support, Kenham had progressed to other City positions, and Franks felt he could have expected better support from the man than had been evident the previous day.

Kenham entered blink-eyed like the owl he resembled, briefcase before him as a shield. Franks nodded him toward a chair and Kenham sat, smiling hopefully. Franks thought, asshole, and didn't bother to respond. Resisting any immediate attack about the previous day, Franks said, "You've made the Swiss arrangements?"

Kenham nodded hopefully—an owl isolating an unsuspecting mouse, thought Franks—and said, "Everything's fixed; waiting for you."

Without the support of the others, Kenham's demeanor was very different, Franks decided. Double bastard, he thought. "What are the details?"

Kenham went into the briefcase and produced a file. "Everything's there," he said, offering it across the desk.

Franks let it lie, refusing the man his escape, conscious as he did so that it wasn't just to recover from what had happened earlier but to reimpose his own superiority—as he'd reimposed it that morning with the managers—to recover his own flaked confidence. He said, "Set it out for me."

Kenham smiled again, hopefully. "The establishment is being created by Maitre Francois Dulac. He's got chambers at Limmatstresse. Number thirty-nine. I've arranged for your private bank account to be transferred to Zurich, too. To the Swiss Banking Corporation on the Paradeplatz." The lawyer gestured toward the unopened file. "The correspondence there will accord with mine to them. Provide the introduction. They'll need passport identification, in addition. It's part of the protection, of course, that I don't know what Dulac will have arranged in the transfer company, in Liechtenstein."

Conscious of the previous day's arrangements, Franks said, "When I'm in Switzerland I shall assign authority for Dulac to advise you in the event of anything happening to me."

"I was going to remind you of the necessity," said the lawyer.

"There's no need," said Franks.

"There wasn't the opportunity for me to express it yesterday, but I'd like to say how much I regret what's happened to you. On a personal basis, I mean. And to say that I'm sure everything is going to resolve itself, black though it may look at the moment."

"Why didn't you say so?" queried Franks at once.

"I just did," said Kenham.

"*Now*," said Franks. "I don't remember any sympathy—any particular support even—in yesterday's meeting."

"You've got everybody's sympathy," insisted Kenham. "But Podmore was quite correct about our responsibilities. None of us could have done anything differently than we did yesterday."

Liar, thought Franks. When the time came—how much he hoped it would come quickly!—he'd dump Kenham as well as Podmore. When the time came he might even dump the bloody lot for the way they'd treated him. Bastards, he thought again. He said, "Don't write me off. Don't imagine—don't any of you imagine—that because of what happened yesterday these businesses are going to slip away from me." It sounded like another defense, he thought.

"No one imagines that," assured Kenham.

The man would tittle-tattle back to the others, Franks knew; he was uncertain whether to disclose that morning's decision to increase the newly elevated director-managers' salaries. Better left until it was utterly irrevocable; so soon it might still be reversed. He would be denied Kenham's reaction, which he regretted. But then Franks realized that he was committed to return, to sign officially the formal documents. By then they'd know what had happened; all of them, not just Kenham. Far better to wait, to savor the irritation of them all. Franks said, "Thank you for setting everything up as efficiently as you have."

"It's my job," said Kenham.

Enjoy it while you've got it, thought Franks. "I still appreciate it," he said.

"I don't envy you," said the solicitor. "In fact, I can't actually imagine what it's like."

"It's not very pleasant," said Franks. "In fact, it's bloody awful."

"If there's anything further that I can do," offered Kenham, "all you have to do is call."

He'd rather trust Rosenberg, Franks decided. He said, "Thank you, yet again."

"*Is* there anything further?"

Franks said, "Only that I want the remaining companies run as efficiently and as well as possible until I get back." Franks decided at that moment that he *would* replace the boards of all the companies; bring in fresh men with fresh ideas and stronger degrees of loyalty. He didn't want to leave Kenham or any of them even as caretakers, although he decided caretakers was a function for which they were ideally suited; church hall caretakers.

Kenham rose, anxious to get away. "We'll meet again when you get back from Switzerland, then?"

Reluctantly, on his part, thought Franks. He said, "Yes. It should only take a day."

"Everything is arranged," repeated Kenham nervously. "There shouldn't be any problems."

"I'm sure there won't."

After the company secretary had left the room, Franks still didn't move. There were staff—personal secretaries even—whom he hadn't greeted, let alone spoken to properly. But if he spoke to them he would have to provide some sort of explanation, and although he thought the FBI was overacting he conceded that to make some sort of general staff announcement would be foolish. It was fortunate that because of the way he worked, he hadn't forged any close staff relationships.

Franks enjoyed emerging from a door that neither Waldo nor Schultz expected, smiling openly at their momentary confusion. Franks supposed by now Rosenberg would have been in contact with the New York district attorney. How would Ronan communicate with the two irritated men approaching him now? They'd be even angrier when it happened.

"You trying to make our job more difficult than it already is, Mr. Franks?" attacked Waldo at once.

"Just doing my job," said Franks, throwing their phrase back at them. Franks felt better today than he had for a long time; more in charge and in control of things. At the moment Waldo and Schultz amused him more than they irritated him.

David's school was the next appointment. They arrived early, and suddenly on the enclosed grounds Waldo and Schultz and their backup were the object of attention. Franks felt the embarrassment was shifted from him. The headmaster, whose name was Henderson, came directly from the dining room, still gowned and with his napkin absentmindedly clutched in his hand. The man became aware of it after they entered his study, staring curiously at it and then gazing around, as if unsure whether to put it down somewhere or keep it in his hand. He thrust it into his pocket and smiled the sort of open-faced smile that Franks couldn't remember having seen for a long time, and said, "After luncheon I suppose it's too late—or maybe too early—to offer you a sherry."

"I think it is," said Franks. "But thank you anyway." He was becoming increasingly proud at having gone so far into the day without a drink. Not that it was a problem—he'd decided that a long time ago—but he couldn't deny he'd been drinking more than usual lately. He recalled the looks that had passed between Waldo and Schultz when he'd ordered the bar at the Dorchester and hoped they had noticed. Why did it matter whether they'd noticed or not? Why did *they* matter?

"How's David?" asked Henderson.

Franks wondered what the headmaster's reaction would be to seeing the child posing proudly with a pistol and a pump-action shotgun. He said, "He's very well. But it's obviously about David that I've come to see you."

"Obviously," agreed the headmaster, brushing aside the fronds of some straying grey hair. "I've actually been quite anxious to hear from you. His sudden recall seemed quite dramatic."

"I'm afraid it is," said Franks.

"Oh?" said Henderson, the greeting-parents' smile slipping.

He probably thinks it's a difficulty in paying the fees, thought Franks. He coughed and then launched into what was becoming practically a recorded message, although again he minimized his own faults in the affair. When he started talking about protection Henderson actually swiveled in his creaking chair and stared out through the window at the waiting cars and the ill-at-ease Americans, taking off his half-rimmed glasses and polishing them with the hastily pocketed napkin.

"Good Lord!" said Henderson when Franks had finished. "Astonishing. Absolutely astonishing."

The man would have made the same reaction at an English batsman achieving six in a test match against the West Indians. Franks said, "I want to emphasize that everything is temporary. I have had to take David away for this term and may have to keep him away for a while longer, but I want him to return and continue his education with you. He's extremely happy here and I think he's doing well."

Henderson started polishing his glasses again, a delaying mannerism. "He's a good pupil and someone we've been happy to have here," said Henderson. "Certainly someone whom I and the form masters and his housemaster regarded as a child with promise . . ."

"I'm delighted you feel that way," said Franks.

"But you must understand that I have to balance my genuine feeling for David against my responsibilities to the school as a whole."

"I'm not sure I understand," said Franks, who thought he did.

"I've over four hundred pupils here. I'm responsible for all of them; for their safety as well as for their education," said the headmaster. "For David's sake—for all of your sake—I sincerely hope that the apparent danger to which the American government thinks you are at the moment subjected is as brief as you have explained to me. I hope—even more sincerely—that however long the period is, that David, at the impressionable age that he is, can withstand it without any prolonged psychological difficulty. . . ."

"I'm sure he can," intruded Franks.

"Knowing the boy, I'm inclined to agree with you. I certainly hope he can," picked up Henderson. "But that's really not the nub of what I'm trying to say, Mr. Franks. I'm not at all sure that I can give you the undertaking here today that there would still be a place at the school for David if there was the risk of any physical assault . . . anything of the like that you've set out to me this afternoon. Of course I would do it for David, if David were the only child involved in my decision. But what about the other four hundred boys and the parents of those other four hundred boys? Let me ask you something. How would you feel if you knew that a school to which you'd entrusted David's safety as well as his education had knowingly accepted a child liable to goodness-knows-what—kidnapping or physical attack—from which your son might be the inadvertent sufferer? Would you be prepared to accept that risk and leave David here? That's what you're asking me to do. You're asking me to put at risk the entire safety and reputation of the school. Isn't that so?"

"No!" protested Franks. "I said I wouldn't consider asking you to accept David—wouldn't consider sending him back to you—unless I was absolutely and utterly convinced of his personal safety. And if his safety is guaranteed, how can that possibly put at risk anyone else in the school?"

"Who's going to give that absolute and utter guarantee, Mr. Franks? Give it to the satisfaction of the parents of my other pupils?"

"What about those other pupils!" demanded Franks suddenly, as the argument came belatedly to him. "I know for a fact that some of them—quite a few—are the children of diplomats attached to embassies in this country. Diplomats and government officials and statesmen in unstable countries, often subjected to coups and uprisings. You have children here now at greater risk—kidnapping was a word you used—than will ever exist for David." Franks guessed that Henderson was wilting and moved to press the advantage. "Isn't that so?" he demanded. "Far greater risk!"

Henderson plucked at the napkin. "I'm not at all sure it's a valid comparison," he said.

"I am," said Franks, gauging the weakening. "It's a direct

222

and valid comparison, which all the other parents—myself until this moment—recognize and accept. . . ." He allowed another pause, and said, "I must be quite honest, Mr. Henderson. I came here today expecting more understanding than I'm so far receiving."

"I'm very sorry that you should feel that way, Mr. Franks," said the headmaster stiffly.

"But I don't consider that my feelings are those that matter," said Franks. "My prime consideration is my son. And continuing the excellent education he has, until now, been able to receive here. I've come to see you today because I considered it was right and proper to do so; because I considered you deserved the explanation."

"And I appreciate the gesture," said Henderson, now completely on the defensive.

"As I would appreciate one from you," picked up Franks at once. It was good to feel dominant in a discussion again, even a discussion with a schoolmaster.

"Do you anticipate a great deal of publicity arising from the matter?"

"I expect some will be inevitable," conceded Franks. "Far more in America than here. But that will be about the crimes being alleged. I do not anticipate any reference to the protection I've spoken about; or why it's considered necessary."

"You understand my concern for the pupils and for the school in general?" persisted Henderson.

"I thought I'd made it clear that I do," said Franks. "Just as I thought I'd made it clear that there will be no cause for that concern when David returns here."

Henderson nodded. "You—and David, of course—have my sympathy, Mr. Franks. I think it is my responsibility to consider both the school and the boy. What I am prepared to do is place the whole matter before the school governors. And I give you my assurance—my absolute assurance—that I will present the arguments that you have put forward today as strongly as possible."

The bloody man had wriggled away, thought Franks. And there was nothing he could do to stop it. He said, "When could I expect a decision?"

Henderson pursed his lips. "A month," he said. "Certainly no longer than six weeks."

Another time limit, thought Franks miserably. "I'll contact you from America," promised Franks. Hastily he added, "Or my lawyer will. A Mr. Rosenberg."

Henderson wrote the name on a jotting pad in front of him

and smiled up, aware of his escape and pleased because of it. "I'm sure everything will work out all right, Mr. Franks. And to David's benefit."

"I hope so," said Franks. "I sincerely hope so."

Franks was far more circumspect at Gabriella's school. He stopped short of actually lying but, cautious from his experience with Henderson, there was a lot he omitted to tell the headmistress, whose name was Tippitt. She was a spinster and fussy and her study smelled strongly of something like lavender or mothballs. He took tea he didn't want, to be polite, and minimized every likely difficulty and embarrassment. He nodded dutifully through what appeared to be the standard lecture about her responsibilities to the school as a whole and assured her that nothing would jeopardize the school, its pupils, or its reputation. The woman ran behind the same barricade as Henderson, insisting she had to put the matter before the school governors, and Franks had to stifle the impotence, knowing there was no way he could argue her around. She even gave him the same time limit as the headmaster.

Back at the hotel suite Franks took the first drink of the day, pleased with his abstinence; to celebrate, he made it a big one. What had he achieved? The meeting with the managers had gone well, but objectively there had been little likelihood of it going any other way. Any more than with Kenham, without the support of the others. Franks had expected to get commitments from both schools, but, maintaining his objectivity, he supposed that had been an unreal hope. He thought he'd argued Henderson around to present a fair case to the governors, but he wasn't so certain about the headmistress. Gabby's was only a prep school, he reassured himself. It wouldn't be the end of the world if they wouldn't take her back. Just irritating. He looked at his watch, calculating the time in America. Was there any point in calling Tina? She'd be interested only in what had happened at the schools, and he didn't have anything positive to tell her about them. She'd ask for his impressions, though, and when he gave them she'd start fighting. Franks decided not to call. She had the number, after all. If she wanted him, she could call.

Franks was at the bar freshening his drink when the sound came at the door. He frowned toward it, starting forward, but it opened before he got there. Waldo was red-faced, in the act of saying something to the following Schultz, which Franks didn't hear. Franks got the impression that Schultz was trying to restrain the fat man but that Waldo wasn't listening.

"Very clever!" erupted Waldo. "Very fucking clever!"

Momentarily Franks didn't understand, his mind still occupied with the other events of the crowded day, and then he remembered the call to Rosenberg. His anger boiled up, to match that of the FBI man. "You want to come into my room, you knock!" he said. "And then you wait! Who the hell do you think you are?"

"I know who I am," said Waldo. "And I know who you are. You've made me the fucking laughingstock of the embassy here."

"You made yourself the laughingstock, Waldo. You arranged the tap on the telephone. And then had to boast about it. Would you have taken it off? Would you?"

Schultz closed the door and stood hesitantly just inside. "Let it go, Harry," he urged his partner. "This isn't going to achieve anything."

Waldo ignored the other American. "No," he admitted, "I wouldn't have taken it off. I'd have kept it on and listened to everything you said because it's my job to do so."

"It's not your job to do so," rejected Franks. "I don't think you've got a job to do here, any of you. I think you're playacting and wasting time. I'm going along with it but only just. And going along with it isn't being treated like you think you can treat me. Understood?"

Waldo came farther into the room, belligerently, and briefly Franks thought the huge man was going to strike him. Instead he stopped, very close, and said, "I want you to understand something! I said I know who you are. And I do. I can smell a crook, and you smell. I know you were in on it. In on everything, right up to your ass. I don't care about any special files; I tracked you and your companies for months and you're as guilty as hell. Okay, so the district attorney chose the path to take and that path lets you off the hook legally. But not as far as I am concerned. I think you should be arraigned with them, with Pascara and Flamini and Dukes." Waldo stopped, gulping air. "You know why I put the tap on? You know why I stick closer to you than shit to a blanket? I think you plan to run. I think this company stuff and school stuff is just so much bullshit. I think you're going to try to run, somewhere, somehow. Let me tell you something. Don't try it. Because you don't stand a chance. Not a fucking chance."

Waldo was standing so close that Franks could actually feel the man's breath as he spat the words out. The American's face

225

was suffused with color, more purple than red, and a vein throbbed in the center of his forehead. Franks' feelings had gone beyond the immediate, instinctive anger and he was glad. Icily calm, his voice very quiet, Franks said, "Get out. Get out of this room. Now! But I want you back here. I want you back here when you've got rid of your hysteria and I want your apology. I told you in the car this morning that the cooperation was off. Then we were just talking about the tap. Now we're talking about you. Any arrangement I made with Ronan is over, right now. I'm not going to deal with a maniac and that's how you're behaving, like a maniac. I'll give you an hour. If you're not back here within an hour then I'm going to call Rosenberg and I'm going to call Ronan and then I'm going to get on a plane out of here— tonight—and your whole fucking case will be around your ankles, where it deserves to be if this is your idea how to work." Franks looked over the man's shoulder, to Schultz. Stretching the contempt, he said, "Get him out! For God's sake get him out of here!"

Waldo was quivering with rage, beyond speech. He started to move forward, toward Franks, but Schultz got beside him, both hands on the man's arm. "Stop it, Harry! For God's sake stop it! He's right; you're behaving like a goddamned maniac!"

A sound came from Waldo, unrecognizable as a word. For several moments he stood rocklike and unmoving, and then, almost appearing unaware of what was happening, he let himself be turned at his partner's urging and led from the room.

When he was pouring at the bar, Franks realized just how much he was shaking. But it hadn't been fear, he decided, pleased. In any physical confrontation he knew full well that Waldo would have beaten him to a pulp, but even when it seemed the man might lash out he hadn't felt frightened. Another awareness came, counteracting Franks' satisfaction. Waldo was wrong and certainly he'd appeared off-balanced, but the FBI man had been convinced of his guilt. How many others, when everything became public, would have a no-smoke-without-fire reaction? He'd been wrong trying to minimize the embarrassment in his meetings with the schoolteachers that afternoon. Franks flushed, hot with a helpless impotence to do anything to make it different. Maybe he deserved to suffer for his stupidity, but he didn't think he deserved to suffer quite this much.

The knock at the door came after thirty minutes and this time there was no barging intrusion. Franks took his time answering. It was Schultz, not Waldo.

226

"Can I come in?" asked the American politely.

"My argument isn't with you," said Franks.

"Please," said Schultz.

Franks hesitated and then moved aside. Schultz entered and then turned back, looking at Franks. Schultz said, "Harry's in a hell of a state. Really bad. I know you wanted it from him but I want to say sorry, instead. He was way out of bounds. He knows it, which makes it worse."

Franks walked back into the room, and said, "Would you like a drink?"

"Yes," smiled Schultz. "Yes, I would. Scotch would be fine."

Franks poured the drink, made another for himself, and said, "What the hell was it all about?"

"It's a personal thing," said Schultz. "I know it shouldn't be—that it never should have happened—but it has. Some damned fool at Washington headquarters thought he had a good idea and assigned Harry to the case, which was a mistake. But Washington doesn't admit its mistakes; although to be fair, there's no way they could know, not unless you start making the sort of waves you set up today with that complaint direct to the district attorney."

"You're not being very clear," said Franks.

"This isn't the first time Harry's gone after Pascara and Flamini," explained Schultz. "He used to work out of the Chicago office. Made a case against them about five years back and didn't get it right. Hurried, I think, because he was up for promotion and saw it as the way to jump a couple of grades. Except that it didn't work out that way. The lawyers blew so many holes in the case it was embarrassing; grand jury threw it out and Harry was the asshole of the year. Promised himself to get even. Kept bothering Washington, to try again. Seems to have convinced them he's some sort of expert on the Flamini and Pascara families. Washington's mistake was in letting him have the second try, because it's become an obsession he can't see around. He was sure he'd made everything watertight this time, not just against those two but against Dukes and you. It was Ronan's idea to offer the deal: make you a witness. Harry argued against it like hell. Ronan said without you they'd probably get off again, which would mean Harry being wrong once more. So he got overruled. Then he got overruled again when Ronan agreed to your coming here. Headquarters has started asking questions about all the fighting between us and the D.A.'s office, and there'll be more questions, because you went direct to Ronan, through your lawyer, today." Schultz gulped at his drink, finishing it. "That's how it is," he said. "I know that doesn't excuse him for what happened in here. But that's how it is."

Schultz accepted a second drink and this time Franks stayed with the one he had. "Let me ask you something," he said.

"What?"

"You worked with him all the time on this?"

"Yes," said Schultz.

"So do you think I'm guilty?" demanded Franks urgently.

"Does what we're talking about now form any part of a conversation you might later have with your lawyer? And he with the district attorney?"

"Of course not!" said Franks. "If it did, I'd deny it."

"I've told you no," said Franks.

"Like Harry, I thought you were as guilty as hell. I couldn't understand why . . . why you had to get involved, I mean. But then, these guys can put the black on someone for a lot of things, so maybe there was pressure. That's what I thought, all the way through the investigation. I guess I still thought it after that first meeting at the Plaza, although maybe I did have some doubts; no, not doubts. Doubts is too strong. Maybe I felt a vague uncertainty. That file you produced was good; dissolving the companies seemed like panic, though."

Rosenberg's caution about the companies' dissolvement, remembered Franks. He said, "You're going up and down, like a seesaw. Do you or do you not—personally—consider that I'm *guilty*?"

"Not anymore," said the FBI man. "Having been with you all the time, seen how you behave, not anymore."

"Not until now!" said Franks, anguished.

"You ever been in an American court, Mr. Franks?"

Franks shook his head. "No."

"I know all about justice," said Schultz. "About men being innocent until proven otherwise. I know about courts; how they're stage-managed and how plea bargaining is done; how deals are made, lesser sentences for lesser charges. If I'd sat on a jury and heard a case made out against you—the sort of case that is made out in court, with a lot of innuendo and a lot of things unsaid that should have been said—then I think I'd have found it difficult to think you were innocent."

Whatever the outcome, he was going to be stigmatized for the rest of his life, Franks thought in stomach-emptying awareness; branded like a medieval criminal, with an identifiable mark

228

on his forehead so that everyone would know who he was and what he had done. Except that he hadn't done anything. He'd said that so many times to himself—as well as to every other accuser—that it was beginning to sound hollow, even to himself. He tried to remember some schoolboy quotation—he thought it was Shakespeare—that said something about somebody protesting too much and decided it was apposite. And it *was* Shakespeare. *Hamlet.* The wrong sex but the right message. *The lady doth protest too much, methinks.* Franks was surprised it had taken him so long to remember; it had been one of the challenges between himself and Nicky, when Enrico was insisting that they study classics. Franks had lost track of the conversation he was having. Trying to recover, he said, "Where does that leave me?"

"In the public mind, some guy who was pretty lucky to get away with it," said Schultz, honestly.

"I'm not going to stand any more shit from Waldo," said Franks. "His problems are his problems; I've got enough of my own. This time, okay. But not anymore."

"Sure," agreed Schultz. The FBI man rotated his glass in his hand and said, "You got any idea about bringing your kids back at some time, to those schools?"

"Anything wrong with keeping my options open?"

"It's not the way, Mr. Franks. You're either in the protection program or you're not. It's not something you pick up and put down. It's new names, new lives, new everything. For good."

"No one in America knows what schools the kids go to," insisted Franks. "Where would the problem be if they came back under new names?" He hadn't discussed new names with either school head. It would be impossible trying to make it work like that. His way was the way, Franks was convinced.

"You're in the big leagues," warned Schultz. "These guys have facilities every bit as good as we do; sometimes better because they can afford better. Don't underestimate them. You've been suckered once; be careful about it happening again."

The American was offering a genuine warning, Franks knew. Perhaps he should acknowledge it with further thought than he'd already given. Thinking back to his conversation with Tomkiss, on the car ride into New York, Franks said, "You ever been involved in this before? The protection program?"

"Once," said Schultz.

"What happened?"

Schultz looked down into his glass. "We set it all up," he

229

said. "New ID, new Social Security number, bank account, house in another part of the country. Everything. It was against three capos in New Jersey. Got our indictments from the grand jury and started planning the celebration. They got to him before the trial. We still don't know how. One day we had him nicely boxed and protected and the next day we didn't; he slipped us visiting his lawyer's office. Got out through a bathroom window. Never saw him again. No one has." Schultz snapped his fingers. "Just like that. That's how the case collapsed, too."

"You mean he was killed?"

Schultz put his empty glass on a side table and declined the gestured offer for more. "I don't know," said Schultz. "No one knows. Some people think he's part of a support in some overhead traffic system. Others that he's doing exactly what we offered him, living under a different identity on mob money. Doesn't really matter. We lost him and we lost the case." Schultz smiled sadly. "It's that sort of story that throws Harry."

"Don't you realize what running would mean?" demanded Franks. "Doesn't Waldo? It would mean abandoning my wife and children!"

"Guy I'm talking about had been married for fifteen years and had three nice kids. Great family man. Kissed them good-bye that morning and never came back. Happens a lot."

"It's not going to happen with me."

"Glad to hear it, Mr. Franks. We've got a lot riding on this."

"Make sure Waldo understands it, too."

"I'll try," promised the American.

The following day, Schultz appeared to have done so. There was an initial embarrassment between Franks and Waldo, but Franks discerned a definite change in attitude. There wasn't the streetwise antagonism from the other man, and he actually appeared more relaxed. They caught the early flight to Zurich, wanting to complete the visit and return in one day. There had clearly been liaison with the Swiss authorities, and officials from the American embassy in Bern were waiting at Zurich.

Francois Dulac, the Swiss lawyer, was a white-haired, smooth-faced, unsmiling man who seemed offended by the crowd surrounding Franks, particularly the escorting police car. He closed the door positively against Waldo and Schultz, and said complainingly, "This isn't the normal way that I am accustomed to do business."

"It's not the way that I am accustomed to doing it, either," assured Franks.

"You have some identification, from Mr. Kenham?"

Franks produced the documentation that the company secretary had provided the previous afternoon. Dulac fitted heavy bifocals into position and read steadily. Then he said, "You have a passport?"

Franks offered it, and the man compared the photograph in it to the man sitting opposite. Franks sat unmoving, as if he were actually posing for a photograph, feeling vaguely stupid.

Dulac returned the passport and said, "It's my understanding you want an omnibus account for a bank holding. And for me to establish from here, but in Liechtenstein, an *actiengesellschaft*."

"Is that possible?" said Franks.

"Of course," said Dulac briskly. "You want me the director named in the companies?"

"Yes," said Franks.

"There is, of course, a fee."

"I understand. Also I want my attachment to the companies, through you, to be in a name other than my own." The moment of commitment to a new identity, thought Franks. He wondered how long it had taken his father to decide; the transportation might have been different—like the circumstances that made the change necessary—but they'd both wandered Europe, running from unseen pursuers.

"That is no problem either," said Dulac. "What do you want it to be?"

The idea had come to him the previous night, after Schultz had left the suite and he'd permitted himself another drink. Franks knew it was sentimental, but the given name had belonged to his father. "Isaacs," he said. "David Isaacs."

"I'll need a sample signature today in that name. And a photograph of yourself to accompany it; that needn't be provided today. I'd accept it from Mr. Kenham."

Franks was suddenly aware of the provision he always made to permit Tina access to any account. He said, "My wife must also have drawing facilities."

"I'll also need sample signatures and photographs," said Dulac. "In the name of Isaacs?"

If he were going to be sentimental, he might as well be completely so and involve his unknown mother, as well. "Rebecca Isaacs," he said. "I'll see they come to you from my American attorney. His name is Rosenberg." Franks paused.

231

Why involve Kenham anymore? He added, "My photograph will come from Mr. Rosenberg, too."

"As you wish," said the Swiss lawyer.

"Something else," continued Franks. "You are already familiar with Mr. Kenham, in London. I want today to draw up a document—a sort of will, I suppose—giving Mr. Kenham and the named members of the boards of my English companies disposal access to the *actiengesellschaft* in the event of my death. But *only* in the event of my death."

"The death of whom?" said the lawyer. "Edmund Franks or David Isaacs?"

Franks wondered if anything ever surprised or shocked this imperturbable man. "Either," he said. "Provable upon production of photographs and a notarized death certificate." Would there have been any reaction from Dulac at a photograph of the blasted-apart Nicky Scargo?

"Some of the documentation has already been prepared," said Dulac. "The access document can be prepared while we go through what is already available."

The man gave brief instructions in German through an intercom and then moved with Franks to another part of the office, where there was a settee and a low table in front of it. They sat side by side while Dulac took him through all the clauses and conditions of the hidden account and companies. Franks initialed each page and signed a total of three. He provided the sample signature and took the forms necessary for Tina, and by the time they finished, the papers giving the London boards access were ready, as Dulac had promised. They remained on the couch and went painstakingly through the newest documents. Again each page had to be initialed and finally signed. Again, there were three copies.

"I will deal with you direct?" queried Dulac.

Franks shook his head. "Through Mr. Rosenberg."

"There are laws in this country to which I have to comply," said Dulac. "Are you the subject of criminal proceedings?"

"I am involved in criminal proceedings," said Franks. "I am not a defendant, nor am I likely to be accused of any crime."

"Mr. Rosenberg will provide an affidavit attesting to that?"

"If you feel it necessary."

"I think it would keep and maintain things in correct order," said the lawyer. He looked through the window, from which the escorting police car was still visible. "It is not usual for clients to come *with* the police," he said.

"The affidavit will come from Mr. Rosenberg with everything else that you've asked for," promised Franks.

They were back in London—Franks still unable to adjust to what Waldo and Schultz felt necessary protection—by early evening. He called and arranged the final directors' meeting for the following day. Just that, and he could return to America, Franks realized. He'd looked forward to the trip, to escaping the Scarsdale imprisonment, but it hadn't felt like an escape at all. At least the continued relaxation with Waldo had remained throughout the day. Deciding to eat in his suite—he didn't feel like going out anyway—he invited the two FBI men to join him. Schultz was the one who accepted for both of them. There was a slight uneasiness at the transition from a strictly business to partially social situation, but Schultz, the chosen mediator, worked hard to relax the group. He told stories on himself for mistakes in investigations—but, considerately, nothing of the sort in which Franks was involved—and then Waldo emerged to do the same, showing the same consideration. Waldo showed pictures of his wife and family—two boys the same ages as David and Gabby—and said he'd promised his wife a going-home present of a tartan skirt, and Schultz hesitatingly disclosed his hobby of campanology and said he regretted that he hadn't been able to visit any of England's famous cathedrals to hear the bells being rung. The meal was very good and the wine was excellent, and as Franks poured the brandies, Waldo finally said, "I'm extremely sorry about yesterday. I was way out of line."

Franks indicated Schultz with his brandy goblet, and said, "John explained a lot. It's forgotten."

"Thanks," said Waldo.

Franks decided he was enjoying himself; for the first time since he couldn't remember when. He'd had a lot to drink—they all had—but he wasn't drunk. None of them were. It had been a convivial, relaxed, pleasant evening, and he'd unwound. As the thought came, Franks knew just how much he'd *needed* to unwind. He asked, "What happens afterward, when it's all over?" He spread his hands. "Does it go on, like this?"

"Usually, for the first few weeks. Kind of settling down; making sure people understand what to do. The scale down is gradual. You've always got contact numbers to call any time, not just for emergencies. But eventually you're on your own."

Franks found it difficult to imagine what it had ever been

233

like for him and Tina and the kids to be on their own. "You personally?" he said.

"I shouldn't think so," said Schultz. "The FBI is involved, of course. Runs the operation. But the marshals are usually the people who do it. It's their job."

"It's going to be difficult for you," declared Waldo abruptly.

"I've already realized that," said Franks.

"That's not what I mean," said Waldo. "For *you*, personally. Normally it's punks; people who don't know any different. They usually end up with a house better than they had in the first place and they're grateful for the pension. . . ." The FBI man looked around the suite. "This isn't our standard," he said. "It's yours. The adjustment for you is going to be a bastard."

He'd unwound; now it was winding-up time again, thought Franks. "I'll learn," he said, unwilling to face reality too quickly.

"I think you've got a lot to learn," said Waldo. "An awful lot."

"I will," insisted Franks stubbornly.

The meeting with the directors was a formality. They'd drawn the agreements as promised, and he produced the access documents as promised, and the formalities were over very quickly.

"We're now effectively running the companies?" said Podmore.

"Yes," agreed Franks. He had the inescapable feeling of being cast adrift.

"Knowing—as you did—that it was going to happen, I'm somewhat surprised you made the salary and advantage agreements that you did with the managers who are being elevated," said the man.

Franks bristled at the lecturing tone but knew it would be wrong to respond angrily to it, like it would have been wrong to have met Waldo's anger with anger. "Extra responsibilities are being imposed upon them, just as they are upon you. Shouldn't that be recognized?"

"Shouldn't we have been the people to recognize it?" came back Podmore.

Fuck the man, thought Franks, the recurring reaction; fuck them all. "Two days ago I was in control of these companies," he said. "I still am, although distanced. Within six months, I shall be back, running them again. I'm grateful for your support but I don't think it would be wise for anyone to imagine a situation anything different from what it actually is, do you?"

234

Waldo and Schultz seemed surprised by his early emergence from the conference room.

"All through?" said Schultz.

"All through," agreed Franks. "It's time to get back to America." To get it over and then get back to something else: normality.

"What now?" asked Waldo.

Franks checked his watch, unnecessarily because he'd already timed the suggestion out. "The last plane," he said, abandoning the thought of the Concorde. "That gives us time to go from here to St. Paul's, which is very close, so that John can hear the bells. And then to Knightsbridge so that you can buy the tartan for your wife. The Scotch Shop is there. Harrod's, too. You can get presents for the kids, as well."

Which is what they did. Franks took them to lunch at Scott's after getting their assurance that the protection wouldn't be too obvious, and back at the hotel he had time enough after packing to call Tina to say he was returning.

"I'm glad it hasn't taken as long as you thought," she said.

"So am I," he said, pleased there was no challenge in her voice.

"Not for that reason," said the woman. "Poppa had a heart attack during the night."

25

Enrico Scargo refused to go to the hospital, with an old man's conviction that hospitals were places where people went to die. Private nurses and resuscitation and monitoring equipment were installed in the house. At first both Tina and Maria moved in. Neither of them got any rest because Mamma insisted on sitting up practically throughout the night as well as day with her husband. So they evolved a routine of alternating between Scarsdale and the Scargos'. When Franks arrived from Kennedy airport, the old man was hooked up to a respirator. Although there was nothing practical he could do, Franks stayed for two days before going into Manhattan to brief Rosenberg on the arrangements he'd made in England and Switzerland and instructing the lawyer what he wanted done. On the way back from the city, Franks decided that although it was an improper thought—certainly not one he'd consider expressing—her father's collapse meant that Tina now had something to fully distract her from the unreality of how they were living. She'd signed the bank papers dismissively—not bothering to ask what they were—and had been quite disinterested in hearing what he'd done on the trip. In fact, reflected Franks, disinterest in him was an accurate description of Tina's current attitude.

Franks went back to the Scarsdale house from Manhattan for the first time since his return from England. David and Gabriella were subdued by their grandfather's illness and there was none of the usual boisterousness of a homecoming or excitement about the presents he brought: a make-it-yourself tank model kit for David and what he belatedly realized was an inappropriate wetting doll for Gabriella. Franks was back early enough in the evening to be with them for their evening meal, and toward the end of it David looked soberly at him and said, "Why did you tell me a lie?"

"What lie?" said Franks, not immediately remembering.

"About Uncle Nicky. You said he might come, but I know he can't because he's dead. Aunty Maria told me."

Franks sighed. He said, "It wasn't a lie to cheat you. I just wanted to talk to Maria about it first, but I didn't have time. What did she tell you?"

"I asked her when he was coming," said the boy. "She said there had been a bad accident and that he'd died."

"Did she say what sort of accident?" asked Franks.

David shook his head. "Just that it was an accident."

"What did happen?" said Gabriella.

Franks hesitated, unwilling to lie a second time, but even more unwilling to talk about shooting, conscious of David's fascination with guns. "Something happened with a car," he said, aware at once of the inadequacy.

"Were other people killed as well?" asked the boy.

"No, only Uncle Nicky," said Franks. The question had been easier than he expected.

"Why doesn't Aunty Maria cry?" asked the girl.

"She has," said Franks. He was beginning to wish he hadn't joined them for their meal.

236

"I haven't seen her," insisted the child.

"She cries by herself. In her room," groped Franks.

"Does that mean she's brave?" said Gabriella.

"Yes," said Franks.

"I'd cry if you died," she said.

"Let's stop talking about people dying," said Franks. "I'm not going to die."

"Promise!" said David, more urgency than usual in the familiar demand.

"I promise," said Franks gently.

"You didn't tell the truth about Uncle Nicky," accused the boy.

Franks leaned across the table for David's hand. "I didn't tell you about Uncle Nicky because I didn't want to upset you; in case you started thinking silly things like that it *could* happen to me. It isn't going to. I'm not going to die, and nothing is going to happen to me."

"Are those men who are here all the time now going to see that it doesn't?" said Gabriella with innocent accuracy. "I thought it was to guard treasure."

Franks tried desperately to remember the explanation he'd given to David. He said. "They're men who are helping me; it's to do with Daddy's job."

"You said there were some bad men who didn't want you to tell on them," said David.

"That's it!" said Franks. "I've got to tell the truth about some bad things and the people here with us now are going to help me do that." He looked up gratefully at Elizabeth's arrival and said, "Bath time!"

Franks escaped at once into the small sitting room. He examined the drinks, momentarily undecided, and then chose the usual martini. He mixed a small pitcher, thinking how well he'd done over the last few days: hardly anything at the Scargos'— certainly never approaching drunkenness—and this the first to-day. He knew he should call to see how things were up there. Time enough later. He carried the drink with him to an easy chair, thinking of the conversation with the children. Not good, he decided; bloody awful, in fact. It was inconceivable to talk about shotgun murders to kids that young, so to lie was unavoidable, but he didn't like risking his relationship with them. Was it at risk? Or was he magnifying something out of proportion? He wished he could talk to someone about it, but couldn't think who.

Tina? She'd gone to her parents' that afternoon. Besides, if he mentioned it, he and Tina wouldn't talk; in minutes they would be arguing.

Franks was at the drinks table refilling his glass when he heard the sound of the car in the driveway outside, and through the window saw that it was Maria. He answered the door for her himself, knowing that she'd sat up most of the previous night with Mamma Scargo and surprised that she didn't look more tired than she did. He kissed her platonically on the cheek and said he had drinks already mixed, and she said, "Terrific!"

Maria sat in the chair he'd earlier occupied and stretched her legs out straight in front of her, kicking off her shoes. He gave her the drink, sat opposite, and said, "How it is up there?"

She pulled down the corners of her mouth and said, "Nothing happening at all, really. Doctor says he's stable, whatever that means. He could be off the respirator by the weekend. This morning the doctor prescribed some tranquilizers and sleeping pills for Mamma but she says she won't take them. Insists she wants to be awake, in case he needs her." She raised her glass and said, "Cheers, if that's an appropriate thing to say."

"I'd better call Tina soon," said Franks. "I told her I was coming back here but I'm not sure if she'll remember."

"She didn't say anything," said Maria.

"How is she?"

Maria appeared surprised by the question. "Okay, I guess. Worried, naturally."

"Everything is getting her down," said Franks. Hadn't he once decided not to discuss Tina with Maria? It seemed a long time ago.

"You can't expect much else," she said.

Franks gestured toward her glass and she nodded acceptance. Franks said, "You don't seem to be letting it get you down so much as she is."

"Maybe I've had my crisis," said the woman. "Maybe Tina thinks she's still got hers to come."

He'd like very much to know what they all had to come, thought Franks. "Whatever she feels, she's not helping much," he said.

She smiled at him and Franks smiled back, arguing pointlessly with himself about why he was doing what he was doing.

"Anything I can do to help?" said Maria.

"I think you're doing it, by listening," said Franks. Recalling the difficulties with the children, Franks talked about that, too, and of his uncertainty at the way he'd responded, welcoming the chance to speak and not be shouted at in return. Was Gabriella still wetting the bed? he wondered. Bloody stupid to have bought that doll.

"I'm sorry if I made things difficult with the kids," she said. "I should have talked about it first to Tina, I guess. It just didn't occur to me."

"I was the person who avoided the issue; I should have warned you," said Franks.

"I can understand why you did want to avoid it," said the woman. "It was unthinking of me and I'm sorry."

They were each overcompensating, Franks recognized. He recognized, too, a tension or an awareness growing between them and wondered if she noticed it.

Maria said, "Europe go okay?"

"Busy," said Franks. "I didn't enjoy all the protection; I felt stupid."

"I've practically stopped noticing," said Maria. "Perhaps I'll take a trip when things have settled down a little. I enjoyed Europe with Nicky."

Mentioning the man—and their honeymoon—didn't seem to cause her any difficulty. He said, "I can arrange anything, practically anywhere you're likely to want to go. All you've got to do is mention it."

"It would be good to get away," said Maria reflectively. "Go somewhere where nobody knew me and sit in the sun and get fat."

"Getting fat doesn't seem to be a problem for you," said Franks, and at once regretted it because it sounded gauche. Hurriedly he said, "Getting away and sitting in the sun certainly sounds good."

Maria looked pointedly at him but didn't speak for several moments. Then she said, "Why don't you try it?" and smiled again.

Franks realized she didn't know everything about his going into the Witnesses Protection Program; he didn't know *everything* about it himself. But that wasn't what she was talking about, anyway. He said, "Do you think this is wise?"

"What?" she said, knowing but wanting him to say it.

"Holding our hands into the fire to see how long it takes to get burned."

"Is that what we're doing?"

"That's what I think we're doing."

"Frightened?"

"I don't know," said Franks. "Are you?"

"I don't know."

Clutching at straws Franks said, "I should telephone Tina."

"Yes," agreed Maria, the more controlled of the two. "You should."

"Why don't you freshen the drinks?" said Franks. "I freshened them the last time."

Maria rose slowly, enjoying his attention upon her but stopped too far away to take his glass. "Halfway," she said. "You've got to come halfway."

Franks leaned forward, holding out his glass for her to take. She held back, in command, knowing it and wanting him to know it too, and then took it from him. Franks used the telephone alongside the chair in which he was sitting, which was a mistake because it meant that he had to conduct a conversation with his wife while the woman for whom he felt a physical ache—and who was aware of it because she looked and saw how obvious it was and smiled yet again—was sitting only a few feet away. It was a desultory, clipped conversation. He asked after her father and she said there wasn't really any change and she asked about his visit to Rosenberg and he said it had all gone as he told her it would. Tina asked if Maria was back and he said she was and he said the children were okay and when was she coming back, and Tina said maybe in three days, when Maria came up to relieve her. He said he'd call tomorrow and she said okay, and as he replaced the receiver Franks realized it had occurred to neither of them to express anything like love. At least the conversation, inconsequential as it was, had subdued his physical arousal.

"There's no change," he said.

"I told you that."

"You hungry? I arranged steaks."

"For both of us?"

"Yes."

"You knew I was coming back then?"

"Tina said you might; it seemed more sensible to prepare than not."

"Is that why you decided to stay here tonight?"

Yes, thought Franks. He said, "I always intended to come back here today; there were so many people up there it was like a railway station."

"I think David's right."

"David?"

"You tell lies."

"You didn't say whether you were hungry."

"Not particularly."

"It's being prepared now."

"We'd better eat some of it then."

"Yes."

It was a meal with little conversation, but they rarely stopped looking at each other in a way that wasn't looking at all but was a kind of touching, without hands. Toward the end of the meal, which they hardly ate, Maria said, "I always wondered if this would happen. I didn't think it would but I always wondered."

"Nothing's happened yet," he said.

"But it's going to."

"Yes," accepted Franks in final, easy surrender. "It's going to."

Maria was suddenly, surprisingly, brisk. "I don't know how it is between you and Tina," she said. "That's between you. It just obviously isn't very good at all. But you should know about Nicky and me."

"Why?"

"Because I want you to," insisted the woman. "Nicky was gay. I suppose I should have known before we got married. I was the personal assistant, for God's sake. As close as that, I would have known about the women and I knew there weren't any. No, that's not true. There were some but not a lot; not as many as there should have been for a bachelor lawyer with a lot of money and a townhouse in Manhattan." For practically the first time during the meal she broke their gaze, fussing with her wineglass. "I know I told you that I wanted whoever did it to suffer. And I do. But Nicky was a bastard for what he did to me. It was an experiment of a sort, I suppose. Respectability required that he was married—before the gossips got it right—and I guess in the early months he tried. *Very* early months; I'd say the first three or four. He could swing both ways. At first I couldn't believe how good it was. Then he answered the question I didn't know he was asking himself and it started going wrong." There was a further pause. "Late-night meetings started to happen; I guessed he was cheating on me because that was the obvious explanation, but I thought he was cheating with some other woman. He still tried, occasionally. He started asking me to be his man. . . . We'd done

241

it before and I didn't think anything of it, and then he kept asking and that's the way it was. . . ." Maria looked up to him and said, "You know what I mean?"

"Yes," said Franks. "I know what you mean. But I don't know why you want to tell me."

"I want it—whatever *it* is—to be right between us. So I don't want you to think of me as some hot bitch wanting to get laid practically before her husband's buried. He made me an offer, you see. Finally he couldn't pretend anymore and we talked it out. All he wanted was discretion. He'd be thoroughly discreet and I could be thoroughly discreet, and to the outside world it would be the perfect, loving marriage."

"That's pretty sick," said Franks.

"Nicky said I'd be surprised how ordinary the situation is."

"Did you agree?" demanded Franks.

"No," she said at once.

Franks held her eyes, saying nothing. Maria shrugged and said, "I guess I would have done, in time. Who wouldn't? But I didn't. I supposed I still loved him; still do, in a funny way. Tried to tell myself that sex wasn't the only thing and that it might come around to be okay, in time. I know it wouldn't have done, of course. We talked about divorce, but he was very frightened of that; respectability again."

"You don't make him sound a very nice guy," said Franks. "I know I've got my own reasons for not thinking so, but it seems to me that you do, too."

"Which means I should hate him; dislike him at least," said Maria. "But the truth is that I never felt like that. Not even on the night he confessed to me, when he cried and held me and said he hated himself for something he couldn't stop. I never felt any dislike or rejection. If there was a feeling at all, I suppose it was a pity. I know he cheated me and I know he used me—just like he cheated and used you, I guess—but I still couldn't hate him. Do you?"

Franks was off-balanced by the question. Of course he did; the bastard had come close to wrecking his life. Just how close he still had to find out. So what other emotion could he have but hatred? But he didn't think that was his feeling. To hate, you had to feel anger and vilify and think all the time of revenge. Franks' thoughts about Nicky were of complete emptiness; a void, as if the man had never existed or occupied any part of his feelings. Why was feeling—any feeling—always so difficult?

"I don't know," he said unwillingly.

"I've told you," said Maria, still brisk. "All of it. Not particularly nice, is it?"

"No," said Franks. "I'm sorry. That it didn't work out better, I mean."

"We've finished eating," she said unnecessarily.

"Yes," he said.

"Do you want to go on sitting here?"

"Why don't we go into the other room and have some brandy?"

"I don't think I want brandy," said Maria.

They were back looking at each other again, touching without feel. Aware of the household staff and of the attentive Elizabeth, Franks said, "You'd better go up ahead of me."

"Don't be long."

"I won't."

Franks took a brandy by himself and kept it a small one. He sat in the same chair in which he'd agreed with Maria that they were going to sleep together. He felt the heat he'd warned her about and realized that if he was going to pull back, like he should pull back, now was the time—the last available time—to do it. There'd been a moment that seemed like a million years ago but really hadn't been when he'd had the chance to pull back, and he was going to regret for the rest of his life that he hadn't done so. Franks drank his brandy, got up from the chair, and went upstairs.

She was already in bed when he went into her room, but when he did she threw back the covers so he could see. She watched while he undressed and he bent over her, not getting at once into bed but starting with his mouth low, just inside her knee and gradually moving up. She shifted to make it easier for him, whimpering with the pleasure of it and then getting ahead of him, snatching at him and forcing him into her, hurrying him to match her, which he couldn't do. She quietened after the first climax, matching his pace, and they came together the second time and only needed to rest briefly before they were able to make love again. Finally, exhausted, they drifted into a half sleep from which Maria recovered first, urging him awake because she needed him again; Franks was surprised—and pleased—that he could match her demands, wanting her as much as she wanted him.

It was near light when he left her at last, to go back to his own room. Franks had slept hardly at all, always vaguely aware of her, but he didn't sleep when he got to bed alone, because he couldn't. What sort of deception was it to have made love to a woman while his wife was away at the bedside of a sick father, and his two children—two trusting, dependent children—were asleep in another part of the house! Franks waited for the remorse to come—*wanted* it to come—but it wouldn't. He felt deceitful and embarrassed, but there wasn't any genuine remorse. Having abandoned practically everything else, Franks refused any longer to stop comparing them. Maria was a much more exciting and accomplished lover than Tina. Was that what he wanted, a wife *and* a mistress? That was a question he couldn't answer. Another, to join all the rest. He didn't know if he wanted Tina and he didn't know if he wanted Maria. Or the additional complication he had created for himself in an already overcomplicated, difficult situation.

In the shower, later, Franks considered confronting Maria and apologizing for a mistake and asking her to forget that it had ever happened and then realized that that was ridiculous and that he didn't want to do it anyway.

They worked to be alone and succeeded in the afternoon, and the lovemaking was better than it had been the previous night. Conscience urged Franks to go up to see Tina and her parents and he did so without experiencing any guilt. Enrico had responded to tests and the doctor was fairly convinced of some sort of recovery but wasn't prepared at that stage to forecast how complete it might be. Tina looked gaunt and tired and had not bothered with any makeup. She seemed impatient and distracted and ill at ease with him. Franks said he didn't think he'd stay, but go back to Scarsdale—sure the guilt would come now, but it didn't—and Tina said that would probably be a good thing and then blurted out that her mother blamed him for Enrico's collapse and didn't want him in the house. It was too much trouble to try to justify himself, and so Franks didn't bother. He got away, back to Scarsdale and Maria.

They slept together that night and made love as anxiously but as well as before. As they lay wetly together afterward Maria said, "Sorry?"

"No," said Franks positively. "Are you?"

"No," said the woman. "You're fantastic."

"So are you."

"I haven't worked out what we've really done yet," Maria admitted. "Just that I think it's wonderful and I don't want it to stop."

"I tried and gave up," said Franks.

"I know this is going to sound pretty stupid and hypocritical in the circumstances, but I don't want to hurt Tina," she said.

"No."

"So we're going to have to be careful." She paused. "Or stop."

"I don't think I want to stop," said Franks.

"I know I don't," said the woman. "But then I've not got a lot to lose, have I?"

"No."

"It's got to be your decision," insisted Maria. "When it's time, you've got to be the one to say."

"All right," accepted Franks. How easy was it going to be?

"I don't know if it's going to happen with you," said Maria. "Maybe not. I think it's already happening with me. So perhaps it would be a good idea for you to call it off before you fall in love."

"I—" started Franks, but she put her fingers across his lips, stopping him. "No," she said. "Don't say it. Don't ever say it, not even if you think it's true, unless you think you can find a way to make it work properly."

They had one more idyllic day before it was time for Maria to exchange duty with Tina. His wife came back clearly on the edge of exhaustion and Franks insisted she remain in bed all day, which she accepted without any argument. Alone downstairs—apart from passing contact with the attended children—Franks missed Maria and found it difficult not to regard Tina as an intruder. She got up that night for dinner and he explained in greater detail what he had done in England and Switzerland, but she seemed to find the necessary concentration difficult.

"Poppa's never going to get completely well," she said.

"Did the doctor tell you that?"

"He doesn't have to; it's obvious."

"We'll get specialists, when the immediate crisis is over," promised Franks.

Tina smiled briefly. "You didn't tell me what happened at the schools."

Intentionally, thought Franks. He tried to make it sound better than he believed it was, waiting for the outburst, but Tina seemed too tired to respond with anything but resigned acceptance.

"You're still exhausted," said Franks. "Why don't you sleep again by yourself tonight?"

245

"It might be a good idea," agreed Tina at once.

Franks wondered if the following day was going to be difficult, in the house and alone with Tina after she was fully rested, but Rosenberg called. The grand jury had been convened. Shortly after that Waldo and Schultz arrived personally, with more agents to strengthen the protection because of the formal notification that would have been made to Dukes, Flamini, and Pascara.

"Now it starts!" declared the huge FBI man.

"*Now?*" queried Tina. "I thought it already had, a long time ago."

Waldo looked curiously at her. "It hasn't begun yet, Mrs. Franks," he said.

PART FOUR

Prophecy is the most gratuitous form of error.

George Eliot
MIDDLEMARCH

26

The grand jury appearance was different from what Franks expected, despite a preappearance briefing from Rosenberg the day before, when he and Tina were driven into Manhattan under heavy escort and installed in the Plaza under the most stringent guard yet. Franks' only awareness of courts was from the dramatized reconstructions in movies and on television; there was, he supposed, some sort of similarity but not as much as he imagined there would be. Although he was warned by Rosenberg that they were unlikely to attend, Franks was still surprised not to see Pascara, Flamini, or Dukes.

He wasn't the first witness, so he queried their nonappearance with Ronan during a break in the presentation of the case before the jury.

"They were invited," confirmed the district attorney. "Law says they've got to be. But people like these rarely show; they can come under examination. Legal advice is nearly always to wait until the actual trial, if there is one."

"What about legal representation now?"

"Not permitted," said Ronan.

Franks had hoped that the break from the guarded monotony of Tina's life would have lifted her, even though the circumstances of the break were what they were. It didn't. She sat away from him in the car bringing them into the city, unspeaking; at the hotel she concerned herself with telephone calls to Scarsdale and Elizabeth, to talk about the children, and went directly to bed after a picked-at meal in the suite. Now, in the prehearing anteroom, she stood as close to the window as Tomkiss would allow, staring out at the city skyline. Franks had the impression that she wasn't seeing anything. Neither of them was called to the stand, the first day or the second, and Tina's hostility, to everything and everybody, worsened.

"Why the hell were we brought in, if they don't want us!" she exploded when they got back to the hotel on the second night.

"All the witnesses had to be assembled, in readiness," said Franks. "Ronan can only make an estimate of how long things are going to take."

"I hope the strength of his case is a damned sight better than his estimates," she said.

"Relax, Tina," he said wearily.

"Relax! How the fuck am I supposed to relax?"

"Do you think it's any easier for me?"

"I think you're enjoying it."

"Don't be ridiculous!" said Franks, exasperated himself now.

"It doesn't seem to be worrying you."

"Of course it's worrying me! I'm just determined not to give in to it; just like I'm determined not to give in to them."

"So now I'm weak!" demanded Tina, able to see a challenge in everything.

When it was all over—the jury hearings and the trial and the period in the protection program—Franks didn't think it was ever going to be possible for things to be the same between him and Tina as they had been before. And it wasn't because of what had arisen between himself and Maria. Franks felt that Tina had failed him. There'd been all the early talk of love and trust and admiration, but when the stress came she just hadn't been able to handle it. She'd cracked—was cracking—and Franks was disappointed. He'd trusted and admired her—loved her, too—and expected more. He said, "If you want an opinion, then yes, you are being weak."

"Thanks!"

"Aren't you?" he insisted. "Where's the support been, from you, since all this began?"

"I've supported you," she said.

"No you haven't," he said. "You want to know how every conversation has begun from you, for weeks now? I. It's always, 'I can't do this,' or 'I can't stand this,' or 'I can't understand how I'm expected . . .' When was the last time you thought beyond 'I,' Tina?"

"So I haven't thought about David and Gabby?"

"We weren't talking about David or Gabby. We were talking about your support for me."

"I thought you were supposed to be able to look after yourself."

Nothing took very long to get back to cliché, he thought. He wondered what Maria was doing up at the Scargos'; it would be

250

tiring for her to stand duty throughout the time that Tina was down here in the city. Disinterested in prolonging yet another dispute—why was disinterest always the prevalent word applying to them!—Franks said, "I think they should reach you tomorrow. And it shouldn't take long; it's only formal stuff about the proxy vote and your unawareness of what they were doing."

"I hope so," she said.

"I'll be giving evidence for much longer," said Franks. "Could run over more than one day; several, in fact. You want to stay down here or go back home?"

Tina looked disparagingly around the suite and back at her husband. "You mean do some shopping at Bergdorf Goodman or Saks and maybe take in a matinee or something, while I wait?"

"I just asked."

"At least I can breathe at home. And I want to get back to Poppa anyway."

Which would relieve Maria. Could she come down, to join him? Now Franks gazed around the suite and thought of the security arrangements in the corridors outside and in the surrounding rooms and realized the emptiness of the hope. He said, "I'll fix it tomorrow with Tomkiss."

He had to, because Tina was the first witness. It was very brief, as Ronan had advised them, and Franks was the next to be called, so there wasn't time for any particular farewell, which was a relief for both of them.

"I'll call," he said.

"All right."

"Hope your father's going on okay," he said.

"Yes."

"Give the children my love."

"Yes," she said again.

Franks wondered whether to kiss her, conscious of the waiting court usher and their FBI protectors, and decided against it. The way he felt—and suspected she did also—would have made the gesture hypocritical.

Franks followed the usher into the hearing, took the oath, and accepted the invitation to be seated. It put him partially facing the district attorney and partially looking toward the grand jury. The first row was predominantly women, just one black at the end, but after that the jury was composed of a majority of men; having reached the third day, they seemed settled in and comfortable with their surroundings. Very quickly Franks found it easy to do the same. Since the law did not allow the absent Pascara, Flamini, or Dukes to be legally represented, there was no cross-examination of his evidence. Franks gave it to Ronan's lead, setting his involvement down in the chronological order in which he'd first given it to the district attorney. Ronan was a painstaking prosecutor, refusing to let Franks hurry and miss detail, and they only got halfway through the account by the time of the evening recess.

Franks was glad to be alone at the hotel, freed from Tina's company. He had a couple of drinks and watched the evening news and had a bottle of wine with his meal, but stopped short of brandy, not wanting to be thickheaded the following morning. Elizabeth answered when he telephoned the Scarsdale house. Franks feigned surprise at realizing that Tina was at her parents' and said dismissively that he might as well talk to Mrs. Scargo to see how things were if she was there. Maria came at once to the telephone.

"How are you?" he said.

"Okay," she said. "You?"

"Okay, I guess."

Would Waldo have put any sort of monitor on the telephone calls? Franks wasn't sure that the man could be trusted. Hoping to warn the woman, he said, "I'm phoning from the hotel, through the switchboard."

"Yes," said Maria.

"How's Poppa Scargo?"

"A lot better. Doctor says he can start eating solids in a couple of days. He's ordered Mamma to bed, though. She's out on her feet."

"You must be tired," he said.

"Not too bad," she said. "I'll be able to get some sleep tonight." There was a pause, and she said, "When do you think you'll be back?"

Franks understood the meaning of the question and was excited by it. "I don't know," he said. "I only started giving evidence today."

"Oh," said Maria.

Franks thought disappointment was obvious in her voice and that Waldo would recognize it if he were listening. Damn the man; it wasn't any of his business. He said, "Maybe I'll be able to get back in a day or two."

"Seems like ages since I've been to Manhattan," said Maria, and Franks knew she was having the same thoughts that he had earlier, about her coming to him.

He said, "The restrictions are pretty stringent; people everywhere."

"I guess there would be," she said, accepting the difficulty.

"Tell the kids I called, will you?" said Franks, feeling he should.

"Of course."

"I'll call to see how they are tomorrow," promised Franks. So he was using David and Gabby as an excuse; so what!

"Of course."

"About this time."

"I'll expect you, then."

"Take care."

"And you." Franks thought the protracted conversation was familiar and then remembered this was how it had been with him and Tina.

"Good-bye then," said Maria.

"Good night."

"Hope things go okay tomorrow."

"It's all pretty formal. No problem really."

"That's good."

"I could even be away in time to get back tomorrow night."

"I'd like that," said Maria, unthinking. She appeared at once to realize what she'd said; there was a heavy silence from her end of the line.

"I'd better go," said Franks.

"Yes," she agreed. "I meant—"

"It doesn't matter," cut off Franks, not wanting her embarrassed with a hurried apology.

"Hear from you tomorrow, then?" she said.

"Or maybe I'll get back."

"Yes."

"Good night."

"Good night."

Franks replaced the telephone but remained looking at it, wondering the reaction if the line was tapped. Damn them, he thought again. It didn't encroach on or endanger any case they were trying to make so it was none of their business. He should telephone Tina. But why? He knew from Maria how the old man was, and he knew from experience what would happen if he and Tina started—or tried to start—talking. Tomorrow would be soon enough. Despite his earlier resolution, Franks ordered brandy and sat with the drink, watching the late night Manhattan news. The grand jury hearing was the lead item, and there was a jostled film of him being taken into the building surrounded by FBI men, led by Tomkiss. The reporter estimated that the hearing would last another week before the jury reached any decision and ended with still pictures of Flamini, Dukes, and Pascara. The newscast would have reached Scarsdale and Franks wondered if Maria was watching. He considered calling again, to ask, but decided against it.

The second day Franks concentrated more upon the jury than he did upon the district attorney, who questioned him, anxious for some reaction or facial indication that might let him know how this group of independent people—the first group of independent people so far to consider the evidence—would regard his part in it. The test was a difficult one. For the most part, now completely accustomed to their surroundings—some, Franks suspected, actually enjoying the albeit hidden notoriety of comprising a grand jury that led television newscasts—the jurors showed no obvious response. But he thought two of the women in the front row looked suspiciously at him as the facts emerged, and a refined, scholarly looking man behind them also appeared to doubt Franks' unawareness of what happened. Franks tried hard not to become unsettled by the impression. Because after all, that was the extent of it—just an impression—and to attempt some sort of explanation in addition to answering Ronan's questions risked making himself appear someone needing a defense instead of exoneration. Increasingly Franks found the restraint a problem, burning—actually red-faced—at the admission of stupidity, conscious how difficult—how frighteningly, horrifyingly difficult—it would be for these uninvolved, unknowing people to decide impartially that he *was* innocent. By the third day of his evidence Franks was nervous and trying hard not to show it, permanently red-faced and knowing how bad it made him look, like the perspiration he couldn't seem to control, even though the air conditioning of the room was good.

He telephoned Tina once and Maria each evening, and at the conclusion of his evidence lunched with Ronan and said he knew it hadn't looked very good.

"It looked fine," assured the district attorney.

"Sweating and blushing?"

"Wouldn't an innocent man—having to admit a mistake—sweat and blush?"

Franks thanked the man for his reassurance, but he didn't believe it. He asked if he could return to Scarsdale now that his evidence was over and Ronan said he'd prefer it if he waited, in case there were some last-minute queries that needed clarification. That night Franks called both Tina and Maria to explain why he was remaining in the city; the conversation with his wife was brief and perfunctory, that with Maria protracted and rambling, neither willing to break the contact and repeating themselves, talking of inconsequential things, just to keep the call going.

It took a full twelve days to present the case to the grand jury. On the thirteenth, the jury returned indictments against each of the three men on every charge for which the district attorney sought prosecution. The formal arrests and declarations of innocence from Pascara, Dukes, and Flamini became a major news story. The media obtained the details, once the indictments were officially returned, and Franks' photograph and all the known biographical material accompanied the stories, in the newspapers and on television. The coverage extended to England, and Franks journeyed to Manhattan on the average twice and sometimes three times a week to have Rosenberg physically with him when he telephoned or telexed his London managers and the various boards.

Lawyers for Pascara and Flamini and Dukes sought bail, which in each case was set at one million dollars, despite objections to their release from custody by Ronan. When the men were freed, Ronan moved for a hearing date under the Speedy Trial Act. Franks was relieved; every discussion with the directors had caused British nervousness at the effect on the business of the concerted and unremitting publicity.

That nervousness came near to something like paranoia three weeks after the conclusion of the grand jury hearings when an apparently accidental explosion—which everyone knew wasn't accidental—destroyed the main engine room of the Caribbean cruise liner, causing five hundred passengers to be evacuated in lifeboats in their nightclothes. It crippled the sailing program for six months. And a week after that a bacillus appeared in the food being served in all their Italian hotels, and in four in France, creating a salmonella outbreak that caused the death of an eight-year-old child in Venice and of an elderly couple in Rome. Italian health authorities closed down eight of the company's hotels and a total of two thousand holidays were lost, in addition to the one thousand that were canceled by people themselves, no longer prepared to risk the vacation.

The snatched times that he could spend with Maria became Franks' only escape from the daily increasing pressures. He stopped caring whether the Scarsdale household or even the FBI

255

protectors knew about it, concerned only to keep it from David and Gabriella. He knew from her openly hostile attitude that Elizabeth was aware of the affair. Tina never made any open accusation.

About the time of the explosion aboard the liner, Maria was with the Scargos. Tina was home. She withdrew one night to the solitary bedroom he'd suggested she occupy that first time, when the affair began. Tina offered no explanation and Franks didn't seek one. The situation continued for a month, and then the decision came from England about the children's schooling.

With deep regret, but bound as they were by their very necessary primary duty to the well-being of their schools, the principals were unable to accept the return of Gabriella or David. Both felt quite confident that adequate and alternative schooling would be available, and that the children would fulfill the promising ability they had so far shown.

Tina was home the day the letters came. She read them, unspeaking, and then looked up at him. "I think it's time a lot of things were sorted out."

"Like what?" said Franks.

"For a start, I want to know everything about this protection program. All I've heard so far is what you understand it to be. I want someone else to explain it to me; I don't care who, just someone who knows."

"And then?"

"I'm going to decide what to do."

"It's too late for a choice," said Franks.

"It might be for you," said Tina. "I don't think it is for me."

They traveled into Manhattan for the meeting because it was the easiest place for everyone to gather. The original intention was to hold it in Rosenberg's office, but then Ronan offered his chambers, which were larger, and they accepted. Rosenberg came with Waldo from the FBI and someone Franks hadn't met before, a man named Myer Berenson, from the U.S. Marshals Service.

It was the first time Ronan and Franks had met since the sabotage to the ship and the hotels. The district attorney said at once, "I'm sincerely very sorry about what's happened. You understand there's nothing I could have done—no precaution I could have initiated—to stop it happening?"

"Yes," said Franks.

256

"Let's talk about what precautions you are capable of," insisted Tina. She had dressed carefully for the encounter, in a businesslike suit, and for the first time in weeks there was about her no resigned acceptance. Instead, her demeanor was brisk and forceful.

"What exactly is it you want to know, Mrs. Franks?" asked Ronan gently.

"Everything about the protection program," said Tina. *"Everything."*

Ronan looked curiously to Franks and then, as he had on the first occasion, toward Waldo, and said, "Would you like to set it out again?"

Now Waldo looked questioningly at Franks and then, as he had on the earlier occasion, recounted all the details. Tina listened, tensed forward on her chair, head slightly to one side. Although he was sure he'd made everything already clear to her, Franks had the impression that she was as incredulous as he had been when he first heard it. Her reaction, when the melting-fat man finished, was very controlled, however.

"A new identity?" she queried.

"The name has already been chosen by your husband," reminded Waldo. "Isaacs."

"And a new home?" she went on.

"Anywhere of your choice in America," said Waldo. "Your being an American citizen, there's no residency difficulty for your husband."

"So overnight we become Mr. and Mrs. Isaacs, in some part of America that we don't know. New bank accounts, new Social Security. Everything."

"Yes," said Ronan.

"I've explained all this," said Franks, beside her. "Every bit of it."

"What about the staff at Scarsdale?" said Tina, ignoring Franks. "What about Elizabeth?"

"Elizabeth?" frowned Ronan.

"She's been with the children since they were born; she is practically part of the household."

"You must understand something, Mrs. Franks," said Berenson. He was an angular, sharp-boned man with a pronounced southern accent. "The object of the program—the entire point of it—*is* protection. Which means cutting links absolutely."

"You're telling me that we'd have to get rid of Elizabeth? Dismiss her after all these years?"

"I'm saying that would be the safest thing to do," said Berenson. "I'm aware from conversations with Mr. Waldo and Mr. Ronan of arrangements your husband has made in Switzerland. Had I been asked before they were made, I would have advised against them, secure and privileged though I understand those arrangements to be. I would have thought your brother's death would have been proof enough of the determination of these people. If that isn't, then surely what's happened to the cruise liner and to the hotels in Europe is warning enough."

"What *is* that warning?" said the woman. "Spell it out for me."

Berenson looked awkwardly at the district attorney and then at Waldo, as if he were seeking some support. Then he said, "It's a very simple warning, Mrs. Franks. Either your husband—and to a much lesser extent you yourself—withdraws from this case or they will destroy you, one way or another."

"My father is very ill," said Tina. "My mother is absolutely dependent upon him. At the moment I'm spending as much time with him as possible. How often, after I become Mrs. Isaacs, would I be able to visit him?"

"It would be extremely difficult," said Ronan, coming in to relieve the pressure on Berenson.

"How *often?*" demanded Tina.

"Not at all, for a long time," said Berenson. "A very long time. These people will be aware of what's happened to your father. It would be an obvious place to concentrate, to trace you and your husband through some contact."

"Are you telling me *never?*"

"I said a very long time, Mrs. Franks."

Tina turned away from the angular man, toward the bulging Waldo. "You're familiar with the scheme?" she said. "Been involved in actual cases of protection?"

"Yes, ma'am," said Waldo cautiously.

"Were kids involved?"

"Once."

"How old?"

"It was a boy. He was about nine, I guess."

"Like David then?"

"About the same," agreed the FBI man.

"So tell me how it's done," seized the woman. "Tell me how you get a nine-year-old boy and explain it all to him. Explain it so that he doesn't think his mother has gone out of her mind and start telling it to anyone who'll listen as a joke. Tell me

258

how you do that without creating some kind of mental distur-
bance?''

Always her objection, from the very first, remembered Franks.
Had she ever intended to go along with it? Or hadn't she believed
him when he'd tried to explain to her what it would be like?

"I agree it won't be easy," said Ronan, coming to the rescue
again.

Tina turned to the district attorney. "Easy! You got any
kids, Mr. Ronan?''

The man nodded, shifting in his chair under the attack.
"Two boys and a girl.''

"Do you think you could do it?" said Tina. "You think you
could convince them to take a new name and a new home and a
new school and never tell the other kids what they'd done or
where they'd been before? Make them understand they'll never
again see their grandparents or anyone else that they've known,
apart from their parents who have a new name as well?''

"I've agreed it won't be easy," said the lawyer.

"That's trite and you know it, Mr. Ronan," said Tina. "I'd
say it would be impossible. Maybe some people enter this program and it works for them; maybe they've got funny minds and
funny kids. I don't think it will work for me. Or the children.''

Ronan came anxiously forward in his chair. "Mrs. Franks,''
he said, still gentle-voiced, "you're established now as a state
witness in a case about to come to trial. You're pledged to
cooperate. The alternative would be for me to subpoena you. I
don't want to call you before the court as a hostile witness.''

"I'm not really concerned how you call me before the
court," she said. She looked briefly sideways to Franks. "I was
not present on the first occasion when the implications of this
scheme were explained. Which is not saying they weren't set out
to me. They were. Maybe I just didn't correctly understand;
certainly I didn't appreciate in the beginning what any of it would
be like. I am not telling you that I am not prepared to give
evidence. I *am* prepared to do that. What I'm not prepared to do
is take myself and my children through some Alice-in-the-looking-
glass charade. They're bewildered enough as it is.''

Ronan's concern switched from Tina to Franks. "We've an
understanding," said the lawyer warningly. "An agreed commitment.''

"I'm aware of that," said Franks, looking not at the district
attorney but at his wife.

Gauging the district attorney's concern that Franks would

259

withdraw if his wife were not prepared to cooperate, Rosenberg said to the man, "Mrs. Franks' evidence is corroboratory; couldn't you proceed without it?"

"It's possible," said Ronan, "although I've already indicated that I don't want to. It's Mr. Franks' attitude in which I'm primarily interested, at the moment."

Rosenberg looked toward the smaller office where he and Franks had talked before and said, "Could I have a moment with Mr. and Mrs. Franks?"

"Take as long as you like," agreed Ronan. "Just remember we've got a deal that I don't intend to get reneged on."

Rosenberg led, with Tina following. As they entered the small room Rosenberg said to Franks, "I could have done with some sort of warning about this."

"I could have done with some sort of warning myself," said Franks.

"You've known how I've felt for a long time," said Tina. "From the start, in fact."

"You never refused," said Franks.

"Well I am now. It's stupid and I won't go along with it. I don't care what happened to Nicky and I don't care what happened to the ship or the hotels. If the FBI or whoever it is wants to give me some protection, then they can do it at my own home." She looked directly to Franks. "I thought the big boast was that we *weren't* running. So what's this, if it isn't running?"

"Mrs. Franks," said Rosenberg, "you heard what the district attorney said. And you *can't* ignore what happened to your brother. Or anything else. Your safety could never be guaranteed—even promised—if you remained in Scarsdale. If you're really thinking about the children, shouldn't you be thinking about protecting them? Physically protecting them, I mean."

She shook her head. "I've thought about it for a long time. Thought about practically nothing else. I'll give evidence. But I won't go into the program."

"Isn't there a further consideration, beyond the children?" the lawyer asked her.

Tina frowned at the man. "'What?"

"Your husband is the chief prosecution witness. The case stands or falls by him. I think if he's pressed, the district attorney might go ahead without you. He certainly couldn't do that in Eddie's case. And Eddie can't stay at Scarsdale. That would be suicide. You surely must accept that."

"So let Eddie go into the program," said Tina shortly.

There was a long silence in the room, with Rosenberg looking for guidance between husband and wife.

"You mean that?" said Franks.

"I wouldn't have said it if I didn't mean it."

"And you understand *what* you're saying?"

"Why don't you take her with you?" said Tina. "Then you wouldn't have to creep around the house at night with your prick in your hand."

Franks looked awkwardly to Rosenberg and then back to Tina. "I think we should talk about this somewhere else," he said.

"Why?" demanded Tina brightly. "You told me everything was out in the open between you and Rosenberg." She actually smiled at the lawyer. "Hasn't my husband told you that he's screwing Maria, my sister-in-law? Nicky's widow. They don't care who knows. You're a lawyer, Mr. Rosenberg; isn't it a criminal offense, like incest, to fuck your own sister-in-law? Or is it just a moral objection?"

It would have been Elizabeth, Franks supposed. Ahead of Rosenberg he said, "Is that why you've staged all this today?"

"No," said Tina. "And it isn't staged. Something staged means something that isn't meant, a performance. And I mean what I am saying."

To Franks, Rosenberg said, "It all comes down to you. Ronan's scared you'll back off and he'll lose his case, like the others that have been lost against these guys before."

"I know," accepted Franks, still looking at Tina. She met his gaze unflinchingly.

"So what are you going to do?" said Rosenberg.

Franks came to the other man at last. "What I always intended to do," he said. "Give evidence and get convictions against them."

Rosenberg looked briefly to Tina and then back to Franks again. "And go into the protection program afterward?"

"Yes," said Franks.

There was another prolonged silence.

"Which means that you and Mrs. Franks will be separating?"

"That's exactly what it means," agreed Franks at once.

On their way back to Scarsdale, Tina said, "You going to take Maria with you?"

"I don't know," he said.

"Do you love her?"

"I don't know that either."

261

"I think you've behaved like a bastard," she said. "An absolute bastard."

Franks snorted a laugh bitterly. "That's the most ridiculous part," he said. "All I tried to do was behave as I thought I should have done."

27

Franks moved out of Scarsdale that night, late, because before he left there was a lot to do. He called Maria first, from his bedroom, although he didn't suppose Tina would have intruded into any of the downstairs rooms. Maria asked him what he was going to do and he told her, and she said she guessed she couldn't stay on any longer at Scarsdale, either. It hadn't occurred to him until then but he said no, he guessed she couldn't.

"Can I come with you?"

Franks didn't respond at once to the question. In Manhattan he'd fantasized about her joining him, but he wasn't sure whether he wanted her with him.

"I see," she said from the other end of the line.

"No, you don't," said Franks quickly. "I was thinking of the danger, because of everything that's happening. Whether I could expect you to run the risk."

"I'm prepared to," she said immediately.

"All right," agreed Franks. "And thank you. I'll arrange it with Tomkiss. I'm leaving them to find a place."

"I'm not sorry," blurted Maria. "About it coming out, I mean."

"Neither am I," said Franks, knowing that was what she wanted him to say.

"I just didn't want to hurt Tina. To hurt anybody," said the woman.

"Neither did I," said Franks. So why had he done it in the first place? Hadn't he sneered a long time ago at men who had to prove something by sleeping around? Yes, thought Franks; a long time ago.

"What shall I do?" asked Maria, relying on him.

"Just come to wherever the FBI people take you," said Franks. "I'll be there."

"Everything is going to work out okay," she said.

That used to be his reassurance, remembered Franks. To Tina. He said, "Sure. I know it is. I'll see you later."

He told Tomkiss what he wanted, alert for the man's reaction because people's reaction to him seemed important these days. The FBI agent just nodded and said sure, he'd fix it, and how long would he be? Franks asked for an hour. Tina and Elizabeth were with the children when he went to their adjoining rooms. Without being asked—without any conversation whatsoever—both the women withdrew. David looked up at him soberly and said, "Mommy's been crying."

"Has she?" said Franks, surprised.

"Is she worried about Poppa?" asked Gabriella.

"Yes," said Franks, seizing the excuse. Hurriedly he said, "I'm going away."

"Where?" frowned the boy.

"Work," lied Franks. "You know how I have to go away."

"So you'll be back?" pressed David.

He couldn't lie, Franks decided. Or tell the truth, either. He wedged himself onto Gabriella's bed and pulled her onto his lap, blinking the sudden blur from his eyes. "Probably not for a long time," he said. "I've got a lot to do and I'm going to be very busy, so you mustn't expect to see me for a long time."

"How long?" demanded David.

"I'm not sure, not yet," said Franks. "So while I'm away you've got to be the man of the house. Look after Mommy for me."

"What about all the men?" asked the girl. "Are they going away too?"

"No," said Franks. "They'll still be here. You've got to look after Mommy inside the house."

"Is that why Mommy was crying, as well as about Poppa? Because you're going away?" pressed David.

"I should think so," said Franks. Why—having sought to feel emotion for so long—was he embarrassed about it now? He nuzzled his face into Gabriella's hair, so that David wouldn't see how close he was to tears, and said, "I want you both to be good now. Understood?"

"Sure," said David.

"Do everything that Mommy tells you."

"Why can't we come with you?" asked Gabriella. "We used to, when you went away to work before."

Would there be a divorce? Arrangements about access and things like that? It was the usual procedure, Franks knew; but his circumstances weren't usual. It was something he was going to have to discuss with Rosenberg. To the child he said, "This is a very difficult job. You can't come, not this time."

"Not at all, not later?" persisted the girl.

"I'll see," avoided Franks.

"Promise?" said David predictably.

Franks swallowed. "Promise," he said awkwardly.

"You all right, Daddy?" said David.

"Gabby's hair has got into my eyes. Made them water," said Franks. He put the child back onto her bed and stood up abruptly. "I've got to go," he said.

"You're going tonight?"

"Yes."

"Come back as soon as you can," said Gabriella.

Franks scrubbed his hand across his eyes, and said, "Your hair really hurts. Remember what I said about being good." He bent quickly, kissed Gabriella first and then David, who didn't try to pull away like he normally did.

Back in the corridor outside Franks had to blink a lot to be able to see clearly, concentrating on the other calls he had to make in an effort to recover from his encounter with the children. He went downstairs to use the telephone in the small sitting room, because the drinks were there, pouring and drinking one in a series of gulps and then making another before moving to the telephone. Podmore seemed to have taken over the de facto chairmanship of the groups in his absence, so Franks bothered only to call him, explaining that he was going to be unavailable at Scarsdale from that night and that any messages should be channeled through Rosenberg. The English lawyer said that the Italian authorities were refusing to reissue health certificates to four of the hotels, and that a labor dispute that seemed to be restricted only to their properties was disrupting business at three of the Spanish hotels. Too, the insurers of the liner were questioning whether to settle the necessary repairs or declare the vessel a write-off. Franks tried to give the instructions on the telephone, hot with frustration at not being able to get on the next plane and personally resolve the difficulties. Which was how he'd always operated and wanted to operate now, troubleshooting the problems as they arose. He made Podmore give an undertaking to

264

remain in close contact with Rosenberg and then called the New York lawyer at home to explain the yet further arrangements he'd made involving the man.

"There are other things that need to be done," warned Rosenberg. "If this is going to be an official separation you'll need to agree on support payments and property division . . . things like that."

"Will you fix it for me?" sighed Franks.

"I'm sorry it's happened," sympathized the American. "Lot of things seem to be happening all at once."

"Too many," agreed Franks. "And thanks."

"Where are you going?"

"I don't know. I'll call you, tomorrow."

Tomkiss and Sheridan were waiting in the car when Franks emerged. Franks turned, keeping the house in sight through the rear window as the vehicle wound down the driveway. He stayed that way until it vanished from view and then slumped in the back.

"It's all fixed," said Tomkiss.

"Good," said Franks.

"You familiar with Kingston?" asked the FBI man.

Franks looked up at the man, paying attention for the first time. "Yes," he said, distantly. "I know Kingston." It was the entrance to the Catskills, where Enrico had stopped when they made the trip there as kids, pointing out the Onteora Trail and then circling the reservoir and identifying Mount Tobias and Mount Tremper and the highest of them all, Slide Mountain. It was on the lower hills of Slide Mountain that Enrico had set the crossing challenge and he'd almost been engulfed in the slurry.

"Borrowed a 'safe house' there, from the CIA. You'll be okay."

Franks realized he'd gone from not being scared to being unconcerned what happened to him. "Good," he repeated automatically.

The house was not actually in Kingston but two miles south, on the road to High Falls. It was surrounded by a wall and the gate was electronically operated, with an intercom set into the wall. Just inside there was a small gatehouse in which Franks saw the figures of at least two men as they drove through. The driveway was lighted, and in the illumination Franks saw what appeared to be junction boxes or some sort of electronic apparatus and guessed the grounds were protected by sensors as well as human guards.

Maria was already there. There was a central hallway, with

four doors leading off, and she was to the left, in what appeared to be the largest room. She was sitting nervously on the very edge of the couch and as he entered she got up, started toward him and then stopped, uncertain.

"Hello," she said.

"Hello."

"I got here about an hour ago."

"Yes."

"Was it bad?"

"Not really," said Franks. "Tina is being very controlled about the whole thing. It wasn't very easy with the children."

"What did you tell them?"

"That I was going away for a long time on business," said Franks. He looked around the room and said, "Is there a drink anywhere?"

Appearing glad of the activity, Maria went to a side cupboard and poured the gin, taking one for herself, too. "That leaves Tina to tell them?" she said as she handed him the glass.

"Maybe it's better that they hear it from her," said Franks, irked by the unspoken accusation. "What happened at the Scargos'?"

Now it was Maria's turn to be awkward. "I didn't tell them anything," she said. "I just told Mamma that I had to get away; let her think it was something to do with Nicky's death."

He smiled sadly at her. "We're both a couple of cowards, aren't we?" he said.

She smiled back. "Seems like it," she said.

"Where are your bags?"

"Upstairs."

"You've already chosen our room then?"

"*Our* room?"

"Isn't it going to be?" he frowned.

"I wanted to hear you say it."

"Nervous?"

"Very," she nodded. "Silly, isn't it? I didn't feel scared at Scarsdale, but now I do."

Knowing that he should—that he should have the moment he came into the house—Franks went to her, and took the glass from her so that she wouldn't spill it, and kissed her. She kissed him back urgently, clutching her arms around his waist. He could feel her shaking and ran his hand through her hair, and said, "Okay. It's all going to be okay."

"I know it is," she said, trying hard. "I know it is."

266

He was a refugee again, thought Franks. He'd imagined—hopefully—that the attitude had left him forever, but it came suddenly and was as positive as it had been that day on the New York dockside and then back again, in Southampton, meeting a father he'd never known nor learned how to know. More positively, in fact. He felt more completely alone and abandoned than he ever remembered feeling before, and it frightened him, so that he physically shivered. Maria felt it and pulled away, frowning up into his face.

"What is it?" she said.

"Nothing."

"You shivered."

"It was nothing."

She remained doubtful, looking up at him expectantly. He said, "Do we look after ourselves here?"

"It seems like it," said Maria. "I've found the kitchen. The refrigerator's stocked."

"Looks like you're making supper then," said Franks, seeking an escape.

"You sure you're okay?"

"Positive."

"I don't want you to say it back—I told you that before—but I think I love you, Eddie Franks," she said.

"I think I love you, too."

"You didn't have to say it."

"I wanted to."

"I wanted you to."

That night and the days that followed provided the first release—a relaxation—for what seemed to Franks to be years. He established telephone contact with Rosenberg and through the New York attorney attempted arm's-length control of the European businesses—frustrated that he couldn't do more—but that was his only irritation. There was the aphrodisiac of the illicit about his relationship with Maria, but he thought it went beyond that, to something more. Maria never criticized—never questioned him—but was content to listen and understand. He told her about the arrangements he had made to protect the European businesses and how he hoped everything would be over in time for him to be able to solve the difficulties personally. Objectively, she suggested that the bacillus attack and the ship sabotage and the union disruptions might have been created precisely to achieve that: his appearance in an unguarded situation. They spent evenings entwined watching television or listening to music and during the

267

day explored the expansive grounds of the CIA installation. During the third week Franks made the demand to Tomkiss, who said he'd have to get higher clearance, which was given, so they were allowed out of the enclosure and wandered along the Esopus and through Stony Hollow into the mountain foothills. There was always an escort of FBI agents and marshals, but Franks found that in Maria's company he was able to forget them, as she appeared to be. He confessed to her the contests that Enrico set him and Nicky, and pointed out Slide Mountain and actually tried to find the slurry slip, although he didn't succeed. They made love every day and often more than once, on the couch in front of the television or actually going to bed in the afternoon. Maria was completely uninhibited, and at her urging he did things with her he would have never considered with Tina. Realizing how highly sexed she was, Franks was astonished she'd remained faithful as long as she had to the unresponsive Nicky.

He held back from attempting any direct telephone contact with Tina, instead asking Rosenberg to arrange any maintenance that she might need. Tina's initial reaction was that she didn't want any support, but Rosenberg persuaded her to engage a lawyer of her own and in consultation with him created an agreement. As well as an interim financial settlement Franks drew from Switzerland, he also made the Scarsdale house over to her in its entirety, the only condition being that she retain the necessary votes that maintained his control in the European shareholding. Tina agreed at once.

Rosenberg argued against overgenerosity, but Franks was insistent. He inquired through the lawyer whether Tina wanted to keep the Henley house in England, and when she said she didn't, instructed the lawyer to place it on the market. Although she said she didn't want to know, because she considered it none of her business, Franks discussed everything with Maria. On each occasion when they talked about it Maria listened but said very little, careful never to judge what he was doing, even when he asked her for her opinion.

The trial was set for the last week in July. There were fresh journeys, alone, into Manhattan, for revision and reconsideration of the evidence. Franks used the trips to see Rosenberg as well, and on the last one learned of Podmore's assessment of the year's trading prospects. In Italy the business was expected to show a drop of seventy-five percent on the previous year, and two hotels were still so polluted that the health authorities were considering their permanent closure. Trading in Spain was down by forty percent and in France by thirty. Overall, their current year's business was reduced by fifty percent and the forecast for the following year, unless there was some way of restoring public confidence, was that the decline would exceed that. Repairing the liner, which had taken three months to settle with the insurance company, was being delayed by industrial disputes in the Amsterdam shipyard, and effectively the vessel's trading potential had to be dismissed for the entire year. Profit forecast, before tax, would certainly show a reduction of four million pounds from the previous year, and the possibility was that the drop would be even greater. If so, then it would be necessary to go into reserves to finance the advertising and refurbishing necessary for the next year. Podmore's covering letter reminded Franks of the time limit that had been agreed for his returning to England to resume control. Franks instructed the American lawyer to reply that he was fully aware of the timing and would be back, as he had undertaken to be.

"You can't promise that," said Rosenberg. "For God's sake, Eddie, when are you going to recognize, after all that's happened, the precautions you're going to have to take?"

"They're near panic, right?" said Franks, gesturing to the bulging file from England that lay between them on Rosenberg's desk.

"Looks like that," agreed the lawyer.

"So what effect would a letter from me create, saying I can't maintain the undertaking? I'm maintaining confidence; it's an essential principle of business."

"So what happens in six months' time? Or rather five and a half months' time, when they'll be pressing for dates?"

"I'll answer that in five and a half months' time," said Franks. "By then the trial will be over and the hotel pollution may be cleared up." Franks stopped as the idea occurred to him. "For Christ's sake, why haven't they thought about it in England!" he erupted angrily. "Tell Podmore to stop pissing about with Italian fumigation and cleaning experts. Tell him to get the best company in Britain to create a team and fly them out to Italy to cleanse every hotel. Tell him to send a photographer and a writer from the publicity department to record every step of the cleaning and when it's successful—but only when it's successful, because if it isn't then it'll backfire—issue a complete release on how a baffling infection was beaten. Tell them to send hygiene specialists and doctors as well, if necessary. It'll cost a lot, but it'll be worth every penny if the publicity is sufficiently wide-spread to restore the confidence that Podmore is so worried about."

Rosenberg made the required note on his pad and said, "Six months is still too soon, Eddie."

"I'm fed up talking about it," refused Franks. Running again, he thought.

Ronan said he wanted Franks in a secure hotel in Manhattan throughout the trial, as he had been for the grand jury hearings, and estimated it could last as long as a month. Maria made a particular effort the night before he left, cooking the beef which she'd learned was his favorite. He told her it was very good, which it was, but he found it difficult to eat, just as she appeared to do.

"You going to be all right by yourself?" he asked.

"Of course. And I won't exactly be by myself, will I?"

Hadn't Tina said something like that, some time? He couldn't remember. He said, "I'll be glad to get the trial over. Then we can get away. Thought where you'd like to go?"

"I'll leave you to decide that."

"Think about it while I'm gone."

"It's going to feel strange without you," said Maria. "I've got used to your being around all the time."

"Maybe it won't last for a month."

"Phone?"

"Every day."

"This will be the first time you've confronted them since the dissolution meeting, won't it?" she said.

"Yes," said Franks. It seemed a lifetime ago, he thought, and then realized it was: Nicky's lifetime.

"Be careful."

"There's hardly anything they can do in a court, is there?"

"There doesn't seem much they can't do."

"They're going to go to jail and then it will all be over," said Franks.

They exhausted themselves that night with love and Maria, always the demanding one, awoke him before it was properly light and they made love again. She sat, unspeaking, while he packed his cases, and remained silent while he carried them downstairs into the hallway.

"Do you want anything to eat?" she said at last.

"Just coffee."

They drank it in the kitchen, sitting opposite one another.

270

She said, "There seemed something final about the way you were packing."

"Don't be silly."

"Do everything they tell you," she said. "The FBI, I mean. Don't take any chances."

"You know I won't."

"I don't ever remember being so happy as I have been here with you. Despite everything outside."

"Or me," said Franks. Was that strictly true? He'd been very contented and settled with Tina when he evolved the long-weekend working routine in England. He must remember to ask Rosenberg how the sale of the Henley house was progressing. He said, "I've got to go."

"Yes."

They stood facing each other, neither moving. Then Franks went to her and kissed her, and she gripped him, and said, her voice muffled into his shoulder, "Hurry back."

There was a tight escort into Manhattan, one car in front and two behind and another man joining Tomkiss and Sheridan actually inside their own vehicle. There was a lot of radio traffic. From the front Franks heard Tomkiss say, "Shit!" The FBI man looked back and said, "Outside the court it's like the Fourth of July, apparently. Photographers and television cameras everywhere. They think it's too dangerous to go in the front; they're going to set up a decoy arrival and we're going to go in through the back."

Which is what they did, Franks huddled in the middle of a complete circle of guards, head bent, hurrying into the building, and up in an elevator to the fifth floor. Once, remembered Franks, he'd been embarrassed by the procedure. He wasn't anymore. He was jostled into an anteroom similar to that he'd used at the grand jury hearings, surprised to see Tina already there. She was apart from the other witnesses. Waldo and Schultz were at the far end of the room, talking to Knap, and there were a number of other men whom Franks had not met before. Franks hesitated and then went over to his wife.

"Hello," he said.

"Hello."

"How's your father?"

"He's out of bed now. We can get him around in a wheel-chair. There's some speech difficulty, but he's being helped by a therapist."

"I wanted to keep in touch," said Franks defensively. "The lawyers said everything should go through them."

"I know," she said.

"How's David? Gabby?"

"David still swears, and Gabby wet the bed three times last week."

"What have you told them about us?"

"The truth, which you didn't seem able to."

"What's that?"

"That we've broken up," she said. "Is Maria with you?"

"Yes."

"How is she?"

"Fine," said Franks. Awkwardly he added, "Thank you."

"I asked the FBI people up at the house where you were. They wouldn't tell me."

"There's no reason you shouldn't know," said Franks. "There's a house, near Kingston. Belongs to the CIA. Lot of electronic surveillance and stuff like that."

"I seem to be getting used to it," said the woman.

"How are you?"

"Okay, I guess," she said, looking directly at him. "You?"

"Okay, I guess."

"David asked last week if he could see you."

"We'll have to arrange something," said Franks. "I want to see him, too. And Gabby, of course. I'll talk to Tomkiss about it."

"I suppose we'd better involve the lawyers, too?"

"Yes," said Franks. "It all seems a bit ridiculous, doesn't it?"

"It has for a long time."

"There've been a lot of attacks on the companies in Europe," he said.

"As well as the liner explosion?"

"Some hotels in Italy and France were poisoned. And there are a lot of labor problems in Spain."

"What are you doing about it?"

"There's nothing I can do at the moment."

"Worried about it?"

"Naturally," said Franks. "Podmore and the others don't seem able to handle it."

"You going to go back?"

"That was always the plan."

272

"Thank you for giving me the Scarsdale house. My lawyer says you're being very generous."

He smiled briefly. "That's what Rosenberg says, too."

"I don't want us to fall out over any settlement," said Tina. "I've always thought it terrible that people who once loved each other should end up hating each other when it comes to dividing things."

"I don't want that, either," said Franks. It was good to be able to talk to Tina without arguing. He thought she looked pale but very pretty.

"I'm determined it won't happen," she said.

"You booked into a hotel here?"

She nodded. "The Plaza, like last time."

"Me, too," said Franks.

"Did Maria come with you?"

"No."

Ronan hurried into the room, interrupting them. The district attorney paused briefly at Waldo and the other men and then continued across the room toward them. Ronan smiled and shook hands, and said, "All set?"

"You tell us," said Franks.

"They've got impressive counsel," said Ronan. "It's going to be a fight."

"Wasn't it always?"

"This time we're going to get them," said the district attorney. "I'm sure of it."

"You'd better be, after what it's entailed," said Franks.

Ronan looked between them, as if he'd forgotten the breakup. To Tina he said, "Thank you for agreeing to testify."

"I don't want to spend too much time away from the children."

"I'll call you as quickly as I can."

Which wasn't that day or several days after, because there was a lengthy opening and then professional, investigative evidence to call, before them. The first night Franks said it was ridiculous for them to eat alone as they were being kept in the same hotel, and Tina agreed and came to his suite for dinner. She said that until the trial was over she didn't know what to do about the children's interrupted education, and for the time being was relying upon FBI-approved tutors who were coming into Scarsdale every day. She asked what he thought about their future schooling and Franks said he'd always thought it would be in

273

England, but if she wanted to remain in America then he didn't mind it being there.

Directly after the meal was finished, Tina said she thought she'd better get back to her own rooms because she had calls to make, and Franks said of course, because he still had to telephone Maria. He walked with Tina to the door, unsure whether there should any parting kiss or a handshake and decided that both would be wrong so he did nothing. Maria said she'd expected him to call earlier. Franks hesitated at telling her about the meal with Tina, and said instead that he'd been tied up. She asked how the case was going and he said he didn't know, because until he was called he wasn't allowed in court, but that Ronan appeared confident. She asked if he'd seen Tina at the court and he said yes: they'd talked about the children and the settlement. Maria asked how she'd looked and Franks said tired but okay. Maria said she loved him and made him promise to call—earlier—the following night, and Franks said he loved her too and promised he would. After he replaced the receiver Franks sat nursing his brandy, asking himself why he'd ducked telling her about Tina. He seemed to duck so much when it came to making personal decisions. Maria had never indicated any doubt or jealousy—in fact had steadfastly refused to put herself between them in any way since the separation—so why couldn't he have told her about the dinner? There was nothing wrong with having eaten with Tina, for God's sake!

A pattern developed between Franks and Tina through the next days. They went separately each day to the courtroom—scurrying through various doors but not always avoiding the photographers and newsmen—and remained together in the waiting room. His rooms at the Plaza became the regular eating place but later than the first night, so that they could make their calls first. In addition to the nightly contact with Maria, Franks kept in touch with Podmore in London, increasingly anxious at the way the businesses were slipping. The English hygiene experts had gone to Italy as he instructed and cleaned the hotels, but four days after their return, there had been fresh outbreaks at five of the premises. Franks talked the problems through with Tina, glad there was someone to whom he could talk. She asked him what he could do about it and Franks said he didn't know, and Tina said—not argumentatively—that she'd never known him unsure about anything before. Franks wasn't annoyed at the observation, recognizing it to be true. There was a lot about the time they spent together that reminded Franks of how it had been before

274

with him and Tina. He *was* content and he *was* relaxed at Kingston with Maria, but there was still an edge to their relationship, a need for him to impress her. He supposed it was because of the newness of everything with her. With Tina, he didn't feel the need to do anything. Was that because he knew her so completely, or because whatever there had been between them was over and it didn't matter to him anymore whether she admired him? Another unanswered question, to join the long list.

Ronan warned them the day before he intended calling them and said Tina would be first. That last night they made their calls, and they ate, as they always did, in his rooms.

"I'll go back to Scarsdale directly after I've given evidence," she said. "I want to get back to the children."

"Of course," said Franks. "Will you tell them you've seen me?"

"Naturally," said Tina, surprised by the question. "There's no reason why I shouldn't."

"Give them my love," said Franks. "And tell them I'll see them soon."

"I don't think it's a good idea to make promises you can't be sure of."

"I don't intend it to be a promise I can't keep," said Franks. He paused and said, "It's all been a bit unnatural—more than a bit—but it's been good to see you again."

"You, too," said Tina. She looked down into her wineglass and then said, "I'm sorry that it had to happen. The breakup, I mean. I've thought about it a lot, since you've gone. Much of it was my fault; most of it. . . ." She smiled up at him sadly, and said, "It was a pity I wasn't able to be stronger."

"I'm sorry it happened, too," said Franks. "I've thought about it as well. Maybe I should have done what Nicky and Poppa wanted."

"No," she said at once. "You did the right thing; *are* doing the right thing. I still think you're very brave. I hope the bastards go down for life for what they've done. And are doing."

"I hope to God it'll stop, if they do go to jail," said Franks with deep feeling.

"I hope so, too. For your sake," said Tina. "I know that there'll still be people around at Scarsdale, but really I expect it to be over for me after I've given evidence tomorrow. It's not going to be for you, is it?"

"I'm expecting it to be," said Franks. "Not at once, but soon."

"Poor darling," she said. "I don't think it's going to be."
Franks looked directly at her, caught more by her use of the
word than by her opinion. She appeared to become aware of it
too and colored slightly. To help her he said, "You sound like all
the rest."
"I know I keep saying it, so that it sounds practically like a
recorded message, but you'll be careful, won't you?"
"Yes."
"There's something else."
"What?"
"Give Maria a message from me. Tell her I don't hate her
for what happened. I don't want to see her or imagine we could
be friends like we were before. But I don't hate her."
"Thank you," said Franks. "That'll mean a lot to her."
"It's been good to be with you again."
"We said that," reminded Franks.
"Yes, we did, didn't we," she said.
No! thought Franks. He could see and certainly feel what
was happening, but he wouldn't let it. He'd made too many
personal mistakes—as well as business mistakes—and he wasn't
going to allow any more. Although he wanted to. The second
awareness alarmed him more than the first. His emotions were
becoming more entangled and knotted than a wool ball dropped
in a kitten's nest; he'd lost the beginning and didn't know where
the end was to be found, but he certainly didn't intend to tangle
the strands any more than they were already. He said, "You're
on the witness stand tomorrow."
"Ouch!"
"Things aren't normal, darling, so don't—" he managed
before he realized the word and stopped. "Shit!" he said.
"I don't want us to break up, Eddie," she said intently. "I
fucked up, badly. I made all the mistakes, and I know I don't
have any right to expect any sort of forgiveness, but that's what
I'm asking for. I didn't know what it was going to be like, seeing
you like this. I was frightened to hell. When you walked into the
witnesses' room that first day I creamed in my pants just at the
sight of you. I love you and the children love you. I'm asking
you to come back. Come back to us however and whenever, and
I promise I won't be stupid anymore. That I'll do all I can to
help, which I realize that I didn't do before. I want—"
"Stop it, Tina!" cut off Franks.
She did and Franks didn't say anything more; they remained
looking at each other across the table. To create some movement,

276

more than for any other reason, he gestured with the brandy bottle, and she nodded acceptance, each waiting for the other to say something first.

Tina broke the silence. "Lucky Maria," she said.

"I don't know!" said Franks. "I just don't know!"

"You do, about me," said Tina.

Around and around goes the ball of wool, thought Franks. He said, "That doesn't make anything any easier."

Tina looked toward the door leading in to the bedroom. "I want to stay tonight," she said.

"Tina, please!" said Franks. No! he thought again. Definitely no.

She played with her brandy glass, not drinking from it. "Short of taking off all my clothes, putting on sackcloth and pouring ashes over my head, I don't know what else I can do," she said.

"You don't have to do any more," he said.

"Which brings it back to you," she said.

"You're pushing me," protested Franks, hating his own ineffectiveness.

"I set out to push you," Tina admitted.

"Don't!"

"All right," she said, backing off. "Just so you know."

"I know," said Franks. "I know."

"I meant what I said, about staying."

"No!"

"You want me to go?"

"Yes."

"This isn't how it's supposed to be in movies and books."

"This isn't movies and books."

"If it were, no one would believe it."

"Please go, Tina."

"Sure," she said.

"You think I'm a shit?"

"No."

"I feel like one."

"Maybe that's how I should feel. You're with Maria now, after all."

"Can I call you? Direct I mean?"

"Of course."

"I'd like to."

"Have you told Maria about our meeting here?"

"She knew you were a witness; that we'd obviously meet."

"That wasn't what I meant."

"No," admitted Franks. "I haven't told her." From the first night he'd delayed the second night, and then he'd decided Maria would suspect him of keeping things from her—which he was—so he decided against doing it at all.

"Why not?"

"Because I didn't."

"That sounds like David when he's petulant."

"I asked you to go."

"I thought you might change your mind."

"I won't."

"Sure?"

"Quite sure."

"You didn't try to make love to me that night on the boat, when you were at Harvard and we went sailing off Martha's Vineyard. Do you remember?"

"I remember," said Franks nostalgically.

"I thought you would. Try to, I mean. I made my mind up to do everything but go the whole way. But you didn't try. I know I thanked you afterward, but I always wished you'd tried. For a long time I thought there might be something wrong with me. That I wasn't attractive or sexy or something."

He poured more brandy for them both, and she said, "Do you really want that?"

"No," he said.

"Why'd you pour it, then?"

"Because I couldn't think of anything to say and it gave me something to do."

"Am I making you uncomfortable?"

"Yes."

"Horny?"

Yes, he thought. He said, "If we're going to solve anything, this isn't the way to do it. It isn't a screwing competition."

The coquettishness went abruptly from her. "No," she conceded. "It isn't, is it?" She tried to brighten. "I always did trust you to do the right thing, remember? Like you're doing now. I don't know what's going to happen between us. I'm glad at least that you're uncertain."

Franks wished that he weren't. He said, "I still care, Tina."

"Nurses and doctors care," she said.

"You're being flip."

"It's a kind of protection."

278

"I'll come up to see you, as soon as I can," said Franks. "The children, too."

"Tell Maria," insisted the woman. "I want her to know."

"Why?"

"I just do."

"Now you sound like David."

Tina stood abruptly. "There won't be time for any proper good-byes at the witnesses' room tomorrow."

"I guess not," said Franks. What was a proper good-bye?

Tina stood with her hands resting on the small table between them, looking down at him. "I want you to kiss me," she said.

Franks stood, keeping the table between them, leaning forward.

"Not like that," said the woman.

Franks came around the obstruction, wanting to reach out for her but holding back.

"I said I wanted you to kiss me."

Franks felt out, tentatively, and she reached for his hands. They didn't come together in any tight embrace but kissed with their bodies scarcely touching, mouths only slightly parted, tongue nervous against tongue. Franks was the first to stand back, breaking the contact.

"I'll go," she said.

"Yes."

"Did I say I loved you?"

"I think you did."

"I thought I'd say it again. Just to make sure you understood."

"Good night, Tina."

"Good night." She came forward quickly, kissing him again, and then turned for the door. He followed to let her out, and in the corridor she said, "Good luck, for tomorrow."

"You, too," he said.

Tina was called first, as Ronan had promised. Her evidence about shareholding division was little more than technical, and her ignorance of the organization within the Bahamian or Bermudan companies so obvious that the lawyers for the three accused men quite quickly abandoned any attempt at unsettling her. It was still before midday when she emerged from the court into the ante-room. It was crowded, and as Tina had predicted the previous night there was no possibility of any sort of proper good-bye. The usher who saw her out stood waiting in the doorway to take Franks into the courtroom.

"I'll be in touch," said Franks.

"I'll be waiting."

He remained in the room, watching his wife make for the corridor between her two FBI escorts, so he wasn't immediately aware of Ronan coming up behind the increasingly impatient usher.

"Ready?" queried the district attorney.

Franks turned. "Ready," he said.

28

Franks' impression as he walked into the courtroom was of entering an arena. From Ronan's opening and the evidence already given he was known to be the principal prosecution witness and was the sole object of attention of everyone in the room. There was a small nameplate on the rostrum identifying the white-haired judge as a man called Basnett. The man looked at him expressionlessly as Franks took the stand and recited the oath. To Franks' left sat the jury, seven men and five women. Directly in front was Ronan at the prosecutor's table. To his left, each with a separate table, sat Flamini, then Pascara, and then Dukes. Each of the accused had two men with him whom Franks assumed were counsel. Luigi Pascara sat directly behind his father, just the rail designating the public section of the court separating them. Luigi met Franks' gaze, staring back with the intense look that Franks remembered from previous occasions, when the man appeared to be memorizing every feature. Franks held the look and completed the oath without faltering. He didn't drop his eyes until, at the invitation from the judge, he sat in the witness box. The public area of the court was crammed with people. The press area was crowded, too, with reporters overflowing into the public area.

Ronan came forward, had Franks formally identify himself, and then with the care that the man had always shown started to take him through the evidence of his entrapment. There was complete silence and very little movement in the courtroom, only the undulating hands of the court recorder at her machine and an occasional cough or shift from the public area. Flamini and Dukes stared at him with the intensity of Luigi Pascara, and the blind man faced toward him, too. Very occasionally there was a whispered consultation between the men and their lawyers, at something that Franks said.

He was scarcely into his evidence at the luncheon adjournment. Everyone stood for the judge's departure, and as people began to drift from the room Franks said to the district attorney, "How's it going?"

"You're doing fine," encouraged the man.

"That wasn't what I meant," said Franks. "The case generally."

"I'm still happy."

Tomkiss was hovering protectively beside the witness stand, and as Franks started to leave he looked toward the accused men. Pascara was sitting, awaiting some guidance, but behind him Luigi looked directly across the court, and as their eyes met the man imperceptibly shook his head, a gesture of sad finality. Matching theatrics with theatrics, Franks openly smiled at him and followed Tomkiss from the court.

Franks' evidence was still incomplete at the evening adjournment. They left through the front entrance, through an explosion of television lights and camera flashes and yelled, unanswered questions. Back at the Plaza, Franks fixed his drink and thought how lonely he felt without Tina's company. Or was it Maria he missed?

He called the safe house at Kingston and had a longer conversation than usual because for the first time in days there was something to talk about. He told her how Luigi Pascara had looked at him and the stupidity of the headshake and how the others had stared at him, too. She asked how he thought the evidence was going, and he told her of Ronan's confidence and said he still had a long way to go before it was complete.

"What's it like, actually confronting them?"

"It's like nothing," said Franks. "Sort of sterile, really."

"Aren't you frightened?"

"No," he said at once. "That's the odd thing about all three of them: none of them look capable of hurting anyone."

"They don't do it personally, do they?" pointed out Maria. "Somebody else does it for them."

Luigi looked capable of killing someone, thought Franks.

"How was Tina?" asked the woman.

"Tina?" asked Franks guiltily.

"You've seen her, haven't you? You told me she was being called to give evidence. I've been waiting for you to talk about it."

Franks was conscious of the strain in her voice. He said, "She's okay. Actually she asked me to give you a message. That she doesn't hate you for what's happened."

"How did you feel?"

"Feel?"

"Seeing her, for the first time."

"Awkward," said Franks. "Poppa's out of bed. Needs help with his speech, apparently."

There was nothing from Maria's end of the line, and Franks waited for her to press further. Instead she said, "Still no idea when you'll get back?"

"No," said Franks, relieved.

"I miss you."

"I miss you, too."

"Honestly?" she demanded.

"Honestly," said Franks. With whom and about what was he being honest? Franks asked himself.

After finishing the call to Maria, Franks remained by the telephone, thinking of Tina. Should he call? He'd intended to when he entered the suite, but after talking to Maria he was undecided. Who deserved his loyalty? And love, for that matter. Tina, who admitted that the breakdown had been her fault? Or Maria, who'd asked for nothing and never taken sides and was prepared to run any sort of physical risk to be with him? Was it possible to love two people? Possible, he supposed. But stupid and selfish to consider it as a sensible question. Franks moved positively away from the telephone, deciding against calling Scarsdale. Twice during the evening the resolve weakened, and twice he managed to resist. He went to court the following morning pleased with his self-control but not quite sure what he had achieved by it.

The entire day was again occupied by Franks' answers to Ronan's questioning. Remembering Maria's question about fear— and the same question from other people—Franks spoke a lot of the time looking directly at the men who'd cheated him, wanting them to recognize it as the challenge it was. He included Luigi in the attention because he wanted that little bastard with his head-shaking artificiality to recognize it more than any of the others. By the afternoon Franks decided they'd realized the point and were unsettled by it, and he was delighted. He actually tried to heighten his contempt.

Franks had concluded his evidence in chief by the evening adjournment, and Ronan said he wanted a conference. Remembering the emptiness of the previous night, without Tina in the suite with him, Franks suggested their eating together. Ronan accepted and Franks extended the invitation to include Waldo and Schultz, because they were housed in the same hotel. They returned there in the same protective group of cars.

Both the FBI men had given their evidence and so were spending their time now in the body of the court. Almost at once, when they reached the suite, Waldo said, "You got to them today."

"I wanted to," said Franks vindictively. "They've pulled every trick they can against me, so now it's their turn to squirm."

"And maybe yours," warned Ronan.

"Me?"

"The cross-examination starts tomorrow," said the district attorney. "We've got a good case, but you're the linchpin that holds everything together. If your evidence can be discredited or destroyed . . . put into doubt in any substantial way . . . then they've got a chance."

"Wait a minute!" said Franks, immediately alarmed. "You saying that after everything that's happened, they could walk away from this?"

"No," said Ronan. "I know we've done well, up to now. And I think that the jury has been impressed by the evidence you've given so far. You know how some of it sounds—how it could seem that you were involved—because we've discussed it. Thus far, I think, we've got the benefit of any doubt they might have. What I'm saying is that, good though it looks, we shouldn't become complacent and imagine we've got the conviction; there's still a way to go yet."

Franks knew that the district attorney was trying to reassure him but he didn't feel reassured. "What are you telling me I ought to do?"

"Just be careful," said Ronan. "There's a lot of tricks that can be pulled inside as well as outside a court. Stay cool, however hard they go at you. They'll bully and they'll pressure and they'll come at you from every way but which, trying to panic you. Don't say anything without first thinking what it is you're saying. That'll be the ploy: to get you angry or confused so that you say something without thinking, something that's not quite right or correct, so that it looks as if you're changing the evidence you've already given.''

"Tripodi is the one to watch," said Schultz, entering the conversation. "He's the young guy with glasses who's representing Flamini. He's out to make a reputation for himself as a trial lawyer.''

"I think you're right," said Waldo. "He gave me more trouble than any of the others.''

"Who are the others?" asked Franks, wanting as much rehearsal as possible.

"The lawyer for Pascara is called Samuelson. Chicago firm, long-established law practice. Represented Pascara before. The elderly, white-haired guy who walks with a limp," said Waldo. "Dukes' lawyer is a young lion, too, although not as good as Tripodi. Name's Collington. Tends to get carried away and fall over himself, which creates a bad impression in front of a jury. Tripodi is cooler than a polar bear's ass.''

Franks realized suddenly that he was being coached, psyched into performing like American football players were encouraged by cheerleaders; and American football was a game Franks had never been able to understand, either. Rah, rah, rah, he thought. To Ronan he said, "You sure you're as confident about this as you say you are?"

"Absolutely," said the district attorney.

"That was too quick.''

"That was the truth.''

There was an interruption while the courses were changed at the table. When the waiters left the suite—escorted by the outside guards—Franks said, "I want to know what's happened. What's happened in the court while I've been outside. I've seen the newscasts and I've read the newspaper accounts and it all seemed to be going well.'' Franks paused, looking to Ronan. "Like you said.'' He allowed another break. He started again, "As far as you people are concerned, this is a case. A good case but still just a case. It goes down if you're lucky, and it gets thrown out of court if you're not. So you can start again and make another one, and maybe you'll get lucky the next time. I don't have that luxury. I committed myself for all the reasons that you know, and now I have the feeling—despite everything you say—that it hasn't gone as well as you expected. And that you're worried. So level with me. What's the problem?''

There was a shuffled exchange of looks between the three other men. Ronan nodded, accepting the responsibility, and said,

"Flamini isn't looking as he should. Pascara and Dukes have got the numbered accounts around their necks, like the weight that's going to pull them under. But it's not so strong against Flamini."

Franks looked to each of them in turn. "But what can I do about that?" he said in growing exasperation. "You've made the case. Assembled the evidence. I can only say what there is to say; what the truth is."

"We're not asking you to say anything more than that," said Ronan. "All I'm trying to do—we're trying to do—is prepare you for what might happen out there in court tomorrow."

Franks looked across the narrow space between himself and the other men. "This could get away from you," he said accusingly.

"It isn't going to happen," said Ronan.

"It could?" insisted Franks.

"It could," conceded the district attorney finally.

It was the opinion that throbbed through Franks' mind as he entered the court the following morning, settled himself in the witness stand, and looked expectantly toward the assembled defense counsel. It was Samuelson who rose to begin the questioning, and as the elderly man limped toward him Franks wondered if they had engaged in a conference like his the previous evening to formulate some combined attack.

The white-haired lawyer stopped short of the witness box, looking not toward Franks but to the jury, examining each of the jurors intently, as if he had not properly seen them before. Very much a theater, thought Franks.

Still not looking directly at him, Samuelson said, "You did a deal, didn't you, Mr. Franks?"

"A deal?" delayed Franks.

"Yes," said the lawyer. "In exchange for no prosecution being made against you, you agreed to testify against my client? And Mr. Flamini and Mr. Dukes?"

"I was cheated and duped by your client and by Flamini and Dukes," said Franks. "As I have already made clear to this court."

"That's not a proper answer to my question," said the lawyer.

"It's a very proper answer to your question," said Franks. He detected the wince that crossed Ronan's face and remembered the previous night's injunction against responding too hastily; it hadn't taken him long to forget.

"No, it's not," persisted Samuelson. "Tell the jury and tell the court, were you at any time threatened with prosecution?"

285

"I was told a case could be brought against me," conceded Franks.

Samuelson allowed a long pause, conveying to the jury the impression of a major admission. "A case could be brought against you?" he said.

"Yes."

"Why was that?"

Franks frowned, refusing to make any rushed response. "I don't understand the question," he said.

"Forgive me, for being so obtuse," apologized the lawyer emptily. "Why could a case have been brought against you?"

"Because the district attorney considered one could have been made, I suppose."

"So why wasn't it?"

"Because, having heard my account of what happened, the district attorney decided I was innocent," said Franks. He detected Ronan's nod of approval and was relieved.

"That isn't what happened at all, is it, Mr. Franks? You were confronted with a choice. Either you testified against my client or you'd be charged yourself. That's how it was, wasn't it, Mr. Franks?"

Franks hesitated, alert for any unseen traps. He said, "During the initial interview—the very first—the district attorney said he considered there was evidence proving my involvement. Having heard my account he revised that opinion."

"He told you that, did he?" demanded Samuelson sharply.

Careful, thought Franks.

"Nothing is obvious until it is proven to be the truth in court, Mr. Franks. Did the district attorney tell you that he considered you innocent?"

Franks tried to find the danger but couldn't, and so he said, "Yes."

"Why?" said the lawyer.

Franks frowned again, at the apparent stupidity of the question. "He believed it."

"Believed it!" pounced Samuelson. He swept out his arm in a flamboyant gesture to embrace the jury and said, "Or was it just to convince the jury here today, to make them think that you were a reliable witness, to be trusted, and not somebody who had escaped a prosecution which the evidence we've heard in the preceding days amply justifies. Somebody, in fact, deserving prosecution far more than my client or anyone else arraigned in this court!"

286

Franks could feel perspiration making an irritating path down his back, and the palms of his hands were wet, too. He said, "I was tricked; the charges prove that."

"Who tricked you?" demanded Samuelson, changing direction.

"Pascara, Flamini, and Dukes," said Franks as forcefully as he could.

"How?" said Samuelson simply.

"How?" echoed Franks too quickly. "I've spent days sitting here telling you how."

"No," refused Samuelson. "You've spent days telling us what you'd like us to believe, and that's altogether different. Tell the jury the circumstances of my client, Mr. Pascara, coming forward to make contact with you. Tell the jury how he set out the idea of the hotel and casino complexes and inveigled you unwittingly into criminal activities."

Franks bridled at the sarcasm but tried to avoid overreacting to it. "That wasn't how it happened," he said badly.

"No!" seized Samuelson, quickly again. "That wasn't how it happened at all, was it, Mr. Franks?"

"I've already explained how the arrangement was made. Through my brother-in-law, Mr. Scargo."

"Now dead and unable to testify," said Samuelson.

"Now murdered and unable to testify," said Franks. "To the convenience of your client!"

"I move that remark struck from the record and the jury instructed to disregard it," protested the lawyer at once. "There is nothing whatsoever to link my client with the assassination of Nicholas Scargo."

"It will be struck from the record," said the judge. He looked from the court recorder to the jury and said, "I also direct you to disregard that." To Franks, the judge said, "You will not make any more improper remarks like that in this court."

"In my opinion—considering the duress and pressure under which I've existed since the beginning of this affair—I do not consider them improper," said Franks.

"Mr. Franks," warned the judge. "You will not argue with me in this court. You will conduct yourself in the manner in which I direct."

"I will tell the truth," said Franks. Fuck the man, he thought; I'll not play puppet to some legal stage direction.

The judge stared down at him, confronted with open insolence. "Be careful, Mr. Franks," said the man. "Be very careful

287

indeed." He looked beyond, at the lawyer, and said, "Continue, Mr. Samuelson."

Franks looked across the court to Ronan, seeking some reaction from the district attorney. The man gazed back blank-faced.

"Whose concept was a hotel chain in the Caribbean islands, Bermuda and the Bahamas?" picked up Samuelson.

Franks considered he'd emerged ahead in the exchange and felt sure that despite the judge's instruction the jury would not be able to dismiss what he'd said from their minds. Overconfident, he said, "As accuracy is essential I think Bermuda is more correctly described as being in the Atlantic."

"I greatly appreciate the correction," said Samuelson with heavy sarcasm, and Franks regretted his own gesture; theatricality was infectious, he thought.

Quickly, not wanting to lose the advantage he considered he'd established, Franks said, "It was my idea to create the hotel group."

"Not Mr. Pascara's?" said Samuelson in apparent surprise.

"No," said Franks tightly.

"Or Mr. Flamini's?"

"No."

"Or Mr. Dukes'?"

"No."

Samuelson intruded another of his dramatic silences, looking back and forth along the assembled jury, inviting their surprise to match his. He said, "So neither Mr. Pascara nor Mr. Flamini nor Mr. Dukes approached you to establish a hotel chain in the Caribbean . . ." There was an aching, artificial pause. "Forgive me, Atlantic, islands of Bermuda or the Bahamas."

"I've made that quite clear," said Franks, wondering how much of his imagined advantage was left.

"You're making a great deal clear, Mr. Franks," said the lawyer. "More with every answer, in fact."

"I'm delighted to be making the truth clearer," fought back Franks.

"I'm delighted, too," responded the experienced lawyer. Beyond the limping man Franks thought he saw Ronan move his head in a gesture of sadness.

Samuelson said, "Your idea. So having had the idea of creating a chain of hotels, what happened then?"

"I've already explained what happened," said Franks. There was a band of wetness around his waist, where the sweat was gathering.

"Explain it again," insisted the lawyer. He allowed a gap. "You've already advised the court of the importance of accuracy, even in the geographic location of islands. So explain it again so that there is complete and utter accuracy."

"I told my brother-in-law what I planned to do. He asked me how I intended to arrange finance and said he would be able to get a better deal in America than I could in England. He mentioned banks and he also said that he knew of private investors, with whom he'd dealt before, who might be interested. I made some inquiries and it appeared that money would be cheaper here than in England. Because of certain international events the money market tightened and the borrowing would have been expensive. So I agreed with my brother-in-law that we should explore the possibility of private investors." And had the chance to pull out, he remembered. Dear God, how much would have been different if he'd only done that!

"*You* decided to approach Mr. Pascara!"

"I did not know the names; any of them," said Franks. "The introduction came through my . . ." He hesitated, thinking. "Through my murdered brother-in-law," he completed.

Samuelson paused, too, glancing toward the judge as if expecting a rebuke. When none came, the lawyer said, "What did you want, Mr. Franks?"

"Want?" queried Franks.

"Why did you have—if indeed this was the way the transaction went—why did you have your brother-in-law approach Mr. Pascara? And the other two accused?"

"As investors," said Franks, his voice indicating the obviousness of the answer.

"For money?" said Samuelson.

"For investment," quibbled Franks.

"Is money important to you, Mr. Franks?"

"It's very difficult to establish businesses without it," avoided Franks easily.

"You have a lot of businesses?"

"Some."

"All profitable?"

Seeing another advantage, Franks said, "They were, until I agreed to testify against Pascara and Flamini and Dukes. Since which time—"

"—I would ask the court—" Samuelson interrupted, but Franks shouted over him.

"Since which time they have been subject to attack and disruption and every effort made financially to ruin me."

To the judge the lawyer said, "The inference of those remarks is obvious to everyone in this court and completely unsubstantiated and I would ask once more that they be expunged from the record and the jury instructed to disregard them."

"Mr. Samuelson," said the judge, "I would agree with you that the innuendo is unfortunate, but you posed the question to invite such a response. It seemed to me that the witness was directly answering the question about the profitability of his other businesses."

The lawyer's sudden burst of color was accentuated by the whiteness of his hair. To Franks he said, "Profit is important to you?"

"Profit is the basis of all business," lectured Franks, increasingly confident.

"Tell the court about the businesses other than those in Bermuda and the Bahamas," invited Samuelson.

"All are concerned with the leisure industry," said Franks.

"That wasn't what I meant, Mr. Franks."

"Perhaps I would be better able to understand the questions if they were posed more specifically."

The other man's color deepened. "Tell the court about the control of those companies."

"In every enterprise—with the holding of my wife who has already given evidence before this court—I maintain individual control."

"Help the court by further explaining what that means."

"It means exactly what I've said," insisted Franks. "I have control of my companies."

"There are no outside shareholders? No public stock issue?"

"No," said Franks, seeing the direction the questioning was taking and unworried by it.

"Why then, on the venture in the Bahamas and Bermuda, were you prepared to abandon the established practice of a lifetime and take in outside investors?"

"I've already made clear that borrowed money was dear. It was a better business arrangement to involve Pascara and Flamini and Dukes."

"But you insisted upon retaining control, didn't you?" demanded Samuelson.

Shit, thought Franks, fully realizing. "Yes," he said.

"So the companies through which these alleged criminal activities were conducted were in no way controlled or administered by my client, Mr. Pascara. You controlled them?"

"I *established* them," said Franks, attempting the qualification. "And the casino proposal came directly from them, not from me."

"Really!" said Samuelson, in artificial surprise. "My recollection . . . ." He stopped, hand against his head, and then limped the entire width of the court to his desk to retrieve a notepad, which he appeared to consult before looking up. "My recollection," he repeated, "is that Mr. Snarsbrook, a minister under indictment for offenses in his own country, told this court that the approach for a casino was made personally by yourself, with no involvement of my client or any other of the accused. The same Mr. Snarsbrook who also told this court of receiving a sum of money with the personal thanks of someone called Eddie." The pause was perfect. "Your name is Edmund and you're more usually referred to as Eddie, isn't that so, Mr. Franks?"

"I have no knowledge, interest or awareness of the bank account from which that payment was made to Snarsbrook," insisted Franks doggedly. "I did not bribe Snarsbrook to set up the casino. The use of the word 'Eddie' is an obvious and blatant entrapment."

"Would you describe yourself, hitherto, as a successful businessman, Mr. Franks?"

"I would like to think so."

"An experienced businessman?"

"Yes."

"Certainly not one to be tricked or cheated."

Franks saw the pit yawning before him but didn't know how to avoid it. "I have already explained, in my main evidence to this court, how for the first time I was tricked and cheated. It never happened before. Nor—believe me—will it ever happen again. I was gullible and I was stupid and I was used."

"By Scargo?"

"Initially, yes."

"The relationship between yourself and Scargo went beyond that of simple brothers-in-law, did it not?"

"Yes."

"You spent a considerable time in the Scargo family; you were evacuated here to America during the European war?"

"Yes."

"I've heard the description given in court that the relationship was, in fact, not that of brothers-*in-law* but as that of brothers?"

"Yes," admitted Franks.

291

"The Scargo family took you in, when you were a refugee? Protected and cared for you?"

"I have also given evidence to that effect."

"You've also given evidence that Nicholas Scargo, someone whom you knew as a brother, ensnared you into a criminal business activity."

"Yes!"

"You'd fallen out; become bitter enemies?"

"No."

"You mean you were friends?"

Never friends, thought Franks. "I thought so," he said, lying knowingly.

"Mr. Franks," said Samuelson, stressing the incredulity, "are you asking this court to accept as the truth that Nicholas Scargo, whom you regarded as a brother and who loved you as a brother in return, set out to deceive and trap you, for no reason that has ever been presented to this court? And that you, an experienced, sensible businessman, allowed that entrapment to take place!"

"That's how it happened," said Franks desperately.

"You're English, are you not?" said Samuelson.

"Yes," said Franks.

"Are you familiar with the writings of an English author called Lewis Carroll?"

Franks shook his head, looking inquiringly toward Ronan, who was also frowning.

"In a work called *Through the Looking Glass,* Carroll had one of his characters, Tweedledee, comment upon logic." Samuelson went to his reminder pad, starting to quote, " 'If it was so, it might be; and if it were so, it would be; but as it isn't, it ain't.' " The lawyer looked up, not bothering to leave his desk. "That, Mr. Franks, is the most apt description of your evidence I can imagine."

Ronan was on his feet, objecting on the grounds of comment rather than questioning, but Samuelson had already sat down, rendering the protest meaningless.

Tripodi rose to continue, but the judge declared the midday adjournment. Franks ate with Ronan, apologizing at once for what had happened. The district attorney insisted that Franks' showing had not been as bad as the man imagined it had been, but Franks was unconvinced. His own opinion was that he'd done extremely badly and nullified any impression he might have created while presenting the main part of his evidence.

"The mistakes you made were genuine ones," said the state lawyer. "You looked like a man unaccustomed to courts; not like someone who was lying."

"More or less confident than before?"

"About the same," said the district attorney.

When the court resumed in the afternoon, Franks thought Tripodi looked like a greyhound impatient to be released from the trap; certainly he came forward with a set-free urgency. Samuelson had been hard, but there had been some leisurely buildup to his cross-examination, which wasn't Tripodi's style.

He thrust a document toward Franks, and said, "Tell the court what that is."

Franks took it, recognized it at once. "Company records," he said.

"Which company?"

"The island hotels."

"What is recorded on page twenty?"

Franks knew, from the volume number, but turned to the page anyway. "The initial discussion about installing a casino at one of the hotels."

"*Initial?*" snatched Tripodi.

"The first board discussion," said Franks.

"But not the first discussion in which you'd been involved, was it, Mr. Franks?"

"I've explained the circumstances of that," said Franks wearily.

"That there had been informal talks, in the absence of Nicky Scargo; that my client and Mr. Pascara and Mr. Dukes were aware of what was going on?"

"Yes!" insisted Franks, with growing exasperation.

"What would you say, Mr. Franks, if I were to tell you that my client has no recollection whatsoever of any talks with you or with anyone else about installing a casino either in Bermuda or on the Bahamas before the date set out in those company records? By which time you'd already been to Las Vegas and to the islands and engaged in detailed talks with a great number of people?"

"I would say that Flamini is a liar," said Franks simply.

"Mr. Flamini contends that you're the liar, Mr. Franks."

"He doesn't have any alternative, does he?"

"He has some interesting evidence, though," said Tripodi, unruffled. "Let's turn to page twenty-two. What's set out there?"

Resigned, Franks went through the appearance of consulting

the records and said, "It sets out the debate concerning the casino installation."

"Sets out the debate concerning the casino installation," echoed Tripodi for emphasis. "Is there not a remark of yours there attesting that in the Bahamas there was a market for a casino . . ." Tripodi looked toward the jury. "And here I quote," he said, " 'above the common denominator.' "

"Yes," said Franks.

"Did you make that remark, at that meeting?"

"I don't remember specifically, but if it's written there I must have done. I signed them as a true record of the meeting."

"Indeed you did, Mr. Franks. And I'm obliged to you for having made that clear to the jury. We are considering a true and accurate record of a meeting at which a discussion was held about a casino, the very first discussion in which my client was involved."

"That's not true!" rejected Franks. "He was at the previous meeting."

"Of which there is no record and of which no one, with the exception of yourself, has any recollection."

"It happened!" said Franks, knowing his desperation was showing.

"According to you," sneered Tripodi. "Read to the jury what is recorded on the tenth line of page twenty-two."

Franks strained down, trying to find the place. "It quotes Flamini saying that each would destroy the other."

"What does that mean?"

Franks saw the chance of recovery and snatched at it. "He was actually quoting me; reiterating my objection to the idea of a casino at all."

"Was he!" said Tripodi, equally as quick. "The early part of the report of that meeting specifies you as saying that the idea of Las Vegas-type casinos would be destructive; it was not an argument against a casino as such."

"It was!" insisted Franks.

"From Mr. Flamini," said Tripodi. "Not from you." He turned to the jury, repeated the page and line number, and said, "I would invite you, members of the jury, to consider the evidence that Mr. Franks agrees to be an accurate record and decide for yourselves—which is, after all, your function—whom to believe on this matter." Coming back to Franks, Tripodi said, "Don't the records that you're holding, on that very page, show Mr. Flamini referring to the idea of a casino as being a risk?"

"Yes," said Franks.

"And isn't it from Mr. Flamini that the idea comes—and I quote again, 'even if we decide to proceed'—to establish a company separate from the hotels, to minimize any risk?"

"Yes," said Franks.

"Turn the page, Mr. Franks," invited the lawyer. "Read for the benefit of the jury the first three lines that begin that page."

Franks turned the page, sighing down at what was written. He looked up forlornly toward Ronan.

Tripodi said, his voice loud and hectoring, "Read the section, Mr. Franks."

Franks went back to the page and read, " 'So you're in favor of a specialized, exclusive casino operation? Your attitude is important, don't forget. You've got the controlling stockholding.' "

"This comes from a document you attest to be a true record?" repeated Tripodi.

"I've already said that," reminded Franks.

"Who made that remark?"

"Flamini."

"To whom?"

"Me."

"Read your response from the document in front of you," ordered Tripodi.

" 'I am in favor but I think the argument for holding the gambling operation under a separate company is a good one. I'd like the ease of severance, if it becomes necessary.' "

"You said that?" insisted Tripodi.

"This is ridiculous," Franks tried to fight back. "Everything is being taken and twisted, out of every context and out of every truth. I went to Las Vegas and I went to Bermuda and the Bahamas as the result of a board discussion. I was discharging my proper duty, as chairman, fully to investigate a situation before committing my board to it. Having made that examination, I was responding to a board meeting as honestly and truthfully as I felt able."

"I don't believe you know the meaning of honesty and truth," said Tripodi.

"Objection!" came in the waiting Ronan at once. "That is not a question but a comment and a highly improper one at that."

"I agree," said the judge. "It will be taken from the record and the jury will discount it. I invite you to behave yourself with more propriety, Mr. Tripodi."

295

"I apologize," said the lawyer, but Franks decided there was no contrition because the man had achieved precisely what he intended. Tripodi waved the copy of the company minutes toward Franks, like a matador enticing a bull to overcommit itself, and said, " 'If, at the end of all the inquiries and negotiations, we decide to go on, then I'd be very pleased to act as chairman' . . ." He looked up. "You said that, didn't you, Mr. Franks?"

"Yes," Franks admitted.

"Because you wanted to go on controlling everything. The hotels that you created, the capital you received from my client, a respectable and honest financier, and then the casino, which you wanted to establish for its illegal potential."

"No!" said Franks. "I did not want to retain control for anything illegal. I wanted to retain control because that's the way I've always worked."

"I'm interested in the way you've always worked," said Tripodi. As Samuelson had before him, the young lawyer made much of crossing the room to his table and notes and taking up his yellow legal pad, searching for a reminder. He smiled up and then recrossed the courtroom. "Who are Peter Armitrage and Winston Graham and Richard Blackstaff and Herbert Wilkinson and James Partridge and Eric de Falco?"

Franks swallowed. "Officials with whom I dealt in the establishment of the hotels in Bermuda and the Bahamas."

"You're an honest man, Mr. Franks?"

"Yes."

"Who would not consider anything illegal or questionable in his business dealings?"

"It's a recognized practice," said Franks, too anxious to defend himself.

"What is, Mr. Franks?"

"Paying commissions, for assistance."

"These people were employees of their island governments?"

"Yes."

"Salaried employees?"

"I presume so."

"Yet you paid them commissions!"

"Like I said, it's a recognized practice."

"Recognized by whom, Mr. Franks?"

"Businessmen. Officials," groped Franks helplessly.

"You know, don't you, that the men I've identified are currently facing trial in their own countries? And that the charge is accepting bribes?"

"Yes," said Franks. "I understand that."

"Bribes supplied by you: an honest, truthful businessman who would never consider anything illegal."

"Properly recorded in the company accounts!"

"*Improperly* recorded in the company accounts, as commissions to people who had no right to receive them and who are facing legal proceedings as a result of being seduced into criminality by you," said the lawyer.

"That isn't the way it was," protested Franks. It was appalling, Franks knew. Absolutely and utterly appalling. Whatever impression he'd managed to create with the jury was being completely destroyed by these men twisting and juggling the facts. Why couldn't Ronan or the judge intervene, to stop it happening!

"You entrapped Mr. Flamini, didn't you?"

"No."

"Persuaded him into an investment and then used that investment to establish a pattern of gross illegality?"

"No."

"And then turned state's evidence to save your own neck?"

"No!"

"You're a crook, aren't you, Mr. Franks? A crook who thinks he's found the way out of a prosecution?"

"I'm not a crook. I'm telling the truth," protested Franks.

Tripodi turned triumphantly to the jury. "Your function, members of the jury, is to decide who is telling the truth in this matter!"

There was another conference but no meal that night, and Ronan didn't bother with any false reassurances. Franks apologized again and the district attorney repeated that some telling points were made in favor of the prosecution case but that some damage had been done to it as well. There would still be an opportunity to reestablish the facts in the jury's mind when the time came for reexamination. Neither Waldo nor Schultz took a very active part in the discussion, but toward the end Waldo said, "The bastards can't get away; they just can't!"

Franks looked toward the fat man and remembered what Schultz had told him in the London hotel room.

Ronan said, "I still don't think they are going to get away."

"I'm not sure, not anymore," said Waldo.

"What could we have done that we haven't?" asked the district attorney. "Nothing's been overlooked in the evidence

297

we've got. And it's *still* a good case. We anticipated what happened today; let's not talk ourselves into believing that it's worse than it is."

Franks felt physically sick after the prosecutor and the FBI men left the room, certainly with no wish to eat. He drank, instead. He called Maria, who had already seen a report on television, and agreed with her that it was as bad as the accounts were making it. She tried to talk him out of his depression and Franks became annoyed at some of the things she said, at her ignorance, at not really knowing or understanding what was happening. He snapped dismissively at her efforts and Maria stopped talking, not arguing back. Franks became irritated at the whole conversation and so he cut it short, but having done so stared around the empty suite and wondered what to do. Impulsively he called Rosenberg at home. The lawyer had also seen the newscasts. He said criminal prosecutions went that way, for and against, and that Franks shouldn't imagine everything was lost simply on the basis of one seemingly bad day.

"Ronan should have done more to protect me," said Franks petulantly.

"There are court limits to what he's able to do," said Rosenberg. "You're up against some very clever defense counsel who know precisely what those limits are and can remain just safely inside them."

"I need you there," said Franks, petulant still.

"To do what?" asked the lawyer. "I can't intervene; take any part. Not publicly at least. I certainly couldn't leap up and down in court, making protests."

"I feel utterly alone out there," complained Franks. "Like I'm naked."

"Then you'd better stop," advised Rosenberg. "That's how they want you to feel. How they intend to get you to make mistakes."

"Can I call, to talk things through?"

"Any time," said Rosenberg. "You know that."

"Anything to talk about from England?"

"No," said Rosenberg. "I'd have mentioned it if there was."

Franks made himself another drink after he finished the conversation with Rosenberg and was in the process of mixing still another one, actually thinking of Tina, when she called him, the telephone ring making him jump.

"It wasn't easy getting through to you," said Tina. "They intercept everything. Did you know that?"

"I guess they would," said Franks. "I'm glad you did."

"I saw the television news. It sounded terrible."

"It was."

"They're not going to get off, are they?"

"They could."

"But that's—" Tina broke off, searching for the words. "It'll mean it's all been for nothing," she said. "Wasted."

"I haven't worked out what it'll mean," said Franks wearily.

"After our talk I thought you might have called," she said.

"I was going to," said Franks. He didn't want to get into this sort of conversation, not tonight.

"Have you thought about it? What I said, I mean."

"Of course I have," he said. "Let's get the hearing over first. Please."

"I warned you I was going to push."

"Not tonight."

"You sound pretty low."

"I am."

"I could come down. I guess it wouldn't be easy, but I could get Tomkiss or somebody to fix it."

He'd enjoyed the evenings with her in the suite, Franks remembered. But it wouldn't just be an evening if she came down, would it? There would be the night as well. He said, "No. It would be too difficult to arrange and I don't think it would be a good idea anyway."

"You sure?"

"Quite sure." To move the conversation on, he said, "How are the children?"

"Okay," said Tina. "I didn't let them watch the newscasts. Gabby hasn't wet the bed for a week."

"That's good," said Franks. He'd wanted to talk to her, just like he'd wanted to talk to Maria, earlier, but now that they were speaking Franks was anxious for the conversation to end. Lying, he said, "I've got a conference, with Ronan. Preparation for tomorrow."

"Of course," she said at once. "You will call?"

"When I get the chance."

"Good luck."

"Thanks."

"Maybe tomorrow will be better," she said.

It was, but only marginally. Collington was as overeager as Waldo had predicted, but he still succeeded with the inferences and innuendo. Dukes' lawyer concentrated upon the Las Vegas

299

visit, and without any documentary evidence the impression again was that Franks initiated the approach to Greenberg, using Dukes as the intermediary.

"You asked Mr. Dukes to arrange meetings for you in Las Vegas, knowing of his existing business involvement in a casino there?"

"It was Dukes' suggestion, not mine."

"It is my intention to call Mr. Greenberg to the stand at some time," disclosed the urgent Collington. "Mr. Greenberg will tell this court that he agreed to meet you when Mr. Dukes asked him as a personal favor. And that personal favor was to provide some advice for someone who wanted to set up an offshore gambling operation."

"The casino idea was Dukes'," insisted Franks.

"Greenberg will testify that it was clear, from all the conversations he had with you, that it was your proposal."

"It was the proposal of the company I was representing."

"The company of which you have already told this court you insisted upon maintaining rigid and personal control," seized Collington. "If it was the proposal of the company, then it had to be *your* proposal, didn't it?"

"I was acting for the others."

"All the inquiries were made to Mr. Greenberg and other casino operators by yourself. Never Mr. Dukes, who was with you. Or Mr. Flamini or Mr. Pascara."

"Of course that was the way it was!" said Franks. "They were setting me up as the front man, weren't they!"

"I suggest that you were setting them up, Mr. Franks," said Collington. "Eager for their finance and, in Mr. Dukes' case, some peripheral contacts, you tricked my client into a criminal enterprise."

"You know—everyone in this court knows—that that wasn't the case," said Franks. He felt tired. Weary and disinterested in the whole thing.

"No, they don't," said Collington. "There's a great deal that people in this court don't yet know," said the lawyer aggressively. "Didn't Snarsbrook make it clear to you in the discussions about a casino—discussions which you and nobody else initiated—that any approval from the island government would reflect their confidence in you personally?"

How he'd responded to and been sucked up by the flattery, Franks remembered bitterly. "He was bribed, too, wasn't he!" he demanded. "The whole thing was a charade, from the begin-

300

ning to end. Snarsbrook had been approached about a casino before I ever got there.''

"Oh, Mr. Franks!'' said Collington, stretching the words to heighten his supposed incredulity. "There has to be a limit to the number of different ways in which you try to distort the truth. *You* approached Snarsbrook, nobody else. Every record of every discussion, which has been obtained from the Bahamian government and which will be introduced into this court when the time comes, shows that Snarsbrook was acting very much on your behalf, the behalf of his paymaster.''

"I did not bribe William Snarsbrook.''

Collington took up a slip of paper from his desk, appeared to study it, and then quoted, " 'Thanks for all your help and assistance, Eddie.' ''

"That is not me.''

"Who is it, then, Mr. Franks? What other person called Eddie wanted a casino in the Bahamas badly enough to pay a three-hundred-thousand-dollar bribe?''

"Dukes and Flamini and Pascara!'' shouted Franks carelessly, his control slipping.

"Are you aware that the given name of my client, Mr. Dukes, is David? And that of Mr. Flamini is Roland? And that of Mr. Pascara is Roberto?''

Collington had run too fast, and Franks saw the opportunity. "I am further aware that Mr. Dukes is also known by the aliases Tony Alberi and Georgio Alcante, and that Flamini is also Frederick Dialcano and Emanuel Calvo, and that Pascara also uses the aliases of Arno Pellacio and Roberto Longurno and Luigi del Angelo. All appear very adept, in fact, at creating names just like that created to make it appear that I bribed Snarsbrook,'' he said.

Collington's face tightened angrily at the aliases and his awareness of the effect they would have on the jury. Beyond the defense lawyer Franks saw Ronan nodding his head in satisfaction and actually smiling in Waldo's direction.

Collington was still questioning at the recess and occupied most of the afternoon trying to make Franks appear the perpetrator of any crime, but Franks didn't think the man succeeded. Ronan confirmed the failure during their evening conference. Franks spoke to both Maria and Tina but again cut the conversations short, feeling he had nothing to say to either and using the already completed meeting with the district attorney as the reason for hanging up.

Franks remained in the witness box for another full three

days, recovering sufficiently during Ronan's reexamination for them to have a restrained celebratory dinner toward the end of the week, but then becoming doubtful again at some renewed questioning from Tripodi. After the completion of his testimony, Franks remained, protected by Waldo and Schultz, in the well of the court, intent upon the evidence. Knap and the other Internal Revenue Investigators were the most impressive, their evidence of bank accounts and credit transfers seemingly dull and pendantic but in reality difficult for any of the defense counsel to contest.

The defense lasted as long as the prosecution, another fortnight. Snarsbrook was called to say he negotiated on behalf of Franks and believed the three-hundred-thousand dollars came from him, and the Bermudan and Bahamian officials whom he'd bribed were paraded and identified him as the man who had arranged their payments. Ronan was unable to shake Snarsbrook, and the facts involving the other government officials were incontestable. Franks' anxiety worsened. It lifted only slightly when all three defense lawyers refused to put their clients on the stand to give evidence. In his closing speech Ronan indicated that they were frightened to undergo any cross-examination; the defense counsel insisted it was because the prosecution had no case to answer anyway.

The jury retired at midday on Tuesday of the fifth week. They made it clear by early evening that they could not reach a verdict and so they were moved, under escort, to a hotel. There they remained for another two days.

Both Maria and Tina offered to come into Manhattan, to be with him, but Franks refused both, pleading the personal danger to both but not sure in his own mind if that was the reason.

The jury indicated verdicts on Friday, and the court was reconvened at eleven in the morning. Franks sat tense and hollow-stomached between Waldo and Schultz, leaning forward.

"Members of the jury, have you reached your verdict?" asked the court official.

"We have," replied the chairman, a stooped, bookish-looking man.

"How do you find on all the charges against Roberto Pascara?"

"Guilty," announced the chairman.

A numbness of relief spread throughout Franks; he was conscious of some sort of whimper or shout forming at the back of his throat and bit against it, hands gripped whitely on the court bench beneath his legs.

302

"How do you find on all the charges against David Dukes?"

"Guilty," said the chairman.

Franks was aware of the shifting movement of excitement from either side, from Waldo and Schultz, but he didn't trust himself to look at either; directly ahead Ronan was having difficulty in remaining still at the victory.

"How do you find on the charges against Roland Flamini?"

"Not guilty," said the stooped man.

There was a moment of complete silence in the court, a shocked suspension of movement from everyone around him. Then, from his left, Franks heard Waldo say, "Son of a bitch!"

29

Florida was Maria's suggestion. Franks said it really didn't matter because he didn't intend remaining there anyway, although he was careful, despite the confusion of the crowded days, not to let Ronan or Waldo or any of the marshals think he was doing anything but fully entering the program. They were provided with a suburban house near St. Petersburg, on the Gulf Coast. It had a screened pool and an inlet from the back canal for a boat if they wanted one. Franks formally adopted the name David Isaacs and obtained a Social Security number and a bank account listed under it; the bank provided the reference when he made credit card applications in the new name. Waldo gave him telephone numbers, both office and home, for any contact, any time, but their protection became the responsibility specifically of the Marshals Service. Myer Berenson, the marshal who'd tried to reassure Tina that day in Ronan's office, traveled personally to Florida to inspect the protection arrangements. His officers were housed in a separate bungalow, linked by a closed circuit television system that covered every approach to the main house, and Berenson assured them it would be monitored twenty-four hours a day. The angular southerner expressed no surprise at finding Franks with a woman different from the one he'd met in the district attorney's office, and Franks guessed the man had been warned; enough people knew, after all. Berenson provided telephone numbers, like Waldo, and there were alarm bleepers for Franks and Maria linking them to the guards' bungalow, in addition to the television protection. Thank God, thought Franks, that it was only temporary.

The precautions seemed greater than they had been at the CIA house, although Franks realized they probably weren't; here everything was concentrated into a far smaller area than it had been at Kingston. He tried, and he knew Maria tried even harder, to recapture what existed for them in the Catskills hideaway. They swam in the pool and Franks—Isaacs—bought a car, and they drove under discreet escort to Naples and to Tampa and one day took an expedition into the Everglades. They made plans to drive around the Gulf and up to New Orleans, which Maria knew and said he'd like and Franks said he wanted to see. The marshals advised against engaging staff during the initial months because anyone they employed would have to know them as Isaacs and would need an explanation for the initial tight security. Maria said she didn't want any help anyway but preferred to keep house by herself. She did it very well. Franks began putting on weight because he was doing absolutely nothing except telephoning. He did that constantly, to Rosenberg in New York and to Podmore in London, desperately trying to keep the businesses intact. The Italian authorities finally closed two of the hotels down. The publicity that the case attracted severely affected everything, according to the pessimistic Podmore. Certainly the figures justified pessimism. The following year's prebookings were down seventy percent—an indicator that had proved reliable in the past—and the New York court case encouraged the English insurers of the liner to query a clause in the policy that excluded willful sabotage; Podmore assured Franks he was initiating court proceedings but it was likely to be a year before a hearing, and in the meantime the Amsterdam repairers had to be paid out of company resources, which were in overdraft because of the non-working of the liner anyway. The revised profit forecast was for a reduction of six million pounds from the previous year. There was never a conversation with Podmore when the English lawyer didn't remind Franks of his committed time limit for a return, and Franks got the impression that the man was sitting in his London office ticking off the dates day by day on a calender constantly in front of him. Franks came to rely absolutely upon Rosenberg, talking everything through with the man, and within a month of their being installed in Florida Rosenberg said, "They're running scared. I don't think they're doing a goddamned thing to keep anything operating as it should be. They just want out, as soon as possible."

"It's not going to happen; but what if they have to offer the companies publicly? It doesn't make sense to run them down," protested Franks. "What price would they get?"

"What price do they want to get?" argued Rosenberg. "They're salaried directors; all they need is enough money left over to pay themselves a salary. They're your companies; you're the loser."

"I always seem to be," said Franks, unhappy at the quickness of the self-pity.

"I could go across, if you want," offered Rosenberg. "I could go with your power of attorney. Kick ass a little."

"Let's leave it run for a while," said Franks. "But thanks." He paused and said, "And I want to kick all the ass myself. You can't imagine how much I'm looking forward to it."

"You're paying for my advice," reminded Rosenberg. "And my advice is that in England everything is fouling up badly."

"I know," said Franks. "I'm going to fix it. Soon."

Franks created a den in a small room off the main sitting room for his business contacts, and Maria respected his privacy. He was grateful, because the calls he made from there weren't all business. He told her about calling Scarsdale, because it was entirely understandable that he would want to retain contact with the children, but he didn't tell her of the sort of conversations he was having with Tina or the increasing dilemma they were creating for him, to go with everything else. Tina fluctuated from the coquettish to the openly sexual and then further demanding. She repeated during every conversation how sorry she was for the breakup, which was entirely her fault, and pleaded with him to make up. As Franks' response to her grew, so did his guilt about Maria. Franks decided that he didn't want to hurt her, and he didn't want to leave her, but he didn't want to stay apart from Tina either, and he was completely fucked up. The strain stretched their relationship. They both recognized it and both tried to pretend that it wasn't happening. They spent evenings like they had at Kingston, wrapped in each other's arms watching television or listening to the music on the elaborate stereo system that Franks installed. He lavished presents upon her, a diamond ring which she studiously avoided putting on her engagement finger, and three weeks later a matching necklace. The gifts were not all ostentatious. He bought her flowers—from street stalls as well as

305

from gift-wrapping florists—and once a T-shirt with the message
"I Love You" and on another occasion, during a trip to Tampa,
a troll doll from a street vendor that cost him only ninety cents.

It was Maria who brought things out into the open. They'd
eaten and she'd cleared away, and they'd decided they didn't
want either television or music. She said, head against his chest
so that she didn't have to look at him, "Don't you think you
should try to see the kids sometime?"

"I've been thinking that," said Franks. Why was he always
using David and Gabby?

"And Tina," added the woman.

Franks didn't reply at once. She deserved honesty as much
as—if not more than—she deserved jewelry and intentionally
cute toys, Franks thought. He said, "I did see her, in New York.
During the trial."

"You told me."

"Not how it really was. We weren't called for quite a long
time. We ate together, talked about things."

"I guessed," said Maria.

"We didn't sleep together," protested Franks urgently.

"She's your wife."

"We *didn't!*" insisted Franks. "You've got to believe me
about that."

"If you tell me then I believe you," said the woman. "Did
you want to?"

"Yes," he said, determined on the honesty at last. "But I
didn't. I didn't because it would have meant cheating on you."
He pulled her around so that she had to look at him. She was
serious-faced and her eyes were filmed. "I *mean* that," he said.

"I do believe you," said Maria. "You been speaking a lot
to her?"

"Quite a lot."

"I've never made any demands upon you, Eddie."

"You didn't," he said.

"And I'm not now, not really. I just want to know. I think
I've a right to know."

"Yes," he said.

"I tried to invent funny rules in talking about love. It was
because I was frightened and because I was nervous. Just like I'm
frightened and nervous now. But that's not why I'm saying that I
love you. I do. I love you so much that when I'm in one part of
this house and you're in another part I ache for you, and if you
go out by yourself in the car I spend all the time in the window,

306

waiting to catch the first sight of your car coming back, and at night sometimes I wake up and I watch you sleeping and I think what it would be like not to be able to wake up and find you next to me and I cry because the hurt is an actual pain. And I'm not talking about any of the danger that all this protection is supposed to be about. I'm talking about your being alive and not having you; of having you drive away one morning and my standing there until it gets dark and not seeing your car come back.''

Franks closed his eyes against the words, overwhelmed by them. How, in God's name, could he choose? And wasn't even to think of it in terms of choice offensive? Obscene even?

Maria's head was back against his chest now, her voice muffled again. ''I know, from all the stories, that at times like these the other woman is supposed to do anything and everything to win. But I'm not going to fight, darling. I'm not going to force you into a corner and try to make you choose me and spend the rest of our life together uncertain whether you did it because you wanted to or because you felt—for whatever reason—that you *had* to. I'll accept whatever decision you make. . . .'' She trailed away and was silent for a long time, but Franks knew she hadn't finished. At last she started again. ''And if you decide that you want to go back to Tina and the children but that you still want me as well, then I'll accept whatever arrangement you want to make. You understand?''

''I understand,'' said Franks, his voice choked. ''Christ, darling!''

''That's how much I love you,'' she said.

Franks knew he should respond and what that response should be, but he'd decided upon honesty and so he didn't speak. Then he said, ''I don't know.''

''I know you don't, my darling,'' she said.

''How *can* you know? And still say what you've just said!''

''I was talking of me. Not you.''

''I think I love you, Maria.''

''And Tina, too?''

''That's what I don't know.''

''What would you say if it were Tina here, in your arms, and she asked the same question about me?''

''I said I don't know,'' said Franks.

''You've got to make the choice, Eddie. Not between us; I've told you already what I'm prepared to do about that. You owe it to Tina to choose. Not just to me. Or yourself.''

She was right, Franks knew; he'd known for a long time. ''I think you're stronger than me,'' he said.

"No, I'm not," she said. "It's easier for me; it always has been." She was silent for a moment and then she said, "I *haven't* made any demands on you, have I, Eddie?"

"Never," he said at once.

"I am now," she said. "Let me know soon; very soon."

The following day Rosenberg called Franks; appeals had been lodged by both Dukes and Pascara. When Franks asked how long the legal process could take, Rosenberg said up to five years, and Franks said he couldn't possibly consider such a period away from England, and Rosenberg said he knew that. Franks asked if he was a necessary participant in any appeal and Rosenberg said that normally it would not have been a requirement but in this case he considered it was. Franks repeated that the European businesses couldn't continue uncontrolled, as they were at present, and Rosenberg repeated that he knew that, too. Within an hour there was a call from Ronan, requesting his guarded presence at any appeal but saying that he wanted another meeting to review all the evidence that had been presented at the first trial to anticipate the tricks that the defense lawyers might try to pull before the court of appeals. Franks agreed to the meeting that Ronan wanted. He contacted Rosenberg again, asking him to be present at the conference, and then telephoned Tina and said he was coming up to Manhattan and wanted to talk to her.

"About what?" she demanded at once.

"I would have thought that was obvious."

"I want you to tell me."

"Us."

"It's taken long enough."

"Don't start!"

"I'm not starting," said Tina in immediate capitulation. "How?"

"I'll speak to Waldo. Is Tomkiss still at the house?"

"He's teaching David baseball."

"Tell him to liaise with Waldo; he'll know when I'm coming up and we can meet."

"I love you, Eddie," said Tina.

Oh Christ! he thought. "It'll be soon," he said. "This week."

"I said I loved you."

"I know what you said. Stop pushing!"

"That's the decision, is it?"

Franks sighed, knuckles against his teeth to stop the outburst. "If that—whatever 'that' means—was it, I wouldn't be coming up to see you, would I?" he said. Yes, he thought. His future with Tina or Maria had nothing to do with his going to Manhattan.

"I want you to know . . ." started the woman. But Franks stopped her. "I *know,* Tina," he said. "Believe me, I know." He hesitated, realizing he was shouting and confirming whatever fear she had. He added, "This week. I'll see you this week."

Although Berenson, who was in charge of the marshal protection, had left his number, it was Waldo whom Franks called. The FBI supervisor knew about the appeals, obviously, and also about the conference with Ronan. He'd liaise, to see that everything was organized; Franks wasn't to worry. The incoming calls over the next two days were constant, from Ronan and Rosenberg and Waldo. Wednesday was chosen for the day.

"You'll come back, won't you?" said Maria when Franks told her. "I mean, whatever decision you make, you'll come back?"

"Don't be silly."

"It *is* silly," said the woman. "You're going up about an appeal, and all I'm worrying about is us."

"No," said Franks. "That's not what's silly. Worrying about my not coming back is silly."

"Don't make promises you can't keep," said Maria.

"I'm not," said Franks.

Franks tried to make love to her the last night, because he knew she would expect him to, and Maria tried to respond, because she knew he would expect her to, and it was awful. In her exasperation she actually punched his shoulder and said, "Oh, shit! Shit! Shit! Shit!"

In the morning he said he didn't know how long he would be away. She said she understood. He said he would be back as soon as he could, and she let the pause into the conversation and said she hoped he would. Franks traveled in the car with two marshals. The traffic across the bridge was lighter than they anticipated, so they reached the Tampa airport in sufficient time to check in and go to the bar for a drink. The relaxation was intentional, explained the guards. This way they weren't attracting attention; making a drama of the departure would be counterproductive because there was no way that Flamini or Pascara or Dukes could have learned of the Florida location. Franks remembered the stupidity of the Kennedy flight and arrival in London and all the pavement-and-alley vigilance of Tomkiss and Sheridan in Manhattan and said he preferred it this way.

He only had one drink at the bar and refused anything in-flight, reflecting how his drinking had diminished since he'd been with Maria despite the continuing pressure. She was a wonderful woman, he decided. More than he—more than any man—could expect.

The flight landed at Kennedy, and Franks thought again how much more sensible the arrival there was this time than the last occasion when he'd arrived in the middle of an FBI crowd. The only concession to security was their clearance, so they emerged out of the Eastern terminal ahead of the other passengers on the flight.

The car was waiting, a discreet black Ford between two other Fords, equally undistinguished. Franks hesitated, waiting for some indication of which vehicle he was expected to ride in, but the black car was the obvious choice and so he made toward it. The first bullet caught him when he neared the rear door. It took away half his skull and part of his brain, so he was already dying. But so efficient was the hit that the second killer, positioned in another part of the parking lot to ensure that Franks was caught in the crossfire, got one Armelite shell into Franks' chest, caving the left lung. Another chipped his right shoulder and took away part of his arm before he fell. He was dead before he struck the ground, and because the first wound was to the head—and brain—he felt nothing.

Epilogue

There was so much evidence that a separate conference table had been moved into Ronan's office to accommodate it, and the district attorney stood over it like a miser gloating over his hoard. "Never," he said disbelievingly. "Never have I seen anything like it." He turned to Waldo, who was at his shoulder. "Who would have thought that an ordinary security filming of Franks' arrival at Kennedy would have actually recorded the assassination in such a way that the identification of the killers was so easy!"

"That was part of the security," reminded the FBI official.

There were still pictures as well, taken after the arrests at Kennedy, and attached to them were other police photographs from previous arrests. Ronan picked up the shots of the two men, gazing down at them. "Joey Aranozza and John Hanna," he said, reading the captions as if for the first time. He looked again to Waldo. "They're not talking, of course?"

The fat man shook his head. "Not a word. They're professionals, from St. Louis. Never expected them to."

"We don't need confessions," said the district attorney. He leaned toward the records upon which were stored the results of all the wire tapping that the FBI had carried out since the Dukes and Pascara convictions, choosing what he wanted to hear. He depressed the tape and smiled, waiting in anticipation.

"Poppa wants it," said a voice. *"Poppa says he wants Franks hit and I should ask your help. I want the best, Mr. Flamini; no mistakes."*

"There've already been too many mistakes, Luigi," replied Flamini. *"Use Aranozza. And Hanna. I'll fix it. They'll blow the bastard away and settle the problem, once and for all."*

"I appreciate it, Mr. Flamini. I'm spreading the word throughout the families. There isn't a state in the union that doesn't have people looking for him."

311

"I'll do what I can there, as well. Talk to people. Don't worry; we'll find him, soon enough."

"My father's an old man; an old, blind man. I don't want him in prison like that."

"He won't be," promised Flamini. *"Without Franks, they haven't got anything."*

Ronan switched off the tape and said, "Who needs confessions, with that! It's all there. Everything." He patted Waldo on the shoulder. "It was a brilliant idea, to put wires on everyone directly after the verdicts. I'm glad you persuaded me to get the warrants."

"This time it's secure, right?" said Schultz. "No escape, no not-guilty verdicts this time?"

Ronan stopped smiling. "John!" he said. "Believe me. This time they're going to go down for life. It's conspiracy to murder, and the evidence is incontestable. This time, definitely no escape. No not-guilty verdicts."

From the district attorney's office Waldo and Schultz went across town, to a bar just off Forty-second Street. "My celebration," announced Waldo, getting to the bar ahead of his partner. Schultz asked for bourbon and Waldo took the same, both doubles.

They touched glasses, and Waldo said, "You heard what the man said. No escape. No not-guilty verdicts."

"I heard what he said," agreed Schultz. "You got them, Harry. Every one of them."

"That's what I said I would do," reminded Waldo. "I said I'd get every one of the bastards. They escaped me once, and it looked like they might again, and I wasn't going to let that happen."

"You sure it's safe?" asked Schultz, allowing the worry to show.

Waldo shook his head at his partner's concern, gesturing to the barman for refills. "Everyone knows how careless Franks was: never took the program seriously. Never *intended* to. He was planning to go back to Europe and we've got the telephone intercepts from the marshal's office to prove it, if we need them. Which we won't. . . ." Waldo accepted the new drinks. "You just heard Luigi Pascara say on the tape that everyone was on the lookout for him, for Christ's sake! And I was careful. I put so many people between myself and the Pascara family, suggesting Florida and then Tampa, that there's no way it could ever be traced back to me. And who wants to? Ronan's got his unbreakable case: why would he want that sort of inquiry?"

312

"I guess you're right," said Schultz.

They drank in silence for several minutes, and then Waldo said, "And I was right about Franks, you know. He was as guilty as hell, just like the others. I said I could smell it, and I could with that bastard. I saw to it that Pascara and Flamini wouldn't beat me again, and I saw to it that Franks got his, in a different way."

This time Schultz bought the drinks.

He raised his glass to the other man and said, "You did well, Harry. You wrapped it all up in one neat package."

"That's what I always intended to do," said Waldo.

A SHEILA MALORY MYSTERY

Mrs. Malory and a Time to Die

Hazel Holt

THORNDIKE PRESS

A part of Gale, Cengage Learning

GALE
CENGAGE Learning

Detroit • New York • San Francisco • New Haven, Conn • Waterville, Maine • London

Lg Print
Holt

LIBRARY OF CONGRESS CATALOGING-IN-PUBLICATION DATA

Holt, Hazel, 1928–
   Mrs. Malory and a time to die : a Sheila Malory mystery / by Hazel Holt.
      p. cm. — (Thorndike Press large print mystery)
   ISBN-13: 978-1-4104-1529-5 (hardcover : alk. paper)
   ISBN-10: 1-4104-1529-5 (hardcover : alk. paper)
   1. Malory, Sheila (Fictitious character)—Fiction. 2. Women detectives—England—Fiction. 3. Riding schools—Fiction. 4. Show jumpers (Persons)—Crimes against—Fiction. 5. City and town life—England—Fiction. 6. Large type books. I. Title.
PR6058.O473M747 2009
823'.914—dc22   2009000216

Published in 2009 by arrangement with NAL Signet, a member of Penguin Group (USA) Inc.

For my granddaughter Natalie
With love and thanks for her help
with all the horsey bits

To every thing there is a season, and a time to every purpose under the heaven: A time to be born, and a time to die.

— Ecclesiastes 3:1

CHAPTER ONE

"Keep his head up, Fiona! Straighten up, Jemma. You're like a sack of potatoes! Poppy, don't check him too soon. That's good, Hannah. Keep him moving!"

I watched, with some affection, the tall woman taking a class of young riders in the ring.

"Jo really is fantastic," I said to my friend Rosemary. "She must be seventy if she's a day. She's so full of energy; she never stops! How does she do it?"

"Oh, metabolism," Rosemary said, "or whatever they call it. Some people have it and some people haven't. I haven't."

"Oh, nor do I, but I do envy people who have. I mean, just looking at all this" — I gestured towards the stables, the fields with horses grazing and the ring set up with jumps in the field below — "makes me long to go for a ride again. After all, I'm younger than Jo, but I just *know* how much I'd ache and how nervous I'd be about injuring myself. Feeble, isn't it?"

"Nonsense," Rosemary replied robustly, "just sensible. Jo's been riding every day of her life for the last goodness knows how many years. You haven't. Anyway," she continued with the candor of an old friend, "you've never been much of a one for taking exercise."

The voice from below went on. "Martha, keep your hands *down*. Don't pull at his mouth like that! Jemma, lower leg *forwards!*"

Clear and mellifluous, each word audible even at this distance, it was a splendid voice, as well it might be. Josephine Howard, as she was then, was used to making herself heard at the back of the upper circle without a microphone. We tend to forget that Jo was one of the leading actresses of her day. Looking at her now, with her brown, weather-beaten face and untidy, cropped gray hair, it's difficult to trace the beauty that illuminated her Rosalind, her Viola and her enchanting Beatrice. Just occasionally a graceful movement or gesture brings back memories. And there's the voice, of course.

"I wonder," I said, "if she ever regrets giving it up — the stage, I mean."

"She seems happy enough," Rosemary said, "and she still adores *him*."

10

At the height of her career Jo had abandoned the theater to marry Charlie Hamilton, and embraced with enthusiasm his world of horses. It wasn't surprising, I suppose; his charm was legendary. In our cynical age, charm is something dubious, almost a pejorative term, but Charlie's was the real thing. It still is. He's one of the nicest people I know and the niceness has survived some pretty awful bad luck.

When he married Jo, he was a brilliant show jumper, Olympic standard. He bred his own horses and rode them magnificently. Until, that is, he had a bad fall and his leg never mended properly. He went on breeding horses, but the business didn't prosper. He was let down badly by some financial backers, and it was Jo who finally called a halt. She persuaded him to come back to Taviscombe, where she'd been born and brought up, and set up the riding school with their remaining capital. Through determination and hard work she'd made it a success, and the quieter life seems to suit them.

Just then we saw Charlie crossing the stable yard. He'd finally and reluctantly taken to a walking stick, which he raised in greeting when he saw us. We waved back, and Rosemary said, "You can see why she

11

does — adore him, I mean."

We watched him fondly as he went into one of the horse boxes. He doesn't ride anymore but still gives the occasional lesson and is always busy with the horses in one way or another.

"When you think," Rosemary went on, "about the sort of life he's had and how unlucky he's been, it's amazing that he never seems bitter or resentful — always cheerful and in good spirits."

"And Jo's the same," I agreed. "I suppose they're content, and how many of us can say that?"

A small group of riders appeared in the distance.

"Oh, good," Rosemary said, "that's Delia's ride coming back. I hoped they'd be back on time because I've got to collect Alex from his piano lesson at half past."

Rosemary's daughter, Jilly (my goddaughter), has a sprained ankle and can't drive, so Rosemary has taken on the task of ferrying her grandchildren to and from the many social and leisure activities that the young seem to need to engage in nowadays.

"*We* were never driven about everywhere," I said. "We went by bus or on our bikes."

"Goodness, yes," Rosemary said, laughing. "Do you remember that time we cycled to the Valley of Rocks and you got a puncture? It started to get dark and our parents were frantic — no phones anywhere, of course, and certainly no mobiles!"

"But it was practically the only time they *did* get frantic," I said. "We had so much more freedom then. And, actually, Michael and your two got about quite a bit on their own."

"I think," Rosemary said thoughtfully, "that was just about the end of the age of innocence. Before all the dreadful tabloid stories and the horrors on television. And there was less traffic even then. I know Jilly gets really anxious when Alex insists on cycling to school." She sighed. "Sad, but I don't think we'll ever get back to the way things were."

The riders had now dismounted, and I saw Delia leading her horse back into the yard.

"Oh dear," Rosemary said, "I hope she's not going to hang around there. I do want to get back for Alex, and once she gets into those stables . . ."

But Delia emerged quite soon.

"Hello, Gran," she said, taking off all the impediments that safety regulations seem to require (I know they're sensible, but I'm always delighted to see the Queen out riding, wearing a head scarf).

Delia acknowledged my presence in the casual way the young do.

"Did you have a nice ride, darling?" Rosemary asked.

"Yes, I had Tsar. I love him; he's very lively."

"That gray one looks nice too," Rosemary said. "He looks just like the old rocking horse I had when I was a child."

Delia looked at her grandmother in horror. "Gran, how could you! Someone might have heard you — *so* embarrassing!"

She wrenched open the rear door of the car, flung her riding things inside and scrambled in after them, presumably in case any of her friends saw her with people who made such uncool remarks. Rosemary looked at me and pulled a face, and I smiled back.

However, in the car — presumably safe from the observation of her peers — Delia held forth at great length about the glories of the ride.

"We had a lovely lot of cantering. Tsar canters really well; he really likes to go. And we got as far as the Giant's Chair this time. You know how last time it was too windy high up there and the horses were getting

14

spooked. Tsar tried to bolt, but I pulled him round all right. Liz said I did really well. Gran, do you think Daddy *will* see about that loan pony we saw advertised? If *you* speak to him, I'm sure he will. Liz said there's room for us to keep him at livery here. Oh yes, and Mummy said I could have another jumping lesson, so I booked in for next Friday, and Charlie said he'd be taking it! Isn't that wicked!"

Not surprisingly, Charlie is something of a hero with the young who frequent the stables, and he's wonderful with them. He and Jo have no children of their own but are always surrounded with a crowd of the young. Mostly girls, of course.

When Rosemary dropped me off at home on her way to pick up Alex ("He's completely unmusical," Rosemary says, "but Jilly thinks piano lessons are somehow good for him — I can't imagine why!"), I let the animals out and, on an impulse, got out one of the old photograph albums that live in the chest in the hall. I turned over the pages and smiled at the pictures of my younger self, formally dressed in boots, breeches and hacking jacket with a shirt and tie, on Prudence, an elderly mare who once lost her head and bolted with me, trying to join the hunt when she heard the sound of the hounds in the distance. There were photographs of Michael in riding gear too, but boys seem to grow out of their horsey phase more quickly than girls, and he soon gave it up in favor of fishing and ferreting. I suppose it won't be long, though, before Alice wants to ride too.

My thoughts were interrupted by the phone. Its ring seemed to have a particularly imperious tone and I wasn't surprised to find that the caller was my friend Anthea. Brunswick Lodge is a large house, the center of most of the social activities of Taviscombe. It is staffed entirely by volunteers who, as is well-known, need a very firm hand to control them. Anthea is that firm hand.

"Where have you been?" she demanded, without any sort of preamble. "I've been trying to get you all afternoon."

"I went with Rosemary to fetch Delia from the riding stables," I said, an apologetic note creeping involuntarily into my voice.

"Oh." From Anthea's tone I gathered she didn't think it was much of an excuse. "Well, anyway, it's about the bring and buy next Wednesday morning. Can you take over? Maureen says she's got to go to visit her mother in hospital in Taunton, though

16

why she can't go in the afternoon, I don't know."

At times like this one doesn't say no to Anthea, and I found myself agreeing to do far more than simply "take over" — providing cakes and scones, for example, and arranging for the trestle tables to be picked up from the Scouts' Hall. I was just about to ring off when Anthea suddenly said, "Oh yes, and talking about the stables, you know Charlie Hamilton, don't you?"

"Well, yes," I said warily.

"I thought it might be a good idea to get him to give a talk about show jumping and all that sort of thing when we start our autumn season. It might bring in some of the younger people. We could do with some young blood. The over-sixties are all very well, but we have to look to the future."

Since Anthea's views on the young are usually condemnatory to put it mildly, this was quite a turnaround. Still, I was determined to not get involved.

"Not really a good idea," I said. "I don't think it would be tactful to ask him to talk about the old days."

"Whyever not?" Anthea is not renowned for her tact.

"Oh, you know, the way everything fell apart for him, the memories must still be very painful."

"What nonsense." I sometimes wonder if Anthea has ruthlessly expunged from *her* memory anything that might give her the slightest feeling of disquiet. "Oh well," she went on, "I'll have a think about it and get back to you."

As it turned out, Ron Murphy, who usually fetches the trestles for us, was away on holiday. ("What he wants to go to *Egypt* for, I don't know," his sister said when I rang. "I blame all these television programs about pyramids and pharaohs and nonsense like that. *I* wouldn't cross the street to see one of those horrible mummy things — morbid, if you ask me!") As a result I had to try to make other arrangements, without success, so I had to fall back on my last hope — Michael.

"I know you're busy, darling," I said, "but it'll take you only half an hour and I'd be so grateful. There'll be someone there to help you load them into the Land Rover."

"I suppose I could manage Thursday evening," Michael said, "but in return, I've a favor to ask you."

"Of *course.* What is it?"

"Will you look after your granddaughter next Friday? Thea and I want to go to Taunton to see poor old Jonah. He's just had his gallbladder out and is feeling a bit low, and frankly, I don't think Alice and hospital visiting are a good mix."

"Very wise. Of course you must go and see Jonah — he's your best friend after all. Do give him my love. And I'd love to have Alice. If it's a nice day, we could go to the beach."

As it turned out we didn't go to the beach because Rosemary rang me that morning in some agitation.

"Sheila, I hate to ask, but could you possibly collect Delia from her riding lesson this afternoon? Jilly's out of action and Roger's taking Alex to the cricket, and now I've just heard from Mother that she's made an appointment to have her eyes tested. Mr. Mackenzie doesn't usually see people in the afternoon, but she persuaded him! And she didn't think to tell me until this morning. I can take Delia to the stables, but if you could collect her at three o'clock and take her back with you, I'll fetch her as soon as I've sorted Mother out."

Since Mrs. Dudley is another person one doesn't say no to, I quite understood Rosemary's predicament.

"No, that's fine. I'm looking after Alice, but I'm sure she'd love to go to see the horses. Unless," I said, "you think Delia might find it *embarrassing.*"

Rosemary laughed. "Apparently it doesn't work like that. Small children are all right — at least small *girls* are. They can be bossed about and patronized. She'll be delighted to have someone to show off to."

We got to the stables early and stood watching Delia in the ring below with two other girls. Charlie stood there, leaning on his stick and calling out instructions while Liz, one of the stable girls, moved forward occasionally to pick up a pole that had been knocked down. Alice was enthralled and tugged at my arm.

"Gran, Gran, can we go down and see them? I want to see the horses!"

"Hallo, Sheila." Jo had come up behind me. "And who have we here?"

"Oh, hello, Jo. This is my granddaughter, Alice."

"Hello, Alice. Would you like to come and see *my* horses?"

Alice, who is usually shy with strangers, took Jo's hand immediately, and they went off towards the stable yard. When I caught up with them, Jo had lifted Alice up to stroke the nose of a large chestnut whose head protruded from one of the loose boxes.

"It's all right," Jo said to me. "Captain's very gentle."

"Captain," Alice said with satisfaction, "*likes* me stroking him." And, as Jo put her down she asked, "Can I ride him?"

"He's too big for you," Jo said. She thought for a moment, and then she called out to the other stable girl, who was filling a hay net, "Pam, could you bring Cracker out into the yard, please."

Pam led a small Exmoor pony from one of the stables and put a saddle and bridle on him. Jo turned to me. "She'll be quite safe on him. Pam will hold him. Is that all right?"

Alice was wild with excitement, so I nodded.

Jo lifted her onto the pony's back and said, "Hold on tight to his mane."

"I want to hold the strings," Alice said, so Jo showed her how to hold the reins, and Pam slowly walked the pony round the yard.

Jo smiled. "A natural. Look how well she's sitting down. How old is she?"

"She's seven, nearly eight," I said.

"The perfect age to start," Jo said. "And no, I'm not touting for customers. I just think, like I said, that she's a natural, and she's obviously enjoying it."

"I'll have to see what Thea and Michael think," I said.

Pam brought Cracker back round the yard towards us. I was amused to see Alice's solemn face, concentrating hard on what she was doing.

"She did very well," Pam said, lifting her down. "She's full of confidence."

"Did you see me, Gran?" Alice was all excitement again. "Can I come ride Cracker again — ride him properly?"

"We'll have to see, darling," I said, but I knew from experience that once Alice had set her mind on something, she was unstoppable.

We collected Delia, and all the way home and while they were both having tea, Delia and Alice talked horses. Or rather Delia laid down the law, and Alice, her fervent acolyte, drank it all in.

When Thea and Michael called to collect her, I explained what had happened (with antiphonal comments from Alice) and told them what Jo had said. With some relief I learned that Thea used to be a keen rider in her youth.

"I've been meaning to get back into it," she said, "but I never got around to it. I'd love to go with Alice."

"Jo's a very good teacher," Michael said,

"and Charlie was wonderful. He could still go hacking when I was learning — that was before his leg got so bad — and it was a terrific experience to go out with him. No, if Jo says Alice is up to it, and if" — he turned to his daughter — "*if* she's a very good girl, then I don't see why we shouldn't give it a try."

"Oh well," Rosemary said when I told her about it, "it had to happen sooner or later. And, really, it's been marvelous this holiday. Delia spends all her time up at the stables — never wants to go anywhere else. Not just riding, but mucking out and cleaning tack, polishing bits and bridles and so forth."

"Most stables are partly run on child labor," I said.

"Very true," Rosemary agreed. "It was so funny, the first time Delia asked Jo if she could help around the stables, Jo agreed and then gave her a bucket of water, some soap and a brush, and told her to scrub down all the tables and things in the tack room."

"Goodness!"

"And Delia was thrilled — Delia, who considers herself martyred if she has to stack the dishwasher, and as for tidying her room . . . !"

I smiled. "Little girls and horses," I said.

"And I can see *I'm* going to be hanging around stables quite a bit myself from now on."

CHAPTER TWO

"Are you going to Dunster Show?" Rosemary asked.

"I don't know; it depends on the weather,"
I replied. "It was pretty miserable last year,
trailing about in the rain and absolutely
ghastly trying to get the car out — all that
mud. Lots of people had to be pulled out
by tractors."

"The forecast isn't bad. Overcast but not
actually wet. I said I'd go with Jilly and the
children. Roger's working, of course. Delia's
mad to see the horses. One of her school
friends is showing her pony and she says
Delia can help her groom it beforehand, so
we'll have to get there early. Do come and
we can lunch together in the Members'
Tent."

"I might go with Michael and Thea, in
the Land Rover so we don't get stuck. I
expect Thea — and Alice now — will want
to watch the jumping. I love watching for a

bit, but they're always hours behind and it goes on forever, so lunch with you would be a marvelous excuse for getting away!"

We've all been going to the show ever since we were children, and every year for the last I don't know how long we've all said we're not going *this* year — it's too exhausting, too crowded, and, anyway, not what it was — but, in the end, we usually do go. It's not just the show itself that draws us, but, really, it's a way of catching up with people we hardly ever see at other times, old friends from way back, people who've moved away, but who come back "one more time," a chance to catch up on the news.

"It's not only Jilly and the children," Rosemary said, "but Mother expects me to go, now that she can't manage to get there herself, to take back the gossip."

"Oh well," I said, "there'll be plenty of that in the Members' Tent. Drinking gin and tonics rather too early in the day does seem to loosen tongues quite remarkably."

The weather wasn't too bad — gray and chilly — a typical English August day, in fact. We got there quite early and wandered round, looking at the livestock — the massive Red Devon cattle and jolly little Dexters, and all the wonderfully woolly Exmoor Horn sheep, the only breed I can recognize.

After a bit we met up with Rosemary and her family, who were sitting on straw bales round the ring, waiting for the horsey events.

"Oh, poor Jilly," I said. "Is your wrist still in plaster?"

"No, it's just bound up now and getting on quite well, but I thought I'd put it in a sling so that, with any luck, people won't jostle me."

"Where's Delia?" Alice demanded.

"She's helping her friend with a pony, but she'll be back here soon," Rosemary said. She made a place for us beside her, and Michael took Alex, who was getting restive at the lack of activity, to look at the tractors and other assorted farm machinery. Delia joined us just as the tannoy was urging the child's pony novice class to "go into the collecting ring *now.*"

"Rachel's awfully nervous," Delia said, addressing Alice as the only person present worthy of the information, "and Muffet — that's her horse, a Welsh mountain pony that is absolutely marvelous — was playing up. I had to hold him while she was plaiting his mane and tail, but he settled down, so I think she'll be all right."

A series of girls rode around the ring, each one criticized sharply by Delia, until Rachel

27

came in on her neat little pony. She walked, trotted and cantered, and then joined the others waiting hopefully to be called up by the judges.

"Oh look," Delia burst out excitedly, "they're calling her up! Oh, wonderful Muffet, he's standing *beautifully!* She's got a third; isn't that brilliant!"

We all clapped enthusiastically as the three winners did their lap of honor, clutching their rosettes. Delia promptly disappeared, presumably to congratulate her friend, and the rest of us settled down to watch the next event.

"It's the hunter mare up to fifteen hands," Thea said, consulting her program, "with own foal at foot. I love this one; the foals are so enchanting! Oh look, isn't that Jo with the chestnut and that lovely little foal? I didn't know they were still breeding horses."

"Just one or two, but not to sell on," I said. "Jo couldn't bear to give up altogether."

We watched Jo's slim figure, elegant in the black jacket and formal gear, so unlike her usual everyday self, and we applauded vigorously when she won her class.

When that was over Rosemary got to her feet. "I must go and walk about a bit. I'm getting stiff. Straw bales weren't meant for the over-sixties. Are you coming, Sheila?"

I looked at Thea inquiringly.

"You go," she said. "I'd rather like to see the jumping, and I'm sure Alice would too. We'll see you for lunch."

Rosemary looked at her watch as we moved away. "Just time for a quick prowl round the stalls; then we'll go for a drink."

I fell victim to a rather nice leather handbag and a new Barbour waterproof hat. Rosemary bought a tweed waistcoat for herself and a cap for Jack ("I always have to take him back a fairing," she said, "though he doesn't deserve it because he never comes himself"), and we made our way through the crowds to the Members' Tent. Although it was still early, the place was quite full. I found a table while Rosemary got the drinks.

"Nice to sit in a proper chair," Rosemary said as she poured the tonic into her glass, "even if it is a bit wobbly. And thank goodness they still have real glasses in here and not those awful plastic things. Now then, who's here?"

Greetings were exchanged with various people and news was shouted across from other tables, against the background roar of conversation.

"Have you ever noticed," I said, "how the canvas walls of the tent seem to magnify the noise? I suppose they act as a sort of sounding board."

"I know. I really couldn't hear properly what Dick Fraser was telling me. Did he really say that Elaine has gone off to Inverness with *Malcolm Hartman?*"

"I think so, though I must say it does seem unlikely! Oh look, there's Charlie. Do wave to him to come and sit here."

Charlie Hamilton, looking rather worn and leaning heavily on his stick, made his way towards us.

"Great heavens, what a crush!" he said as he sat down gratefully. "I always forget how crowded everywhere is."

"I'll get some drinks," I said. "Whiskey for you, Charlie?"

When I got back, Rosemary was saying how glad we were that Jo had won her class, and how splendid she looked.

Charlie smiled. "The old girl still turns out pretty well," he said, "and we're very pleased with Starlight. She's come on beautifully, and that's a really nice little foal she dropped."

"I'm so glad you haven't given up breeding altogether," I said.

"Well, it creates a bit more interest for

Jo," Charlie said, "and I like to see the young ones about." He turned to Rosemary. "Your Delia's coming along well."

"She's mad keen," Rosemary said, "and, of course, she's longing for her own pony. I expect she'll wear Jilly and Roger down. I don't know how much longer they'll be able to hold out!"

"I think I might know of a loan pony," Charlie said. "I'll make some inquiries. . . ."

He broke off as he spotted two people coming in. "Oh, there's Esther and Simon. Is there room for them to join us?"

Esther Nicholson is Jo's sister, but totally unlike her in every way. Where Jo is tall and elegant, Esther is short and plump; where Jo is cool and witty, Esther is fidgety and never stops talking. Jo went away and made a brilliant career for herself; Esther stayed at home and, after a brief spell as a receptionist, married Gordon Nicholson, the dentist she worked for. Simon is their son, and more like his aunt (whom he's devoted to) than either of his parents. He's an accountant and looks after the books at the stables.

"Hello," Rosemary said. "Lovely to see you. Pull up a couple of chairs, Simon. There's plenty of room here."

"Well," Esther said, flopping down into a

chair and arranging a collection of plastic bags round her feet, "I've never known it so crowded. You can hardly get into some of the trade tents. I'm sure the girl in the produce tent didn't pack that honeycomb properly; she was so busy." She bent down and rummaged in one of the bags. "No, it seems to be all right, but it's in the bag with the smoked-trout pâté and the wild-boar sausages, and you wouldn't want honey all over *those,* now would you? Simon, I'll have a gin and tonic if you can get to the bar."

"How about everyone else?" Simon asked.

Rosemary and I shook our heads, and Charlie said, "I'll wait till lunch, thanks all the same."

"It gets worse every year," Esther went on. "I don't think I'll come again. It's not what it was — not like the old days. It's getting too commercial — and not a proper band, just taped music and all those motor bikes doing acrobatics or whatever it is they do. Anyway, it's nice to see you both. How have you been keeping? I saw Jilly just now, Rosemary. She had her arm in a sling. Has she broken it? And I didn't expect to see Michael here, Sheila. I thought lawyers never took a day off — too busy making money!" She laughed. "Did you see Jo and that horse of hers? She really is getting too old for all that, Charlie. I don't know why you let her do it."

Knowing Esther of old, none of us felt it necessary to answer what were obviously rhetorical questions. Fortunately, Simon came back with the drinks, so she was obliged to stop talking while she drank her gin and tonic.

"Well, *you've* taken a day off," Rosemary said to Simon, smiling. Simon used to work for Jack's firm of accountants when he first started out and Rosemary has always had a soft spot for him. We both feel sorry for him having to cope with Esther. Gordon has more or less given up and, at home at least, has gone into a kind of monosyllabic retreat, giving all his energies to outside activities like the Rotarians and the local council.

"I usually take a week of my leave around now," he said. "I'm going to spend a few days in London."

"Theaters and galleries?" I asked.

"This and that," Simon said. "I haven't decided yet."

"Oh, Simon's not a one for museums and all that," Esther broke in. "We used to take him to all sorts of things when he was little. Do you remember, Simon, when we used to stay with Aunt Mavis?" She turned to me. "She's Gordon's older sister, married a

33

consultant — orthopedics, always pays well! — and they have a house in Richmond, huge great place; must be worth a fortune now. No," she went on, "Simon never took any interest in that kind of thing. Vicky, now, she loved it all, but then she's always been the clever one." Vicky is Simon's sister and their mother's favorite. "She got a first, you know, at Oxford — such a pity she never did anything *with* it, going into the BBC like that."

"But she's done awfully well," Rosemary said. "She's a producer now, isn't she?"

"Yes," Esther said, "but only *radio.*"

Vicky is very ambitious and simply couldn't wait to go away to London, without the slightest qualm about leaving Simon to bear the brunt of things at home. I do feel sorry for him. He's so good with both his parents and doesn't really have much of a life — just work and home and doing things around the stables. I know he likes being there with Jo and Charlie, so I suppose that's something. He did have a nice girl-friend, Julie Phillips, the daughter of one of the partners of his firm, but her job took her away to London and long-distance relationships never seem to work. That was more than a year ago and, as far as I know, he hasn't found anyone since. I did wonder, though, when he said he was going to London, whether he was going to see her.

Jo came in then and we all congratulated her on her first prize.

"Yes, I'm really pleased with Starlight," she said. "I think she's going to be something special. Freddy Barnet — he's one of the judges — he said that she's really first class. You know him, Charlie; we met him at the Bath and West last year. Oh, thank you, Simon." She turned and smiled at him as he handed her a drink. "Just what I needed! Liz is seeing to Starlight — we have to stay on for the President's Cup — but I must go and take over when I've had some lunch. I couldn't eat anything first thing — too nervous."

"Like a first night?" Rosemary suggested.

"Oh, worse, though that was always bad enough. But even for quite a small show it's worse because it's the horse as well, not just you."

The mention of lunch reminded me that I had to go and find my family, so I got up.

"I'd better come too," Rosemary said, "and drag Jilly and the children away from those horses and get some food into them!"

After lunch I wandered around for a bit, but quite soon I began to feel tired and was glad when Thea said, "I think Alice has had enough. Do you feel like coming away now?"

When I got home and had fed the animals (if I've been out all day their reproach takes the form of constant and repeated demands for food), I went upstairs to look for my old tweed hacking jacket, which I had promised to give to Thea now that she'd started riding again. It was many years since I'd worn it and I finally ran it to earth at the back of the cupboard in the spare room. It really is amazing the things one comes across if you're a hoarder like me. I found garments I'd had before Michael was born. Needless to say I couldn't get into any of them. I left them in a pile on the bed so that I'd be obliged to pack them all up for the charity shop. I suppose they're fashionable again by now — retro, I think the term is.

I tried on the hacking jacket and found that, amazingly, it still fitted me, and for one mad moment I thought perhaps I might start riding again, but common sense prevailed and I decided I really must have it cleaned before handing it on to Thea. I noted with resignation that Foss had curled up and was resolutely asleep among the clothes on the bed, and went downstairs to make myself a cup of tea.

■ ■ ■ ■

A few days later I took the newly cleaned jacket round to Thea and asked her how she'd been getting on at the stables.

"The first few times were agony afterwards," she said. "All those muscles I haven't used for years! But it's fine now. Except that everything I learned now seems to be out of date."

"How could it be?" I asked.

"You know how it was *so* important to use your knees to control your horse? Well, it isn't now."

"Good heavens!"

"No, now it seems you have to use the whole of your lower leg. Well, you can imagine how difficult *that* is. I mean, all your instincts are to do things the way you always have."

"How awful."

"I think I'm getting the hang of it now. I've been out a couple of times with Liz, who tactfully reminded me, and once with Jo, who yelled at me when I forgot!"

I laughed. "At least Alice will be learning properly from scratch. Has she had any lessons yet?"

"Yes, a couple. On a leading rein, of

37

course, though Jo, who's taking a real interest in her, thinks it won't be long before she can go on her own in the ring. Oh, I must show you something." She went away and came back with some very small jodhpurs and a pair of boots. "There! Aren't they gorgeous! I know it was silly of me, but she's so keen and was longing for the proper gear. Michael says I'm mad and we ought to wait and see how she gets on, but I was in that shop in Porlock where they have all the riding stuff and I couldn't resist!"

"Well," I said, "we won't have to worry now about what to give her for birthdays and Christmas."

"As long as it's not her own pony. Though I've no doubt Jo will have thoughts about that too!"

"How was Jo; is she all right? I thought she looked really tired at the show. I know she'd just been showing her horse and all that, but, just for a moment she really looked her age."

"No, she seemed all right when I saw her. She was a bit — well, I don't know quite what — not put out exactly, but disconcerted, I suppose. She'd heard from Vicky, who's making a radio program and wants to tape an interview with her."

"And?"

"I gather it's to be about the theater — past actors and so forth. Well, you know how Jo never likes talking about all that."

"No, I sometimes think she regrets her time as an actress and doesn't want to be reminded about it. I remember Anthea once asked her to give a talk about her life in the theater at Brunswick Lodge and Jo was really quite rude to her. Anthea was absolutely amazed, because you know how amiable Jo always is. But she shut Anthea up, and that takes a lot of doing!"

"Oh well, perhaps she'll put Vicky off."

"I don't know about that. From what I remember, Vicky can be just as persistent as Anthea, and she does have the advantage of being Jo's niece. It will be interesting to see if she can pull it off."

CHAPTER THREE

"Do you feel like coming with me to collect some chickens?" Thea asked me when she rang.

"Chickens?"

"Yes, I've always wanted to keep them, ever since I was a child, so, when I saw an advert for a chicken house in the *Free Press,* I thought why not!"

"Well, good for you. What does Michael think about it?"

"Since he knows *he* won't have to do anything about the actual hens, he's all for it. Anyway, he's installed the chicken house and put up a wire-netting pen, so I'm all set. I'm starting off with twelve to see how it goes."

"Splendid. Yes, I'd love to come. When?"

"Alice is spending the day with her friend Jessica tomorrow. Jessica's mother, bless her, is taking them both swimming and then back to lunch, so I thought that would be a good time to go. Could you come about ten thirty? I'm afraid we'll have to go in the Land Rover, so I pray this place isn't up a dreadfully narrow lane, because I'm hopeless at backing up in it!"

There was a narrow lane, leading up to the rather scruffy-looking farmhouse high up, out over the moor, but fortunately no one else seemed to be using it that particular morning. A young woman, followed by a little girl, came out as we drove into the yard.

"You for the chicken, then?" she asked. "Dave left them all ready."

We followed her to a corner of the yard where there were two crates, each containing six rust-colored fowl, who clucked hysterically when the woman picked them up and swung them into the back of the Land Rover.

"Are they all right?" Thea asked anxiously.

"They'll soon settle down; don't you fret. If you can bring the crates back . . ."

The child, who had watched the whole proceedings with her finger in her mouth, took it out and pointed in the direction of the agitated birds.

"Chicken!" she said. "Chicken cross!"

Then, apparently overcome by her own temerity, she retreated behind her mother.

"We'll bring the crates back at the weekend if that's all right," Thea said. She handed over some money to the young woman, and we got back into the Land Rover and drove away.

After a little while I said, "I can't hear any noise from the chickens. Do you think they're all right?"

"I think so. Apparently they can't stand up while I'm driving, so they sit down and presumably await their fate with a sort of Asian stoicism. They'll be fine when we get them home."

And, indeed, they were. After a brief inspection of the pen they pecked happily away at the corn Thea gave them and went into the chicken house as easily as if they'd always lived there.

"Well, that was good," I said. "I was afraid they might be temperamental."

"Oh, these are Warrens," Thea said, "not high-class, fancy birds — what Michael calls industrial grade — but uncomplicated and very good layers."

"That's all right, then. Are they going to be safe in there? I mean, what about foxes?"

"There's a sort of electric fence." She indicated the strands of wire going round the pen that she'd had to step over when she was seeing to them.

"Goodness," I said, "is it dangerous?"

"No, it's fine." She stooped to switch something on. "It gives quite a mild shock, enough to stop a fox or anything like that, but not too bad for humans. It runs off a battery. It's the big ones, you know, like the ones round fields, which run off the mains, that you have to be careful of. Anyway, they seem all right. I'll let them settle down for a bit and come back and look at them later. Let's go and have a cup of tea. I'm absolutely dying for one."

As I drove back home I thought about the way the wheel had come full circle, and how Thea had chosen to give up a successful career in the law to stay at home and cultivate the domestic virtues. I suppose it's a matter of temperament, and for some people it's perfectly possible to get complete satisfaction from that sort of life, while it would drive others mad. The trouble is, it seems to me, that, given the financial pressures of modern society, not many women *have* the option of choosing. In a way I didn't actually have a choice. My mother was an invalid for some years before she died, so I stayed at home to look after her, and after Michael too when he was young. But I was lucky; I had quite a bit of freelance work — writing books, articles, reviews and so forth — so I had the best of both worlds. And now I was finding that being a grandmother was both pleasurable and demanding.

The next day I decided that being able to do what I like when I like is very useful. My cousin (well, second cousin, really) Fred Prior telephoned to say he was back in England for a few days and asked if I would have lunch with him tomorrow. All Fred's arrangements tend to be ad hoc. He's some years older than I am, and more my parents' friend than mine. We hadn't seen each other for many years until he came back into my life quite recently. He's amazing for his age, full of energy and fun, with a wicked sense of humor, and we get on famously. He and his much-younger second wife now live in the south of France but, when he comes back to Bristol for business reasons, he always rings me and we have a splendid lunch together.

Nowadays I tend to avoid motorways, so on this occasion I decided to go to Bristol by train. As usual I arrived early for the train. Michael always used to say that if he counted up all the hours he'd spent waiting with me on railway platforms, he could have *written War and Peace,* let alone read it.

There was only one other person on the platform when I arrived, a tall figure, instantly recognizable.

"Hello, Jo," I said. "Fancy seeing you here."

She turned quickly and seemed surprised and somehow disconcerted at being addressed, but then she said, "Sheila! Do forgive me; I was miles away!"

"Are you going to Bristol too?"

"Yes, I've got some tiresome business to see to. How about you?"

"Oh, lunch with my cousin — Fred Prior. Do you remember him?"

"Vaguely from down here. I used to see more of his first wife, Amanda, when she got married to Vernon Russell, the producer. They used to have rather grand parties at their house in Hampstead. And there was a son, wasn't there? He went into the profession, I seem to remember. He was a Charlie too — that's right, Charlie Prior."

"Actually, he gave up the stage, or acting, at least, and now he's a very successful agent."

"Good for him. That's a sensible move. There are too many actors! And what about Fred? He married again too, didn't he?"

"Yes, someone much younger, called Louise. She's half French, and they live in Antibes now. Fred's given up the Bristol house, but he comes over occasionally to see to things."

"I couldn't do that," Jo declared. "I couldn't live anywhere but England."

"Oh, nor could I. Abroad's all very well for holidays, but not for *living,* and, really, I don't think I'd want to live anywhere but Taviscombe — not just for the people, friends and family, but it's the only place where I really feel comfortable, if you know what I mean."

"Absolutely. That's why I came back here after — after we decided to set up the stables. It was a really bad time for us both. I just wanted to come home, I suppose."

I looked at Jo curiously. I'd never heard her mention that part of her life; all I knew had come from Simon, and Esther, of course. I was flattered, somehow, that she'd actually felt easy enough with me to mention it.

"I know what you mean," I said, feeling the urge to repay confidence with confidence. "When Mother died, and Peter, I wouldn't have been able to bear it anywhere else — not just the support from friends, but, well, it's something about your own *place,* somewhere you feel you belong."

Jo gave me one of her rare smiles. "Exactly," she said.

When the train came in, our reserved seats were in different carriages, so I didn't see her get off at Temple Mead station. But when Fred, who had come to meet me, and I were walking past the taxi rank, she was standing there, and I pointed her out to him.

"Yes, still the same old Jo Howard," he said. "She's worn well. I'd recognize her anywhere. But the poor old girl doesn't seem very happy — looks as if she's got the troubles of the world on her shoulders!"

Indeed, she did look drawn and anxious, and I wondered what sort of tiresome business it was that had brought her to Bristol.

The next time I saw her, though, I was glad to see that she was her old self again. I'd gone with Thea to watch Alice have a riding lesson at the stables and Jo was taking a class of older girls over the jumps, her voice ringing out cheerfully as she encouraged them.

"Here comes Cracker," Thea said as Liz led out the small Exmoor pony. Alice hesitated for a moment and then went resolutely towards them. She went to the mounting block and when she got onto the pony herself without any help, she turned and gave us a triumphant smile.

47

"She's still on a leading rein, of course," Thea said, "but she can rise to the trot now — there, look!"

Smiling indulgently, we watched her for a while, and then I said, "You stay here and I'll go and pay Peggy for her lesson."

I made my way through the stable block, past the tack room and into the office, though "office" is a rather grand name for the ramshackle wooden structure built onto one side of the tack room. Peggy wasn't there, but Charlie was, seated at a makeshift desk, making heavy weather of some forms. He looked up as I came in.

"Hello, Sheila. How are you with all this lot?" He waved an official-looking booklet in the air. "Honestly, what with insurance, health and safety and God knows what else, I might as well be a bloody civil servant!"

"Oh don't!" I said. "I'm hopeless. I dash at them without reading them properly and then I find I've filled them in all wrong and they end up with masses of crossings out. Fortunately, Michael can't bear to see the mess I make of them, so he takes them away and sorts them for me."

Charlie smiled. "To be fair," he said, "Simon deals with most of our stuff, but he's still away and these have to go off before he gets back. He's a good lad; I don't know

48

what we'd do without him, and he'll never take a penny for all the work he does for us."

"Oh well," I said. "Family."

Charlie sighed. "It's just as well," he said. "I don't know that we could afford to pay an accountant. Running a stable's an expensive business. That's why we've tried to expand the livery side. Weekenders and people like that will pay a fair amount for their riding, but then *that* means you've got to spruce things up a bit, make them feel they're getting value for money, and getting it all costs. Have you seen the price of hay now?"

I had to admit I hadn't.

"Criminal!" he said. "We've got a fair bit of pasture here, of course, but, even with that, the feed bills are terrible. And there's labor, of course. Liz and Peggy are marvelous workers and Jo slaves away every hour that God sends, and even I try to do my bit, but it's a struggle!"

"Well," I said, putting a couple of notes down on the desk, "here's a tiny bit towards it — the money for Alice's lesson."

He laughed. "Sorry, Sheila. I didn't mean to go on like that. You caught me at the wrong time; I'm not usually so dismal!"

"Oh, don't apologize. I know it does help

sometimes to get things off your chest."

"I don't mind so much for myself," Charlie said. "I'd be quite happy with a few horses and a couple of regulars, but Jo cares so much about it. Anyway, thanks for this." He picked up the money, stood up, unlocked a small safe and put the notes into a cash box. "Every little bit helps!"

"You seem to have quite a few youngsters now," I said. "I imagine they'll be regulars for a while yet."

"Some of them will," Charlie said with a smile, "but some of them will discover boys and that will be the end of it."

"Oh well," I said, "you'll have Alice for a good many years. She's absolutely obsessed!"

"Jo says she's coming along very nicely." He broke off as there was a sudden noise and the sound of hooves clattering against wood. He limped out into the stable and I followed. Peggy was trying to calm down a large chestnut hunter that kept rearing up.

"Shorten the rein," Charlie said, "and bring his head round. That's it. Good girl. Now he'll go into his stall. Take it gently."

He followed them and went over to the horse, stroking it and talking to it quietly. After a while he had a few words with Peggy and went out into the yard.

"That was Tarquin," he said to me, "just come in for livery and hasn't settled down properly yet. He's a bit temperamental and right now he's got a touch of laminitis, and that always makes them jumpy."

"Does he belong to a weekender?" I asked.

"As a matter of fact, no. He belongs to one of Gordon's council friends, Dan Webster. He's quite experienced; used to hunt with the D&S. But he's not a very good judge of horses; he goes for the showily good-looking ones. I think Tarquin's going to be a bit too much for him to handle, even when we've sorted out the laminitis."

"He's a very handsome creature," I said. "I can see how he might appeal."

"Oh well, we'll just have to do the best we can."

I stood in the doorway and looked out beyond the yard at the ring with the young riders and their ponies, then farther down, across the fields where some of the horses were grazing peacefully in the afternoon sunlight, towards the woods and in the distance to the hills, which were just beginning to turn purple and gold with the heather and gorse.

"It really is a glorious spot," I said to Charlie.

"I know," he said quietly. "We're very

lucky. Whatever happens, we have to keep hold of it somehow."

I went back to tea with Thea and Alice and, when Alice had finally exhausted every aspect of her ride ("And did you see me, Gran? I dismounted all by myself. I took both my feet out of the stirrups, like Liz said — you have to take them *right* out, and then you can get down. . . ."), I told Thea I thought Jo and Charlie might be having financial difficulties.

"It may just have been general grumbling," I said. "I mean, we all like to have a bit of a moan, but I have the feeling it was more than that and they're really worried."

"I thought riding stables simply coined money," Thea said. "They certainly charge enough!"

"Well, the expenses are high and it's all labor-intensive."

"But think of all that child labor — all those young girls who hang around, longing to be allowed to *do* something for the horses, however menial."

I thought of Delia scrubbing down the shelves and laughed. "Yes, there is that, but there's the feed and the equipment — saddles are a horrendous price, so Rosemary tells me. Apparently Roger is quite happy to look for a pony for Delia, and Jilly, who's not at all keen, keeps producing advertisements from Delia's horsey magazines to prove how hideously expensive everything is. And then, of course, they grow out of things so quickly — ponies as well as riding boots!"

"True."

"Anyway, Charlie seemed really worried. I've never seen him so down; you know how cheerful he usually is. And, come to think of it, when I saw Jo that time I went to Bristol, she looked very anxious about something and she did say she was there on business. Perhaps that was something to do with the stables."

"Trying to raise a loan do you think? Surely it can't be as bad as that. I mean, they own the land, don't they?"

"Oh yes. Well, I've never heard anything about it from either of them, but I'm sure Esther told me they used what money was left when Charlie had to sell up, to buy the whole setup, all those years ago, which I'm sure included the land. But they'd hate to have to sell a single field — well, I'm sure Jo would. Though I think, from what he said, Charlie would be perfectly happy to carry on in quite a small way."

"Jo's a perfectionist," Thea said. "She loves whatever she does and has to be the best — no half measures for her!"

"I know. I often wonder if that's part of the reason she gave up the stage. I mean, she'd done all the great classic roles and, after a certain age, there aren't that many parts for a woman. I don't think she could have borne to — well, come down from those heights."

Thea considered this for a moment and said, "You may be right. I don't suppose we'll ever know. Jo's never been one for talking about herself."

"No. Come to think of it, all we know about her life since she left Taviscombe we've heard from Esther, and Jo would never tell her anything really personal like that!"

Alice, who had just come back into the room, said, "When I have *my* pony, it can go and live at the stables with Cracker, can't it, Mummy?"

"Oh dear," I said to Thea, "it's started already. How long will you be able to hold out!"

CHAPTER FOUR

Every year I mean to buy my spring bulbs nice and early, but, what with one thing and another, I never seem to get around to it. When I finally do, there's practically nothing left except the rather forlorn piles of peeling daffodils, scruffy hyacinths and dried-up crocuses that have been picked over and discarded by other shoppers. Since I had a free afternoon for once, I went straight round to the garden center while the whole bulb situation was still uppermost on my mind.

Confronted by tempting boxes of newly arrived stock, I quite lost my head, filling the brown paper bags provided with practically every variety and every color on offer. I was just trying to decide between the merits of dwarf and parrot tulips when a voice behind me said, "You're going to be busy with that lot!"

Rapidly brought down to earth, I turned

to answer Esther Nicholson. "Yes, I know," I said lightly. "I do seem to have gone a bit mad."

"But," she went on, "I don't suppose you still do your own gardening — it's not so easy when you get to our age."

"As a matter of fact," I said, annoyed at being classed with Esther, who is at least five years older than I am, if not more, "I do *all* the garden. Well," I added with a nod towards the truth, "except the heavy digging, of course. Reg Carter does that for me."

"Oh, do you find him satisfactory? We used to have him, but he wasn't very reliable."

"I've always found him absolutely fine," I said, conveniently forgetting the times I'd been maddened by his erratic timekeeping. I do find that conversation with Esther tends to bring out the worst in me. "Anyway," I went on, "how are you and Gordon?" I put my wire basket with the bulbs in it down on the floor, knowing from past experience that Esther always answers such trivial questions very fully.

"Oh, Gordon's been very busy. A lot of council stuff, you know, and then there's the Rotarians, of course. He's president this year and he's having to organize the trip to

56

Belgium."

"How nice. Are you going?"

"I suppose I shall have to. I wouldn't have bothered if he hadn't been president, but you know how it is; it's expected of you. We've got to go through the Channel Tunnel and I can't say I fancy that — I mean, all that way under the sea! And Brussels, that's not very exciting. One of the trips is round the European Union buildings — not what you'd go abroad for, is it?"

"There's all that lovely Belgian chocolate," I suggested.

"Not with Gordon's heart and his cholesterol level, there isn't. No, I really don't feel like going anywhere just now."

"Really?"

"Between ourselves, I'm worried about Simon. He's working too hard, brings stuff home, up till all hours with that computer of his. I've seen the light on in his room at two o'clock, or three, even. I told him, you'll wear yourself out; you've got to get your proper rest. But of course he never listens; says he's fine. But he's looking really washed-out."

"But he's just been on holiday, surely . . ."

Esther gave a short laugh. "Much good it did him. He looked even worse when he got back. I said to him I don't know what you've been doing up in London, my lad, but it's certainly done you no good at all! But all he said was he had some late nights seeing friends." She sighed. "All those BBC types, friends of Vicky's, I suppose. He was staying with her. I hoped she might have talked some sense into him, but she's just the same; no idea of looking after herself. I'll be glad to have her down with me for a week — give her regular meals, not all these ready meals and takeaways that they seem to live on. Indian and Chinese — well, I tried Indian food once; you couldn't taste anything, it was so hot! As for Chinese — well, goodness knows what's in *that!* And now they all seem to be eating Japanese stuff, raw fish, if you can believe it! You can't tell me that's natural, or healthy either."

"Well," I said, hoping to stem the culinary tide, "you'll be able to give her some lovely home-cooked food when she comes to stay."

"Roast lamb — she's always liked my roast lamb, and of course it's local, so we know where it *comes* from, and a nice cabbage from the garden and one of my apple tarts — the Bramleys will be just about ready by then."

"I'm sure she'll love that," I said, shifting my weight from one foot to the other and trying to look interested.

"Mind you," Esther went on, "I'm not prejudiced. When we go to France or Italy I always like the food there — well, almost all, some of it's a bit rich — but we've had some very nice meals in Paris and Florence. I always avoid the veal, of course — those poor little calves — but that's more Germany and Austria, isn't it? Escalopes and so forth."

"Yes, well . . . ," I said, tentatively trying to make a move.

"But" — Esther leaned towards me as if to increase the confidential nature of what she had to say — "the person I'm most worried about is Jo."

"Really?"

"She's not herself at all. She's getting very vague; hardly seems to take in anything I say to her. It looks as if her mind's elsewhere half the time. And she doesn't remember half the things I've been telling her about. I told her about our trip to Brussels only last week, but when I mentioned it yesterday she obviously hadn't taken in anything I'd said! I'm beginning to wonder if she's going into Alzheimer's. She's quite a bit older than I, you know."

"Surely not! She always seems so full of life and so much on the ball!"

Esther shook her head. "I think Charlie's

worried about her too, though he denied there was anything wrong when I asked him."

"I'm sure everything's all right," I said reassuringly.

"Well, we'll see. Goodness, is that the time? I mustn't stand here chatting to you like this!" Having neatly put me in the wrong, she swept off to the checkout, where she caused a considerable holdup by having to go back to the shelves to hunt for a certain type of insecticide, which, it turned out, had been banned by the EU some months ago.

When I got home I put the bulbs carefully away in the larder (you're supposed to keep them cool) until I could empty the planters. I'd just put the kettle on when there was a ring at the door; it was Rosemary.

"Sorry to descend on you like this," she said, "but I was on my way back from Porlock and I thought I'd just pop in to see if you feel like coming out for lunch one day this week. It's been a really tiresome couple of days and I feel the need for a little treat."

"Oh dear, what's happened?"

"Well, it's Mother mostly — when is it not! She's been in one of her redecorating moods."

"Not painting and wallpapering!"

"No, not quite as bad as that, but curtains and covers. She says she can't *bear* to live with the present ones any longer."

"But she had those only eighteen months ago. I distinctly remember your having to go to Exeter to get some fabric she'd seen in a magazine."

"Don't remind me! No, this time it's something that chum of hers, Mrs. Watson, saw in a shop in Taunton. So I had to go and get a sample for her to see — several samples actually, because Mrs. Watson's description was so vague it could have been any one of half a dozen."

"And?"

"And, of course, none of them were right for her and, of *course,* it was my fault for being so stupid and not finding the right one. Honestly, Sheila, I almost *said* something, but what's the use? It's water off a duck's back with Mother!"

"Here," I said, passing her a cup of tea and pushing a plate of chocolate wafers towards her, "comfort food! So what happened?"

"Oh, she thought she might like that William Morris willow pattern fabric, so I dashed out and ordered some and phoned little Martha Cronin to come and measure up, all very quickly before she could change her mind."

"She might still change it."

"No, not now — money has been spent!"

"Poor you! And, yes, I'd love to come out to lunch. Would Thursday be all right? We might go to that new place in Lynton. They say it's very good and it's a nice little run to get there."

Rosemary leaned back in her chair and bit into a biscuit. "I mustn't stay too long; I've got to go and pick up Delia from the stables. She wants to get in as many rides as she can before school starts again and the nights start drawing in."

"I know — it's frightening how quickly the days get shorter. I always feel that after July it's downhill all the way to winter! Is Delia having a ride or a lesson?"

"Oh, a lesson. She's mad about jumping just now and Jo is a wonderful teacher."

"How do you think Jo is these days?" I asked.

"She seems fine. Why do you ask?"

"When I saw her last she looked a bit drawn and pale, and I've just had a dismal conversation about her with Esther."

I told her what Esther had said and Rosemary laughed. "I should think Jo *hadn't* been listening to Esther going on about

62

Brussels! I mean, the only thing to do when Esther gets going is to think about something else until she stops. And, anyway, you know what she's like about saying how worried she is about everyone!"

"Well, she was certainly going on about Simon and Vicky as well."

"Oh, poor Simon — that boy is a saint. Anyone else would have moved out ages ago, but I think he feels it's only his being at home that keeps that family on some sort of even keel. So, what's the worry this time?"

"Oh, bringing work home, up till all hours at his computer — that sort of thing."

"Actually," Rosemary said thoughtfully, "I'm not really surprised — about bringing work home, I mean. Simon's good at his job, very thorough and reliable — Jack said he could trust him to cope with anything — but, because he's so thorough, he is a bit slow. The way things are nowadays, with everyone expecting things to be done absolutely at once, he may very well feel he's getting behind and needs to catch up at home."

"It really is dreadful," I said, "the way there's no *time* to do things properly. Not just business but doctors, even, having only ten minutes to give to each patient — though, thank goodness Dr. Macdonald belongs to the old school and jolly well gives it as long as it takes!"

"Still," Rosemary said, "I do hope Simon isn't overdoing things. He's got enough to put up with at home without having worries at work. I know Esther always exaggerates, but even so, I don't like to think of him looking ill."

I was able to judge for myself at the weekend when I went with Thea to collect Alice from the stables. As we drove up, a car parked beside us and Simon got out. He greeted us cheerfully and said, "It's such a beautiful day, I thought I'd have a ride and blow the cobwebs away. It's ages since I've been out."

"I didn't know you rode," I said.

"It would be difficult not to with Jo and Charlie around. They insisted on giving me lessons when I was practically a toddler! I'm not very good — nothing fancy, just a bit of mild hacking."

"Well," I said, looking appreciatively at his tweed jacket, boots and riding hat, "you're certainly properly turned out."

He laughed. "Jo wouldn't allow anything less."

We all went into the yard and looked down into the ring where Alice, now off a leading rein, was performing quite creditably with Liz.

"Is that your little girl?" Simon asked Thea.

She nodded. "Jo's idea, of course; she's a great enthusiast! But Alice loves it."

"Good for Alice," Simon said. He waved his hand and went off into the stables.

"Well," I said, "he looks all right to me."

"Who does?"

"Simon — Esther said she was worried about him and that he wasn't looking well."

"Oh, Esther! She's never happy unless she's got something to worry about. Simon's perfectly fine. Oh, Alice is coming in now; shall we go and meet her?"

That evening, when I was cooking Foss's fish in the microwave, I suddenly thought of what Esther had said about Simon looking worse after his holiday, and I wondered if he'd gone to London to try to get back with his girlfriend (What was her name? Annie? Rosie? something like that) and she'd turned him down. Perhaps he'd had enough of being the good son at home and wanted, at the age of — what was it? — thirtysomething, to get a life of his own at last. Certainly he's devoted himself to Esther and Gordon for a very long time. Not many young men of his age would have done as much.

The ping of the microwave put an end to these unprofitable thoughts. Foss, attracted by the smell of fish, suddenly materialized at my elbow on the worktop and Tris, who doesn't like fish, turned up nevertheless, knowing that I wouldn't dare feed one without the other. I put some fish into Foss's saucer and took it over to the tap to run a little cold water on it to cool it down. I removed Foss from the sink, where he had been keeping an eye on things, and put him and the saucer down on the floor. In response to Tris's impatient whine, I shook some dry food into his dish, gave a perfunctory squirt of air freshener to dispel the fish smell and took myself off to the sitting room for a quiet glass of sherry before I started making my own supper.

Rosemary and I set off in high spirits for our lunch together. It was a beautiful day and the drive across the moor to Lynton was especially fine with the moorland clothed in purple and gold.

"A real Mrs. Alexander day," I said to Rosemary.

"A what?"

"You know, the hymn 'All things bright and beautiful' . . . 'the purple-headed mountain' bit and all that. She wrote it when she was staying down here."

"Oh yes, at Dunster, wasn't it?"

"Yes — 'The rich man in his castle, the poor man at the gate' — the verse we're not allowed to sing nowadays. Silly nonsense — I ask you, who's going to be offended by it? It's of its period. I mean, half of literature's politically incorrect if you look at it the wrong way!"

"I suppose so."

"Anyway, I always sing that verse silently under my breath when we have the hymn."

"It's very popular at funerals nowadays, have you noticed?"

"Yes, you're right — I suppose people think that, without *that* verse, it's sort of ecologically friendly!"

In spite of the good write-ups it had had, the restaurant wasn't very full, but we were early.

"They make a great thing about all the produce they use being locally sourced," Rosemary said, looking at the menu. "I suppose that's a good thing, unless you want an avocado. What are you going to have?"

"I don't know. I can never make up my mind until I know what other people are having. What are you?" I asked.

"I'll have the steak and ale pie," Rosemary said. "I'm getting very lazy about making

67

pastry nowadays, so that will be a treat."

"I think I'll have the meatballs. I haven't had one for ages and homemade ones are very delicious. Mother used to do them for Father — he adored them — but I've never attempted them; they're really complicated to make. And a glass of wine, do you think?"

We gave our orders to the waitress and sat peacefully drinking our wine.

"Can you remember the name of Simon's girlfriend?" I asked Rosemary. "You know, the one who went to London. I was trying to think of it the other day."

"Oh, you mean Julie Phillips, Harold Phillips's daughter. Why?"

"I was just wondering why they broke up. They seemed very devoted and I thought they were on the verge of getting engaged, when she suddenly went away."

"I never really knew. I must say they did seem perfectly suited, so I was surprised. I believe they had a row about something and she went and got herself a job in London."

"It seems a bit drastic. What could the row have been about?"

"I don't know. I did ask Jack if he'd heard anything, but you know what men are like; they haven't any idea of what's happening right under their noses!" Rosemary said.

"It does seem a shame." I looked at my

watch. "They're taking a long time with our food."

Eventually the waitress appeared with two of those large soup plates that are the trendy thing to serve food in nowadays and we looked at their contents in disbelief. The food was absolutely disgusting.

"Steak and ale pie be blowed," Rosemary said. "It's a ladle full of stew with a piece of puff pastry — *bought* puff pastry," she said, trying a piece of it, "plonked down on top."

I poked at the small cannonball of brown, compacted matter sitting on a bed of lumpy mash, surrounded by grayish gravy. "Mine is even more horrible," I said. "I'm not even going to attempt it."

I waved the waitress over and asked for the bill. She looked at our untouched plates.

"Not worth waiting half an hour for," Rosemary said.

"I'm sorry," the waitress said. "Nobody's ever complained before. Would you like to speak to the chef?"

"I think that would be a waste of time," Rosemary said grimly.

Outside, we looked at each other and started to laugh. "So much for our treat!" I said. "Come on, let's go and get some fish-and-chips!"

CHAPTER FIVE

"I'm afraid it's going to be a good plum year," I said to Michael when he called to leave me some eggs. "The Early Rivers are quite ripe now — some of them are dropping — and the Victorias won't be far behind."

"We could come over at the weekend and help pick them, if that's all right," he said.

"That would be marvelous. I do hope Thea will be able to use a good lot of them. I suppose I'll have to make some jam. I'll try to make a bit of room in the freezer for the Victorias, but there are so many, and this year everyone will have plums and it'll be difficult to get rid of them!"

"Oh, I'm sure I can find some takers. Anyway, I'd better get off — I'm due back in the office."

"Thank Thea for the eggs — I'm so glad they've started to lay!" I said.

"Yes, she's really thrilled. Mind you, with

the price of feed and corn, I suspect each egg will be worth its weight in gold."

"Still, better than a pan of fowl food on the stove. I can still remember the ghastly smell when I was a child and my aunt Edith kept chickens!"

"I can just remember her. She used to keep her hat on when she came to lunch with Grandma."

"Ladies did then. Extraordinary to think of it now."

The fruits of the earth are wonderful, of course, but when I contemplate the bowed-down plum trees and their harvest, soon to be followed by the apples and pears, not to mention the abundance of runner beans and courgettes, all clamoring to be picked *now*, then I do wish nature would arrange a decent interval between these things.

I was in the pet shop — well, it's more than that really, selling horsey things and feed for a variety of animals — looking at the notice board. It's always full of interesting things. Advertisements for horse boxes and hay and Muscovy ducks and chicken houses, along-side requests for ("good") homes for kittens ("two marmalade boys and a sweet tabby girl") and rescue dogs ("Patch — likes riding in cars") and notices of charity rides and dog shows. I was just considering a small poster that read ADVANCE NOTICE: MOUNTED GAMES WORLD PAIRS CHAMPIONSHIP when Jo came in and stood beside me.

"What is it?" she asked. "The double horse trailer or the retired greyhound?"

"Neither," I said, laughing. "I do rather long for a retired greyhound, but my two would never allow it! I love looking at these advertisements — such richness!"

"There's certainly a lot going on," Jo said. "That reminds me, we're having an open day at the stables next Saturday afternoon. Is there any chance of Alice coming for a lesson then? I think it might encourage people to bring their young ones if they see her. I know it sounds a bit commercial, asking you like this, but I do really want to get as many people as possible interested. I just came in to put up a notice." She indicated a flyer in her hand.

"I think it's a splendid idea and I'm sure Alice will be delighted. She'd like to live at the stables if we'd let her!"

"That's marvelous. If you'd have a word with Thea, I'll ring her about times when I've got everything sorted out," Jo said.

"Fine. Oh, by the way, I don't suppose you'd like some plums. I've got a lot of really nice eating Victorias — it does seem such a shame to freeze them."

"Lovely. They're Charlie's favorite. He'll be delighted. We've got only apple trees and a few unproductive pears."

"Right, I'll bring them on Saturday, then."

As I knew she would be, Alice was thrilled at being part of the open day.

Thea was equally pleased though rather less vocal. "Michael keeps muttering about making Alice into a terrible little show-off," Thea said, "but I know he's delighted that Jo wants her there!"

I picked out the nicest plums for Charlie and took them along with me on the Saturday. There were quite a few people there, watching Delia and several other girls putting the horses over the jumps in one of the fields.

"They look pretty good, don't they?" Rosemary said. "Not exactly Horse of the Year Show, but quite professional."

"Absolutely splendid," I said. "I do hope it brings Jo in some more customers. Is Jilly here?"

"No, Alex has some sort of virus, so she's had to stay with him. They were afraid Delia might have caught it and wouldn't be able to come today. She's been driving them all mad about it, as you can imagine. Roger's here, though. He's actually got a weekend off." Rosemary's son-in-law, Roger, is now a police superintendent, so his work patterns are rather complicated. "He's over there talking to Charlie."

"Oh right — I'll just go and give him these plums. I'll see you in a minute."

Charlie was delighted with the plums and ate one right away. "My favorites," he said. "The nicest fruit there is and such a short season. Thank you, Sheila. They're wonderful."

"It looks as if the open day's a success," I said.

"Yes, we've had a few inquiries about livery and several bookings for lessons. I think it'll make a difference."

"Delia looks splendid," I said to Roger.

"I was just telling Charlie how grateful we are that she's taken to riding so enthusiastically," he said. "It makes her much more bearable to live with. I can't imagine how parents of other teenage girls survive!"

Just then Gordon Nicholson came up. He acknowledged Roger and me with a brief nod, but addressed himself to Charlie. "I want," he said, "to talk to you about Tarquin. What is your opinion of him? What is the situation — do we need to call the vet in?"

"It's only a slight case of laminitis," Charlie was saying as they went towards the stables. "We can cure it perfectly well by diet."

Roger and I moved away. "Tiresome man," Roger said. "I bet Charlie regrets taking that horse on for Dan Webster."

"I expect he felt he had to, since he's Gordon's friend and Gordon's Charlie's brother-in-law."

"I suppose so, but I bet they both want special rates. Gordon's always been very tight with money and I've no doubt he's told Dan that he can fix it!"

"Poor Charlie," I said. "He's too nice for his own good."

We'd joined Rosemary by this point and she added, "Goodness, yes. Gordon Nicholson is a ghastly man. Mother has all sorts of stories about his business dealings. I know Esther is a bore and a pest, but I can't help feeling sorry for her, married to a man like that!"

After a while Thea joined us and there were murmurs of appreciation from the visitors as Alice went round the ring on Cracker. "Oh look, isn't that *sweet!*" "What a dear little pony," "That little girl is riding it so well; isn't she clever!"

Thea looked at me and pulled a face. "Thank goodness she's too far away to hear any of that," she muttered, "or she'd be even more pleased with herself."

There was quite a storm in the night and it was still raining heavily in the morning. I was annoyed, though not surprised, to find a pool of water on the floor of the larder. That part of the house is a sort of extension, built in Victorian times. It has a slate roof, unlike the original structure, which is thatched. Some of the slates are loose and, when the rain falls from a certain direction, it comes through into the larder. I mopped the floor dry and put down an old saucepan to catch the drips. Whenever this happens I always remember Jane Austen, in one of her letters, bemoaning the fact that the rain had come into the storeroom and soaked everything — in her case it was a blocked gutter. *Plus ça change* . . .

Foss, who believes that no activity can be accomplished without his presence, came in and sat beside the saucepan, watching and waiting for each raindrop as it descended. I left him to it and went to ring Michael, who had promised a while ago to get a ladder and fix the slates.

"Only if you can spare the time," I said. "I know how busy you are at weekends. It'll be all right when the rain stops. It's just that I'm a bit worried about what will happen to the ceiling if it gets really saturated."

Michael, bless him, came after lunch. Fortunately the rain had stopped, so I wasn't so worried about him climbing up a ladder and the slates being slippery.

"There now," he said, coming in again, "I think that's all right. A couple of slates had slipped, but I've got them fixed back securely. Any chance of a cup of tea?"

While we were having it, I said, "I'm so sorry you missed seeing Alice yesterday. Everyone said how good she looked on that pony!"

"I know, but it was the last match of the season, so I had to go. Not that I did much good — out for sixteen, cleaned bowled! But I've certainly heard all about it from Alice — at great length!"

I laughed. "Everyone did make a big fuss of her. But I know Jo was pleased. Apparently several people asked about children's lessons after they saw Alice's."

"Thea says that they — Jo and Charlie — are worried about money."

"Well, horses are expensive, you know — the upkeep. And I imagine there's a limit to how much you can charge, even the week-enders."

"They own all those fields, right up to the new plantation, don't they?" he asked. "Surely they don't need them all for pasture?"

"Probably not, and I believe they do rent out a couple. But I know Jo would hate to *sell* any of them."

"Anyway," Michael said, reaching for the last piece of shortbread, "they'd only get the agricultural price. You'd never get planning permission for land round there."

"I should hope not indeed!" I said, "and certainly Jo would never, ever consider it, however desperate they were."

"Well," Michael said with the optimism we all feel about affairs that don't immediately concern us, "I daresay they'll pull through. It's a perfectly good business as far as I can see."

"Perhaps," I said hopefully, "the open day will bring them in a lot more people."

One of the more irritating things in life is the sudden realization that you've lost a filling; it seems almost impossible not to keep poking at the hole with your tongue. Fortunately my dentist, Jim Robinson, had a cancellation and was able to see me the very next day. Jim is an old friend and a great gossip, which is fine, except that it's difficult to comment on the latest bit of news when your mouth is full of cotton wool, or you're poised to wince at the whirring of the drill and the unpleasantness of the water spray.

"We've got a new dentist coming soon," Jim said, poking experimentally at the hole in my tooth, "a South African — nice chap. It'll take some of the strain off Gordon Nicholson and me. Since old Waddell died, there's just been the two of us — not enough for a place the size of Taviscombe."

I mumbled something that I hoped would indicate appreciation of his position.

"And Gordon's not been putting in the hours, from what I heard. Only there part of the week." He applied the drill and April, his assistant, sprayed water vigorously onto the tooth. "Do you know a chap called Dan Webster? Have a rinse away."

Given this respite, I said, "I think I've met him once or twice, but I can't say I know him. Why?"

"They say he and Gordon are involved in some sort of business deal; I don't know what."

"Really? I haven't heard anything about that."

"I've heard Webster has just bought a big place and some land up beyond Upper Barton — must have cost a packet."

April handed him the stuff she'd been mixing, and he poked the cotton wool rolls into my mouth and began to fill the tooth.

"It's all a bit of a mystery," Jim said. "I mean, *is* Gordon carrying on with the practice or is he going in full-time with whatever this new thing is?" I tried to express interest in this speculation by raising my eyebrows, though I don't think he noticed. "This Webster fellow, I think he's into property in some way and Gordon's on the council; that may be something to do with it!"

He took out the cotton wool, and I rinsed away the bits of filling before saying, "Oh, I don't think Gordon would do anything underhanded; he's always been a terrific one for abiding by the rules. A real sea green incorruptible!"

Jim looked startled and I said, "You know, the French Revolution — Robespierre, or at least I think it's Robespierre. . . . No, I can't believe Gordon would do anything wrong that's connected with his council work; he cares too much about his position as a councillor."

"True," Jim said thoughtfully, "*and* he's

president of Rotary this year. He certainly wouldn't get involved with anything that might jeopardize that. Still, I would like to know what he's up to, especially with this new man coming; I need to know where we all are. Right, then, that's you sorted out. Don't bite on it for a couple of hours."

After I left the surgery I felt the need for a little quiet relaxation, so I drove down, past the harbor, to the end of the seafront. To my annoyance, the council has decided in its wisdom that the seagulls might annoy the visitors, so it has caused the railings where the seagulls have always perched to be treated with some noxious substance to keep them away. Of course it doesn't. They (the seagulls) perch on the shingle, rising in a noisy crowd whenever they spot someone who (in defiance of the notice posted by the aforementioned council) might have come to feed them. But I miss the line of gulls — neat little terns and large bully-boy herring gulls — alert and interested, occasionally making little forays, but returning to keep an eye on the passersby, waiting to see what they might offer.

I stood by the rails, looking out to the sea, and considering what Jim had said about Gordon and Dan Webster. I didn't believe that Gordon, however greedy he might be for money, would risk the position and reputation he's built up over the years. He likes being a big fish in a small pond, and his position on the council, and on the committees of other organizations, means a lot to him. He loves the idea of making rules for other people (it wouldn't surprise me if the seagull embargo was his idea), extending the sort of control he believes he exercises over his own family to the public at large.

Of course, it's possible that whatever Dan Webster wanted from Gordon was perfectly aboveboard and honest. But I couldn't really think of anything Gordon might have or do that could be valuable to an entrepreneur (for want of a better word) like Dan Webster. Gordon was comfortably off, but he didn't have the sort of money that would make him a possible investor in a really big project.

Looking out over the sea I saw threatening black clouds darkening the horizon. The gulls on the beach, apparently sensing the approaching storm, rose all together and flew off round the corner of the bay, and the first large drops of rain drove me back into the car. By the time I got home it was raining heavily and the sky was really dark. When I'd fed the animals, I made myself a light supper of steamed fish and mashed potatoes, because of my new filling, and sat down with it in front of the television. But the lights flickered from time to time and the rumble of thunder seemed to be getting nearer. Tris, who hates thunderstorms, sat pressed close by my feet and quivered at each lightning flash.

I went to bed early, taking the animals with me. Tris lay on the bottom of the bed, making little whimpering sounds when the noise of the thunder was too much for him. Foss, who loves excitement of any kind, inserted himself behind the drawn curtains on the windowsill, where he watched the storm with the interest of a small child at a firework display. I couldn't get to sleep and lay there in the dark, not even able to see the time because the brief power cuts caused by the storm meant that my electric clock was affected and was now flashing madly on and off. After a while I put on the light, switched off the clock and looked at my watch. It was only just after midnight. With a sigh I picked up my copy of *Pillars of the House* and immersed myself in the lives of the Underwood family until the storm had passed over and I was able to sleep.

The next morning I had hoped to have a

little lie-in, but now that the storm was over the animals were anxious to get on with their lives and saw no reason to be diverted from their usual regime, so we were all downstairs by eight o'clock, they with their bowls of food and I with a very necessary cup of coffee. When I went to let them out, I saw it was a beautiful morning and last night's raindrops were sparkling in the sun.

Inspired by the brightness and freshness of the morning, I had a great clear-out in the kitchen, sweeping away the detritus of daily living from the work-top — all the packets of dry animal food, a dish of withered apples and overripe bananas, a bowl half full of drippings I'd meant to put out for the birds, a packet of biscuits and a couple of storage tins that should have been put away in the larder, and the animals' antiflea spray — and wiped down every surface I could reach. After all that, averting my eyes from the cooker, I made myself another cup of coffee and had a nice sit-down with the daily paper.

It was late afternoon when Rosemary rang. Her voice was a little unsteady.

"Sheila, the most awful thing has happened. Charlie's dead."

CHAPTER SIX

For a moment I didn't take in what Rosemary was saying.

"Dead?"

"Yes, but it's worse than that, Sheila. He's been killed."

"Killed," I echoed stupidly.

"In the stables. He was hit over the head — it looks like a burglary that went wrong."

"That's — that's horrible! When was this?"

"This morning — very early on. Simon rang a little while ago to tell me."

"What happened?"

"Apparently he got up when it was just light to see to the horses — they'd been restless in the night . . . that awful storm. Liz had the same idea and she arrived early. She went into the office to put her things down before going to see to the horses and she found him there. He was slumped on the desk and there was this awful wound on the side of his head."

"Oh no!"

"She said there was a very faint pulse — you know Jo made both girls do that first aid course — so she rang for an ambulance straightaway and then she rang up to the house to let Jo know what had happened."

"Poor Jo. How could she bear it?" I asked.

"Liz said she was very calm and when the ambulance arrived, she went with him, of course. But he died on the way to the hospital without regaining consciousness."

"Where's Jo now?"

"At home. She rang Simon and he fetched her from the hospital. He'll stay with her tonight."

"Thank goodness for that."

"The police were all over the place. Apparently the safe — you know that small safe in the office — was open but the money, yesterday's takings, was still there, so I suppose whoever it was panicked when he saw what he'd done and ran away."

"Oh dear," I said wearily, "what a terrible waste of a wonderful life."

"I know. Charlie of all people, so kind and bright and intelligent and — oh, everything! It doesn't bear thinking about."

But, of course, it was all I could think about that evening. I knew the sort of numbness that Jo must be feeling, the denial and the feeling that somehow it should be possible to turn back the clock and make everything all right. And I knew, too, the pain of waking up each morning and re-alizing all over again the awful fact of death, and the terrible emptiness. But when Peter died, I had Michael, still quite young, someone I had to make an effort for, some-one to give some sort of meaning to my life. Jo had no children. True, Simon was de-voted to her and she to him, but it wasn't, couldn't ever be, the same.

Rosemary rang again next morning. "I wish I knew what to do about Jo. I'd like to go and see her, but I suppose it's too soon?"

"I think she'd like some time on her own," I said. "In a little while I'm sure she'll be glad to see people, but not just yet."

"I'm sure you're right; it's just that one wants to *do* something. Anyway, she's got Simon. Oh, I do hope Esther doesn't go rushing round! Though I'm sure Simon can keep her away. Poor Esther, I know she'd mean well, like we all do, but I know the last thing I'd want in these circumstances would be Esther wittering on."

"The last thing!"

"Do Michael and Thea know?" Rosemary asked.

"I rang them. They were dreadfully shocked and upset. Charlie meant so much to everyone, even people who didn't know him that well. Michael's their solicitor, so he'll be involved, though I suppose if there's a police inquiry, it won't be for a while."

"When I rang Jilly last night I had a word with Roger. Of course, he'd heard officially. He says Bob Morris will be looking into it, being the man on the spot. Bob's got his promotion, Roger said — he's an inspector now."

"Oh, that's good. Bob's a nice person, very sympathetic and kind. If anyone's got to talk to Jo about all this, I'm glad it's him."

The following morning I ran into Liz as I was coming out of the chemist and was able to ask her how Jo was.

"She's being marvelous," Liz said. "Well, you know Jo. She's dreadfully upset — you can see that — but she's trying to carry on as usual."

"I suppose you've got to when there are animals around," I said.

"Peggy and I can cope, but she says she needs to keep busy."

"I don't suppose it helps to have the police around asking questions."

"They've been pretty good. Bob Morris is

nice. His daughter rides with us, so he knows his way around the stables — that helps. And knowing Charlie and Jo too."

"Of course." I hesitated. "What exactly happened?"

"I turned up at the stables early because I thought the horses would be spooked by the storm. I went straight to the office and that's where I found poor Charlie. It was so awful. It was . . ." Liz stopped and shook her head as if she couldn't say any more.

"I'm sorry," I said. "I shouldn't have asked you."

"No, it's all right." She paused for a moment and then went on. "He was lying across the desk and there was this terrible wound on the side of his head. They think he was hit with an iron bar or something. Can you believe anyone would do a thing like that? He was alive, but only just. I rang for the ambulance and they were very quick, but — but he didn't make it to the hospital, poor Charlie."

There were tears in her eyes and I put my hand on her arm. "I'm so sorry," I said. "We all loved him."

She nodded. "Everybody did. I can't imagine what it will be like there without him. And all for nothing — not even for the money. He'd opened the safe, the door was open, but the money was still inside. We usually take it out in the evening, when we close down, but that time we were busy and Charlie said leave it and I'll see to it in the morning. If only . . ."

"I know."

"The horses knew something had happened," Liz said. "It wasn't just the storm; they were so restless, I'm sure they knew."

"Certainly, if someone had been prowling around they'd have been upset."

"Yes, that's right. Anyway, I must get on. I came out only to get some paracetamol for Jo. She's got a rotten headache and we've run out."

"Give her my love. I'll be round to see her soon, but I didn't want to intrude."

"I think she'd like to see you — anyone who knew Charlie — you know."

It's peculiar, really; some days you can go round the shops and never see anyone you know, but other days you bump into several people all in one morning. In quick succession I saw Thea (on her way to pick up Alice from her friend Emma's), Anthea (who wanted me to fill in for Maureen at the next coffee morning) and, finally, Rosemary, who said, "Come and have some lunch at the Buttery. I'm absolutely shattered. I've just been taking Mother to buy a new pair of shoes and you can imagine what *that* was like!"

"Did you find any that she liked?"

Rosemary gave a hollow laugh. "What do you think!"

"Difficult?"

"Difficult. The floor of the shop was *strewn* with shoes and the poor girl — it was Shelley, you know, Mrs. Carter's daughter — was at her wits' end but trying desperately to be polite." She sighed. "I doubt if I'll ever be able to enter that shop again!"

It was quite early when we got to the Buttery and not too crowded.

"I'm going to have soup and an *enormous* piece of chocolate gâteau," Rosemary said. "And I'll be obliged if you'll have the same so that I can be indulgent without feeling guilty."

"Actually, I could do with a little indulgence myself," I said. "I saw Liz earlier on and asked her about poor Charlie. It was awful; she was very upset — so I feel the need of a little something myself."

We carried our trays down to the far end of the room where it was quiet.

"Did Liz say how Jo is?" Rosemary asked.

"Coping, of course. Carrying on as usual, as you'd expect. Liz thinks it would be all right to go to see her. Actually, Alice has a lesson on Saturday — I don't imagine they'll have canceled it — so I'll just go along then. Why don't you come too?"

"Yes, that would be best."

"I wonder when the funeral will be," Rosemary said.

"I suppose there'll have to be a postmortem, after the way he died, so I don't expect it'll be for a while."

"I imagine Simon will help her make all the arrangements. He's been so good, like a son to her — better than some sons, actually — and I'm so glad she's got someone like him to support her." She broke off and muttered, "Oh no!"

Esther's voice behind me said, "I thought I saw you two lurking down here. Do you mind if I join you?" Without waiting for an answer (and what answer could there be?), she put her tray on the table, moved my shopping bag from the spare chair and sat down.

"I don't often come here; I mean, it's just snacks really, not proper food, isn't it? But I had to do some shopping and get Gordon's suit from the cleaners, and I've got an appointment with Mr. Davis about my new glasses at two thirty, so it didn't seem worthwhile going home. Oh dear, the pastry on this quiche is very hard. I don't think I

92

can eat that! Perhaps I should have had the soup like you — what is it?"

"Onion and potato," I said. "It's home-made and very good."

"Oh, I can't eat anything with onion. It gives me dreadful indigestion; the same with garlic. In a restaurant, whatever they may say, I can tell in a moment if there's even a *whiff* of garlic in anything!"

Esther settled herself more comfortably and began picking at the quiche. "So, wasn't it dreadful about poor Charlie! Of course, the moment I heard — Simon rang me — I went round straight-away." Rosemary and I exchanged glances. "I mean, I had to see if there was anything I could do for Jo. The police had gone when I got there, but there was still all that tape stuff they put round things. I was going up to the house — well, I thought Jo would be resting, I mean, after a shock like that, but, do you know, she was there in the stables seeing to the horses!"

"Well," I said, "when there are animals . . ."

"But she's got those two girls for all that sort of thing."

"She probably wanted to keep busy," Rosemary said, "to keep her mind off things."

"I don't see how mucking out stables

would take your mind off a dreadful thing like that! No, I said to her, 'You should be lying down. You go up to the house and I'll make you a nice cup of tea.' But she said Peggy had just made some and would I like a cup. Just as though nothing had happened." She pushed her plate to one side and drank a little of her coffee. "No, what it is, she's in denial — that's what they call it now, isn't it? She can't bring herself to face up to it. Well, it's not surprising — Charlie was her life, really; she gave up her career for him, after all. If she'd gone on in the theater she'd have been a dame by now." She paused for a moment to allow us to take in the magnificent implications of this fact. "Still, I suppose they were happy, or as happy as anyone is nowadays."

"Oh yes," I said, "they were very happy."

Esther spooned some sugar into her cup and stirred it vigorously. "This coffee's very strong. No, what I mean to say is that she only took up all this horse business because of Charlie and now she can give it up. After all, she's seventy-four — quite a bit older than me, and, goodness knows, I get tired sometimes. All this hard work, looking after all those horses, is heavy work and too much for someone that age."

"She couldn't bear to give up," Rosemary

said. "The stables are her life, just like Charlie was; they'll mean everything to her now that he's gone."

"That's all very well, but she'll have to give up sometime. From what I hear, those stables are practically running at a loss."

"That's as may be," Rosemary persisted, "but she'll carry on to the bitter end if need be."

"Anyway," I said, "there's every chance she can turn things round. She's got a lot of new people coming for lessons and livery."

"Yes, but now Charlie's gone," Esther said, "she'll have to get someone to replace him, and that will cost money."

"You couldn't replace Charlie," I said sadly. "But I'm sure she'll manage. Liz and Peggy are splendid girls and she has a lot of voluntary help from all those horse-mad youngsters, and, of course, Simon is a great help."

"Oh, Simon — he's always up there. It's that or work," Esther said. "I often say to him he ought to be getting out more, but, of course he never listens to me. Boys are so difficult. Not that Vicky is much better. Thinks of nothing but work. She's in America now. Simon rang her to tell her about Charlie, but she can't get back for the funeral. You'd have thought a family

95

crisis like that would come first, but she said she's on a deadline, whatever that may mean."

"If she's in America," Rosemary said, "she might not be able to get a flight anyway. Of course, we don't know when the funeral's going to be, and the postmortem will hold things up."

"It's perfectly awful," Esther said, "all this business with the police and everything. It's bad enough for poor Jo without all this."

"And she's perfectly right," Rosemary said when Esther had gone. "It must make things ten times worse — churning up her feelings with every question, not being able to lay him to rest properly."

"I know. And if they do manage to catch the person who did this horrible thing, there'll be the trial and the whole business brought up all over again."

I collected Alice on Saturday afternoon and drove her to the stables. As she was getting her things out of the back of the car she said, "Gran, Delia said that Charlie was dead. Is he?"

"I'm afraid so, darling."

"So we won't see him ever again?"

"I'm afraid not."

She considered this for a moment. "That's

sad," she said.

I was pleased to see that the stables seemed to be as busy as usual, with quite a few people about and Liz and Peggy leading out the horses and adjusting the girths, just, as Esther said, as if nothing had happened. I looked around for Jo and saw that she was in the yard at the back of the stables, bent over the engine of their ancient Land Rover. In addition to her other skills, Jo is also a useful amateur mechanic.

Just then Rosemary arrived with Delia, who immediately took charge of Alice and led her off to the stables. We heard her say, "It's all right, Alice. I can tack up Cracker for you if Peggy's busy."

Rosemary smiled and I said, "Alice thinks she's wonderful; it's 'Delia says this' and 'Delia says that' all day long."

"We're just grateful — especially Alex — that Delia's got someone else to boss around!"

Just then they came out and we watched while Delia helped Alice to mount and then spent a long time meticulously checking the girth and adjusting the stirrups. Finally she took hold of the bridle and led the pony off into the ring, then handed her over to Peggy.

"Very professional," I said. "No, really, she's quite excellent."

"She says she doesn't want to do A levels and go to university — just wants to work with horses. We're hoping she'll grow out of it!"

"Well, there are horse management courses at some universities, I believe."

"Oh well, there's plenty of time yet." She looked around. "Have you seen Jo?"

"She's round the back fiddling with the Land Rover. What do you think — shall we go and have a word, or shall we leave it till later?"

"Oh, let's go now, I think, don't you?"

As we walked slowly towards her, Jo looked up and, wiping her hands on a piece of rag, slammed shut the bonnet of the Land Rover.

"Hello, you two," she greeted us, smiling.

"You look busy," I said.

"Oh well, got to keep the old girl on the road for a bit longer."

"Jo," Rosemary said, "we're so very sorry about Charlie. Such a terrible thing to have happened, especially a brutal attack like that . . ."

Jo shook her head. "No," she said, "it wasn't. We've had the postmortem report and it turns out that it was an accident after all."

CHAPTER SEVEN

At first neither of us spoke. Then Rosemary said, "What do you mean? How could it be an accident?"

Jo opened the back door of the Land Rover and threw the piece of dirty rag inside.

"It's complicated," she said, "but we've more or less managed to piece together what happened. The postmortem showed that the injury was caused by a horseshoe. It had to be Tarquin — we examined his feet and found traces of blood."

"But how . . . ?" I said.

"Charlie was worried about the horses after that storm, so he went down to the stables very early, while it was still dark. He went into the office to switch the lights on — that was probably when he opened the safe, since he'd been going to bring the takings back to the house — and then went in to see Tarquin, who he knew would have been the one most upset by the storm. Tarquin would have been restless — nervous from the storm and uncomfortable with the laminitis that affects his feet. Charlie would have bent down to examine them and, in doing so, knocked over a bucket — we found it rolled over to one corner of the stall. That, on top of everything else, must have startled Tarquin so that he reared up and caught Charlie a blow on the side of the head."

"But how did he get to the office?" I asked.

"Apparently it's perfectly possible to move after a blow to the head. It doesn't necessarily affect you straightaway. So he probably got up and went into the office to phone for help and then — then collapsed."

Her voice shook slightly and Rosemary said quickly, "Oh, Jo, I'm so sorry. This must be awful for you, to go over it like this."

Jo shook her head. "No," she said, "it's all right. Somehow when I talk about it, it doesn't seem as if I'm talking about Charlie, just some other person. And really, you know, it's such a blessing."

"A blessing?" I asked.

"Yes. When I thought he'd been killed by someone, deliberately and violently, that was almost the worst thing of all. Do you see what I mean? Charlie — who loved everyone and whom everyone loved — it seemed a sort of negation of all he'd been, his whole life, a *terrible* ending to it. But now I can accept it for what it was, an accident that could have happened to anyone."

"Will you get Dan Webster to take the horse away?" Rosemary asked.

"No, why should I? It wasn't Tarquin's fault; he didn't *mean* to do it. Actually, we've been making a lot of progress with him. He's a good horse at bottom; it's just that he hasn't been treated properly. Liz has been working with him and he's taken to her very well. I really believe we can get him sorted out. Charlie would have wanted us to try, anyway."

"Well," Rosemary said, "I think you're being marvelous. I don't know how you can be so strong."

Jo smiled. "You carry on. The stables mean — meant — a lot to Charlie and me. It's never been just a business. It's the people and the horses and — oh, I don't know — the whole way of life, I suppose. He wouldn't want me to let everything go, now would he? Talking of which, I'd better get on; I've got a class waiting for me. See you later perhaps."

She moved away, down to the lower ring where Liz was putting up the jumps.

"She is amazing," Rosemary said. "Not getting rid of the horse and everything. How could she do it?"

"Well, I understand about the horse," I said, "and about being glad that it was an accident, but I do admire the calm way she goes about things."

"She's never been one to show her feelings, of course. I don't know how these things work, but I suppose all that sort of thing went into her acting."

"Oh yes," I said, "there was plenty of feeling there. Do you remember the way she spoke the willow cabin speech in *Twelfth Night* and the 'patience on a monument' bit? So moving!"

"And the young girl in *The Seagull,* goodness, that was fantastic. She was really brilliant. I can't imagine how she could bear to give it up!"

"Oh well. Charlie. It was a — what's the phrase? — a *coup de foudre.* She was simply bowled over by him, and stayed that way to the end. That's why it's so extraordinary that she's taking it so well."

We moved back towards the stables as Alice was coming back on Cracker.

"Gran, Gran, did you see me? Can you watch me dismount? You take *both* your feet out of the stirrups at once and then you get off like this!"

Peggy led the pony away as Delia appeared from the stables and said to Rosemary, "Can I stay for an extra hour? Liz said I could help her mix the feeds and fill the hay nets."

"I'm sorry, darling; I've got to be back before four," Rosemary said. She turned to me. "Mother's expecting me. She's got these two old chums coming to tea and I promised to take her some cream for the scones."

"Oh, Gran!" Delia said. "They're so busy here with it being a Saturday and they do need some help, especially now that Charlie . . ."

"It's all right," I said to Rosemary, "I can wait and take Delia back. I'll just give Jilly a ring and say we'll be a bit later. And you'd better go. Mustn't keep your mother waiting for the cream!"

Rosemary pulled a face and went.

On the way back in the car later on, I said to Delia, "What exactly *is* laminitis?"

She considered for a moment. "It's something that usually affects ponies, but some horses are subject to it. It's often caused by the horse eating too much new sweet grass in the spring, or the second growth at this time of the year. That's probably how Tarquin got it before he came to us. It causes a painful burning sensation in the hooves, which are very sensitive. You cure it mainly by diet and medication and also by poultices. I expect that's what poor Charlie was going to do when he was looking at Tarquin's hooves."

"Goodness," I said, "aren't you knowledgeable!"

"Oh, I've got a lot of books about horse management and horse diseases," Delia said. "It's very interesting. Actually, Tarquin's getting much better. Liz has put special boots on him — that helps, you know — so he should be quite all right soon. Liz says that Jo might buy him from Mr. Webster. I hope she does. I don't think Mr. Webster really likes horses and he hardly ever rides Tarquin — not that he could now with the laminitis, but before. I think he just wanted a good-looking horse to show off — that's what Liz says anyway."

I thought about what Esther's reaction would be to the news that Jo had bought the horse that had killed her husband, but then Esther would never allow Simon and Vicky to have a pet animal when they were children "because of the hairs all over the furniture."

"Liz is very good with Tarquin. She knows

a lot about all sorts of horsey things." Delia turned round to address Alice. "She says she thinks you're getting along very well and perhaps you might be able to go out on one of the shorter rides soon. If you do, I'll come on that one with you — though, of course I usually go on the two-hour ones — and I can keep an eye on you. I expect you'd like that."

Overcome by this magnificent prospect, Alice, most unusually robbed of speech, nodded silently.

The church was full for Charlie's funeral. Not just local friends, but people from the horse world so eminent that even I recognized them. There was a general buzz of conversation, almost as if it were a social occasion. Charlie would have liked that. I went with Thea and Michael (lawyers always seem able to get time off for funerals) and when Rosemary came in she sat by us.

"Such a lot of people!" she whispered, "but I suppose he *was* such a well-known figure. So nice to think that people haven't forgotten him."

I was pleased to see, in the little procession that followed the coffin, that Simon, Liz and Peggy were gathered round Jo — her chosen family really — while Esther and

Gordon walked separately behind. I was pleased too that Jo had chosen the proper *Book of Common Prayer* service. The beautiful language, soothing and familiar, felt so much more fitting to me than the determinedly cheery language of some contemporary services, though I suppose many people do find comfort in them. Horses for courses, as Charlie would say.

It was a surprise, though, to find that one of the hymns Jo had chosen was Newman's "Lead, Kindly Light." With so many people filling the church with their singing, the words came through with a freshness and immediacy.

I loved the garish day, and, spite of fears,
Pride ruled my will; remember not past
  years.
So long thy power hath blest me, sure it
  still
Will lead me on
O'er moor and fen, o'er crag and torrent,
  till
The night is gone.

Was that a summing up of Charlie's life? I hadn't thought of Jo as having a strong faith. I couldn't remember seeing her in church, though of course, Sunday is always a busy day at the stables. But maybe she has something of that splendid Victorian certainty, different from the vague hope that is the most many of us feel. Perhaps she really believes that one day she and Charlie will be reunited in some celestial city. I hope so.

Afterwards, when we were gathered with drinks and sandwiches in the local hotel, talking affectionately of Charlie, the atmosphere was definitely partylike. There was a buzz of chatter, with sudden little bursts of laughter as one person after another recalled some anecdote or incident. "I remember when . . . ," they began, and Charlie's life seemed to unroll from their memories of him.

Looking round, I saw Jo standing on her own at the table where the drinks and things were laid out, and I went over to speak to her. She was pouring herself a cup of coffee and looked up as I approached.

"I think it went well," she said.

"It went wonderfully, and now," I said, nodding towards the room full of people, "it's turning into a splendid party."

Jo smiled. "He'd have been so pleased. He loved to see people enjoying themselves." She looked around. "I was very touched that so many people came, and a lot of them from the old days. Dear Charlie, it's wonderful that they still remember him. . . ." Her voice broke a little and the cup rattled in its saucer as her hand shook. She put it down quickly on the table and said, "I'm sorry, Sheila. It's been rather an emotional time." She laid her hand on my arm. "Thank you for coming," she said, and moved away.

As Michael, Thea and I were about to leave, Simon came over and spoke to us.

"It was a good turnout, wasn't it? I'm so glad for Jo's sake. She's been wonderful, of course, but it's all been so complicated, determining the cause of death and all that confusion. Thanks, Michael, for dealing with all the legal stuff — much appreciated. Now we must try to carry on."

"How are things at the stables?" I asked.

"Quite good really, in the actual day-to-day running of things. Liz and Peggy are brilliant and I try to put in a few hours when I can, just helping out — as well as doing the books and so forth. Jo, of course, is fantastic — never stops. I worry about her sometimes, but I do see that's what keeps her going. And we're all determined to keep up the standard; Charlie would have expected that." Simon smiled. "And we feel that somehow he's still in charge."

■ ■ ■ ■

I'd arranged to have lunch with an old school friend, Rhonda Jackson. She lives quite a long way away in Devon, so we usually meet halfway at South Molton. We met at one of the restaurants that seem to have sprung up in the small market town now that a large number of fashionable Londoners have bought second homes down there. This one is in a mews behind the main street and has made a feature of its original stables origin. The menu is equally fashionable.

"What on earth are pumpkin gnocchi?" Rhonda demanded. She's always been very forthright and has what someone once described as the sort of voice that lost us the Empire, so that heads were turned in our direction. "And young leaves of *what?*" she went on.

"I quite fancy the crusted sea bass with celariac puree," I said.

"I shall have the fish cakes," Rhonda said, "though why they have to be Thai with chili dip beats me! Anyway, how're Rosemary and that terrible old mother of hers?"

I gave her the latest Taviscombe news and, of course, she wanted to know all about Jo and Charlie.

"Such an extraordinary thing to have happened," she said. "I never did trust horses. Enormous brutes — stand on your feet as soon as look at you! And I never understood about Jo. I mean, there she was, acting at the National and the RSC, on top of her profession, traveling all over the world — a wonderful life. You could have knocked me down with a feather when I heard she'd thrown it all up and gone back to Taviscombe of all places!"

"It was her home," I said mildly.

"But *Taviscombe*, such a dead and alive hole. I must say I couldn't wait to get out!" I refrained from commenting on the aliveness or otherwise of Newton Abbott, where Rhonda now lives.

"I must say it's always seemed a bit odd to me," she continued. "I wondered if there was something behind it all."

"What sort of thing?" I asked.

"Oh, I don't know — something to do with her career. You should know; you were always the one who was mad about the theater. Mind you, we never knew her really well in the old days, did we? She was a jump older than us. Now, *Esther* was still at school when we were. She was a prefect — do you remember?"

"Yes," I said with feeling, "I certainly do."

"Goodness, she was bossy — worse than the staff, really. I remember that time when Phyllis Shaw threw her school hat up onto the roof of the bus shelter while we were waiting for the school bus and Esther made her climb up to get it — said Phyllis had damaged the good name of the school!"

"I'd forgotten that," I said, "but I do remember how, when Rosemary and I sneaked off from that museum trip in Exeter to go shopping, she caught us coming back and meanly reported us to Miss Martin. Actually, Miss Martin was a good sport — and I think would rather have liked to have gone shopping herself — and only gave us an order mark."

"Still," Rhonda said, prodding her fish cake experimentally, "I'm really sorry for poor Jo. Of course there are no children — that makes it much worse for her."

"Her nephew is very devoted to her," I said. "He lives in Taviscombe and has been marvelous over all this."

"I'm sure he has. But," she went on with the authority of the mother of four, "it's not the same as your own, is it? I don't know why they call this a *Thai* fish cake — it's only cod with bits in it."

"Jo's been wonderful," I said. "Carrying

111

on as usual, though she must miss Charlie dreadfully; they were so close."

"I'd have thought she might sell up," Rhonda said, looking at the menu. "I think I'll go mad and have a pudding — that fish cake wasn't very filling. The pear and almond tart sounds all right. I can't be bothered to make pastry anymore. How about you?"

I shook my head. "Not for me. No, I'm sure Jo will never sell the stables; they're part of her life with Charlie. Anyway, I think it's the work that's helping her through."

"Oh well, it takes all sorts I suppose. But she's getting on a bit and it's hard work; she won't be able to carry on forever."

When I parted from Rhonda ("No really, you paid last time"; "Oh all right, but next time is on me"), I thought I'd drive back over Withypool Common. It was a beautiful afternoon, still bright, summer weather, though the heather was fading and tipped with brown, and the grass was no longer green and fresh, but dusty and close-cropped where the sheep had been feeding. Yet the sky was a light, clear blue and the sun felt warm through the windscreen of the car.

Considering it was still the school holidays, there wasn't much traffic, and very few people had stopped in the lay-bys on the hill. But, as I approached the turning that leads down to Landacre, I saw two cars parked on the verge: an old Land Rover and a smart new Mitsubishi four-by-four. Driving past, I realized that it was Jo's Land Rover, but there was no sign of her, nor of the other driver. Presumably she was seeing someone about a horse; it was a perfectly reasonable explanation. But the fact of seeing someone (or their car) in an unexpected place always evokes a faint prick of curiosity. I was puzzling about it until, out on the open moor, the sight of a large herd of ponies silhouetted dramatically against the sky drove all other thoughts from my mind.

CHAPTER EIGHT

A few days later I had to go up to Kirkby Lonsdale for several weeks. My cousin Marjorie had fallen and broken her arm rather badly, and her sister, Bridget, who lives with her and who would normally have been able to look after her, had gone to Australia to be with her daughter, who was expecting her first baby.

"It's frightfully good of you to offer, Sheila. I know she's got lots of friends and splendid neighbors," Bridget said, when she rang me from Melbourne, "but she really does need someone to monitor her insulin injections and, anyway, I'd feel *so* much better if there was someone actually sleeping in the house. I feel awful about being away just when she needs me, but Jenny's due any day now. . . ."

I took Tris with me, and Foss went to stay with Michael and Thea, to disrupt their household and tyrannize over their little cat,

Smoke. In a way, I wasn't sorry to be going away. Somehow too much seemed to be going on in Taviscombe and I felt it would be nice to have a break and live in a completely different environment for a while. Marjorie and I always get on well and I was looking forward to being in the Lake District again.

At first Marjorie really did need a lot of attention and several visits back and forth to the hospital to adjust the horrible metalwork frame on her poor arm; it was a challenge to find garments she could wear and getting her up and dressed took at least half an hour. But after a while she was well enough to come out for little drives so that I could revisit my favorite places.

"It's wonderful to be out of the house again," she said as we sat looking out at the still waters of Coniston. "I was beginning to feel quite claustrophobic."

"You went to the hospital on Monday," I said.

"That's not *out*. I mean, just being a little bit back to normal."

"Do you feel like some tea?" I asked. "I seem to remember there's a nice place quite near here, if it's still open this late in the season."

"I meant to ask you the other day," Marjorie said as I buttered a scone and cut it up

115

for her, "why your friend Jo gave up the stage like that."

"Well, she met Charlie. . . ."

"*Such* a pity! I remember seeing her at Stratford, years ago, when I used to take the English sixth to see their set plays when they were doing them there. What always struck me was how *different* she was."

"Different?"

"Well, you know how some actresses — and actors too — are always the same, always themselves, if you know what I mean. But she was always different in every part she took. When you saw her in *Twelfth Night* and then in *Hamlet* — well, they might not have been the same actress."

"Yes, I do know what you mean. I suppose it's just that she was a brilliant actress."

"I'll always remember her and James Carlyle in *Hamlet.* Now, he was a *marvelous* actor. But it was a most peculiar production; they made Hamlet absolutely selfish and self-obsessed, not sympathetic at all. She was wonderful as Ophelia. She did the mad scene so beautifully, but the bit I remember most was the nunnery scene with Hamlet. I've never seen anything so cruel and unpleasant as his rejection of her! I suppose it was all part of the production, and it was certainly very memorable — well, look how it's stayed in my mind all these years!"

"I never saw that production and I don't think I'd like an unsympathetic Hamlet."

"It certainly got my sixth form talking!"

"I did see James Carlyle's *Macbeth*," I said. "That was with his wife, Jane Neville. He was better than she was, very charismatic, but she wasn't really up to it. Splendid in light comedy, but she wasn't really a Shakespearean actress."

"Those husband and wife things don't always work when one is better than the other. Is there any more tea in the pot? I think I could manage another cup."

The weather was amazingly kind and we made other trips — to Thirlmere and Buttermere, Derwentwater and Ullswater — all full of happy memories for me. It was late in the season and there weren't too many people about (one always wishes that places like the Lake District could be conveniently emptied for the duration of one's visit), just the red and blue anoraks of the ramblers dotting the landscape in the distance or cramming onto the ferries at Windermere.

On my last day we went to Rydal Water and then on to Grasmere so that I could have another look at Dove Cottage.

"It's a good thing to have visitors," Marjorie said. "Somehow, left to yourself, you

117

never go to places like this, on your own doorstep."

By a fortunate chance we had the cottage to ourselves, so I was able to wander round at will and picture not William but Dorothy Wordsworth walking many miles about the countryside in all winds and weathers with William, copying out William's poems by inadequate lamplight, keeping house for William in this uncomfortable, inconvenient cottage, with the added burden of frequent visits from Coleridge, not the easiest of guests. No wonder her diary often recorded, "Laid down with a headache."

"I suppose if you're very fond of someone," Marjorie said when I spoke of this, "you don't mind what you do or where you are as long as you're with them."

Bridget came home at last ("Yes, it was a boy, eight pounds and red hair! Jenny's fine. It was wonderful to see her and Greg and Andrew — that's what they're calling him. You've been an absolute angel, Sheila, and I can't thank you enough."), and I was able to go home.

I must say I did feel better for the break.

"A change of scene," I said to Rosemary, "that's what they say, and I really feel as if I've had a holiday, though it was quite hard work with poor Marjorie. That awful metal contraption meant she couldn't do anything much. But she was very good about it all and it was nice to see her again, better on her own, really. I'm very fond of her and of Bridget, but somehow, not together. And, although Marjorie's house is very comfortable, there's nothing like your own bed, is there? So what's the news? Have I missed anything important?"

"Not really," Rosemary said, pouring us both another cup of coffee. "Mother's ignored my advice and is having her sitting room decorated after all. So she's living in the dining room and making life hell for poor Elsie and, of course, for poor little Mr. Burge who's *doing* the decorating — keeps changing her mind, all the usual things. She did hint that it would be more convenient if she came to stay with us while it was all happening, but I *totally* ignored that. Jack would have divorced me if I'd said yes! I think she knew that and didn't press it."

"Poor you! How about Jo? How is she managing?" I asked.

"Seems to be fine. Simon was up there quite a bit, but he's at home more just now because they're worried about Gordon."

"Worried?"

"Well, you know he's had a heart condition for years, and it seems to have got worse lately. But you know what men are like. Esther's been at him to go and see Dr. Macdonald and he kept putting it off. When he did finally go, Dr. Macdonald said he wanted him to see a specialist and have some more tests, but — it makes me so cross — Gordon says he's too busy at the moment and he'll think about it! So selfish when he *knows* how worried Esther is."

"We've always known he's selfish, but I'd have thought he'd want to have it seen to for his own sake."

"Oh, you know how they are — keep on saying that they're fine and get irritated when you try to persuade them to be sensible. Jack's just the same; he'll never do anything about his bad back. I've offered to make an appointment for him with that wonderful chiropractor Jilly found when my neck was so bad, but he tells me not to fuss, and then goes on moaning and groaning about it. I think he enjoys being a martyr."

"It can't be easy for Esther; I should think Gordon's difficult enough when he's well. I'm glad she has some support from Simon."

"I really think he's trying to do too much. He looked absolutely exhausted when I saw him last week. Poor boy, he does his best, but Gordon's disagreeable and Esther would drive anyone mad — and then there's his job. I think the time he spends up at the stables, however hard he may work there, is the only relaxation he gets!"

"Yes, it can't be easy. It all falls on him now that Vicky's in London."

"Oh, I nearly forgot," Rosemary said. "I thought I'd better warn you — Anthea's got this new idea for raising money for the kitchen at Brunswick Lodge."

"For heaven's sake," I exclaimed. "We had that new sink and they replaced the entire work-top only last year!"

"I know, but Anthea says we ought to have a dishwasher and a microwave."

"I agree about the microwave," I said, "and that would cost virtually nothing, but why do we need a dishwasher when we've got so many helpers? Anyway, it's mainly cups and saucers and glasses."

"Ah," said Rosemary, "*that's* Anthea's idea."

"What do you mean?" I asked warily.

"She wants us to do light lunches, so, of course, there'd be lots more washing up."

"At Brunswick Lodge?"

"Yes."

"She must be mad! Who on earth is going to cook them?"

"She says that people will cook things like

shepherd's pie and lasagna — things that can be heated up in the microwave — at home, and then do salads and so forth at the lodge."

"Leaving aside the complete impossibility of organizing something like that, *who*," I demanded, "is going to be there every day to serve these lunches? For heaven's sake, it's difficult enough to find stewards and people to do the weekly coffee mornings!"

"I thought you wouldn't be keen," Rosemary said, laughing. "Anyway, don't be cross with me; I'm merely the unwilling messenger. As I said, I'm just warning you so that she doesn't take you by surprise!"

It's amazing, really, how much there is to do when you've been away. Little things like restarting the milk and the papers, and finding that you're out of basics like flour and marmalade, things you meant to get before you left and never did. And then there were the animals, of course. Although I knew from Thea that Foss had had a marvelous time with them, being thoroughly spoiled, sleeping on Alice's bed ("Poor, darling Foss, he's *lonely*"), bossing around Smoke and enjoying a feud with the large black cat next door, nevertheless, when I brought him home, he treated me as a monster who had cast him into exile. He remained aloof for several days, only approaching to pick disdainfully at the choicest foods I cooked for him by way of expiation. He wasn't much better with Tris, clouting him over the nose when his erstwhile playmate went to greet him and pointedly ignoring him for the rest of the day. Poor Tris, who, compared with a wily Siamese, is a simple soul, couldn't understand what he'd done wrong and cast anxious glances in my direction, asking for reassurance. But things got back to normal eventually.

I spent quite a lot of time vacuuming and polishing. It's amazing how dismal the house looks when you've been away — not dirty exactly, just a bit musty and generally neglected. I flung open all the windows (which Foss adored, coming and going as the fancy took him and startling me by suddenly appearing on unexpected windowsills) to let in the fresh air, which, now that summer was over, had a hint of autumn. For a few days I was too busy to do any real shopping but, when I was reduced to defrosting an undated package from the freezer that was labeled only CASSEROLE for my supper, I thought I really ought to go and stock up.

I was just on my way to see if I could find the tinned tomatoes when I saw Anthea at the other end of the aisle. I did a sharp U-turn to escape her and came face-to-face with Esther.

"Oh, you're back then," she greeted me. "Did you have a nice holiday?"

"Well, it wasn't a holiday exactly. . . ."

"The Lake District — it was the Lake District, Rosemary said, wasn't it? — is very nice, though I expect it was full of tourists. I believe it's what some call a honey trap. Gordon and I went a couple of years ago. Well, he had a patient who moved up there and who invited us both for a few days when we were on our way to Edinburgh when Gordon had to go to that conference."

"Really."

"They were very kind — Gordon's patients, that is — and took us around to see everything. Though to be honest, one lake is very like another, and when you've seen one you've seen the lot!"

"I was actually up there to look after my cousin who broke her arm rather badly. . . ."

"Oh, arms are so difficult, aren't they? It's easier with legs — I mean, with them you can't move about very well, but at least you can brush your teeth and comb your hair!"

"I know. . . ."

"I remember when Gordon broke his wrist — that was when he had that car ac-

cident years ago — he was absolutely helpless for ages. Such a performance *that* was!"

"How is Gordon? Rosemary said he
hadn't been well."

"No, his heart's playing up again. He
really ought to see a specialist — Dr. Macdonald was quite annoyed with him when
he put it off — but he's been very seedy off
and on for several weeks now. You know,
one day he's fine, the next he's feeling really
bad. He says it's all this medication he's on,
those beta-blockers. He's always complaining about taking those — you get all these
side effects. Anyway, I put my foot down
and I made an appointment for him to see
Dr. Macdonald next week to arrange things.
It can't be before then because *he's* off on a
conference; that's all doctors seem to do
these days. Gordon was cross with me for
going behind his back like that, but I think,
although he wouldn't admit it, he was quite
relieved."

"I'm so glad. I'm sure you did the right
thing."

"Oh, you know what men are like — say
they don't want to make a fuss and then
expect you to run around after them when
it turns nasty. I know when Gordon had a
bad cold last year he *would* go to a council
meeting, even though it was a dreadful

night, wind and rain and I don't know what. Of course he wouldn't listen to me, would he, and it turned into bronchitis and we had a terrible time of it."

"I know; they can be maddening. . . ."

"Simon's just as bad. He looks really off-color. I'm sure they're working him too hard at work, but he does try to do what he can for Gordon, doing the accounts and so forth and, now that Gordon's not too well, he's been doing some letters for him and writing up council notes, that sort of thing. I don't understand any of it, but I'm sure it must be a help."

"Rosemary said she thought Simon looked a bit tired."

"I keep telling him he's doing too much, but of course he doesn't take any notice of what I say."

"Boys don't really, do they?" I backed away and wheeled my trolley in the opposite direction. "I hope all goes well," I said as I made my escape.

What with dodging Anthea and trying not to reencounter Esther, it took me some time to do my shopping. When I got outside it was pouring with rain and thoroughly dismal, so I abandoned any idea of doing more shopping in the town and went straight home. After I'd unpacked my shopping (a job I hate) and had a bit of lunch, I felt restless. There were certainly things I *ought* to do — two books to be reviewed mutely reproached me from my desk — but somehow I couldn't settle to anything. I roamed about the house, annoying the animals (Tris had turned his back on the weather and was curled up in his basket; Foss was perched on the arm of the sofa, watching the snooker on television) and finally ended up in the kitchen.

On an impulse I decided to do some cooking — something detailed and fiddly that would occupy a lot of time. I put on the radio and got out the things to make a lemon meringue pie and began to measure out the flour to make the pastry. There is something satisfying about cooking something you don't *have* to. Grating the lemon rind and slowly and carefully stirring the egg and lemon mixture in the double saucepan were a positive pleasure, though they were tasks I normally found irritating. I whisked up the egg whites for the meringue, while lending half an ear to two men earnestly discussing a possible interest rate rise, but, important though I'm sure that was, somehow it seemed less important just then than achieving exactly the right consistency of soft peaks by my whisking.

After the pies were finished and baked, I regarded them with pleasure. I'd made enough for two and it gave me satisfaction to think that I would give one of them to the children who would really enjoy it (it was Thea's favorite). I felt a moment of pity for Jo who had no one now to make some special treat for, and for Esther, who would probably never even think of doing such a thing.

CHAPTER NINE

When I called to leave the lemon meringue pie for Thea, she greeted me eagerly. "Oh good, I was just going to ring you. Could you do me a favor? My washing machine's finally given up the ghost. Well, I say 'finally,' but we seem to have had it only a couple of years. I bought a new one, but they can only deliver it on Friday afternoon — and of course they can't give me an exact time — and Alice has a riding lesson then. So would you mind collecting her from school and taking her to the stables?"

"Yes, of course. And how maddening about your washing machine. Things simply don't last nowadays. What is it they call it — built-in obsolescence? I was just saying to Rosemary the other day, when my fridge packed up, that the one Peter and I had when we were first married lasted more than thirty years! No, it'll be lovely to see her. What time's the lesson?"

"Four thirty. Is that all right?"

"Splendid. I can take her back with me and give her a sandwich to keep her going, and if you give me her jodhpurs and things, she can change then. Are you all right for washing until Friday? Would you like me to take anything back and put it in my machine?"

"No, it's fine. Actually, it's quite a relief *not* to be able to do any washing for a bit. I'm always putting stuff into the machine, forgetting that it's simply piling up the ironing!"

Fortunately, Alice is still at the age when being fetched from school is perfectly acceptable (unlike Delia who, Rosemary tells me, regards being collected by any adult as a brutal attempt to embarrass her in front of her friends), and she greeted me with enthusiasm.

"Hello, Gran. Are you going to come and see me ride? Cracker really knows me now — he's so sweet — and Liz says I can go on a proper long ride soon. Have you got my things? *And* my crop — not that I need a crop with Cracker; he's so good."

When we arrived at the stables, although it was early, there was another car there. It was a Mitsubishi Shogun, like the one I'd seen out beyond Withypool parked beside Jo's Land Rover. Alice gathered her things together and, as we went into the stable yard, Dan Webster came out of the office. He turned in the doorway and I heard him say, "I'll stay in touch — you never know!" He greeted me with a wave of the hand, got into the Shogun and drove away.

Alice saw Peggy in one of the stables and ran off to join her. I sat on one of the mounting blocks, waiting for her to emerge. After a short while Jo came out of the office. She looked tired and not very well.

"Hallo," I said. "Are you all right?"

She smiled. "I'm fine. It's just been a tiring day, one thing after another; you know how it is."

"I saw Dan Webster leaving," I said. "Was he one of the tiring things?"

"In a way. I'm buying Tarquin off him, but there's some difficulty about the horse passport, silly bureaucratic nonsense, so it's all a bit complicated and, as I said, just one more thing!"

"I don't expect Dan Webster is the easiest person to do business with anyway," I said.

"Oh, he's quite keen to make the sale. I don't think he'd find many buyers; poor Tarquin has a reputation now, of course. Unfair, really, there's no vice in him; it's just that he was badly handled before he came here. Liz is doing a marvelous job on him. Anyway, I know that's what Charlie would have wanted."

"You're probably right," I said doubtfully.

"I'm sure I am." She smiled and, as several children in jodhpurs arrived, she looked at her watch. "I must be off. I've got a lesson. Nice to see you."

I dutifully watched Alice going round and round the ring under Peggy's careful eye, but my mind kept wandering to Dan Webster and what the meeting up on the moor had been about and what he had meant by "You never know."

We seemed to be having an Indian summer and, although I'd meant to put away all my summer clothes, it was still warm enough to keep on wearing them. This year at least, as Rosemary said, we're getting some *use* out of our summer things. In spite of being in the southwest, Taviscombe can be quite chilly. I can distinctly remember, when Michael was small, wearing a sheepskin coat one August day when I was watching him build sand castles on the beach. Still, I suppose if all they say about global warming is true, then we'll have no more use for our heavy sweaters and winter coats.

I'd just decided, as a compromise, to put away my summer dresses and keep out the skirts and tops, when the phone rang. It was Rosemary.

"Simon's just rung to say that Gordon died last night."

"Good heavens! I had heard that he wasn't well, but I'd no idea. . . . What was it, heart?"

"Yes. It was quite sudden. Of course, he should have been having those tests, or at least seeing Dr. Macdonald, but he kept putting things off."

"What happened?"

"He went off to a council meeting; apparently he seemed quite all right then. He was late back — they're used to that, but after a while Esther started to fret about keeping his supper hot, so Simon went out to see if he was coming and saw that his car was parked in the drive. He went out and found Gordon collapsed over the wheel. Simon phoned an ambulance, of course, but he was dead when they arrived."

"How awful — poor Esther!"

"I know. Simon says she's still in shock; doesn't seem to have taken it in."

"No, I'm sure one doesn't. Sudden death may be the most merciful way to go, but it's wretched for those left behind."

133

"Fortunately Simon's there to see to everything and Vicky's coming home from London."

"Has Simon told Jo?" I asked.

"Yes — he said it was difficult — you know, with Charlie just gone."

"Of course. They're both widows now, though I don't really think of Jo as a widow, do you? I feel as if Charlie's still there with her somehow."

"In a nice sort of way — yes, I know what you mean. A loving presence. Not like poor Gordon. Though," Rosemary added, "I don't know why I say poor Gordon. I disliked him when he was alive and the fact that he's dead hasn't changed my opinion of him."

"Poor Esther, though," I said. "She'll be lost without him. I don't think she ever made a real decision in her life — everything was referred to him."

"Poor Simon, if you really get down to it," Rosemary said. "He'll never be able to escape now — I mean, Vicky will be going back to London after the funeral, and then there'll be just him and Esther."

"I don't suppose you know when the funeral will be?"

"No, I don't think Simon's fixed it yet; it's still early days."

I rang Esther later that day, just to see if there was anything I could do — though, goodness knows, there's little enough that anyone *can* do, or say, for that matter.

"That's very kind of you, Sheila," she said. She sounded somehow muted and uncertain. "I don't think there is. Simon's been very good and Vicky will be here tomorrow. I thought I ought to go to Taunton to get a hat. Well, I've got quite a nice one, but it's navy and that's not quite the same as black, is it? Though, of course I do have a navy coat. . . . but Gordon was very definite about things like that. He always wore black for funerals — not just a black tie, but a black overcoat, even in summer, over a dark suit. He said it was paying proper respect and he wouldn't like me not to. I've got a black coat. It's a lightweight summer coat, but it *is* black, and I've got a black-and-white silk dress — or do you think black and white wouldn't be suitable?"

"I think it would be fine," I said, "and I have a black hat if you'd like to borrow it. It would save you going all the way to Taunton. Actually, come to think of it, I've two black hats — one straw and one felt. I suppose the straw one would be better if you're wearing a summer coat. Anyway, I could bring them for you to try."

"Oh, would you, Sheila; that's very kind. But what about you?"

I didn't admit that I hadn't intended to wear a hat at all. "Oh, I've got a navy one — a very *dark* navy, so that would be all right for me."

I took the hats round the next afternoon and found Esther less subdued, but still not really her old self. When we went up to her bedroom to try on the hats, I was touched to see that Gordon's pajamas were lying folded on one of the pillows and his hair brushes were still on the dressing table.

"What do you think, Sheila, will this coat do? It's quite full — what we used to call a duster coat, isn't it?" She went over to one of the wardrobes and took out the black-and-white dress for me to see. "Do you think this is all right? The coat will cover up the dress completely in the church, though I suppose I'll have to take it off afterwards at the — what do you call it? Not reception?"

"I don't know," I said. "The Irish say 'wake' of course, but it doesn't seem suitable in this case. People just say 'afterwards at' wherever it is."

"Simon thought the Westfield would be suitable. Gordon always says it's the best hotel in Taviscombe."

"Yes, that would be splendid. It's quite near the church, so everyone can walk there."

Esther sat down at the dressing table and tried on the hats.

"I think the straw one," she said, "or what do you think? The felt one is more off the face. I never did have the face for a hat. Jo did. She had a big Garbo hat in pink felt. It had a big brim that came down all one side of her face. I remember she said it made her look mysterious, whatever that might have meant. She had it all those years ago when she went off to London."

"I think the straw one will be better," I said.

"Yes, you're right; I'll wear that one."

I mentally noted that this was the first time in all our acquaintance that Esther had asked for my opinion and had actually taken it. "That's fine," I said, "but I'll leave both of them in case you change your mind."

She put the hats down and looked at them doubtfully; then she got up and said, "Shall we have a cup of tea?"

"That would be nice."

I followed her into the kitchen while she put the kettle on, and when the tea was made she said, "Shall we have it out here? Gordon doesn't like us to eat or drink in the kitchen. He says, 'What do we have a dining room for?' "

"I don't think a cup of tea counts," I said.

"Oh" — she moved over to one of the cupboards — "would you like some biscuits, or there's a cake I got from Stenners the other day, before . . . but it's been in a cake tin, so I'm sure it's quite fresh."

"No, really, just a cup of tea will be fine."

She sat down and poured the tea while I tried to think of something to say.

"Vicky's coming home tomorrow," she said.

"That's nice."

"She said she should be able to stay for a full week because she wants to see Jo about some program or other — but I'd have thought her father's funeral would be quite enough reason for staying."

"I expect she just wants to get her program sorted out. I imagine she's under quite a bit of pressure in her job."

"I suppose so," Esther said absently. She was silent for a while and then she said quite suddenly, "I miss him so. I don't know what I'm going to do without him. How am I going to bear it, Sheila? How am I going to go on?" She was crying now, not sobbing, but quietly crying, tears pouring down her face.

I put my hand on hers. "You get used to

it. No, that's not true; you never get used to it, but you learn to accept it. When Peter died, I was lucky to have Michael. You have Simon and Vicky; they'll get you through."

"If only he'd seen Dr. Macdonald, if *only* he'd listened to me — he might have been here now. He wasn't old; he had years ahead of him. It need never have happened; he could have had a bypass, a new heart, even. . . ." She fumbled for a handkerchief and wiped her eyes. "I'm sorry, Sheila, giving way like that."

"Don't be silly," I said. "It's good for you to give way. Here, drink your tea; it will make you feel better. Shall I stay with you until Simon comes home?"

"No, I'm all right. Anyway, I've got to get on with supper. I've got some nice lamb chops, Simon's favorite — and I thought I'd make an apple pie for tomorrow when Vicky comes. I don't suppose she does much cooking in that flat of hers."

Seeing Esther more or less restored to her proper self, I left and on the way home I thought about how the two sisters had each reacted to their sudden loss. I suppose it was inevitable that someone as erratic as Esther should have become vague and disorientated while Jo, the strong one, had collected herself quickly and, to all intents and purposes, got on with her life. I mentioned this to Rosemary when I met her in the library the next day.

"Well, considering how wonderful Charlie was, I think it's fantastic that Jo is coping so well," she said. "Of course, it helps to have to keep busy — the stables are a lot of hard work — and I expect she feels she's keeping things going for Charlie's sake. I suppose what I mean is that Jo and Charlie were partners in everything, whereas poor old Esther was completely under horrible Gordon's thumb. She had no sort of life of her own, did she? So she's got nothing to fill the gap."

"There's Simon and Vicky," I said. "Though, of course, they've always been sort of peripheral to her life and her devotion to Gordon. She'll be quite well off, I should think. Perhaps she could travel."

"Can you imagine it?"

"Well, no, not really, not unless she took Simon with her, and that would defeat the whole object of the exercise, which is somehow to arrange things so that Simon gets a life of his own."

"It's a pity Vicky lives in London."

"Oh, Vicky's the selfish one — and ambitious too. She wouldn't let any family feeling get in the way of her career. Esther was quite hurt that all she seems to be interested in, when she comes down for the funeral, is getting Jo to do some program or other."

"Poor Esther. Goodness, is that the time. Mother expects me at twelve and I haven't found a book for her yet. I'll have to take this life of the Queen Mother. I'm sure she's read it, but she's read so many of them she may not remember!"

Gordon's funeral was very different from Charlie's. The church was, indeed, quite full.

"Everyone on the council is here," Rosemary said, looking round, "and most of the Rotarians."

But the atmosphere was stiff and formal rather than warm and loving; people were here because they felt they *ought* to be, not because they wanted to be. I saw Dan Webster come in and make his way to a pew at the front, across the aisle from the one set aside for the family. He was the only person sitting there, most people having modestly crowded into the pews at the back.

"You're wearing a hat!" Rosemary said suddenly.

"I felt I had to," I said. "Esther was making such a thing about what sort of hat *she* would wear. It's really uncomfortable; it's pressing on my ear. Oh, here they come."

Esther came down the aisle with Simon, Vicky and Jo — I saw, without surprise, that she was wearing the felt hat, not the straw one — and the service began. There were several addresses by members of the council and other public bodies, all stressing the good works that Gordon had been associated with, so that I felt it was beginning to resemble a company report rather than a funeral service. The hymn was "Abide with Me," which always makes me so choked up that I can't sing the words; Rosemary nudged me when we got to the line "Change and decay in all around I see," because it's one of our favorite quotations.

Then it was all over and we trooped off down the road to the Westfield Hotel where a lavish buffet was set out, though I, for one, didn't feel like eating anything. Indeed, only the council members and other similar guests seemed inclined to do so. The men (and they were mostly men) piled their plates high and, with full glasses, retreated to the far corner of the room where they appeared to be embarked upon some sort of business meeting. Perhaps it was the most suitable thing to do, since I'm sure they were the ones who would miss Gordon most. Now it would be someone else who would make up a quorum, make a resolution or pass a motion.

"Here," Rosemary said, handing me a glass of wine. "We'll have a couple of these and then go and have a word with Esther."

I noticed that Vicky had cornered Jo and was talking to her earnestly. But Jo was standing there impassively, seeming to let the flood of talk wash over her. I smiled to myself, knowing that she would be more than a match for her niece and no amount of talk would persuade her to do anything she didn't want to do.

Esther was over by the door with Simon by her side. We went across and said all those useless things one does on such occasions.

"I think it went off very well," Esther said.

"It was a splendid service," I said, "and the church was very full."

"Mr. Broadbank was there," Esther said. Mr. Broadbank is our MP. "He couldn't come on here because he had to get back to London — for the House, you know — but it was good of him to come. Gordon would have liked that; he did a lot for the party, of course. . . ." Her attention wandered as she saw someone else approaching, and she turned to greet them.

"Thank you for coming," Simon said.

"Please call round and see her sometime. I know she'd appreciate that."

It was good to be outside in the fresh air.

"Come on," Rosemary said. "I snaffled a few of those not-very-nice sandwiches. Let's go down to the seafront and feed the seagulls."

CHAPTER TEN

It's always silly to shop on a Saturday if you don't have to. The supermarket checkouts are slower, the queue at the post office is longer and in the smaller shops the Saturday staff don't know where things are kept. I'd just decided to give up and go home when it suddenly started to rain quite heavily. Fortunately, I was quite near the Buttery, so I took shelter inside with a cup of coffee. A lot of people had had the same idea and it was very crowded. I was standing for a moment with my cup held insecurely in a hand already weighed down with shopping bags, when I heard someone call my name. It was Simon beckoning me to join him and his sister, Vicky.

"Oh, thank you so much," I said, putting my cup down and prizing off the handles of the bags that were now cutting into my fingers. "It's not usually quite as crowded as this, but the rain has driven everyone indoors."

We spoke for a while about the funeral and I asked Vicky how long she was staying.

"Oh, I've got to go back on Monday. I'm recording on Tuesday."

"What's the program?" I asked.

"It's a docudrama about the Bloomsbury set. I've got Laurel Makepeace as Virginia Woolf and Matthew Franklin as Lytton Strachey, so it's really quite an interesting production."

"It sounds marvelous," I said. "I'll look forward to hearing it. Your mother said you were hoping to have a word with Jo. Do you want her to talk about horses or something?"

Vicky smiled — a rather superior smile, reminiscent of her father. "*Not* horses," she said. "I'm contracted to do a series of arts programs. I don't know if you heard my program on Stravinsky; it had a very good notice in the *Spectator.* No, I'm planning something on the London postwar theater, and I want Jo to talk to me about her time at the Old Vic and at Stratford with James Carlyle and Jane Neville."

"It sounds fascinating."

"Well, it would be," Vicky said irritably, "if Jo would cooperate, but she's being very tiresome. She says it's all a long time ago

146

and she can't remember anything interesting. It's nonsense. All actors love talking about their past triumphs, and she certainly had a lot of those."

"Perhaps," Simon put in gently, "she doesn't want to think about the past; well, *that* past, before she met Charlie, that is — especially now."

"I think Simon's right," I said. "The only time she wants to think about is her time with Charlie."

"Well, I think it's very selfish of her," Vicky said. "It wouldn't take long — just a couple of hours with a tape recorder; surely that's not too much to ask from a member of the family!"

Simon and I carefully avoided looking at each other.

"I'm sure you'll find someone else," he said. "Jane Neville's still around, isn't she?"

"Yes, and I've got something lined up with her, but it would have been so convenient to do Jo while I'm down here anyway."

"I think the rain has stopped now," I said, "so I'd better be getting along."

"We'll stay here a bit longer," Simon said. "We're keeping out of the way while Mother's preparing a special lunch — roast beef, Yorkshire, the lot. We have instructions to be back promptly at one thirty and I only hope we can do justice to it all!"

"It sounds lovely," I said, "and I'm sure it's giving her a lot of pleasure to do it."

A few weeks later I had a phone call from my cousin Hilda. She'd been at Bletchley Park during the war and now, she told me, there was to be a sort of reunion of some of the surviving members of the team.

"How lovely," I said. "You'll enjoy that."

"Oh, I can't possibly go."

"Why not?"

"For goodness' sake, Sheila, you of all people should know why I can't."

It was Tolly, of course. For most of her long life Hilda has steadfastly avoided animals, deriding those who are devoted to them. But in her fourth decade Hilda was obliged to take over the care of a small Siamese kitten and, on Hilda's part at least, it was love at first sight, and her life has revolved around him ever since.

"I can't possibly leave Tolly."

"No, of course not." I knew better than to suggest a cattery or a helpful neighbor. "Well, actually, I could do with a break," I said. "Shall I come?"

It was perfectly obvious to both of us that Hilda had rung me expecting precisely this response, though, of course, she'd never

148

admit it.

"I wouldn't dream of it," she said. "You have such a busy life; you could hardly drop everything at a moment's notice."

"No, really," I said, "I'd love to have a few days in London — lots of things I want to do. It'll be a splendid opportunity to see people."

"I couldn't possibly let you."

"And I'd really like to look up a few things in the Senate House Library."

"Oh well, in that case . . ."

"When would you like me to come?"

"Thursday of next week," Hilda said briskly, abandoning any pretence of casualness. "It's a weekend meeting, but I'd need you here all day on Friday so that Tolly can get used to you while I'm still here."

"Honestly," Rosemary said, "you and your cousins — first it was Marjorie and now it's Hilda — using you as an invalid and cat sitter!"

"Oh, I don't mind. I enjoyed being up in the Lake District and it's ages since I had a trip to London. Mind you, the responsibility of looking after Tolly is a bit frightening. Anyway, you can't talk — all you do for Jilly and the children, not to mention your mother!"

"Oh, *don't* mention Mother," Rosemary said. "She's decided she needs a new winter coat — goodness knows why; she hardly ever goes out now. Luckily, Estelle lets me take several for Mother to choose from, but it means going back and forth umpteen times, and you know how sarcastic Estelle can be."

Estelle is the owner of our long-established dress shop (you wouldn't dare to call it a boutique), a formidable figure who has cowed many generations of customers. Only Rosemary's mother, Mrs. Dudley, has ever stood up to her and browbeaten her into submission.

"Oh, poor you, caught between the devil and the deep blue sea, though, of course, I wouldn't dream of saying which was which."

Rosemary laughed. "Oh well," she said. "Anyway, I expect you'd like me to have Tris while you're away?"

"Would you? That would be marvelous. He'll be much happier playing with your Alpha than getting overexcited about Thea's chickens. Foss, of course, simply ignores them."

"That's fine then. Drop him off on the way to the station."

"Bless you, now I can go away with a tranquil mind — well, not tranquil exactly when I think of what a responsibility it's going to be looking after Tolly! Oh dear, I must dash. I'm collecting Alice from the stables and giving her her tea. Thea's got a dinner party this evening — a couple of Michael's colleagues — so she's up to her eyes."

It was a lovely afternoon at the stables and I stood peacefully leaning on the rails, looking down into the ring where Alice, under Peggy's watchful eye, was cantering cautiously round on Cracker. There was a clatter of hooves behind me and Jo came out of the yard on Tarquin. She waved to me and rode off. They certainly made a splendid picture: the superb horse with its confident rider moving easily across the fields in the late-afternoon sunshine.

"They're great together." Liz came up behind me, echoing my thoughts.

"He's a beautiful animal," I said, "but is he all right now? Safe to ride, I mean."

"He's pretty highly strung and it's fairly obvious that he hasn't been properly handled, but he's fine now with Jo and me. Actually, I think it's been good for Jo to work with him like that. She'd stopped going out much, with the rides and so forth, but she's out every day now on Tarquin."

"It seemed strange to me at first, how she could bear to keep him — after Charlie —

151

but I do see now that it's been a good thing for her. That and working in the stables generally."

"Well, you know, it's her life and somehow there's the connection with Charlie — we all feel that."

"You and Peggy have been wonderful, the way you've supported her," I said.

"Well," Liz spoke quietly, "the stables are my life too. I had a miserable childhood. My parents were divorced and I hated my stepfather and left home as soon as I could. I'd always been mad about horses and although I was only sixteen and pretty useless, they took me on and looked after me and taught me everything I know. Jo and Charlie have been my family." She stopped abruptly, as if she had said too much and, indeed, I'd never known her to talk about herself before. "I'd better get the jumps set up. I've got a class coming soon. Your Alice is doing very well. She's a natural."

"She's horse mad too," I said, and Liz smiled as she went down into the field to put up the apparatus.

I enjoyed being in London, though I do find that every time I go there it's changed and, usually, to my elderly mind, not for the better — change and decay, indeed. Hilda's little mews house in Holland Park, which she bought for a song just after the war, is now part of a very desirable area, and her neighbors, instead of the agreeable mix of all ages and classes they used to be, are now universally young and affluent. The little corner shop, dark and inconvenient, but friendly and a cheerful meeting place, is now a specialty cheese shop, and the news-agent next door is an exclusive boutique, which appears to sell only (unbelievably expensive) handbags.

Tolly greeted me amiably enough. Possibly he remembered me (as Hilda maintained), but he probably just recognized a born slave and was prepared to accept me as such.

"I've written out his daily schedule," Hilda said, presenting me with several closely printed sheets. "Meal times and so forth. He only has tinned food, organic, of course, once a day for breakfast and I like to rotate the various varieties, so I've put stickers with the appropriate day on each of the tins on his shelf in the larder. I've cooked the fish and chicken; it's in the fridge, and you just heat it up in the microwave. I usually do it for twenty seconds on high and then let it cool down a little naturally so it's *just* warm, which is how he likes it." She con-sulted the papers again. "Now, I let him out first thing and try to get him in after half an hour, and the same in the afternoon, if you happen to be in, but *never* after three thirty. He sleeps on my bed, of course, though while I'm away he may just come and sleep on yours for company." She handed me the papers. "Have a look through this while I go and make a cup of tea, and then if there's anything you want to ask me . . ."

Tolly jumped up onto the table beside me and sat looking smug. When I stroked his head he nipped my hand, not out of malice, you understand, but merely to indicate my place in the hierarchy.

Hilda came back with the tea tray, which she put down beside Tolly. He inspected the milk jug but, deciding it wasn't worth investigating fully, he jumped down and went upstairs.

"I'll be back on Tuesday," Hilda said, "just after lunch. My train gets in at two fifteen. I've left my telephone number beside the phone. It's my mobile number, so you will, of course, ring me if there's any sort of problem at *any* time. Now," she continued, pouring the tea, "how are the children? As you know, they came to see me a little while ago. Dear Michael and Thea, it was lovely to see them and I was most impressed with Alice, such a nice child. She was very good at playing with Tolly and he quite took to her."

Fortunately, it rained most of the time I was in London, so Tolly didn't want to go out and I was spared the agony of not being able to get him in. For myself, I went to several exhibitions and once to a matinee of a new play that had been greatly praised, but which I found dull and overwritten. I wondered idly how Jo would have fared in the theater of today and decided that she'd been wise to get out when she did.

For the sake of telling Hilda that I had, I spent the Monday afternoon in the Senate House Library, looking up some things I felt I might need for an article I'd been putting off writing. I'd just got back and was thinking I might indulge myself by going out to supper at the very trendy bistro nearby, when the phone rang. It was Rosemary.

"Hello," I said, surprised. "I thought you'd be Hilda. She's been ringing up at least once a day since she left to check on Tolly's well-being."

"No, it's me." She sounded very subdued.

"What's the matter? Is something wrong? Is it the children?"

"No, no, they're fine," Rosemary said hastily, "and Tris too. It's just — just I

155

thought you'd want to know. It's Jo; she's dead."

"Dead? What happened? Was it that horse?"

"Horse?"

"Tarquin, the one who killed Charlie. Did he throw her? I *knew* she should never have taken it on."

"No, nothing like that. She was electrocuted."

"*What?* How?"

"She always goes in last thing to switch on the electric fences — they leave them on at night. The switch is in the office. Apparently there was some sort of fault — I don't know the details — and she was electrocuted. Liz found her when she arrived for work."

"How awful for her, poor girl," I said, remembering the brief conversation I'd had with Liz just before I came away.

"Yes, it must have been terrible. But she kept her head and switched everything off at the mains, then tried to revive Jo. She couldn't, so she called an ambulance, but there was nothing they could do; it was too late."

"I can't believe it. First Charlie, now Jo — it's like some horrible curse on the place."

"Simon is dreadfully upset. You know how

fond he was of Jo, more than Esther really, though I suppose I shouldn't say so."

"I know," I agreed. "So what's happening?"

"Well, since it was some sort of accidental death I suppose there'll have to be an inquest. I must ask Roger."

"Have they closed the stables?"

"Well, they had to yesterday, when it happened, but Liz said that Jo would have wanted her to carry on, so she and Peggy are coping. I'm sure they're right."

"It's what Jo said when Charlie died," I remembered, "so I'm sure that *is* what she'd want."

"It's going to be hard work, running those stables with just the two of them," Rosemary said, "and it would probably cost more than they can afford to employ somebody. Simon's going to be up there every evening and at weekends, and, of course, all the young girls, like Delia, love helping out, but it's not a very satisfactory way to run a business."

"Oh, I'm sure they'll keep it going somehow," I said. "There's so much enthusiasm there."

But after Rosemary had rung off, I began to wonder just how they would manage and tried to think of various ways it could be done. After half an hour of fruitless thought I realized I'd been dwelling on that side of things to avoid thinking about Jo. It seemed inconceivable that she should be gone too, when we'd barely become accustomed to the idea of Charlie's death. And such a bizarre way to die — as Charlie's had been.

I didn't sleep much that night, turning facts and conjectures over and over in my mind. In the morning I felt thoroughly wretched, and my mood wasn't helped by Tolly who, taking advantage of the rain having stopped, went out straight after breakfast and didn't reappear until just before Hilda was due back. What with roaming the streets looking for him, going back and forth to the door hoping he might suddenly appear and wondering what on earth I'd say to Hilda if anything had happened to him, I was in a bad state when Tolly finally strolled in. I just had time to give him his fish before I heard the taxi.

After the first enthusiastic greeting (on Hilda's part; Tolly was distinctly offhand), I made a cup of tea and heard all about the reunion. It had obviously been a great success from Hilda's point of view since (according to her) all the others were in advanced stages of decrepitude (physical and mental).

"Elinor Bradshaw looked an absolute *wreck.* Her face has just caved in, a mass of wrinkles — quite extraordinary, considering how much time and trouble she used to devote to her appearance. Mavis Foster is hobbling about on two sticks and Bryan Adams's memory has practically gone. He simply didn't remember some of the procedures that used to be second nature to us all! Stone-deaf too and wouldn't wear a hearing aid."

I looked at Hilda, upright and healthy, in full possession of all her faculties, and thought how irritating she must have been to all her contemporaries gathered there. While she was having her second cup of tea I told her about Jo.

"What an unnecessary way to die," was her comment. "I remember her in *Twelfth Night.* She was the best Viola I have ever seen."

"So you see," I said, "I don't think I can stay until Friday. I really ought to get back tomorrow."

"Is there anything useful you can do for anyone at all by going back?" Hilda demanded.

"Well, no, but . . ."

"Then don't be ridiculous," she said firmly. "Stay. I have several things planned for us to do in the next few days."

And, of course, when Hilda is firm, there is no option but to obey.

CHAPTER ELEVEN

"I simply can't believe it," I said to Rosemary when she brought Tris home. "It's just too much to take in. First Charlie's accident, and now Jo's, both at the stables."

"I know, and both such unlikely things to happen."

"What exactly *did* happen to Jo?" I asked. "You said she was just switching on the electric fences?"

"Well, I don't really know the layout there," Rosemary said, "but the switch for the fences is in the office along with some other switches. Apparently there's a lot of separate wiring for them all — a regular tangle, Simon says. He said he did tell Jo, once, that he thought it was dangerous and that the whole place ought to be rewired. Anyway, as far as I can gather, there was a fault in the wiring for the fences and — well — when she switched it on, it killed her."

"And she must have lain there all night —

how horrible."

"Yes, poor Liz was terribly upset, thinking that if she'd only found Jo earlier she might have been saved."

"Hilda said it was an unnecessary way to die," I said, "which I thought was unfeeling of her, but she's right; it *was* an avoidable accident, which somehow makes it even more tragic."

"I know. And Simon feels responsible in a way — he thinks he should have insisted on her getting it sorted out. But, really, I suppose she had so much on her mind that she simply put it to one side, as you do. Simon was busy just then — he's Gordon's executor — and then there was Esther. . . ."

"Of course, there's Gordon too. Good heavens — three deaths in one family, and in such a short space of time. It's like a Greek tragedy! Well, hardly that, but you know what I mean."

"It is extraordinary, and it all comes onto Simon's shoulders."

"How is Esther taking it — Jo's death, I mean?" I asked.

"She's upset, of course, but I think she's still trying to get used to Gordon being dead, so it hasn't really registered with her yet."

"I suppose we don't know yet when the

funeral is to be?"

"Well, I suppose there'll have to be an inquest, so I don't think it'll be for a bit."

"No, I suppose not. Will Vicky come down from London? I wonder. She didn't for Charlie's funeral."

"Oh, she's here at the moment. She had to come down; something about her signature being needed for some documents. Apparently Gordon set up a complicated trust for Vicky and Simon — a way of avoiding death duties — and, of course, anything to do with money and Vicky's onto it like a shot. It was just before Jo died and I think Vicky was still hoping to get her to do something for that program of hers."

"Vicky can be very persistent, but I expect she was disappointed. Jo was really firm about not wanting to do it."

"Vicky's so like her father in some ways," Rosemary said, "self-centered and determined to get her own way, *and* the money thing — not a bit like Simon. I think he takes after Gordon's cousin Clive — you remember him?"

"Yes, I do, vaguely. He was much older than us, so we didn't have much to do with him, but I seem to remember he was rather nice."

"Mother always said that he wanted to

marry Jo," Rosemary said, "and, when she turned him down — she was years younger than he — he went to Australia."

"To mend his broken heart?"

"Something like that. Not that he did, poor chap — he was drowned in a sailing accident in New South Wales."

I was just attempting to make sense of the notes I'd taken in the Senate House Library, when Michael turned up with some eggs.

"Oh, lovely, now I can have a Spanish omelet for supper," I said. "Are the hens laying still? They tend to fall off a bit at this time of the year, don't they? Hang on while I turn off my computer and I'll come and make you a cup of tea."

Michael followed me into the study and looked disapprovingly at my electric fire.

"That's dangerous," he said.

"What, the fire? It was really quite cold today, but I didn't want to put all the heating on."

"No, not the fire itself, but you really oughtn't to have that trailing lead on it."

"I wanted it near me to keep my feet warm. My circulation's really miserable these days."

"Well, it's not safe like that," Michael said firmly.

"I suppose you're right," I agreed. "And after poor Jo — well it's a lesson to us all to be more careful with electrical things."

"What you really need," Michael went on, "is a point on the other side of your desk. If you had it there it would be away from the plugs and things for your computer."

"Yes, well, I'll have to see to it."

"As a matter of fact, Steve is doing some wiring for us at the moment."

"Oh," I said, "whereabouts?"

"It's outside lighting to help us see to the chickens when it gets dark early and we hope, if we leave it on, it might discourage the foxes."

"What a good idea!"

"Anyway," Michael said, reverting to his theme, "you really must have this seen to. I'll get Steve to give you a ring to say when he can come."

I was in the kitchen at Brunswick Lodge unpacking the cakes I'd brought for the Wednesday coffee morning, when Anthea appeared.

"Oh good," she said, "you're back. You always seem to be away on holiday these days."

I considered explaining to Anthea that they hadn't been holidays exactly, but I refrained, partly because it would take too long, but mostly because I knew she wouldn't listen anyway.

"I wanted to have a word," Anthea went on. "I'm rallying all the support I can get."

"Oh," I said warily.

"It's this dreadful business of poor Jo Hamilton. I was really shocked when I heard. But it's a lesson to us all. So I thought about our electrical wiring here."

"It's all right, isn't it?" I asked. "Surely we had someone in a few months ago to put some more points in."

"Yes, we did," Anthea said impatiently, "but that's not what I mean. This is an old house and I think the whole system needs a thorough overhaul."

"Well, I suppose it might. . . ."

"It's not just the helpers," she said. "We do hold events here, so members of the public are at risk too."

"I think 'at risk' is going a bit far," I said.

"Health and Safety," Anthea said impressively. "We might be liable for all sorts of things."

"But we have insurance, don't we?"

"Oh, I'm sure that doesn't count if it's a government thing. But what's important," she repeated, "is to have the whole system overhauled."

"I'm sure it's not necessary," I said feebly, knowing from bitter experience that if Anthea had an idea in her head it was virtually impossible to dislodge it. "Besides," I added, "it would cost the earth. We simply don't have the funds."

She smiled patronizingly. "That's where my scheme comes in."

"Oh?"

It's perfectly simple. We will apply for lottery money."

"But we'd never get *that*," I said. "It's for big projects — stately homes, Victorian piers, that sort of thing."

"Not a bit of it. I saw on the television the other day some villagers got it for extending their village hall. Now if *they* can get it to put up an extension to a wooden hut, then Brunswick Lodge, a historic house, certainly deserves it."

"Well, I suppose. . . ."

"I haven't got all the information yet. I thought I would sound out public opinion first."

That, of course, was sheer sophistry, since, in my long experience, Anthea has never been known to consider any opinion other than her own.

"Well," I said cautiously, "I suppose it wouldn't hurt to give it a try."

"The thing is," Anthea said, "I believe we would have to raise a proportion of the money ourselves."

"What sort of proportion?"

"Oh, I don't know," she said impatiently. "That's a minor point. The thing is to get the ball rolling as soon as possible."

"Well yes, if you think . . ."

"Good. I've spoken to all the trustees and most of the committee — I'd have come to you before if you hadn't been away — and they all think it's a marvelous idea."

"I'm sure they do," I said. And, indeed, I knew they would all be delighted to have extra funds if someone else did the work, though they would reserve the right to criticize and complain at every stage of the proceedings.

"So I'll write away and get all the forms and things. It really is important that we get something done about that wiring. Poor Esther, *another* death in the family; she must be dreadfully upset. She didn't send the ginger cake she promised for the bring and buy sale, but, of course, I quite understood."

Having a son who shoots and plays cricket is marvelous; it opens up a whole range of people who engage in useful activities. Michael's mates now include doctors, dentists, plumbers, carpenters, electricians, computer wizards, and (should you need them) game-keepers and slaughterhouse workers — just to give a general cross section — who will all turn up and *do* things for you when you need them. Michael, on his part, provides general legal advice as part of the give-and-take. Steve is one of the cricketing fraternity (useful medium-pace bowler who can bat a bit) and he duly turned up the following day.

"I've got a job on at Porlock," he said, accepting a cup of tea and a biscuit, "so I thought I'd drop in on my way and see what the problem is."

"Just another point, really," I said, "but, actually, what I'd really like is for you to move most of the points higher up. I find bending right down a bit of a problem now. And with the angle they're at, I can get the plugs in all right, but I find pulling them *out* quite difficult."

"No problem, Mrs. M. I can put battens in at waist height if you like."

"That's marvelous. And I do feel now that I ought to pull plugs out at night, just to be sure, after what happened to poor Jo Hamilton. That really was a terrible thing, an accident that should never have happened."

Steve shook his head. "I'm not so sure," he said.

"What do you mean, not sure?"

"Well, I don't know if I should be telling you this, but when it happened, Bob Morris, who's in charge — he's an inspector now; done very well — anyway, he asked me to have a look at the wiring up there at the stables. Bob used to play for Taviscombe, you remember, a couple of seasons ago — wicketkeeper, a really safe pair of hands — and we're mates, so it was sort of unofficial, if you know what I mean." I nodded. "Well, anyhow, I went up there and you wouldn't *believe* the state of that wiring." I made a murmur of horror. "What you might call real spaghetti — wires all tangled up; you wouldn't credit it!"

He paused for me to take in the enormity of what he was saying.

"Really?" I said.

He leaned forward as if to emphasize the confidential nature of what he was about to say. "When I'd sorted that lot out, guess what I found?" I shook my head. "That lead — the one for the electric fences — it was frayed all right; easy to see how it could have shorted and killed someone. But" he paused to give the full effect — "*but,* that fraying was never just ordinary wear and tear. Oh,

170

it might have looked like it to a layman's eye, as they say, but I could tell. It had been frayed deliberately!"

"Are you sure?" I asked.

"As sure as I'm sitting here. Deliberately. If you knew what you were looking for, you could just see the marks where someone had been at it with a knife."

"But that's terrible."

"Exactly, that's what Bob Morris said to me when I told him. 'That's terrible, Steve,' he said. 'That means this wasn't an accidental death at all. This could be murder.' He said, 'Would you stand up in court and say that lead had been tampered with?' and I said 'Yes, I take my oath it had.' "

"But it's impossible. Who on earth would want to kill Jo? Everyone loved her!"

Steve shook his head. "Well, you never know, do you. Like they say, human nature's a terrible thing. Well, I must be off. Mrs. Henderson'll be wondering what's become of me. I'll give you a ring sometime next week about those points."

When he'd gone I sat for quite a while trying to take in the implications of what he'd said. It had been bad enough to face the fact that Jo was dead without this terrible new possibility. I could think of no one (apart from Charlie) who was so well liked, no one less likely to be — I could hardly bring myself to even think the word — murdered. But Steve was a good electrician, very experienced and unlikely to make a mistake, and certainly not in a situation like this.

Tris, who'd been sitting quietly at my feet, began to make little whining noises, which meant that he wanted to go out. Foss, suddenly materializing beside him, jumped up onto the table, to the imminent danger of the tea things, making his own vocal demands. I got up slowly and took the tray over to the sink and let the animals out into the garden. On an impulse I phoned Thea.

"Steve's just been here to see about the points for me," I said.

"Oh good, Michael said he'd rung him. He's very good. He did a marvelous job for us with that outdoor light. It's made such a difference."

"Yes, I'm sure it has. Actually, when he was here he said something about Jo's accident at the stables." I told her what Steve had told me about the wiring. "And now Bob Morris thinks Jo was — was killed deliberately."

"I don't believe it," Thea said. "Not Jo — who'd want to kill her? It's ridiculous."

"I know, but Steve was absolutely positive

and there's no way he'd have said anything if it wasn't true."

"No, I suppose not, but it's an awful thought. I wonder what's happening. You know Bob Morris, don't you? Could you ask him?"

"I'm not quite sure how I could approach him, but I'll think about it. Roger would be the one to ask, of course, but his work is in Taunton now."

But, as it happened, I ran into Roger quite by chance early on Sunday morning, both of us dog walking on the beach.

"Hallo," he said, looking up at the threatening sky. "I thought I might be the only one out today, but I know the weather doesn't normally put you off."

"Oh, Tris loves the beach and it's one of the few places I can let him run free. Anyway, it's always a pleasure to walk here when there's virtually no one about." We stood silently for a moment looking at the empty beach and the sea until I said, "Actually, I'm so glad I saw you. I wondered if you knew what's happening about Jo's death."

Roger smiled. "I thought you might ask me that. Well, as you know, I've got nothing to do with the case. Bob Morris is in charge for the moment. They might send CID down if they think it's necessary, but we've got a lot of faith in having the local man investigating — and, anyway, there's the usual manpower shortage. No, Bob's a good chap and will do a thorough job."

"I did hear," I said tentatively, "that it's possible it might not have been an accident. Something about the wiring . . ."

"Now, how did you hear about that?" Roger said, looking at me quizzically. "No, don't tell me — it's probably something I shouldn't know. Yes, there was a query about that, so, of course, we sent in forensics to have a special look at it and they agreed that it might have been tampered with."

"So, what then? Is it murder?"

"For the moment it's being classified as suspicious death, but it depends how the inquiries go if it needs to be upgraded to murder."

"But Roger, you knew Jo. Who would want to kill her? No one would want her dead!"

He shook his head. "I know, it does sound unlikely, but I'm afraid one thing experience has taught me is that in the case of murder, no matter how improbable it seems, there is always someone who wanted the victim dead."

CHAPTER TWELVE

Life goes on. It was half term and Alice had been promised a couple of rides. I said I'd take her for the second one.

"Gran," Alice said as we drove to the stables, "Mummy said Jo's died and that's why she wasn't there on Monday."

"I'm afraid so, darling."

"Like Charlie died?"

"Yes, like Charlie."

"Will she be with Charlie now?"

"I expect so, darling."

"Liz was very sad on Monday. She'd been crying. I expect she loved Jo very much."

When I'd handed Alice over to Peggy and went to pay for her ride, I found the door of the office locked and Liz in the tack room. She was in tears. I made a move as if to go away, but she motioned me to come back.

"No, please," she said. "I'm sorry. Don't go away."

"Poor Liz," I said, "it must be very hard

for you."

She felt for a crumpled tissue in her shirt pocket and wiped her eyes. "It's been awful," she said, "but I was just beginning to come to terms with it when I got the news."

"What news?"

"About Jo's will and —," She broke off. "And she's left me the house and a share in the stables." The tears came again. "I never thought — it's too much — I don't want any of that. I just want her back."

"I'm sure you do," I said gently, "but you must do your best to carry on for her and remember how much she must have thought of you to leave you things she cared about so much."

She nodded. "I know, but I just can't help . . ."

"I know."

"But the house — it should have gone to Simon. He was her family."

"She obviously thought of you as family too. And, really, she knew that Simon couldn't leave his mother and move in here, not now his father is dead."

"No, but . . ."

"And," I continued, "she knew someone had to live here, on the premises, to look after things, day or night, and she knew she could trust you to do that."

"Yes, of course, you're right." Liz gave herself a little shake (a characteristic gesture) and mopped her eyes again. "That's what she wanted me to do and I mustn't let her down."

"I'm sure Simon feels the same."

"Yes, I think he does. He said we must do what she wanted. He was very kind. He's been wonderful ever since — you know. Up here every spare minute he has from his job. We couldn't have managed without him. He says we can't afford to hire anyone else and that's all right; I'm sure we can manage. Peggy's been great, working all hours for no extra money."

"Are you still busy?"

"Most of our regulars still come, but a few people have canceled. I suppose they think it's not safe or something."

"Things will sort themselves out."

"That's what Simon says. He says we must have a proper meeting soon, the three of us, to plan for the future, but — well, we've been so busy."

"I'm sure Simon will manage things; he's very methodical."

"Yes, he's brilliant."

I was silent for a moment. Then I asked, "Have the police finished here now?"

"I think so. Inspector Morris came at the

beginning — you know — and asked me how I found Jo and that sort of thing. He came several times to look at things in the office. Then a couple of people came back with him and they examined it as well, something to do with the wiring. Inspector Morris wanted to know if anyone had checked the wiring or the switch lately, but I couldn't tell him. I suppose they might have done, but you know how it is here; we're in and out all the time and don't take much notice of things." She stopped suddenly. "If only we *had* noticed something wrong, Jo wouldn't have died — that's awful!"

"The office is locked now?"

"Yes, Inspector Morris asked us to keep it locked. Until he'd finished making inquiries, he said. Anyway," she went on, "I don't think any of us want to use it now."

There was a knock on the door and a woman and a young girl came in to make a booking, so I put the money for Alice's ride on the shelf that Liz was using for a desk and went outside. Peggy was calling out instructions to the children riding round the ring, just as Jo used to do.

"Sit deep in the saddle, Jemma. Keep your contact, Poppy. Your reins are like washing lines! Fiona, squeeze; don't *kick*. Heels *down,* Alice — you're not keeping your balance — that's better."

It all seemed so timeless, somehow, as if, any moment, Charlie would come limping out of the stable block and Jo would lead Tarquin out into the sunshine. They'd seemed so secure, happy in their own little world; hard to believe that it and they had gone forever. After a while Peggy led the children back out of the ring; Alice dismounted and led Cracker over to where I was standing.

"Gran, Peggy said I can go in with Fiona and help with the tack."

I looked at Peggy, who nodded. "All right," I said, "but not too long, because Mummy will be expecting us back for tea."

The children went off into the stable yard and I turned to Peggy.

"It must be difficult, just the two of you doing everything," I said.

She shrugged. "We manage," she said. "A lot of the kids like helping and they're pretty useful, and Simon comes in every day. But we miss Jo, not just for the stable work, but in lots of ways — well, you can imagine."

"Of course. I think you're all doing wonderfully."

"It's hit Liz hardest. I've got my own family, but Jo and Charlie were her family and

179

you can see she's lost without them."

"I gather the police haven't finished with the office yet," I said tentatively.

"No. Inspector Morris — He's a friend of my uncle Chris; they both used to be on the skittles team for the Stag's Head out at Roadwater — he says the inquiry is ongoing, whatever that means. I suppose they're still trying to find out what happened. He's been back and forth several times — well, it was a dreadful thing to happen."

"Indeed it was and I'm sure he wants to get to the bottom of it. Liz didn't seem to know much about how things are going."

"She's still in a state. If you think about it, she found Charlie and then she was the one to find poor Jo. It's no wonder it's all got to her. She gets through the work — works all the hours God sends, but it's all about the horses and the stables. I don't think she's taken in half of what's happening."

"Poor girl. She's very lucky to have you to support her."

"We all support each other, the kids as well, because it's what Jo and Charlie would want."

"I'm sure it is," I agreed.

We both stood for a while in silence, looking out across the fields to where a small group of riders were emerging from the woods beyond.

"There's the four o'clock ride," Peggy said. "I'd better go and open the gates for them."

I watched while they came in and to my surprise I saw that one of the riders was Vicky. When they got back into the yard, Vicky dismounted and handed the reins to Peggy with a cursory word of thanks and turned to me.

"I didn't expect to see you here, Sheila. Are you *still* riding?"

I wasn't terribly keen on the "still," but I smiled and explained that I was collecting Alice.

"I thought I'd get back in the saddle," she said, "though I know I'll be hellish stiff tomorrow. Still, now it's all in the family, it's free! Trust Simon to get all this — but he always was Jo's favorite."

"He's putting in a lot of work," I said repressively. "He's up here all hours."

"Well, he knows he's got to keep the business going if he wants to get anything for it."

"Oh no, I'm sure he wouldn't dream of selling it."

"Maybe you're right. Daddy always said that for an accountant, he had absolutely

181

no business sense."

"How long are you down here for?" I asked.

"Just until the weekend. I've got a lot on my plate with this program and now that Jo's gone, I'll have to find someone else to cover that period."

"But she didn't agree, did she? I thought she had reservations about it."

"I was working on her," Vicky said. "Actually, I came up here to see her the day before she died and I think she was beginning to change her mind. Pity."

"It was a tragic accident," I said, "absolutely tragic."

"Yes, terrible," she said absently, "but I would have thought it was perfectly obvious how it happened — that whole office was chaotic — so I can't see why the police are questioning everybody like this."

"Are they?"

"Simon, of course, because he was always up here, but why should they want to talk to me? I don't know anything about the wiring, or whatever it was. And coming and bothering Mother like that! I mean, she's been right out of it since Daddy died, and I don't know if she's really taken in what's happened to Jo. She's been very upset."

"Poor Esther, I'm so sorry," I said, "but I

suppose they do have to make inquiries where there are unusual circumstances."

"Unusual?" Vicky said sharply. "It was an accident."

"Yes, but there has to be an inquest."

"A lot of nonsense. Well, I hope they don't expect me to stay down here for that. I'm up to my eyes at the moment. Not only this theater program, but I've scheduled one about women Victorian novelists. There's been a lot of interest ever since that TV *Jane Eyre,* and what was that Gaskell one?"

"North and South."

"That's it." She eyed me speculatively. "You know about these people — you've written books and stuff about them. How would you like to take part in the program?"

"Oh, I don't think so," I said firmly. "It's not my sort of thing at all."

"It would be good for the sales of your books," Vicky said, "all good publicity."

"My books are mostly bought by libraries, so I don't think . . ."

"Well, give it some thought. I wouldn't be able to get down here to record anything, but you could easily go to the Bristol studios."

"No, really," I said, starting to move away. "I'd better go and retrieve Alice or she'll be here all night."

183

■ ■ ■ ■

Michael got back just as I'd finished having tea with Thea and Alice and saw me out to my car.

"When did you last check the oil and tires?" he asked.

"I don't know — a while back."

"Give me the keys. I'll do it for you now."

"Thank you, darling. I would be grateful. I rather wanted to have a word with you," I went on as he opened the bonnet, "that's if it isn't all still confidential."

"All what?"

"About Jo's will. I had a chat with Liz today and she told me that Jo had left her the house and a share in the stables."

"Yes, that's right. Everything else goes to Simon — the rest of the share of the stables and all the land."

"Nothing to Esther or Vicky?"

"No. Jo never did get on with Vicky and I suppose she thought Esther would be looked after by Gordon. She made a new will quite recently, just after Charlie died. But no surprises really."

"Liz was surprised about the house, and a bit upset."

"Why on earth was she upset?"

"Well, she felt she shouldn't have had it. She said it was too much and Simon ought to have had everything — that sort of thing. She was very emotional."

Michael wiped the dipstick on a tissue I handed him and shut the bonnet. "I'll never understand women," he said. "Why can't they ever accept things as they are instead of agonizing over them!"

"Well, poor Liz is in a bit of a state just now. I mean, Charlie gone and then Jo, and, although *she'd* thought of them as her family, the fact that they weren't really made her feel the house should have gone to Jo's actual relations."

"It wouldn't have been in the will if Jo hadn't wanted her to have it." He opened the boot and took out the foot pump.

"I know, and that's what I told her, of course, but I suppose people don't think logically at times like this. And it won't be any easier if Bob Morris decides to make it a murder inquiry."

"Yes, Thea told me what Steve said about the wiring. But the thought that anyone would want to murder Jo is, well, ridiculous."

"That's what I thought, but Roger says they're treating it as a suspicious death, so *someone* must think it's a possibility."

"I still think it's rubbish. This front tire's a bit down. I'll just pump it up."

When I got back I let the animals out into the garden to give myself a little peace to get my supper. I'd eaten rather too much of Thea's gorgeous Victoria sponge to be really hungry and I'd just decided that a plain boiled egg was all I wanted, when the phone rang. It was Rosemary.

"Sorry to be the bearer of bad tidings," she said, "but Mother asked — no *told* — me to ask you to go to tea there next Friday."

I laughed. "I promise not to shoot the messenger," I said, "and of course I'd love to go to tea. I've been feeling a bit guilty about not having seen her for a long time. Has she got over that nasty cold?"

"It did pull her down quite a bit, but she won a great battle with Dr. Macdonald and that set her up wonderfully."

"Battle?"

"Yes, she said she wanted an antibiotic and he said, quite rightly, that they don't do anything for colds."

"But?"

"But Mother did the usual — weak chest, threat of pleurisy if not pneumonia, appalling state of the Health Service, so much for patient choice, criminal lack of government spending on the elderly, et cetera, et cetera."

"So?"

"So, of course, he gave her the mildest possible tablets and she made a splendid recovery, which she, of course, attributed to the antibiotic, but was really her triumph over him!"

I laughed. "She's an example to us all! I'll look forward to hearing all about it next Friday."

"I think," Rosemary said, "she wants to question you about Jo."

"What has she heard?"

"Something about the wiring and it not being an accident."

"How on earth did she hear about that?" I asked.

"You know Mother's system of intelligence gathering. But really, Sheila, is it true? Is there some doubt about it?"

"I think so; no, I'm sure. Steve Webber — you know, the electrician — told me he thought the wire in the office had been cut deliberately, and he's very reliable. I mean, he wouldn't have said anything unless he was certain. And I had a word with Roger when I met him dog walking and he said they were treating it as a suspicious death."

"I can't imagine anyone wanting Jo dead," Rosemary said.

"That's what we all feel," I said, "but, if what Steve says is true — and Roger said the forensic people have checked as well — then I suppose we simply have to consider the possibility, however unlikely."

CHAPTER THIRTEEN

I was flicking through the program pages of the *Radio Times* when I saw that one of the satellite stations was doing a rerun of the *Inspector Ivor* series, with my old friend David Beaumont. David's a childhood friend who became an actor and is now running a sort of Shakespeare institute in Stratford-upon-Avon. We've always stayed in touch, and sometimes I go and stay with him in his lovely little cottage opposite the Memorial Theatre to catch up on the gossip. On an impulse I rang him.

"Hello, darling," the deep, familiar voice greeted me. "I was just thinking about you. Well, you and poor Jo Howard. I heard it on the news and there was a nice obit in the *Guardian*. What a ghastly thing to happen. You must all have been devastated."

"We were. Still are, really. You played with her, didn't you?" I said, giving him the cue that would, I knew, produce the anecdotes I wanted.

"Yes, of course I did, my first proper part: Osric in the Carlyle *Hamlet,* here at Stratford. Her Ophelia was quite wonderful — technically perfect with that little extra something, *so* rare to combine the two. Ellen could, of course, but hardly anybody now — perhaps Vanessa. She was just coming to that point — enough experience, all the big roles, but hadn't lost the freshness — when she could do no wrong. Everything she touched was magic. The critics *adored* her and her name could sell any production."

"Was that the only time you played with her?"

"Well, yes, she gave it all up, absolutely mad. None of us could believe it at the time."

"When she married Charlie Hamilton?"

"Oh no, before that."

"Really?"

"About a year before."

"Do you know why?"

There was a pause at the other end. "Well, darling, there *were* rumors."

"Rumors?"

"About her and John Carlyle."

"Oh?"

"Just greenroom gossip. You know what it's like with a permanent company. Jane wasn't around; she was abroad filming. Do you remember her, Jane Neville? I believe she's practically gaga now, living at Denville Hall anyway. She had absolutely *scathing* notices for her Lady Macbeth, even worse than Tynan on Vivien Leigh, total madness, of course. I mean, she was splendid in *School for Scandal* and a lovely Gwendolen in *The Importance*. She did that mannered stuff very well, but to think she could play Shakespeare, let alone Lady Macbeth . . . Well, think of Marie Tempest playing Goneril!"

"So did they?" I asked, trying to bring him back to the point. "Have an affair — Jo and John Carlyle?"

"Oh yes."

"But surely that wasn't enough to make her give up acting!"

"It was a bit more than that, though I believe Jane had her suspicions. John wasn't the best of husbands, and she did all she could to wreck Jo's career. Jane had a lot of influence. Her father, Arthur Neville, was in management, you see."

"So what was it? You said it was a bit more than the affair."

Another pause. "Well, they're all dead or

191

as good as, so I suppose it won't matter if I tell you. It was after a performance. I found John had left his watch in the greenroom. It was a *very* expensive one — given him by Jane and very lovingly inscribed — so I thought I'd better take it to him in his dressing room. The door was a bit ajar and I heard voices, so I was about to go away, but then I heard Jo's voice. She sounded absolutely distraught. I knew I *ought* to go away. It was unforgivable to listen, but, well, I was young and curious, so I stayed where I was."

"And?"

"I heard John telling her to control herself — his voice was really unpleasant — and after a while she was quiet. Then he said, quite coldly, 'I've told you, you'll have to get rid of it.' He could really be a swine if something upset him. A lot of directors found him very difficult. I know for a fact that after that production of *Winter's Tale,* Guthrie swore he'd never work with him again."

"So what happened? What did Jo say?"

"I couldn't hear her words. Her voice was very muffled as if she was crying, but then I heard him say, 'There's no other way. You know that; you're not a fool. I know of a clinic and I'll pay for it, so if you're sensible and discreet, no one need ever find out. You

know it makes sense, for both our careers.'
His voice was softer then. He was obviously
trying to persuade her — he *could* be very
persuasive when he wanted."

"So what did she say?"

"I don't know. I heard someone coming.
so I had to go, but it was perfectly obvious
what was going on."

"You mean she was pregnant and he
wanted her to get rid of it?"

"What else?"

"How horrible."

"Typical though. He was always tremen-
dously ambitious and it was just coming up
to crunch time for the National Theatre. He
thought he had a chance there and so, of
course, he didn't want any sort of scandal.
Still," David said with some satisfaction,
"I'm glad to say that Larry beat him to it
and got the job."

"Yes, I see. So did she, I wonder?"

"Did she what?"

"Did Jo have an abortion? It wasn't easy
in those days."

"I don't know. After *Hamlet* I went to the
Birmingham Rep — really very lucky. The
Dauphin in *St. Joan* and Konstantin in *The
Seagull* — we got some marvelous notices,
even in the national press, and I made some
really good contacts. So I rather lost touch

and, as far as I can remember, the gossip never really amounted to anything in the end."

"But she still gave up the theater? A year before she married Charlie?"

"Round about a year. So, it did occur to me that perhaps she *did* have the baby."

"And put it up for adoption? No, that's not like Jo!"

"Well, as you rightly said, darling, things were very different then."

"I suppose so. . . ."

"Well, it was all a long time ago," David said, "so we'll never know now. But what I *do* want to know is when are you coming to stay? It's a good time of year. The main *swarms* of Japanese with cameras and French schoolchildren with their horrid backpacks have gone and I've got some gorgeous new exhibits to show you. A dear old soul in Warwick left us some absolutely marvelous set designs for the Beerbohm Tree *Dream* and a couple of scripts — real treasures."

"I'd love to come, David. I'm a bit tied up just now, but the minute I'm free I'll give you a ring. It'll be something to look forward to."

When I put the phone down I sat for a while trying to take in what David had told me. Marjorie's description of Jo and John Carlyle in the nunnery scene came into my mind. The animosity must have been very strong to have come over like that on stage.

Poor Jo. My heart ached for her. As David said, things were very different in those days. It was a miserable business, whether the illegal operation was done by a back-street abortionist or in an expensive clinic where money changed hands and no questions were asked. And keeping an illegitimate child wasn't easy. The social stigma was immense. It must have often seemed easier to bear the pain of having the baby adopted than to face the condemnation of society and, even more, the stigma that would be attached to your child. The Jo I knew was very strong, but even she might have finally decided she couldn't cope, especially if she intended to carry on with her career — though she never did. It was very puzzling, but, as David said, it was all a long time ago and we'd probably never know now what had happened. Still, there was a nagging feeling at the back of my mind that it was just possible that Jo's child, now grown up, could exist and might one day have wanted to find his, or her, real mother.

■ ■ ■ ■

The next day Steve came to change my electricity points.

"Well, I've put that new one in where you needed it and I've moved all the others up to make it easier for you," he said. "There's not a lot of making good — a bit of plastic wood and a lick of paint is all it needs. You'd better come and see if they're what you wanted."

I made a tour of the points with him, making, as one does, appreciative and admiring comments at each one.

"That's splendid," I said when we had finally finished, "just what I wanted; it'll make life *so* much easier! Now, do come and have a cup of tea. You'll need one after all that hard work!"

As I poured the tea and cut some slices of fruit cake, Steve said, "Funny thing about that inquest, wasn't it?"

"Inquest? What inquest?" I asked.

"For poor Mrs. Hamilton."

"Really — have they held it, then?"

"Last Friday."

"I'd no idea — I hadn't heard. I suppose it'll be in this week's *Free Press*. What happened?"

"Well," Steve said, stirring his tea vigorously, "you know what I said about that wiring, and how I told Bob Morris? So, I naturally thought I'd be called to say what I'd found." He added another spoonful of sugar to his tea and stirred it again. "But not a bit of it!"

"Really?"

"No. Bob goes and gets in the what-you-call-them — the *forensic* people to look at it again and they say it could have been an accident after all."

"But you said the wire had been cut."

"And I still say that's what it looked like to me — and I've been twenty years in the trade." He took a large bite of fruit cake. "It seems," he said, his sarcastic tone slightly muffled by a mouthful of crumbs, "it *seems* that there was a heavy, metal cash box they used to keep on that bench where the wiring and the switches were, and they said the sharp edge of that could have cut the wire."

"I suppose it might have done," I said. "It's just possible."

"Possible, perhaps," Steve said scornfully, "but is it likely? I ask you!"

"Well . . ."

"Any road, that's what *they* said, so I wasn't called to say what I thought, and the coroner, Major Barrington, that silly old fool, said it was accidental death."

"I see."

"But I saw what I saw, whatever they may say, and you can take it from me, Mrs. M, we haven't heard the last of it."

After he'd gone and while I was washing up and putting away the cake tin, my immediate feeling was one of relief. Of course it had been an accident, another tragic accident, just like Charlie's had been. Of course no one could possibly have wanted to kill Jo. Like everyone said, the whole idea was ridiculous. We could put away the feelings of distress and anxiety all the speculation had aroused and simply mourn the loss of a good friend.

Foss, who'd been banished outside to prevent him from taking part in Steve's activities, suddenly appeared at the window, demanding to be let in. I opened the door and took down a tin of cat food. Tris, who was fast asleep in his basket, woke up instantly at the sound of a saucer being put down and, with a short, sharp bark, claimed his equal rights. As I shook the dog biscuits into his bowl I felt as if a load had been lifted from my mind.

Later, when I set off to collect Alice, I felt more cheerful about going to the stables than I had ever since Jo's death. When I got there I was surprised to see Roger, leaning on the fence leading down to the ring.

"Hello," I said. "Fancy seeing you here."

He smiled. "I've been detailed to collect my daughter," he said. "How about you?"

"I'm collecting Alice — grandmother's privilege. Actually," I went on, "for a moment, when I saw you here, I wondered if it was something to do with Jo's death."

"No, that's all done and dusted. The coroner's verdict was accidental death."

"So I gather. But I thought you told me that the forensic people thought the wiring might have been tampered with."

"So they did, but then they discovered that a heavy, metal cash box had often been dumped down on some of the wiring — people really are so careless — and that could easily have caused the cut. After that there was no reason to suspect foul play — especially against someone like Jo!"

"I'm so glad," I said. "It gave me a horrible feeling to think that anyone might have wanted to harm her. I'm sure Simon and Liz are so relieved. They've got enough to worry about, running this place."

"They certainly have. I wouldn't like to have to cope with all those teenage girls."

I smiled. "Is Delia giving you a hard time?"

"Let's just say that Jilly and I have been thinking quite seriously about boarding school!"

"You don't mean it."

"No, I know it's only what our Mrs. Mac calls a 'phrase' she's going through and she'll come out the other end our own sweet daughter, but it's hard to live with. Alex is so much easier."

"Ah, just you wait until Alex is seventeen. That I *do* know about! Motor bikes," I said darkly, "and things like that."

The riders had come back while we were talking and Delia walked over, deep in conversation with Alice. Well, not conversation exactly, more like a monologue, which Alice was listening to with rapt attention.

"So you see," Delia was saying, "that's why it's easiest to slow your pony down with half halts — pull and let loose."

She graciously informed me that Alice was doing nicely and if she remembered to sit deeper in the saddle, she'd do very well. When she saw her father, however, she said, "Daddy, how *could* you come out in that *terrible* jacket!" and scrambled quickly into the car before anyone could associate her with such a dreadful sartorial mistake.

Roger pulled a face, waved to me and drove away.

Alice was tugging at my sleeve. "Gran, can I just go and help Peggy with the feed buckets? She said I could."

"Yes, all right, but don't be long."

"That's good. We need all the free labor we can get." Simon had come up behind me. "Thank heaven for little girls. I'm not sure we could function without them!"

"Well," I said, smiling, "it does appear to be mutually beneficial. Seriously though, how's it going?"

He shrugged. "I think we can manage to keep going, if we can get a few more liveries and don't lose any more clients."

"Liz said some of them have canceled."

"Only to be expected, I suppose — two fatal accidents, bound to put people off. But most people have been very loyal."

"I'm sure they want you to succeed, for Jo's sake," I said. "Actually, Simon, I haven't had a proper chance to tell you how very sorry I am about it all. I know how close you were to her and how badly you must miss her. And I'm so glad all this business with the police has been sorted out. That must have been so painful for you."

"Yes," he said, "it was difficult."

"Do you have a date for the funeral?"

"It's not quite settled yet. We've only just had permission to . . ." He had difficulty in finishing the sentence.

"Yes, of course," I said quickly. "I'm sure a lot of people will want to come. She was greatly loved."

"Yes."

"I think," I said, "I'd better go and sort out Alice. I'm sure she'd *sleep* here if she could!"

As I went into the stable yard I felt worried about Simon. He looked absolutely exhausted and was obviously in a highly emotional state. Given his burden of the stables as well as his own demanding job, not to mention looking after his mother following his father's death, I suppose it wasn't surprising. But I still felt there was something else preying on his mind.

I prized a reluctant Alice away from the delights of the hay nets and got her into the car.

I was driving down the track away from the stables when I had to pull over onto the grass to let a large Mitsubishi four-by-four go by. As the driver raised his hand to thank me, I saw that it was Dan Webster.

CHAPTER FOURTEEN

I like to take flowers to Mrs. Dudley when I visit her, but, since she has very definite views on the matter, it's always difficult to know *which* flowers. Not roses or carnations (unnatural nowadays, no scent), not lilies or chrysanthemums (funeral flowers), certainly not geberas (vulgar). Fortunately, I found some rather nice, properly scented freesias that I hoped might be acceptable.

"Freesias, how very nice," she said approvingly, and I breathed a sigh of relief. "Give them to Elsie and tell her to put them in the *tall* cut-glass vase."

I made my way into the kitchen and handed the flowers over to Elsie, who has been with Mrs. Dudley for as long as I can remember, remains cheerful at all times and is, thank goodness, impervious to her moods and general irascibility.

"How is she," I asked, "after that nasty cold?"

"A bit pulled down," Elsie said as she filled the required vase with water and arranged the flowers, "but she's picking up nicely, and Dr. Macdonald is very pleased with her. Of course, she does miss having her little lunch parties, but it really was getting to be too much for her."

"She's still amazing for her age," I said.

"There." Elsie handed me the vase. "If you'd take that in, I'll bring the tea. The kettle's just on the boil."

I took the flowers back into the sitting room and, as directed, put them down carefully ("On that little mat please, Sheila.") on the table by the window.

Mrs. Dudley is the only person I know now who actually has people to tea in the old-fashioned, formal way. I looked with pleasure at the small table laid with a white, lace-edged cloth, the delicate china and the knives and spoons with their mother-of-pearl handles. There were two sorts of tiny sandwiches (cucumber, and egg and cress), scones with clotted cream and jam, and two sorts of cake (an iced sponge and a rich fruit cake). Elsie had surpassed herself. She came in with the large silver teapot and the smaller hot-water jug on a tray. The tea ceremony is, in its way, as traditional as any Japanese one: a little hot water poured into the cup, rinsed round to warm it and poured into the slop basin; the heavy teapot (which I knew from past experience always dribbled just a little) that had to be held at a certain angle away from the cloth so that it wouldn't drip on it; the milk in last, of course, and the sugar always to be offered and always refused.

Mrs. Dudley watched the proceedings with an attentive eye and gave a tiny nod of approval when I'd accomplished it satisfactorily. She then put me through the customary, brisk inquiry about Michael, Thea and Alice, which I knew was merely skirmishing before she got down to the real business of the meeting, as it were.

"So what's all this about Josephine Hamilton, then?"

"I expect you heard that the inquest said it was accidental death."

"And what do you think?"

"Well — I think it probably was."

"Probably? That's not what I heard."

"Well," I said again, "there was some problem about the wire being cut, but that was all explained at the inquest, and the coroner was quite satisfied."

Mrs. Dudley gave a short laugh. "Marcus Barrington! He's about as much use as a chocolate fireguard!"

I looked at her in amazement at this colloquial turn of phrase.

"I believe that's what dear Delia calls it — it struck me as a very colorful and accurate metaphor. I certainly wouldn't trust *his* judgment on any legal matter. How he came to be appointed coroner is, and always will be, a mystery to me."

"Still," I said, getting involved in a discussion I didn't really want, as always happens with Mrs. Dudley, "I do think it *was* most likely an accident. I mean, who would want to kill poor Jo? Everyone loved her."

"Not everyone." She paused to spread a scone with cream and jam. "Not everyone by any means."

"Who? Who could possibly dislike Jo?"

"Esther Nicholson for one."

"Esther? But she's Jo's sister!"

"What has that got to do with it?" Mrs. Dudley said sharply.

"But why?"

"She has always been bitterly jealous of her — the beautiful, talented older sister. Even as a young girl Esther was plain and very dull. You must remember that."

"Well, yes," I said, remembering guiltily several occasions in our youth when Esther had been excluded from some activity or other because someone said she was "dim" or "boring." "I suppose she must have felt left out sometimes."

"Exactly. And, of course, her parents made it very plain that Josephine was their favorite. I remember Margaret Howard saying frequently what a disappointment Esther was after her brilliant older sister."

"Poor Esther," I said. "I'm afraid we weren't very nice to her."

"And then there was the business with Gordon Nicholson."

"Gordon?"

"Oh yes, he was madly in love with Josephine; begged her to marry him several times."

"I never knew that."

"Well, he was hardly likely to publish his disappointment. It would have been a good match. He was a professional man and his family was very well off. Have you heard of Nicholson's, the builders? Arnold Nicholson, Gordon's father, worked his way up from nothing — *his* father was a common laborer — so it wasn't a good family, but he made a great deal of money building those houses out beyond the marshes. He got the land for a song. He always had an eye for the main chance. Gordon takes after him in that way."

I thought of the talk about Gordon's deals

with Dan Webster. "Yes," I said, "he's always had a head for business. But I can see why Jo rejected him — very much not her sort of person. It would have been impossible!"

"The Howards didn't see it in that way. They were very upset that Josephine had refused such a good offer, especially since she'd refused his cousin Clive before. They weren't at all well off. If you remember, Desmond Howard was only a bank clerk and they thought it would have been a marvelous match for their daughter."

"But still — I can't imagine it, Jo and Gordon!"

"They put a certain amount of pressure on her, and that is why she went off to London."

"I see. But then Esther went to work for Gordon."

"That was some years later. I believe she had always had some sort of romantic ideas about him, her sister's young man — I believe that often happens — and he was still unmarried."

"And you think he married her as second best?"

"I believe that often happens too."

"Poor Esther."

"Well, I suppose she had got what she wanted." Mrs. Dudley paused. "Sheila dear, will you very kindly cut me a piece of sponge — no, a little larger than that — and have some yourself. You've eaten almost nothing. I do hope you are not on one of those stupid diets."

I cut myself a piece of sponge and assured her that, indeed, I was making an excellent tea.

"Of course," Mrs. Dudley went on, "getting what we want is not always what we *thought* we wanted."

I considered this aphoristic statement for a moment and then said, "It couldn't work, of course. If Esther knew that Jo was the love of his life and he'd only married her as a sort of substitute, she'd always feel inferior. And I suppose it was bad enough when Jo was in London leading that glamorous life, but, in a way it must have been much worse when she came back to Taviscombe with Charlie — who was so charismatic — and was there under Esther's nose every day, so to speak."

Mrs. Dudley nodded. "Exactly. And it hasn't helped that Simon, her own son, obviously preferred the company of his aunt to that of his mother."

"Oh dear." I absently took another slice of sponge. "I can see why Esther might very well hate her sister, but I really can't see her *killing* her."

"You think she is too stupid to choose such a recherché method?"

"Well, yes — it does seem a little, well, *inventive* for Esther."

"Ah," Mrs. Dudley said triumphantly, "but I happen to know that she had just had some electrical work done and that the electrician had warned her about the dangers of having wiring in a place where it might become damaged."

"Steve Webber?"

"He did happen to mention it when he came to put in a new switch for me."

"He doesn't think Jo's death was an accident," I said, resisting the temptation to lick the icing from my fingers, and wiping them decorously on my table napkin. "He thinks the wire was cut deliberately."

"Precisely," Mrs. Dudley said, "and he is a very experienced electrician."

"But at the inquest they said it was probably that heavy, metal cash box that cut the wire."

"Oh, the inquest!" Mrs. Dudley waved it aside. "I have no opinion of that ridiculous procedure. I've no doubt it suited them to call it an accident — less bother all round, typical of the slipshod way things are done today."

I ignored this slight on the criminal justice system. "But Esther!" I protested. "No, I really can't believe that."

"She adored that tiresome husband of hers and you must have noticed how oddly she has been behaving since he died."

"Well, yes, in a way, but that's only natural. It must have been a dreadful shock to have him collapsing like that."

"The man had had a serious heart condition for years. It can hardly have been unexpected, even to someone as stupid as Esther Nicholson."

"But she hardly ever went to the stables; she may not have gone that day."

"Has anyone asked her?"

"I suppose Inspector Morris may have done."

"*Inspector* Morris," Mrs. Dudley said scornfully. "What use is he? Why is Roger not looking into things?"

"He's based in Taunton now," I said apologetically, "though he is still taking an interest in it."

"That is all very well, but with a murderer on the loose, are we in Taviscombe to be considered less worthy of protection than the people of *Taunton*?"

There seemed to be no answer to that and, with Mrs. Dudley now in full Lady Bracknell mode, I was glad that Elsie came in just then to remove the tea things so that I could decently take my leave.

"Dear Sheila," Mrs. Dudley said as I bent to kiss her, "remember, all this dieting is bad for the health, especially at your age."

"Your mother really does know how to put the knife in," I said to Rosemary when I reported back to her. "That remark about dieting was pure malice!"

"You really should be used to it after nearly sixty years," Rosemary said, laughing.

"I know," I said ruefully, "but she gets to me every time. And what's all this about picking up phrases from Delia? I couldn't believe my ears!"

"Oh, that's Delia's latest ploy, spending time with Great-Grandma. It drives Jilly and Roger mad, which, of course, it's meant to. 'She's always beautifully behaved with *me*,' Mother says whenever any of us complain about how impossible Delia is. And 'She reminds me very much of what I was like at her age.' I mean, come on!"

"Oh dear, the deviousness of little girls," I said.

"She stuffs herself with cakes and things when she's there, just when Jill's trying so hard to get the children to eat healthily. Mother simply encourages her, of course, and Delia always comes away with extra pocket money — for doing well at school, that sort of thing!"

"Well, I suppose it's a new interest for your mother."

"Oh, by the way," Rosemary said, "Simon's been able to fix the date for Jo's funeral. It's going to be on the twenty-ninth at two thirty. St. James's, of course, and then at the County, like Charlie's do. Poor boy, that's the third funeral he's had to arrange. Jo wasn't up to doing Charlie's, so Simon did that, as well as his father's. I think it's all getting to him. He really did look awful when I saw him yesterday."

"Poor Simon," I said. "Everyone does rely on him. I'll go with Thea, of course, and I expect Michael will be able to get away."

But, as it happened I wasn't able to go to Jo's funeral. The day before, I came down with the particularly horrible feverish cold that had been going round Taviscombe — the sort of cold when all you can do is crawl miserably into bed and stay there. I did manage to phone Rosemary to tell her.

"Is there anything I can do?" she asked. "I could easily pop round this morning."

"No, it's fine," I croaked. "Thea, bless her,

has been in and seen to the animals, and she's making me hot drinks and soup and things. Do please tell Simon how sorry I am not to be there, but I really can't make it. My throat's raw and I'm at the streaming stage. I've gone through one box of tissues already. Thea's made me some lemon and honey and I'm living on aspirin and Vick . . ." I broke off with a fit of coughing, and Rosemary, murmuring comforting words, rang off.

Putting down the phone, I sipped some of the lemon and honey, took some more aspirin and moved a reluctant Foss from under the duvet so that I could pull it up over my head and try to get some sleep.

I felt marginally better the next day and able to listen quite sensibly to Rosemary's account of the funeral.

"It was exactly the same as Charlie's, same hymns and everything. Simon told me that's what she wanted. Some of the same horsey people were there and some theater people — I recognized a few of them — and one of them said a few words. The church was more or less full and most people went on afterwards."

"I'm so glad," I said. "I just wish I could have been there too."

"I tell you who wasn't," Rosemary said.

"Who?"

"Esther."

"Really!"

"Apparently she wasn't well enough — she has the same bug as you. So really it was just Simon, Liz and Peggy. Oh, and Vicky. I think she was a bit put out at the girls from the stables being counted as 'family,' but they certainly had more right than she has."

"Especially Liz. She was almost like a daughter to Jo and Charlie."

"I think that's always riled Vicky. Apparently she was *very* put out that Liz had been left the house as well as a share of the stables."

"She really is so like Gordon — money, money, money!"

"And she was networking — if that's what they call it — after the funeral, chatting up some of the theater people. I think she wanted them for this program of hers, the one Jo wouldn't do. Oh yes, and she was asking after you, something she wants *you* for."

"Well, at least I've avoided that," I said. "But I would have liked to be there, just to say good-bye to Jo."

"Anyway, how are you?" Rosemary asked.

"I think the worst's over," I said cautiously. "It was pretty violent but mercifully short. My head feels full of cotton wool and my sinuses are all bunged up, but my temperature's down, so I can function enough to get up and see to the animals. And Thea's been marvelous. She's brought me some gorgeous fish pie for my supper, just what I feel like."

"Well, don't go overdoing things. You must take care" — she paused — "especially at *your* age, as Mother would doubtless say."

But I should have realized that I wasn't going to escape Vicky that easily. I'd just put the fish pie in the microwave to warm it up when she rang.

"Oh, Sheila, I was sorry to miss you at the funeral," she said, "because we need to finalize your contribution to my Victorian writers program."

In my weakened state I hardly felt equal to protesting that I hadn't agreed to any contribution. She went on to outline the "scope," as she called it, of the program and what she needed me to say ". . . in relation to the other contributors. I've been so lucky to get Christine Marshall — she wrote that excellent book on the Brontës; it was *very* well reviewed — and Freda Anderson on George Eliot. So if you concentrate on Mrs. Gaskell, along the lines I've indicated, and just *touch* on Charlotte Yonge . . . I won't want much on her — all that religion puts people off. So if you could, let me have a script, about four thousand words, though we can cut it if necessary, by the beginning of next week. I'll book a parking space for you. That's splendid."

She'd rung off before I could make any effective protest, so I just gave up and switched on the microwave, feeling somehow that she'd quite spoiled my pleasure in the fish pie.

CHAPTER FIFTEEN

When, a week later, I got to the BBC studios in Bristol, I found Vicky very much in charge.

"I had to come down for a special meeting this morning," she said importantly, "so it was convenient to stay on to do your piece. I've booked a studio."

I have to admit that Vicky's very good at her job. She did the recording briskly and efficiently, with only a few interruptions, mostly technical and about sound levels and so forth.

"Right," she said when we'd finished, "I've got a spare half hour, so shall we go and get a cup of tea and a bun in the canteen? That's unless you'd rather have a polystirene cup of not-very-nice coffee from the machine."

I opted gratefully for the tea and a rather nice slice of Dundee cake. For a while Vicky talked about the program and about other programs she had done or was proposing to do, and I listened in a sort of daze. I listened more attentively when she began talking about Jo.

"It's absolutely ridiculous that she should have left the house to that girl. A valuable property like that should have gone to one of the family. I didn't expect her to leave me anything — we never got on; Simon was always her favorite — but to leave it to a stable girl!"

"I think Liz was rather more than a stable girl," I said placatingly. "Really, she's devoted her life to the place."

"Well, she's got a share of the business. I'd have thought that was more than enough."

"Simon seems quite happy about the arrangement."

"Oh, Simon — he's hopeless about any sort of business."

"He is an accountant," I said. "That's business, after all."

Vicky gave a short laugh. "Not a very good one, from what I've heard. Mother says he's always having trouble trying to keep up with things at work. Mind you, he never wanted to go into accountancy. Father made him."

"What did he want to do?" I asked.

"Oh, he had some silly idea of helping Jo

and Charlie. You can imagine what Father thought about that!"

I could imagine it very well. "Perhaps he'd have been happier doing that."

"Happier!" Vicky said scornfully. "What's that got to do with it? No, my little brother's always been a bit odd. There was that girlfriend — what was her name? — Julie something. We quite thought they'd get engaged. It would have been a good match; her father was one of the partners. But that came to nothing."

"I thought she went away to London," I said.

"Yes, she did, but that was after she'd broken it off with Simon. We never knew why. And I'd like to know what he does in London when he comes up to stay with me. Oh, I know he goes to a few theaters, but some evenings he doesn't, and he's out nearly every afternoon. When I ask him where he's been, he just says walking round London."

"Well, perhaps he is. I must say I like just wandering around looking at things when I'm up there."

"Oh, that's different — you write books," Vicky said, as if that covered any sort of eccentricity.

"Well, he's certainly putting a lot of time

in at the stables," I said.

"I suppose he might marry that girl," Vicky said thoughtfully. "At least it would keep that house in the family."

Driving back up Whiteladies Road I decided I didn't want to face the motorway, so I went up onto the Downs to take the old-fashioned A38 home. As I scrabbled in my purse for the money for the toll on the suspension bridge, I considered what Vicky had said about Simon. I could see why she couldn't understand Simon's wish to "walk about London," something she would never have thought of doing. Simon, I now realized, has always been something of a dreamer; pushed by his father into a career he disliked and wasn't good at, he must have often felt the need to escape from the realities of life. I suppose that's why he spent so much time at the stables. I wondered what the future held for him now that his father had died.

Going out of Bristol I suddenly remembered seeing Jo at Temple Mead station and how drawn and anxious she had looked when she thought she was unobserved. I wondered what the "tiresome business" was that she had to face that day. I'd learned so much about her life since she died that I began to feel as if I'd never really known her. But then, how could we possibly say that we knew anybody? It was all too confusing, so I found some soothing music on the radio and concentrated on my driving.

When I got back home the animals rushed out madly into the garden as if they'd been shut up in the house for days rather than hours. I saw with some irritation that it was now raining, so I'd have muddy paw marks all over the kitchen. It had been a long day; I suddenly felt very tired, too tired even to make a cup of tea or pour a drink, and simply sat at the kitchen table, not moving. It occurred to me that I'd been getting old without really noticing it and after doing something unusual, out of my old routine, I no longer had the resilience to pick myself up straightaway. A sharp bark (Tris wanting to come in) got me to my feet and, reaching for his towel, I went to let him in.

"So how did you get on?"

Rosemary and I have the habit, and have had for years, of phoning each other most mornings. Thea or Michael, bless them, ring every day to see if I'm "all right," but it's not quite the same. Just chat I suppose, but it's an exchange of news, thoughts and a good moan, something you can only really share with someone of your own generation, especially someone you've grown up with.

"Oh, it went quite well," I said. "Whatever reservations I might have about Vicky — and I can't say I care for her as a person — she's very good at her job, very professional. But *so* different from Simon!"

"Oh, she's always taken after Gordon, though I can't say Simon takes after Esther, thank goodness!"

"No, he's always seemed the odd one out in that family. I mean, he's always been wonderfully patient with Esther and has tried hard to be a good son, but somehow . . ."

"I know what you mean," Rosemary said. "You sort of feel he's never fitted in."

"Vicky was telling me about how he used to spend days, when he was staying with her, just wandering around London. That is the sort of thing *we* would enjoy, but can you imagine Gordon or Esther doing it! Or Vicky, of course. She was very scornful."

"She would be."

"She did say that Simon was pushed into his accountancy job by Gordon. Simon never wanted to do it."

"Oh, he hates it. Jack used to tell me how terribly difficult Simon found it all when he was just starting with his firm. He took ages to pick things up and was very slow. Jack, bless him, felt sorry for the boy and did his best to help. By the time Simon left to go to Frobisher and King — I think Gordon exerted a bit of influence to get him in there — he was more or less competent. But it's obvious he's pretty miserable and should never have been forced into it."

"Perhaps now Gordon's dead, Simon can do something else. I don't suppose Esther would mind, and, anyway, he's in his thirties for goodness' sake; he doesn't have to consult her!"

"But what would he do? Accountancy's all he's trained for."

"He could take over the stables," I suggested. "He spends all his spare time there and now he owns the biggest share of them — well, why not?"

"It's a thought. Jo would have liked that. I wonder if that's what she had in mind."

"I don't see why he couldn't make a go of it," I said. "He's been riding all his life, though I don't know about teaching people, and he's been doing the books already, so he'd go on seeing to that side of things."

We discussed this possibility enthusiastically for some time, planning a splendid new life for Simon, until Rosemary said, "It would be perfect, but I wonder if Gordon hasn't sapped his confidence too much for him to change direction now."

"You know him best. You could sound him out — see if he's been thinking about it."

"I might just do that," Rosemary said.

I'd only just put the phone down when Thea rang.

"Sheila, could you do me a favor? Could you take Alice and me up to the stables on Saturday afternoon? My car's got to go in to have the transmission seen to and I can't have the Land Rover because Michael's got a clay shoot."

"Of course, I'd love to. How nice that you and Alice are riding together now."

"Well, it's her first proper one-hour ride, off the leading rein, so I thought I'd go along. Anyway, I do enjoy it, especially now I don't get so stiff every time."

I was quite glad to have a reason for going to the stables to see how things were going there.

"It's only an hour," I said to Thea as we arrived, "so it's not worth going away and coming back. I've got a book."

"Come *along* Mummy!" Alice said, tugging at Thea's arm. "Gran, come and see Cracker. He really knows me now."

I followed them into the stable yard. "You

225

carry on, Thea," I said, as Peggy led the horses out. "I'll go and pay for the ride — my treat."

I watched them out of sight and then went into the office. Simon was sitting at the desk. I noticed that the tangle of wires had now been boxed in and there was a new set of switches. I wondered how Simon felt, sitting there. But I suppose life does go on and they needed the office.

"Hello," I said. "I've come to pay for Thea and Alice's ride."

Simon looked up from some papers he'd been studying and smiled. "Hello, Sheila. How are you? Rosemary said you hadn't been well."

"Oh, I'm fine now. It was that horrible bug that was going around. I was so sorry not to be able to get to the funeral. Jo was a good friend and I would have liked to say good-bye."

"It was very well attended. People came from all over."

"I'm so glad."

There was an awkward silence; then I said, "How are things going here? Liz and Peggy seem to have everything well in hand."

"Yes." He took up the subject gratefully. "They've been marvelous — Liz especially. I think we can make a go of it. We've got plans for riding holidays for the young. I thought we could use those outbuildings at the back and make a sort of dormitory. Peggy assures me all young girls want to sleep in dormitories! Other stables do it. It's a good source of income in itself and can bring new people in on a permanent basis." He spoke enthusiastically. "Or, at least," he went on, reverting to his own more hesitant manner, "that's what they tell me."

"I think it's a splendid idea," I said, "and I can think of several little girls of my acquaintance who'll be nagging their parents as soon as you've got it up and running."

He smiled. "I'll get you to spread the word as soon as we have it sorted out."

"Anyway," I said, "I must let you get on." I put the money for the ride down on the desk and went away.

I got back into the car and began to read my book in a desultory way, but I couldn't concentrate, so I put it away and looked around me. Simon had come out of the office and was standing with Liz, deep in conversation as they looked down across the fields. She was talking very earnestly about something, and he was smiling and nodding. At one point he put his arm round her shoulder in a friendly gesture, and the look she gave him made it suddenly very obvious to me how she felt about him. I wondered whether Simon even noticed it; probably not. He patted her shoulder absently, smiled again and went back into the office. Liz stood for several minutes, quite still, leaning on the rail; then she too went inside, into the stable yard.

I was still considering what I'd seen, when I was aware of another vehicle approaching. In my rear mirror I saw that it was Dan Webster's Mitsubishi. Some instinct made me crouch lower in my seat and appear to be buried in my book, though I needn't have bothered since he took no notice and went briskly past me into the office.

On an impulse I got out of the car, shutting the door as quietly as I could, and went up towards the stables. Cautiously, I edged as near as I could get to the door in the hope of hearing something, but, although I could catch the murmur of voices, I couldn't make out any of the conversation. I stood there for a moment and then, feeling rather ridiculous, I moved away. When Liz came out I was standing by the gate leading to the bridle path.

"Hello," she greeted me. "Are you waiting for Alice?"

"Alice and Thea," I said, thankful that she hadn't seen me doing my amateur spy act. "They're both out today. It's a beautiful day for it."

"Mm." She raised her face to the sun and smiled happily. "It's a perfect day."

We chatted for a while about nothing in particular, both of us content just to bask in the sunshine, gazing over the peaceful countryside. Our mood was broken by the appearance of Dan Webster coming out of the office. He was obviously not in a good mood and, as he left, he called back over his shoulder, "Well, just you think about it. We both have a great deal more to discuss. I'll be back."

He got into his car, slamming the door with some violence, and drove away.

"What a disagreeable man," I said.

Liz nodded but didn't say anything.

"I'm sure Jo was keen to get Tarquin away from him," I suggested.

"He's a beautiful horse," Liz said, "and he's come on wonderfully. He just needed proper handling."

"Well, he's certainly better away from that man," I said. "Does he still ride from here?"

"No, I don't think he rides at all now. Jo said he only did it to get in with the hunting set — something to do with business, I think."

I wanted very much to ask what sort of business he had with Simon, but I couldn't think of any way of introducing such a question casually into the conversation. The appearance of the riders brought an end to it anyway, and I was left to speculate.

Alice was very full of her ride and Thea almost as enthusiastic.

"It's ridiculous not to take advantage of the nice weather while it lasts. Soon it'll be winter and horribly cold and wet," she said. "I think I'll just go and make another booking for us both."

When she came out again she was looking very puzzled.

"I don't know what's the matter with Simon," she said. "He seemed miles away — hardly took in what I was saying. I had to ask him for a booking a couple of times until it got through to him."

"How extraordinary," I said. "He was quite all right when I saw him before."

"He looked as if something had upset him quite badly. He pulled himself together and apologized, but it was all a bit odd. Anyway, shall we go back and have some tea? You'll stay, won't you, Sheila?"

Alice hung on my arm. "Do come to tea,

Gran, and then I can tell you all about Cracker. He trotted really *fast*. . . ."

When I got home I mulled over what I'd heard about Dan Webster and what he could have been talking to Simon about. What, indeed, had he been saying to leave Simon so upset? Jim Robinson had said that Webster was into property, presumably in a big way, but I couldn't imagine how that might affect Simon. True, he'd inherited the stables and the land all round, but I didn't think small riding stables would tempt someone like Dan Webster, and no one could ever get planning permission to build in the fields, so it couldn't be that. I remembered seeing his Mitsubishi up on the moors beside Jo's Land Rover. Obviously whatever it was that Webster wanted he'd been pursuing for a long time, since I didn't think, somehow, that particular meeting had just been about Tarquin. It all seemed very strange.

My thoughts were rudely interrupted by a noise from the kitchen. Foss, in an attempt to get at an impertinent blue tit that had been pecking at the putty in the window, had leapt onto the windowsill, knocking down a handsome coleus plant I'd been nurturing, and smashing the pot. Undeterred by this, he was still on the windowsill, chittering angrily at the birds on the feeder.

As I resignedly swept up the soil and pottery fragments, I suddenly thought of Liz and the smile she had given Simon. It occurred to me that Vicky's suggestion, though given for the wrong reason, might very well be a happy ending for both of them.

CHAPTER SIXTEEN

"I was going to circulate the lottery information," Anthea said, backing me up into a corner in the post office, "but Muriel, who said she'd do the photocopying, had to go up to Reading because her sister's had a fall and there's no one else to look after their father. George *says* he'll get it done for us — he's got a photocopier at home, so it won't cost us anything — but he's not very reliable. Anyway, Derek is going to see to the application itself. He used to be something very high up in insurance, so I suppose he should be competent to do that. It's been most annoying — all these delays when I really wanted us to get moving *quickly.* There will be so many applications and we mustn't miss our chance, but push ahead."

Anthea obviously saw the whole lottery system as a kind of race where the prizes would go to the fastest, who would gain their advantage by elbowing the other competitors out of the way.

"I'm sure Derek will do it admirably," I said, seizing the least controversial thread of her narrative.

"But what we *must* do," she continued, "is to start to raise our share of the money as soon as possible. I'm calling a committee meeting for next week — Tuesday, I thought — and I do hope people will come with a lot of good ideas."

"I don't think I can manage Tuesday," I said.

Anthea gave an exclamation of impatience. "It's always the same," she said crossly. "It's practically impossible to arrange any sort of meeting at a time to suit everyone. Don't tell me you're off on holiday again!"

"No, nothing like that. It's just that I've got several appointments fixed for that day and I really can't cancel them."

"Oh, is that all," Anthea said, brushing my excuse to one side. "We can have the meeting in the evening, then. I'm sure you'll be able manage that! Say seven o'clock?"

"Oh, not seven," I said. "Don't you re-member, all the people who eat in the evening do find that difficult — you either have to eat too early or too late."

"Oh really, such nonsense! I have my main

meal at midday — so much better for you. Well, in that case we'll make it six; it won't go on that long."

"No," I said doubtfully, remembering several acrimonious meetings that had gone on until very late in the evening. "No, that should be fine."

"I'll give George a reminder so that you can all have the lottery information before the meeting. And remember," Anthea said briskly, "lots of new, bright ideas!"

"Actually," I said, "do we know how much money we need to raise? I mean, what's the whole thing going to cost? How much are we applying for?"

"That's another thing," Anthea said with some annoyance. "Steve Webber was going to come and give me an estimate, but when I rang, his wife said he'd gone off to Barnstaple to do some big electrical job there and wouldn't be back for a fortnight."

"In that case," I suggested, "wouldn't it be better to wait until we've got the estimate before we have the meeting? I mean, Derek can't make an application until we know how much we actually want."

"Not at all," Anthea said firmly. "We need to have plans made so that we can start raising our part of the money as soon as possible."

Fortunately the post office queue, which had been building up while this conversation was going on, now impinged on our space and gave me an excuse for bringing our talk to a conclusion.

"So," I said to Michael when he came round to saw up an old apple tree that had fallen down in the garden, "poor Derek's been lumbered with this lottery thing. I should think he must regret being retired, what with all the jobs around the house that Edna has been saving up for him over the years, and now Anthea nagging him!"

"And his work on the parish council," Michael said. "I suppose it's the usual case of the willing horse."

"I don't think anyone forced to do something by Anthea could be called willing," I said.

"Oh yes, I meant to tell you," Michael went on. "He told me that the council — I mean the planning committee of the District Council — have decided to change the District Plan to redesignate some of the land near the stables from agricultural to potential-development use. This means that it *could* be built on."

"Really? I haven't seen anything about it in the *Free Press*."

"No, they have to let the parish councils know first — and some other people too; I can't remember who — before the public get to know about it."

"So, technically, someone could build houses on the fields round the stables. That's awful!"

"Well, Jo and Charlie, and now Simon, own all the fields immediately next to the stables. Simon would never sell, so it should be all right."

"I suppose so. But, all the same, it's horrid to think of houses, or worse, in those beautiful fields."

"It's not a conservation area," Michael said, "and people have to live somewhere."

"Yes, I know that, but there's a lot of places on the outskirts of Taviscombe where they've been building already, so a few more houses over there wouldn't make any difference. And this is agricultural land — pasture anyway."

"Well, as I said, Simon won't sell and those fields go right up to the edge of the woods, so that particular spot is safe."

"Thank goodness."

"I expect the council will grant planning permission if the developer, whoever it is, promises to build a certain amount of affordable housing. It's the sort of deal they make."

"Of course!" I said. "That's what that horrible man Dan Webster must have wanted!"

"Dan Webster?"

"Yes, I've seen him up at the stables several times, to see Simon, and Jo too. I'm sure he was pestering them to sell those fields. He sounded really unpleasant when he was up there talking to Simon a few days ago."

"Unpleasant?"

"Yes, as he was going I heard him say there was a great deal still to discuss, and he said he'd be back. It sounded quite threatening, and Thea said Simon seemed really upset when she saw him afterwards."

"It's certainly the sort of deal Webster might want to make. It's the kind of thing he does. They say he usually gets what he wants somehow or other. But I don't think we need worry about Simon. I'm sure he'd never give in to someone like Webster. Anyway, I must get on. I think I'll have to use the band saw on this lot. It's not very sharp, but it's better than the big one."

As I went into the house to make Michael a cup of tea, I thought about Simon and wondered about his ability to stand up to Dan Webster. I was sure he wouldn't want to sell the fields, but I wondered just how well he might stand up to that sort of bullying. Jo would have done. Presumably that was what Webster wanted when they met up on the moor; it would hardly have been about Tarquin. No, Jo would have seen him off. But if Simon had been as upset as Thea said he was when he'd had just a short meeting with Webster, how would he cope with "I'll be back," which was obviously going to be a continuing attack. I wondered if there was anyone who could bolster up Simon's self-confidence and stiffen his resistance. I thought I might have a word with Rosemary, who knows him better than most.

Tuesday's meeting at Brunswick Lodge went off more or less as I'd expected. Although George had managed to photocopy the lottery information, there was a certain amount of grumbling about not knowing how much the job would cost.

"We need the actual *figures*," Derek kept saying. "It's not good asking me to do anything without them, because I can't."

"How can we know what to raise," Maureen said plaintively, "if we don't know the *proportion* required?"

The phrase obviously pleased her since she repeated it several times, as Derek kept reiterating his need for the figures. Anthea, not one to encourage democratic comment, simply ignored them and, raising her voice slightly, brought the meeting to order.

"What we have to do," she said firmly, "is to consider all possible ways of raising our share of the money — whatever," she said, glancing sternly at Maureen, "that may be. Now, I do hope all of you have come armed with some original ideas."

As usual, after such a request, there was dead silence all round the table.

"Well, come along," Anthea said impatiently. "Surely *somebody's* done some thinking and come up with something."

Gradually the usual suggestions emerged: raffles, auctions, bring and buy sales, sponsored walks, a concert. All such ideas were tentatively proposed by one member and promptly disparaged by the rest.

"This is getting us nowhere," Anthea said. "Sheila, you haven't said anything yet. Surely you've got some suggestion to make!"

"Well," I said, "why don't we simply ask for donations? People will usually give you something if you ask them directly, and I'm sure we'd make just as much money that way."

There was a brief moment's shocked

silence at this revolutionary idea, and then Anthea said scathingly, "Well, really, if you're just going to make silly suggestions like that . . ."

"Why don't we have a break for a cup of tea?" Maureen suggested. "I'll just go and put the kettle on."

She went off into the kitchen, closely followed by Derek's wife, Edna, a reluctant member of the committee who only ever came to the meetings to make sure Derek wasn't going to be put upon (her words) by Anthea. While we were having our tea, people broke up into little groups and I went over to talk to Derek.

"Derek," I said, "have you ever come across a man called Dan Webster?"

His expression changed from its usual bland amiability to a positive scowl.

"Yes, I have," he said, "and I hope he's not a friend of yours because a nastier piece of work I've yet to meet."

"No," I said hastily, "certainly not. In fact I think he's trying to put pressure on a friend and I'm rather worried."

"Putting pressure on people is something he does all the time," Derek said. "That place of his up at Upper Barton, now that's a case in point."

"Really?"

"Yes. It belonged to elderly friends of mine, and when Edgar died last year we all wondered what Margaret — that's his wife — would do. It was much too big for her and really, to be honest, needed a lot done to it. But this Webster man heard about it and badgered her to sell it to him. Now, there was no need for her to make a big decision like that straightaway — at a time like that when she was still grieving. But he kept on at her; said she wouldn't get a good price for it because of all the work it needed; hassled her until she gave in. Unfortunately, we were away just then, visiting our son in Canada, and when her nephew up in Doncaster — they didn't have any children — got to hear about it, it was too late. Webster paid a fair price, but it was the way he went about it that made us so mad."

"They say he always gets what he wants," I said, "somehow or other."

"Like I said, nasty piece of work. There was another thing too."

"Really?"

"I didn't deal with it myself, but a colleague of mine said that he bought a big old house just outside Taunton. It was very run-down and would have taken a fortune to put right. Anyway, Webster applied for permission to pull it down, but it was a grade two–listed building, so he didn't get it. Then it started to get vandalized — I wouldn't have put it past him to have organized that — and then there was a fire. The whole house wasn't burnt down, but there was a lot of damage. That's when my colleague was involved over the insurance. Finally it got into such a state that it was downright dangerous and *had* to be pulled down, which, of course, is what he'd wanted in the first place."

"You think he arranged the whole thing?" I asked.

"Well, let's say I think he helped things along. Nothing could be proved, of course. People like Webster are good at covering their tracks."

"I can imagine. So what happened?"

"There was quite a bit of land with the house, so he had some plans drawn up with a couple of starter homes as a sop to the council and built half a dozen fair-sized houses on the site."

"And made a great deal of money?"

"Exactly. So tell your friend to be careful."

Anthea, who'd been getting restless at the prolonged tea-drinking, made efforts to chivy us all back to the meeting, but George looked at his watch and said he had to be going, and several other people said they had to go too. Anthea was engaged in some sort of argument with Maureen ("For goodness' sake, the proportion doesn't *matter!*"), so I took the opportunity to slip away while her back was turned.

I hadn't had an opportunity to talk to Rosemary about Simon, but when I ran into her at the garden center, it seemed like a good moment.

"I've found these gorgeous hellebores," she said. "Wonderful, *sinister* colors they'll have, and, although I usually have a malign effect on practically everything I plant, I really couldn't resist. How about you? Have you found anything?"

"Not really. I just wanted some more heathers to fill in the gaps on that bank by the gate. It's always nice to have something blooming in the winter. Actually, have you got time for a coffee? There's something I want to talk to you about."

"There's nothing special I should be doing and they do rather nice Danish pastries in the café here."

When we were sitting down Rosemary said, "So, what is it?"

"Have you seen anything of Simon lately?" I asked.

"I saw him last weekend when I went to collect Delia from the stables — she practically *lives* there now — and he was there then."

"He does spend a lot of time up there now."

"Well, he is a part owner and they do need his help — not just at weekends either."

"You haven't found out," I asked, "if he's had any thoughts about working at the stables full-time?"

"Well, I did sort of broach the subject when I saw him, but he just said he didn't think they could afford for him to take a salary out of the business, so he felt he had to soldier on with the accountancy."

"Such a pity," I said.

"Well, I suppose the money from his proper job does help, though he and Liz do seem to have some really good ideas about expanding the business. They seem to be getting on really well. I sometimes wonder. . . ."

"Oh, she's obviously deeply devoted to him," I said, and I told her what Vicky had said.

"It's the right idea," Rosemary agreed, "if for the wrong reason — *typical* Vicky — and it would be perfect for both of them. Just what Simon needs, a nice girl looking up to him and thinking he's marvelous."

I smiled. "She certainly does that all right. But there's something else I'm really worried about." I explained what Michael had said about the change of use of the land around the stables and what Derek had told me about Dan Webster. "If he wants to develop that land — and I'm sure he's got his eye on it — he'll keep on at Simon. He's such a *strong* character and could be really threatening. I don't know if Simon can stand up to him."

"Simon cared so much for Jo and Charlie," Rosemary said, "he couldn't betray them like that."

"Well, Thea said Simon was very upset when she saw him just after Dan Webster had been there, and Derek said Webster was the sort of man who always got what he wanted. I'm afraid he's just going to *hound* poor Simon until he gives in."

"Not," Rosemary said firmly, "if we all stand by him and buoy him up. I'll have a word with Jack. I know Simon respects his advice."

"And I'll get Michael to see if there's anything in the will that might stop him selling," I said.

"Cheer up," Rosemary said. "I'm sure that all of us together will be a match for Dan

Webster! Meanwhile," she went on, "I'll keep an eye on Liz and Simon and see if I can promote *that* little affair. A Christmas wedding would be nice."

"There are times, Rosemary Dudley," I said, "when you remind me irresistibly of your mother."

CHAPTER SEVENTEEN

I'd been having Sunday lunch with Michael and Thea and, while Thea and Alice were outside seeing to the chickens, I took the opportunity to have a word with Michael. I told him how worried I was about Dan Webster and asked him if there was anything in Jo's will that might prevent Simon's selling the land.

"No, it was left to him absolutely," Michael said. "It would have been unusual for her to have done anything else."

"It's just that I think the Webster man had been trying to get Jo to sell and she might have wanted to make sure that Simon couldn't."

"But the change of use has only just been granted," Michael said, "so there'd have been no point in his trying to buy the land then, before Jo died."

"But, just suppose," I said, "that Webster had got wind of the council's decision, before it was made public; he'd have been one step ahead of anyone else."

"Well, yes, but . . ."

"And Dan Webster was hand in glove with Gordon, who was on the planning committee, so it's not impossible that he *did* know what was going to happen."

"I'm sure that's slanderous," Michael said. "Promise me you won't go around saying things like that!"

"No, really. If you think about it, Webster might have been acting with Gordon — a sort of front man because Gordon couldn't be seen to be profiting from a council decision. And then Gordon died, so Webster was able to have the whole scheme to himself. That's probably when he started to try to put the pressure on Jo. But *she* wasn't having it."

"So?"

"So, it was probably obvious that Jo would leave the stables and land to Simon, who Webster would think was an easy target."

"So?"

"*So,* perhaps Webster killed her."

"Oh, for goodness' sake, Ma," Michael said, "I thought you'd given up the idea of it being murder, after the inquest and after everything the coroner said."

"Mrs. Dudley doesn't think Marcus Barrington is competent," I said provocatively. "She said she wouldn't trust his judgment on any legal matter."

"Oh really . . ."

"She said he was no more use than a chocolate fireguard."

"What!"

"I know. Apparently she's taken to picking up the latest colloquialisms from Delia."

"Good heavens."

"But seriously, it isn't *that* far-fetched. Webster's well-known for getting what he wants at any cost. It would have been quite easy. There's often no one in the office, especially when the rides are out, and he's been around the stables quite a lot with all the business about that horse."

"No, Ma," Michael said firmly, "I refuse to consider any of that and I strongly advise you to forget all about it."

I couldn't argue anymore because Alice came rushing in with a basket.

"Gran, do look. I've been collecting the eggs and there are some here for you!"

"Gently, Alice," Thea said, "or you'll break them. Only three today — they're starting to go off lay, but do have them. I'll go and find an egg box for them."

But as I took my eggs home I was still turning over in my mind the possibility that

Dan Webster might have had something to do with Jo's death, though, for the moment at least, I didn't see any way of proving it.

I saw Roger a few days later at a concert at Brunswick Lodge. Anthea was mercifully having one of her feuds with Wendy Parker, who organizes them and was pointedly absent, so I didn't have to spend my time avoiding her and could concentrate on talking to Roger in the interval.

"I suppose the police aren't taking any more action about Jo's death," I said.

"Not after the inquest," Roger said. "That made it pretty clear it was an accident."

"And everybody's happy that it was?" I asked tentatively.

Roger looked at me sternly. "Now Sheila, don't try to make something out of nothing, just so you'll have something to worry away at!"

"No, no," I said hastily. "I suppose it's just having two accidents in the same place, one so soon after another."

"Just two tragic accidents," Roger said. "And in a place like a stable, especially with temperamental horses around, there's always a chance of something like that. As for poor Jo's death, well, that was obviously an accident waiting to happen."

"I suppose so. And Inspector Morris is quite satisfied?"

"Yes," Roger said firmly, "quite satisfied. Now, do you want another glass of this rather thin red wine or shall we get back to our seats? I'm looking forward to the Schumann. You don't very often have a chance to hear it."

Faced with such a determined effort to close the subject, I hardly felt it was possible to introduce my suspicions of Dan Webster. All through the rest of the concert I was turning over in my mind how I could find *something* that might back up my suspicions. But I realized, in the light of our conversation, that it would have to be something really conclusive to persuade Roger (and Bob Morris) to take me seriously.

The maddening thing about supermarkets is the way that, just when you think you know where everything is, they immediately move things around. Our local branch had recently had a refit (presumably for their convenience since it obviously wasn't for ours), and I was trying to discover where they'd put the olive oil, when someone behind me said wearily, "I don't suppose you've come across the cheese biscuits anywhere?"

I turned round and found that it was Eileen Butler, an old friend.

"Hello," I said. "How are you? It's been ages since I saw you."

"Oh, soldiering on. You know how it is. It's been a busy time of the year and I'm only just getting back to normal."

Eileen is married to a farmer, whose fields adjoin those belonging to the stables.

"Of course, you do farm holidays, don't you?"

"Well, you have to do something these days, farming being how it is."

"It must be hard work."

"It's not bad, but you have to be around all the time. I did want to get to poor Jo Hamilton's funeral — that was a dreadful thing — but we had some people coming in that day, so I couldn't get away."

"Yes, it was a terrible shock, especially so soon after Charlie's death."

"They were good neighbors and good friends. We'll miss them."

"I'm sure you'll get along with Jo's nephew, Simon, who's taken over the stables. Do you know him?"

"We've seen him around for years, off and on, and had the occasional chat. He seems a pleasant young man. As a matter of fact,

Will's been meaning to go over there and have a talk with him about something."

"Really?"

She hesitated for a moment, and then she said, "How well do you know him? It's a rather delicate matter and I know Will's worried about how he might react."

"Oh, Simon's a thoroughly nice person," I said. "I'm sure he'll be helpful if there's a problem."

"Will's had an offer for some of his fields. There's been some sort of new planning thing that means the land can be built on."

"Was the offer made by someone called Dan Webster?" I asked.

Eileen looked at me in surprise. "Yes, as a matter of fact it was. Do you know him?"

"Only by sight, but I've been hearing a lot about him lately." I hesitated. "So, how does Will feel about selling?"

"Oh no, he wouldn't hear of it. Said his mind was made up, even though this Webster man was very persistent and kept telephoning and coming round to the farm."

"Good for Will."

"Ours isn't a very big farm, as you know, and we couldn't afford to lose that many fields and still carry on. It's not so much Will — though it's always been his life and he does get a bit depressed at how things are going — but it's for the boys. Well, for Johnny; Craig's off to Bristol, working as a surveyor. But Johnny's never wanted to do anything else, ever since he was a toddler, following Will around the farm and riding in the cab of the tractor. He's wonderful with the animals. We still have a few beef cattle and some sheep; visitors like to see animals around the place when they're staying. No, Will would never agree to selling any of the land, even though this man offered a very fancy price."

"I can imagine."

"And, anyway, we wouldn't want a lot of houses or goodness knows what right next to us."

"No, I can see that."

"But we're wondering what Simon's going to do. I mean, Dan Webster's sure to have made him an offer and, well, if he accepts, then where will the houses be built? I mean, it'll be very awkward if they're right up against our fields."

"It would certainly affect your farm holidays," I said, "as well as everything else."

"That's right." She looked at me inquiringly. "So what do you think Simon's likely to do?"

"I'm sure he wouldn't want to sell," I said, "but, of course, I don't know the circumstances. He's only just taken over the stables, after all, so I suppose he's still finding his feet there."

Eileen nodded. "I can see that. Oh well, we'll just have to see what he says to Will."

"I do hope it all works out for you," I said. "I'd hate to think of that man getting his hands on any of that land."

"What have you heard about him?"

"Just that he's a bully who likes to get his own way — a few things like that. I'm so glad Will is standing up to him."

I told Rosemary about my talk with Eileen.

"Well, good for them," she said. "Jack hasn't had a chance to speak to Simon yet, but I really can't believe he would ever sell those fields. I mean, from a practical point of view, apart from anything else, they need them for the horses. Grazing's expensive, and if they mean to expand . . ."

"Exactly. I'm sure it'll be all right. Besides," I added as a sudden thought struck me, "Simon must have inherited something from Gordon. There was a lot of money there and surely he won't have left everything to Esther."

"I think," Rosemary said, "he set up trusts for Vicky and for Simon, tying up the money somehow."

"Typical!" I said. "Making things difficult. For goodness' sake, they're not children, not even particularly young now. Just when Simon could use that money for the stables."

"I suppose," Rosemary said thoughtfully, "Gordon did it so that Simon couldn't give up accountancy."

"Imposing his wishes from beyond the grave! Can't Simon break the trust somehow?"

"I don't know. It probably hasn't occurred to him to try. You know how oppressed he was by his father."

"He might borrow from the bank against his expectations," I said. "I must ask Michael if that's possible."

"Talking of Simon and Gordon," Rosemary said, "have you seen Esther lately?"

"No, not for quite a while, which is odd, really, because I was forever running into her. How about you?"

"Well, yes I did. I saw her in the chemist — I wanted one of those heat patches for Jack's bad back, but, of course, he'll never use it — and I thought she looked very strained."

"Strained?"

"You know, sort of tense and anxious."

"Did you speak to her?"

"Very briefly; she didn't seem to want to talk."

"*That's* not like her!"

"Exactly. No, I asked her how she was, but, instead of going on like she usually does, she just said she was quite well and that was more or less that. It was even odder because I saw she'd been collecting some sort of medication, and you know how she loves telling you every last detail about any sort of illness she has."

"Very odd."

"I did ask her to come round for coffee one morning, but she said she was rather busy just now, and that's not like her either."

"I suppose she's still getting over Gordon's death," I said. "It wasn't that long ago and it must have hit her very hard."

Strangely enough I ran into Esther the very next day. I'd gone down to the harbor, as I often do after I've finished the shopping, and I was sitting in the car, looking at a large container ship making its way slowly up the Bristol Channel, when I saw a figure leaning on the seawall. For a moment I didn't recognize her because it was the last place I'd have expected to see Esther, but there was no doubt it was her. On an impulse I got out of the car and went towards her.

"Hello," I said brightly. "Fancy seeing you here."

She turned and looked at me blankly for a moment and then said, "I wanted some peace and quiet."

"Oh, I'm sorry," I said hastily, and moved as if to go away. Then I stopped and said, "Esther, are you all right?"

Again the blank stare, and then, "I can't sleep. They've given me some tablets but they don't work. Or if I do sleep I have bad dreams."

"What sort of bad dreams?" I asked.

"About her."

"Her?"

"Jo. I can't get it out of my head."

"What is it?"

"Jo and Gordon. Just before he died . . ." Her voice trailed away.

"Surely not," I said.

"Oh yes, it's true. I followed him — to the stables."

"He did occasionally go up there," I said, "something to do with his friend Dan Webster's horse."

"Not the stables, her house. Several times."

"I'm sure there was a perfectly simple explanation."

259

She gave a bitter laugh. "Oh yes. She'd lost Charlie, so she wanted Gordon back."

"Look, Esther, I'm sure you've got it wrong. Jo wouldn't . . ."

"You don't know her like I do. She always wanted everything, even things I had that she didn't really want."

I shook my head. "I can't believe it," I said. "And, Gordon . . ."

"It wasn't his fault," Esther said quickly. "She had this hold over him, like she always did. Like she did in the old days. Just had to lift her little finger and he went running — every man did."

"Gordon married you," I said, "and you had two lovely children."

"And she took Simon away. All the time up at those stables, hardly ever at home, doing things for her. She was jealous because she didn't have any children, so she took Simon. Not Vicky though. Vicky saw through her," she said. "She knew what Jo was up to; she wasn't taken in."

Her voice rose sharply and a man walking his dog turned and looked at us curiously. I was worried about her. She was obviously in a bad state and I wondered how I was going to get her home.

"Gordon, poor Gordon," she went on. "He didn't know what he was doing." She looked at me pleadingly. "He did love me; he really did. But it was the same, just like it used to be; he couldn't help himself. Only *then* she went away. She wasn't going anywhere this time."

"Esther," I said, coaxing her, "don't you think you ought to go home? It's getting cold. There's quite a wind now."

She ignored me and stood looking out at the dull gray water. Then she said, quietly, almost resignedly, "I hated her. I've always hated her. I'm really glad she's dead."

CHAPTER EIGHTEEN

For a moment I was silent. There didn't seem anything I could say.

"I was always second best," she went on in that same, quiet tone, "for Gordon and for Simon. I was used to that, I suppose, but then, after all those years, when I thought I was safe, she took him back. She won — just like she always did."

"No, really Esther," I said, "I'm sure you've got it wrong. Gordon may have gone to see Jo, but I think it was something to do with some land he wanted her to sell."

She ignored me; it was as if I hadn't spoken. "She could always make people do what she wanted. Everyone was fooled by that manner of hers, but I knew. . . ."

Realizing that it was useless to argue with her, I concentrated on trying to get her home.

"Is your car here, or did you walk?" I asked.

That mundane question seemed to rouse her a little and she said, "I think I walked — yes, I wanted to get out of the house, to get some fresh air."

"Well, look, my car's just over there. Let me drive you home. I think it might be going to rain. The wind's getting up too. Look, the sea's quite choppy."

Talking at random I managed to lead her over to the car and got her in. As we drove back she was silent and seemed quite passive. At the house I helped her take off her coat and persuaded her to stay in the sitting room while I went out to the kitchen to put the kettle on. While I was waiting for it to boil, I rang Simon on my mobile.

"Can you possibly get away and come home? Your mother's not well — I found her down by the harbor — she's very upset. I've got her home, but I don't like to leave her alone."

I made the tea and went back to find that Esther was sitting just as I'd left her. She drank her tea like an obedient child and we sat in silence for a while until, to my great relief, I heard Simon arrive. I went out into the hall and drew him to one side.

"I think she's having some kind of a breakdown. She was saying all sorts of wild things about your father and Jo. Really agitated. She's quiet now, but I didn't know what to do. Perhaps she should see a doctor?"

He nodded. "Yes, I think it's come to that. She's been like this several times since Father died and I did hope she'd get over it as time went on. Perhaps she should have professional help. But I can cope for the moment. Anyway, thank you, Sheila. I'm really grateful for all you've done."

We went into the sitting room and I said brightly, "Well, I'll be off now. Simon's here. I expect he'd like a cup of tea too."

She turned her head and gave me a vague smile. "It was nice to see you, Sheila. Do call in again when you're passing."

When I got home I felt I needed something stronger than tea, so I had a glass of sherry before making myself some lunch. I was still attempting to think through what Esther had said, but the animals chose to be difficult, wanting to be let out and then, almost immediately, in again, demanding extra food and attention, and making it impossible for me to concentrate on anything. I was just, finally, sitting down with a ham sandwich when the telephone rang. It was Simon.

"I thought I'd just let you know that I've got her to go and lie down for a bit," he said. "She wouldn't have any lunch, but I thought that if she managed to have a little sleep, she might be more herself when she woke up."

"She said she hadn't been sleeping," I said. "Perhaps that's part of the trouble."

"Dr. Macdonald prescribed some sleeping tablets, but she said they made things worse and stopped taking them."

"She told me they gave her nightmares," I said. "About Jo."

He sighed. "Oh dear, it's so difficult. She has this stupid idea, about Jo and Father. There's nothing in it, of course," he added hastily.

"No, of course not," I agreed, "but it seems like an obsession with her."

"Yes. And you're right. She does need some sort of professional help. That is, if she'll take it. Anyway, I'll ask Dr. Macdonald what he thinks. He'll know whom to consult."

"That's the best thing. You've got enough on your shoulders just now. Can't Vicky help?"

"Well, you know how difficult it is for her, being a freelance and so forth."

"I don't see why you should bear all the burden yourself," I said sharply.

"I'll have to consult her anyway," he said,

"before I make any arrangements for Mother. But I wanted to thank you again for looking after her. She hasn't gone wandering like that before. I'll somehow have to try to keep an eye on her."

"If there's anything I can do," I said, "you only have to ask."

"Bless you, Sheila. I'm so grateful." He paused. "I'd rather people didn't know. . . ."

"Of course not," I said. "I quite understand."

The thing that was uppermost in my mind, as I finally got to eat my sandwich, was the fact that Esther had followed Gordon. It seemed to show the sort of initiative — if that's what you could call it — that I hadn't expected of her. And if she'd always been resentful of Jo and the fact that Gordon had taken her as second best and had lived with that all these years, what, I wondered, had suddenly brought her to the point of this kind of obsessive jealousy? What had sparked it off? The fact of Charlie's death perhaps left Jo available again; but was that enough?

Tris's bark and a ring at the door interrupted these thoughts. It was Rosemary.

"Sorry to drop in, but Delia's got an hour's ride and it didn't seem worth going all the way home and then coming back

266

again, so I thought I'd come and beg a cup of tea from you." She looked at me critically. "Are you all right? You look sort of confused and woolly. Is anything the matter?"

Rosemary and I always tell each other everything, and, anyway, Rosemary is Esther's friend too, so, as we went into the kitchen, I told her what had happened.

"Oh, poor Esther. It sounds as if she's really breaking up."

"She was fairly odd and emotional when I went to see her just before Gordon's funeral," I said. "But this is much worse."

"And all that stuff about Jo," Rosemary said. "She must have been brooding about it for years."

"I know. That's what's puzzled me. What made her suddenly do something as bizarre as following Gordon?"

"Well, perhaps she overheard part of a phone call — something like that — and got the wrong idea. I mean, any sort of connection between Jo and Gordon would have been enough."

"That's true," I said, pouring the tea. "Poor Esther, always trying to compete with Jo and knowing how impossible it was. I suppose that's why she made herself a sort of slave to Gordon. Whatever he wanted always came first; everything he did was always perfect. Remember how she used to go on about him?"

"Dreadfully sad, really. But really awful now. I think I prefer Esther being irritating rather than Esther being pathetic."

"I suppose Gordon was trying to bully Jo into selling that land. That would be why he went up to the house rather than seeing her at the stables. Well, I'm sure he — and Dan Webster — got nothing out of Jo. I did try to tell Esther about it, but she didn't want to hear; she was so obsessed with her own theory."

"I do hope Simon can get some sort of help for her," Rosemary said. "It must be such a worry for him."

"He said he'd have to consult Vicky first. I do hope she doesn't cause any difficulties. After all, she's not around; Simon will have to cope with it all."

"Some sort of psychiatric help, I suppose," Rosemary said thoughtfully. "Vicky would have to agree."

"Do you think actually psychiatric?" I asked.

"Or possibly counseling — whatever that means nowadays. But she is obviously getting worse."

"Do you think," I said slowly, "with all

that hate she had for Jo, she might have tried to do something to — well, to harm her?"

"You mean," Rosemary said bluntly, "did she kill her?"

"Well, yes."

"Are you still thinking it wasn't an accident?"

"You must admit it's a possibility."

"But Esther! Totally out of character!"

"Well, she did creep about following Gordon. You must admit that was out of character too."

"Yes, but . . ."

"And, after Gordon died, when she was in that funny sort of mood, she could easily have found some excuse for going up there, and you know how that office is left empty half the time with people out taking lessons or rides."

"It still doesn't sound like Esther to me."

"And," I said, "she didn't go to Jo's funeral."

"Well, nor did you," Rosemary said, "and you didn't kill Jo. She was ill like you."

"She could have pretended to be ill; it wouldn't have been difficult. Simon, and even Vicky, knew she'd been acting a bit strangely. They'd have been quite glad she didn't go."

"No really," Rosemary said, "I know you

always like to find mysteries in everything, but I honestly don't believe that Esther killed Jo — or that anyone did for that matter."

"Oh well, perhaps you're right," I said reluctantly.

Rosemary looked at her watch. "I'd better get going. Though Delia wouldn't care if I never turned up."

"Do you mind if I come with you?" I asked. "I'd rather like to have an excuse for seeing how things are at the stables. You can drop me off at the end of the lane on your way back."

As we were approaching the stables I saw a familiar Mitsubishi driving away.

"That's Dan Webster," I said, craning my neck to make sure who the driver was. "I suppose he's been up here to persecute Simon again about selling those fields."

"Simon's no more likely to sell than Jo was," Rosemary said confidently.

Delia wasn't back yet, so I followed Rosemary into the office when she went to pay for the ride. Simon was sitting at the desk, studying some papers. He looked up when we went in.

"Hello, Sheila," he said, looking surprised at seeing me and obviously feeling that some explanation was needed for his presence at the stables during office hours. "I thought I might as well come up here; it was a bit late to go back to the office. But I got Mother settled all right before I left."

"That's good," I said.

"Simon," Rosemary broke in, "was Dan Webster up here trying to make you sell him those fields?"

"Dan Webster?" he said, rather taken aback by her tone. "Well, yes, as a matter of fact he was."

"And you're not selling?"

"No. No, of course not. I've told him so."

"He was round at the Butlers'," I said, "bullying them. But they're standing firm."

"Yes, I know," Simon said. "Will came here yesterday to tell me all about it. He was offering them fantastic prices."

"And he'd make fantastic profits," I said, "if he could get hold of this land for development now that there's this change-of-use thing from the council."

"He'd need planning permission," he said.

"Well, I don't think *that* would be a problem for Dan Webster," I said. "He's bound to have a councilor or two in his pocket — he's that sort of man." I stopped suddenly. "I'm sorry, Simon," I said. "I'd forgotten he was a sort of business partner of your father."

Simon smiled ruefully. "I'm quite aware of the sort of dealings my father was involved in," he said, "and I know what the general opinion of him was."

"Well, anyway," Rosemary said impatiently, "as long as neither you nor Will Butler will sell, the Webster man will have to look elsewhere for his nasty little schemes."

"I think it was really noble of the Butlers to hold out," I said. "They're terribly stretched financially and the sort of money he must have offered would have been a lifesaver for them. Thank goodness there are still people like them."

"And Simon, too," Rosemary said, smiling at him. "A hefty cash injection would have been very useful here at the stables. But you held out."

"Well," he said, shuffling the papers on his desk together and putting them away in a drawer, "even if I'd been tempted, I couldn't let Jo down. She'd never have sold."

"Well done, Simon," Rosemary said. "And speaking of money, here's what I owe you for Delia's ride. We'd better go and see if she's back yet."

When we got outside, the riders were

back, but there was no sign of Delia.

"She's probably in the yard helping Liz and Peggy," Rosemary said. "I'd better go and root her out."

"Just before you go," I said, "what did you think of Simon, just now?"

"Simon? What do you mean?"

"Didn't you think he looked a bit uneasy?"

"Well, he looked tired, poor boy, but he's had quite a day, what with his mother going walk-about and then Dan Webster. . . ."

"Yes, I know, but did you think he sounded quite *sure* about Webster? I'm sure he's not thinking of selling," I said hastily, as I could see Rosemary rushing to the defense of her favorite, "but I got the impression that there was something about the affair he wasn't telling us. Something about his father, perhaps."

"That wouldn't surprise me."

"Well, you know, it's always been possible that since Gordon knew about this change of use long before it was made public, he could easily have told Webster about it so that they could make a nice little deal together."

"Probably."

"And, of course, that's what Gordon was going to see Jo about when Esther followed him."

"That's the thing that really gets me!" Rosemary said. "Esther of all people! How do you think she did it without Gordon knowing? I mean, she's not exactly my idea of a private eye."

"Well, I suppose he'd have said he was going to a council meeting and she'd have been suspicious, and when he drove off she got in her car and followed him. If he didn't go in the direction of the council offices but turned the other way, she'd know he was going to Jo's, so she could follow at a distance, if you see what I mean."

"I suppose so," Rosemary said grudgingly. "But it all sounds too clever for Esther!"

"I daresay when you're as jealous and obsessed as she was, you can do anything, however out of character it might seem. Anyway, after Gordon died, then Webster took over and tried to persuade Jo to sell, and when *she* died, Webster probably thought Simon would be easier to persuade. In fact . . ."

"No, Sheila. Not back to *your* obsession. Jo's death was an accident, whether it was more convenient for Dan Webster or not."

"Possibly."

I would have argued the point more fully, but Delia suddenly emerged from the stable yard and Rosemary seized the opportunity

274

to hustle her into the car, where she held forth from the backseat.

"Gran, do you know, Peggy says I should be able to enter next year's Golden Horseshoes competition. I'll be old enough then. Only the ten-mile ride — or perhaps the fifteen if the going's good. So, will you sponsor me? Most people give a pound a mile. And would you sponsor me too, Mrs. Malory? And you could bring Alice to one of the checkpoints to see me. I'm sure she'd like that. It's very exciting. Of course, she won't be able to do it for years, but it would be good for her to see how it's done. This year, of course, it poured with rain and they had to cancel part of the course. Only a few people managed the thirty-five-mile course, but they were mostly sponsored by professional firms and things, which isn't really fair, is it?"

I escaped from this flow of information as Rosemary dropped me off at the end of my lane. As I walked back to the house I tried to remember what had made me think that Simon had been holding something back from us. There was nothing I could put my finger on, just the feeling that he was uneasy talking about it, a vague thought that there was something else. . . . I opened the front door and in the general coming and going, in and out, of the animals I lost track of the thought, whatever it was.

Chapter Nineteen

I'd fallen into a sort of postlunch doze, something that seems to happen to me more and more, when I was woken by the insistent ringing of the phone. I picked it up and heard Anthea's agitated voice.

"It's dreadful news," she said, "absolutely dreadful!"

"What is?" I asked, still only half awake and not yet capable of taking in any news, however dreadful.

"The lottery grant," Anthea said impatiently. "They've turned us down!"

"I'm sorry," I said inadequately.

"After all our hard work on the application — and Derek had lined up two independent referees as well for the next stage — it's really heartbreaking."

"How awful. Did they say why they've refused?"

"Oh, some bureaucratic nonsense — I couldn't be bothered with it. Of course," she went on, lowering her voice, "it's because we're not an inner city, not *deprived.* I know how these things work."

"Oh, I'm sure it's nothing like that," I said.

"Anyway," Anthea went on, "we're not giving up."

"But if . . ."

"We'll raise the money ourselves. After all, it's very necessary." She went into her usual getting-things-done mode and I listened with only half an ear. "Vital work . . . Health and Safety regulations . . . all pull together . . . committee meeting . . ." I came to abruptly when I heard her say sharply, "Well, Sheila, *can* you manage next Friday?"

"Oh," I said hastily, "I'm not sure. I'll look it up on the calendar and let you know."

"Very well," she said grudgingly. "And do you agree?"

"Agree?"

"About my idea for a sponsored walk. People raise thousands for them!"

"Well, yes, but for important things like cancer research, not for rewiring an old building."

"I can't imagine why you think making the wiring safe isn't important," Anthea said severely. "I'd have thought that considering what happened to poor Jo Hamilton — after all, she was a friend of yours — you'd be as

278

anxious as I am to get it done!"

"Of course I am, but . . ."

"And all the committee will take part. We must set an example."

"I don't know how long the walk's going to be," I said, "but I'm afraid my knee can't manage more than a couple of hundred yards nowadays."

She made an exclamation of annoyance. "Oh well, you'll have to be a steward then; they stand about at intervals round the course with bottles of water, timing people. We'll arrange all that next Friday. The important thing is to get things moving."

"Yes . . ."

"I'm glad we've sorted things out. I'll get onto Maureen now and tell her that you agree with me that the sponsored walk is the best way to go. I'll get back to you when I know what she thinks. Good-bye."

"For heaven's sake — a sponsored *walk!*" I said as I put down the phone. Tris, who'd been lying peacefully in front of the electric fire, heard the last word and raised his head, looking hopeful, and then collapsed back again as I sat down on the sofa. Foss, now occupying my armchair, opened one eye, curled his tail round his nose and went back to sleep. I was thoroughly irritated by Anthea, and finding that my after-lunch coffee was now stone cold was the last straw. I slumped back on the sofa, knowing there were a thousand things I ought to be doing in the house and garden, but not feeling like doing any of them.

The phone's ringing again increased my irritation. For a moment I let it ring, sure it was Anthea getting back to me, but habit is strong and I've never been able *not* to answer the phone when it rings. I picked it up and said a cross "Hello." But it wasn't Anthea; it was Rosemary and she sounded upset.

"Oh, Sheila, I'm so glad you're in. I need to speak to you, but not on the phone. Could you come round?"

"Now?"

"Please."

"What is it?"

"I'll tell you when you come."

She rang off and I replaced my receiver slowly, wondering what on earth it was all about. As I drove round there, I considered the various possibilities from something awful happening to one of the family (God forbid) to Mrs. Dudley being more intransigent than usual. By the time I got there I was really worried.

"What on earth's happened?" I demanded as Rosemary opened the door. "Is it one of the children?"

"No, nothing like that, but I didn't want to talk about it over the phone. Come on in and I'll put the kettle on."

Reassured by this, I followed Rosemary into the kitchen and sat down at the table while she filled the kettle.

"So, what on earth is it?"

"It's Simon."

"Simon? What's happened?"

"Well, you know Martin Krieger — Jack plays golf with him."

"I've met him once or twice. Some sort of high-powered businessman."

"That's the one. I don't know exactly what his business is, something to do with exports, but anyway, whatever it is, he has to entertain a lot of his overseas customers. What they mostly like to do is go to that rather plushy casino in Taunton."

"So?"

"So he's seen Simon there a couple of times."

"It can't be. He must have made a mistake."

"No, he knows Simon quite well — Simon's firm does his audit." Rosemary poured a cup of tea and pushed a plate of biscuits towards me. "The thing is," she went on, "he said Simon was on his own each time and was — what was the phrase he used? — 'worryingly absorbed in the play.' So much so that he didn't see Martin. After the first time Martin kept an eye on him and saw that, though he did win occasionally, he went on gambling until everything was gone."

"How awful. When was this?"

"A while ago, before Jo died."

"So do you think it's serious?"

"Well, you know how fond Jack is of Simon — we both are — so he asked him to lunch and had it out with him."

"What did Simon say? Did he admit it?"

"At first he said he's only been once or twice, just to see what it was like. But after Jack pressed him, he more or less broke down and came out with the whole story. Apparently it started by chance when he logged on to some sort of poker thing on the Internet."

"I've heard about that," I said. "There was quite a bit about it in the papers a few weeks ago."

"That was just the beginning. He got really hooked, playing this wretched thing every night."

"Goodness, yes. I remember Esther saying he was up till all hours on his computer, but she thought it was work he'd brought home."

"Anyway," Rosemary said, "he started to go to this casino in Taunton, and casinos in London too when he went up to stay with Vicky."

"*Not* just wandering around London looking at things!" I said.

"Exactly."

"But the money?"

"Well, of course, he was dreadfully in debt — both credit cards to the limit and a loan from one of those companies — you know the ones that advertise."

"*Stupid* boy! So what did he do?"

"Apparently Jo came to his rescue. She lent him — gave really — enough to clear his debts on the understanding that he'd go to this Gamblers Anonymous place, and he said he would."

"And has he?"

"He says he has." She poured us both another cup of tea. "But Jack says he's not sure Simon's really given up gambling. He said he felt Simon was evasive — nothing you could put your finger on, but . . ."

"I know. That's what I felt when we asked him about Dan Webster — you remember — just a sort of *feeling*."

"Yes, you said. But we really don't know

what to do now. Jack says we can't go on persecuting the boy about it; otherwise he'll never tell us anything. But we can't just stand by and let him make a real mess of his life."

"It was really splendid of Jo," I said, "to bail him out like that. Especially when money was pretty tight."

"She had something of her own, and" — Rosemary hesitated for a moment — "and she gave him the money from Charlie's life insurance."

"Good heavens!"

"I know."

"That's quite something!"

"Well, that's what you do for your child," Rosemary said, "and Simon was the nearest thing she had to a child of her own. But I expect it's made the situation at the stables even more difficult."

"And that's another reason why Simon's got to pull himself together and make a go of things there. He owes that to Jo."

"That's what Jack told him."

"But of course," I said slowly, "if he *hasn't* given up and is in debt again, then perhaps he might be considering Webster's offer."

"Oh don't! I keep thinking of that. He couldn't — could he?"

"I suppose it depends how deeply he's in

debt. He might be really desperate and there's no one else to bail him out this time."

"What about the money Gordon left him and Vicky?"

"I don't know how easy it would be to break the trust. And, anyway, it would probably take ages and it would depend whom he's in debt *to.*"

"You mean it might be someone . . . ?"

"Well, you do hear such awful things when people get mixed up in gambling and I don't think it just happens in television plays!"

"Oh don't!"

"I can't think of any way we can find out if he's still gambling, can you?"

"Actually, I can. I'll ask him."

"But Jack said . . ."

"Yes, but it would be different if I asked, not so *formal,* if you see what I mean."

"True. Yes," I went on, warming to the idea, "I think Simon's a bit nervous of men — even Jack. Something to do with his father, I expect. But he would respond to you. Now that Jo's gone, you are the one he'd turn to."

"Right, then," Rosemary said with sudden resolution. "Delia's got a two-hour ride tomorrow. I'll tell Jilly I'll take her to the stables. Two hours — longer if Delia starts cleaning the tack — should be long enough to have a proper talk." She leaned back in her chair and sighed. "Oh dear, *what* a mess. Why can't people lead straightforward lives!"

"If he is in debt," I said, "what will you and Jack do about it?"

"I don't know. Help somehow, I suppose — a proper loan, perhaps. Jack will know. The important thing is to find out exactly what's happened."

When I got home I was quite exhausted. What with one thing and another it had been a peculiar day. Above all there was the awful feeling I had when Rosemary told me about Simon's problem. It was a feeling that I must keep to myself because I could never even suggest to Rosemary the possibility that if Simon was in debt and desperate and Jo had no more money to give him . . . I couldn't even formulate the thought in my mind, but it nagged away all evening. It was impossible, I was sure, that whatever the circumstances, Simon would even contemplate — no, he could never. . . .

I didn't sleep very well that night and I was just finishing a very early breakfast when Rosemary rang.

"Sheila, look, I don't think I can do this

thing with Simon on my own. Will you come with me?"

"Of course I will, but are you sure? Won't it stop him opening up to you if I'm there?"

"No. I don't think so. You're an old friend and you were a very good friend of Jo too. And if he *is* still gambling and he promises to give it up, then you'll be another witness."

"I suppose so."

"And," Rosemary said, "I want you there so that I don't give up too soon; so that I really push him!"

"Fair enough. What time?"

"Delia's ride is at two, so about quarter to?"

"I'll be ready."

But will I really be ready? I wondered, when she'd rung off. I had to prepare myself somehow. On an impulse I put Tris into the car and went down to the beach. Even in the summer Taviscombe beach is almost always empty and this morning there was only one other dog walker in the far distance. The tide was right out — it looked as if you could almost walk all the way to Wales across the channel — and it was pleasant to walk on the hard, ribbed sand. I took a deep breath and tried to face the unthinkable.

If Simon was really in debt — really *badly*

in debt again — and there was no more money to come from Jo . . . Well, then, he must have known that she would have left him everything — not just the stables, but the chance of the money that Dan Webster would pay for the fields. She would certainly have told him about that. He'd have gone through Gordon's papers and would probably have found stuff on the council's decision about the change of use of those fields before they'd been made public. So he'd have known just how *much* money Webster would have been prepared to pay. If he was desperate, *really* desperate, could he have wished . . . ? She was no longer young; she was unhappy, grieving for Charlie. Would it have been so impossible to convince himself that she might want to die? He was in and out of the stables all the time; it would have been so easy for him to have tampered with the wiring. . . .

Tris was running, barking at a large seagull that regarded him with contempt as he flew slowly away. I faced the possibility that a person I knew and liked might have planned the death — no, put it brutally — the *murder* of someone he loved. Gambling, I suppose, is a form of madness; you're not yourself — how could you be? — and when you're not yourself, you might be capable of something you wouldn't ever contemplate when you were in your right mind. Yes, Simon might have killed Jo. I'd faced the thought. But I didn't see how I was ever going to present that thought to Rosemary.

The other dog walker was approaching. I recognized the dog, running on ahead, before I recognized the owner. It was Roger.

"Hello, Sheila. You're out early!"

"So are you."

"It's such a lovely morning, I couldn't resist."

"Yes, it is," I agreed, suddenly realizing that he was right and that it was one of those perfect autumn mornings that still hold the warmth and brightness of summer.

Roger looked at me curiously. "Are you all right?" he asked. "You look a bit worried."

"No," I said hastily. Roger was the last person I could share my suspicions with. "I was just brooding about Anthea's latest idea — for a sponsored walk."

"Good God! Well, no one's going to persuade me to do more than put up the money for someone else to do it!"

"You'd better avoid Anthea then. You're just the sort of person she's looking for."

"I'll willingly sacrifice Delia and Alex," he said, "even Jilly!"

Tris had come running back to me. Roger's terrier, though perfectly amiable, played more energetically than Tris could manage. I bent to put his lead on.

"I'd better take this one home," I said. "He looks worn out!"

"Nice to see you," Roger said as he moved off. "I'll remember what you said about Anthea!"

What would Roger say, I wondered, if he knew what I'd been thinking? He'd laugh, I suppose, and wouldn't take it seriously. Jo's death was an accident — everyone said so; the coroner said so. I should put the thought out of my mind. Or, at least, see what Simon had to say this afternoon.

CHAPTER TWENTY

Rosemary and I were both a bit on edge when she called for me the next day and were, I think, glad of Delia's flow of chat to cover up our silences.

"Emily's got this awful allergy thing — she comes out in ghastly blotches — and they thought she might be allergic to some horsey thing, so she was *dreadfully* upset, but it turned out to be a food allergy, so that was all right. Actually, there's a girl in my form who's gluten intolerant *and* lactose intolerant and when she goes out to tea she has to take her food with her in a sealed plastic box. . . ."

When we got to the stables and Delia had gone off on her ride, Rosemary looked at me and said, "Right. Let's do it." She knocked on the door of the office and we went in, closing the door behind us.

"Can I pay for Delia's ride now?" Rosemary said, putting some money down on the desk.

Simon looked up and smiled. "Hello," he said, "good to see you."

There was silence for a moment and then I said, "How's your mother?"

"Oh, good news. She seems much calmer now and a splendid thing has happened. Vicky's got to go to Montreal — some program she's doing about Canadian women writers — and Mother's going with her. Do you remember our cousin Phyllis? She and Mother were very close at one time, and then Phyllis married a Canadian and went out there. Anyway, he died last year and she's been on at Mother for ages to go out for a visit, so she agreed to go out with Vicky and stay for a while."

"That's marvelous," I said. "It'll do her the world of good."

We were silent again and Simon looked at us inquiringly.

"I'm sorry to go on about it, Simon," Rosemary said abruptly, "but we're really very worried about this gambling thing. Have you really given it up? Yes," she added, "Sheila knows all about it. You know she's fond of you too and is as worried as we are."

"I told you," Simon said, "I'm on top of it now."

"But there is something, isn't there?" I

said tentatively. "I've felt it too — something that's really bothering you. Please, won't you tell us so that we can help?"

"No — really — there's nothing. . . ."

"That's nonsense and you know it." It was Rosemary at her most forceful. "Simon, we've known you all your life. It's perfectly obvious something is very wrong and it's tearing you to bits. If you really are coping with the gambling and it's something else, then *please* tell us. You know how much we care about you. You can tell us anything!"

Silence fell again as Simon sat motionless, not looking at us, staring down at the desk. Then quite suddenly he got up and went over to the small safe, opened it and took out a large brown envelope, which he put down in front of us.

"All right," he said very quietly, "perhaps you should know." He opened the envelope and took out a sheaf of foolscap pages covered with Jo's distinctive handwriting. "You were both her very good friends. I think she would like you to know how it was."

He laid the pages down on the desk.

"I'll leave you both to read it and then you'll understand."

He drew up another chair beside the one at the desk and went out of the office.

"What on earth . . . ," I began.

"Let's just read it," Rosemary said, and we sat side by side, reading together as we used to do sometimes when we were girls, sharing a favorite book. It was in the form of a letter.

Darling Simon:

I know you'll be shocked and saddened by the fact of my death and the way I died, but I must explain it all to you so that you'll see it was the best way. When I was young I had a foolish affair and couldn't cope with the pregnancy that finished it. I had an abortion, but, in those days, it was illegal and often done by unqualified people. Something went wrong and it left me not able to have children. I told Charlie about it before we were married and he, bless him, was loving and supportive but, of course, there was a great gap in our lives. You, dear Simon, filled that gap for us and we'll always be grateful to you.

A while ago I began to suspect that I was developing Parkinson's. I didn't want to burden Charlie with the worry of it, so I went to see a specialist in Bristol and he confirmed it. It's been getting worse, but the symptoms weren't bad enough for me to tell Charlie before he died, so, thank God, he never knew. But I've always led such an active life and I couldn't bear the thought of becoming less active and, in the end, helpless, so I decided I didn't want to go on. I think you'll understand that and forgive me the sadness I know it will cause you.

You'll probably have guessed, though I never actually told you, that there's been a certain amount of pressure on me by Dan Webster and your father to sell our fields. Of course, I said it was impossible and I'd never do it. Unfortunately, some years ago when Charlie set up as a breeder — after his accident — he was going through a very bad time and desperately needed money to keep going. He was tempted, just the once, to do something illegal, something that affected the outcome of a race. He never did it again, and he gave up soon after and we moved down here. Anyway, somehow Gordon found out about it and threatened to make it public if I didn't sell the fields to him. Charlie was dead by then, of course, but I'd do anything to protect his good name, and Gordon knew that.

I knew if I refused outright, Gordon

wouldn't hesitate to carry out his threat, so I tried to play for time. Years ago, before I went to London, Gordon asked me to marry him. Of course, I refused, but he's always had a sort of "thing" for me; I often used to worry that Esther knew about it and was unhappy. I took to inviting him up to the house in the evening, to have a drink, I said, and talk things through. I knew, as we all did, that his heart was bad and he was taking those beta-blocker things. Well, I read in the paper about someone who died after being given potassium while he was taking beta-blockers, and it gave me an idea. I'd got some potassium tablets; Charlie was given them to counteract the diuretic he was taking, and they were soluble and slightly fizzy and quite tasteless. So it was quite easy to put them in Gordon's gin and tonics when I made them for him.

So, yes, I killed your father and I am sorry because he was your father, though I know you and he never got on, but you do see how important it was for me to protect Charlie's good name, and Gordon was a sick man and he'd have died soon in any case. It's just that I needed him to die before I did.

You'll probably wonder why I chose such a strange way to die. I did it because I wanted it to look like an accident so that you'd get the insurance. I thought I might manage some sort of riding accident, but I realized that might damage the stables. Then one day I got a nasty shock from the electric kettle in the office when I was making the tea and that gave me the idea.

I've left a part share in the stables to Liz, as well as the house. If you've been a son to me, in recent years she's been the daughter I never had. Forgive a foolish woman, but I always hoped you two might make a go of it one day. If you ever do, remember you have my blessing!

I know I'm leaving the stables in good hands and I know you'll keep the promise you made me about the gambling. I trust you and I know you won't let me down.

You'd better keep this letter safe just in case there's any sort of complication. I'm sorry it's so disjointed and incoherent, but I've had to write it in bits as and when I could.

Darling Simon, I love you very much and I do hope you'll forgive the pain I've caused you. But I'm sure you'll understand why I couldn't go on. It's not just the Parkinson's, but doing without Charlie is too much for me to bear. What is it that hymn says? ". . . One step enough for me." You know why I have to do this.

All my love,

Jo

P.S. I think I'd like you to show this letter to Liz. I want her to know how it was.

When we had finished reading, we both had tears in our eyes.

"Poor Jo," I said.

"Poor Jo," Rosemary agreed, "and poor Simon too. What he must have gone through!"

The door opened and Simon came in. Rosemary held out her hands to him and he grasped them tightly.

"You poor boy," Rosemary said. "What a burden to place on your shoulders."

"She had no one else," Simon said quietly, "and she wanted me to know."

"And Liz," I said.

"Liz was wonderful when I showed her the letter," he said. "She's got me through. I couldn't have coped without her. And not just this" — he gestured towards the papers on the desk — "but the gambling thing as well. She drives me to the Gamblers Anonymous meetings, waits in the car and drives me back. She has faith in me. I know I mustn't let her down."

"That's wonderful," Rosemary said.

"Actually," Simon went on, "when Mother goes to Canada, I'm going to move in to the house here. Jo was right — we belong together."

"And Jo," Rosemary said, "what a sad, awful mess it all is. How can you deal with it? What can you do?"

Simon shook his head. "There's nothing I can do, except keep faith with her."

"But to take her life like that!"

"It was her choice," I said. "It would have been worse for her to go on."

"I suppose so," Rosemary said reluctantly. "But, Simon, what about your father? What about Gordon?"

"I've agonized about that," he said, "but what good would it do to tell anyone now? Jo's dead and just think what it would do to Mother. Father and Jo! It would tip her right over the edge, now, just when she seems to be getting back to normal."

"That's perfectly true," I said.

Simon gave me a grateful look. "Besides," he said, "we don't *know* those potassium tablets killed him. He was very ill anyway. And if those tablets were prescribed for Charlie, they might very well have been out of date."

"Yes," Rosemary said eagerly, "that's quite possible."

"That just leaves the insurance," I said.

Simon gave a short laugh. "Oh, that's not a problem," he said. "Apparently there was something in the small print in the policy about negligence and due care having to be taken and so forth. After the coroner said it was an accident waiting to happen, they were very reluctant to pay out."

"That wretched Marcus Barrington!" I exclaimed.

"And given the circumstances," Simon went on, "I didn't feel I could press them on that."

"Just as well," Rosemary said. "It might have left you liable to all sorts of things if anyone found out about Jo."

"You won't say anything about any of this?" Simon said quickly. "Please."

"Well, I'll tell Jack, of course," Rosemary said. "I'm sure he'll be all right."

"And Sheila?" Simon looked at me anxiously.

"Of course not," I said.

"Thank you. For Jo's sake as well as mine."

We all sat there for a moment in silence. Then Simon said, "I can't begin to tell you how much it's helped me, telling you about it, showing you the letter — all that. I suppose it's sharing the burden, and explaining how things have been — well, it's helped me get things in perspective in a sort of way."

"You know we only want to help," Rosemary said.

"Actually," Simon said thoughtfully, "I think Jo would be pleased you knew. After all, you were among her oldest and best friends, and she would have been glad *I* had friends I could turn to. Liz is wonderful — she was marvelous about Jo and the letter and everything — but she's very young, and sometimes I worry about the age difference between us. And I know I'll be grateful to be able to talk occasionally about all this with — well, can I say older and wiser friends."

"Anytime, you know that," Rosemary said, getting to her feet. "Delia will be back from her ride. We'd better go."

"Anything we can do," I said, joining her at the door, "don't hesitate to ask."

Somehow being outside in the open air

was an enormous relief. We went over and, leaning on the gate, looked out across the fields.

"Will Jack really be all right?" I asked.

"If I point out that the tablets had been prescribed for Charlie and were really *old*," Rosemary said, "then I'm sure he'll see that it was just wishful thinking on Jo's part."

"Anyway," I said, "Simon's right. It wouldn't do any good to show anyone else the letter and it would certainly do untold harm."

"I'm sure he'll keep it safe just in *case* there's ever a query — if anyone else was blamed, anything like that."

"Oh, I'm sure he will."

Rosemary sighed. "Simon's always been a bit weak. I suppose it's because he's always been frightened of his father and felt he was a disappointment to him."

"Well, now that he's got Liz," I said, "who looks up to him and thinks he's marvelous, I think he'll blossom, get some confidence at last. And I wouldn't be surprised if he only started this gambling thing because he was lonely and felt inadequate. That's something else that having Liz will help."

We silently considered this possibility.

"It's desperately sad about Jo," Rosemary said. "I can't imagine how she carried on as if everything were normal, when all that was going on!"

"Well, she was an actress," I said, "and a very good one. That was the last part she had to play."

"I never suspected the Parkinson's, did you?"

"No, not really, though now I know, looking back I suppose there were signs — the way she looked tired and strained sometimes, not riding so much. Come to think of it, that time I saw her in Bristol at Temple Mead station, she looked dreadful. I suppose she was on her way to see the specialist. No, she'd have hated being really ill, and I know how desperately she missed Charlie. I can see why she wanted to go."

We were silent again and as I looked down across the field, I had a moment of déjà vu. In the slanting rays of the late-afternoon sun I saw a tall figure on a superb horse coming towards us. But, as the figure grew nearer, I saw that it was Liz on Tarquin. We opened the gate for her; she dismounted and thanked us, smiled and led the horse into the stable yard.

"She looks so happy," I said.

"Life goes on," Rosemary said.

"Yes, life goes on," I agreed. "Thank goodness."

ABOUT THE AUTHOR

Hazel Holt was a personal friend and literary adviser to Barbara Pym, and is Pym's official biographer. A former television critic and features writer, she lives in Somerset, England.